ISRAELA

ISRAELA

BATYA CASPER

TATE PUBLISHING & Enterprises

Published by Tate Publishing & Enterprises, LLC
127 E. Trade Center Terrace | Mustang, Oklahoma 73064 USA
1.888.361.9473 | www.tatepublishing.com

Tate Publishing is committed to excellence in the publishing industry. The company reflects the philosophy established by the founders, based on Psalm 68:11,
"The Lord gave the word and great was the company of those who published it."

Published in the United States of America

ISBN: 978-1-61777-828-5
1. Fiction, Literary   2. Fiction, Contemporary Women
11.07.01

In honor of Sammy,
With respect and affection.

DEDICATION

I dedicate this book to my children, whose courage I watch with awe, whose journeys I follow with pride, whose love and encouragement I cherish.

ACKNOWLEDGMENTS

Heartfelt thanks to Susan Snowden, Alan Adelson, Jan Lurie, and Carol Gaskin for their professionalism and their care.

Particular gratitude to Lou Aronica for his profound understanding of the craft of fiction and for his guidance.

Thanks to my dear friend Greg Smith, whose generosity of time, together with his attention to detail, saved me from more than a blunder or two. Thanks to Joann who helped me every step of the way and to Caroline, Miriam, Ella and Benjamin for their encouragement and for reading my manuscript at such an early stage.

Thanks, too, to Sheridan Irick, my editor; Kenna Davis, who created the cover I love so much; and the rest of the wonderful staff at Tate Publishing for their calm demeanors, unwavering professionalism, and kept promises.

Thanks from the innermost recesses of my heart to my sons, who've accompanied me along this path with their love, their critical eyes, and their extraordinary editorial sensitivities.

Thank you to Arie for his close reading, astute comments, and love.

The eternal hourglass of existence is turned upside down again and again, and you with it...!

—Friedrich Nietzsche

BOOK ONE

RATIBA

1966

I had wanted an old time, authentic wedding, with Ibrahim riding through his village on horseback. *You can't get more romantic than that,* I thought. Ibrahim laughed at me, claiming I was the only person he'd ever met who'd want such an outmoded ceremony, telling me I was a contradiction of willfulness and sentimentality, sounding like my sister who was always muttering things like that about me. For his part, Ibrahim wanted me to wear the traditional wedding dress that his mother had worn, which was really old-fashioned, that his father had kept for a hundred years and more in a wooden box, specifically for that purpose. Much to our surprise, Kasim wouldn't let me. "No," he told Ibrahim. "Your mother's dress won't be worn again." I wanted to ask why not but didn't. Instead we sent to Haifa for a dress that was fluffy white, that my sister and I embroidered just the same—rows of red and gold stitches down the bodice, making me look like a hybrid.

I begged my father-in-law, "Please," I said, "don't hire a hall for the ceremony. Let us marry on the slope of the hill among the trees and the evening breezes at the back of your house." But Kasim refused. "We're not poor," he said. "We need to entertain our friends in style."

So we congregate in Ibrahim's village, west of Jerusalem, in the presence of Kasim's family and friends, in a rented hall where toasters and dishes and sets of silverware grow into a marriage-mountain in their tinsel wrappings on the table near the door, where gobs of blue-and-gold plaster cover the walls, where painted flowers gather dust in the corners, and a crown in the center of the sky-blue ceiling hangs during the ceremony, immediately and ominously, over our heads. When I enter, the women, my sister playing her part among them, vent their excitement in a burst of ululations, scaring a thousand devils out of me, as my mother would have said, because I wasn't expecting it; then the atmosphere eases, for which I'm more than grateful, as drums and a lone, weeping lute play around us like doves of sound. I clamp onto my sister's arm, first stifling the need to squeak like a mouse the way I do when I'm excited, then, just as suddenly, repressing the urge to cry, refusing to let go of my sister, to let her move away. *This is the defining moment of my life,* I tell myself, biting my lip till it hurts. *Don't botch it.* We gather for the ceremony.

For the second time in two weeks, Kasim separates me from my sister, draws me to one side.

"You are a good woman," he says. What's the matter with him? I'm not even twenty-one. "Tell me now," he says. "It's not too late. Would your parents have blessed this union?"

It's hot. Overcrowded. The hall is way too narrow. Why is he pestering me about parents? About "unions," as though I was some national entity? Why now, again, at the last minute? If I were to change my mind, would he send everyone home?

"Of course," I say.

"Good," says my father-in-law and disappears into the crowd.

Kasim addresses us in front of his guests: "The marriage of a man and a woman," he says, "is the meeting of two souls. From this day on, you are like the wheels of a carriage. If you work in rhythm with each other, knowing each other's every thought, anticipating each other's every move, you and your children will be happy."

Ibrahim is holding both my hands now, looking only at me. I see nothing, hear nothing, care about nothing but him, my husband, my husband's orange eyes until, like a bullet shot to heaven, the women pierce the air again with their voices, protecting us from harm.

The women are chanting *al zaghareed,* congratulating me on my choice of husband and on my decision, from this point on, to tend to his needs. Men are gathered down the center of the room, dancing. Women cluster around, clapping, throwing seeds at us. The singer is wailing way too loudly now, the music pounding in my ears. For a moment, my heart catches as a fishhook in my chest, frozen by the absence of my parents, refusing to beat, refusing to release its flow of blood.

"Raula," I gasp through the din, "I can't. I can't do this."

"What can't you do?"

"This. Can't do it. Can't breathe."

She laughs out loud as though I'm joking. Then, in an undertone so I have to read her lips to hear her, "This is no time to panic," she tells me. "Focus on Ibrahim." And thrusting me toward him between the two lines of dancing men, my beloved sister spins me around until nothing remains in my mind but my love of my groom and my immediate need to remain upright.

Friends have gathered around Kasim. He looks at my sister and me and tells them, "In the absence of Ratiba's parents, I felt reassured when I met Raula that my son is marrying into a good Muslim family. Raula's manner of speech," he says, "set my mind at ease." Yes, I think, my stuffy father-in-law has a problem with me.

My sister is mingling with my husband's family, people she doesn't even know, handing round glass dishes of dates, of figs, listening attentively, laughing her wonderfully light laugh as they talk, drawing everyone, especially my new brother-in-law and his wife, to her with her charm and her haunting gray eyes. I am trussed up in my self-embroidered wedding dress next to Ibrahim, who is busy being kissed by all the men at our wedding, feeling like a queen bee, Ibrahim looking foreign and adult in his suit. His relatives are circling around me, *oohing* and *aahing*, extending their hands, frightened to touch, believing perhaps that I might sting them, wishing us well. My hairpins are digging into my scalp. My new shoes are pinching my toes; I should have worn them in before the wedding. I want to take them off, to change back into pants.

A ragged line of mustached men dance *al debkeh*. Kasim's neighbor is blatantly inspecting my sister for his son as he moves, his wife joining in his game, nodding, elbowing me, smiling in approval. How are they to know she will disappear after the wedding, abandoning our aspirations, I'll tell them, for the temptations of the United States? I'll tell Ibrahim too, on a weekly, monthly basis. For some reason, he'll never tire of asking, "What happened to Raula?" he'll ask. "Why doesn't she write?"

"She does," I'll lie, and he'll ask why I never write back.

We move outside to the patio on the slope of the hill. The patio, it turns out, is larger than the hall. Raula helps the women carry trays of cracked wheat and lamb, the aroma wafting after them as they go, sets them on the sheets that cover the ground.

"See?" Kasim says, leaning into me. I have never seen him smile before. "You have your trees, your evening breezes." Raula—I just love the way my sister's name rolls over my tongue—carries the *baklava* and coffee from guest to guest, and to us, the bride and groom, as we nestle close to each other, immersed now in our own company, responding only peripherally to the good wishes of our guests. Love songs are pumped through a loudspeaker. Under cover of the music, I whisper my question to Ibrahim. "Some day, in the future, if ever you stop feeling this way about me, will you tell me?" Kissing me ever so lightly, like the brush of a butterfly on my neck, then gazing wickedly into my eyes, he says, "I won't need to. You'll know."

ORIT

Shuli said I fell into this world, like many of my generation, from the back alley, off the outstretched arm of my mother. That's the way Shuli said things. Nevertheless, much later as a young adult, I was lucky enough to visit Rome. There, in the center of the magnificent Sistine Chapel ceiling, I saw God's arm stretched out to man's, and I recognized those arms as my conduit to life.

Shuli was my mother. She was gentle when you caught her attention. The trouble is that wasn't such an easy thing to do. Because Shuli was never fully there, was always concentrating on other things—other than me, that is. I was four years old. I trailed after her from room to room, the metal blinds of our apartment pulled down against the heat, sprinkling eyes of light across the floor that winked and watched me, moving the shadow monsters that lived beneath my bed, under the table, behind the chair, in the corner—

a giant one in the corner, next to the plant, waiting to pounce. I was clutching Boobie, my comfort blanket, for protection. I'd given Boobie a gender. She smelled like me. I dragged her behind me on the floor, so she collected dust and fluff and little bits of things on the way. Really what I was doing was waiting for Shuli to notice me, to pick me up. But when she finally lifted her head out of the storage chest where she was sorting out clothes and saw me with my arms stretched toward her, she gave a start as though I'd frightened her. When she did that, I jumped too and started to howl.

"I thought you were still sleeping, Ority," she said "Why didn't you tell me you were there?" But I'd been whimpering for a while. I knew because I could feel the snot and the tears being smeared round my face by my free hand. She picked me up.

"Yehuda," she told my aba, "put music on," and she became my ima again. "Come, babush," she cooed. "Dance with me." She wrapped me completely in those long arms of hers that wound around my back and all the way round her too. That's how long they were. We glided across the room, stepping on the shadow monsters, killing them, her curtain of hair caressing me like wings, I swaying and dipping in the safety of her arms to the strains of Aba's music; she smelling of the lavender lotion that stood as a permanent fixture on the bathroom sink and never ran out.

There was a gentleness to Shuli that stayed with her, like the bathroom lotion, right up to her last, stubborn, miserable days, way after she'd stopped dancing, when she was lying on my dead aba's bed refusing to walk or talk. But after two minutes of that, she said, "Okay. Orit, sweetness, that's enough. Go play." She plopped me down again as though the music had been turned off, as though I was a purse or a scarf she no longer needed. So I sat on the stone floor, in the blinded room, and waited for her to notice me again.

Aba walked in, also on his way to some more important chore. He lifted me, raised the shades so that its tiny eyes raced together back into the ceiling, like those animals that Aba said rush into the sea when it's their time for the next world, and the day was there. He set me in the corner of the sofa, tied each of my fingers with colored threads and bits of torn handkerchief, drew faces on them with his colored pens.

"This finger is Ima," he said, hugging me, teaching me also, as always, the Arabic name for mother—*ommy*. "When you grow up," he told me, "you'll speak Arabic just as well as Hebrew."

Next to Shuli, my aba was my favorite person in the whole world. He stuck a cotton ball on my Ima-finger for hair and gave it her voice. Then, "This one is me," he, said, adding the Arabic for father—*abee*—and a thimble. "This one is little Ruti." He emitted a crying sound like my baby sister, making me laugh. "Play with us. We are at a party, and we have to dance and eat yummy cake. See? See us lick off the crumbs?" When he wanted to leave me to work at his desk, my aba, said, "One of your finger people is sad and lonely, Ority, and the others are trying to make him happy. How would you make him happy?" He covered me with Boobie, my comfort blanket, placed my thumb, like a stopper, in my mouth for me to suck on so I had to pull it out quickly before baby Ruti's face rubbed off. He put songs on the record player for me to listen to with my family of fingers. I didn't know that my finger family would develop into my life's work.

"A woman on a bus gave you to me while I was still in Europe," Shuli told me, when I was old enough for first grade. "When she sat down next to me, I thought you were a bunch of clothes the woman was clutching to her breast. Later, when I stepped onto the curb with you on my arm, I couldn't remember what the woman looked like, what she wore, whether her eyes were blue or brown, or even whether she was tall or not. I would never have been able to identify her for the authorities."

Shuli wouldn't tell me who "authorities" were, or why she'd need to identify a stranger on the bus for them. Still, I loved this story. Every night, as she'd bend over my bed, I'd spread my Boobie blanket over mother Shuli's knee and beg her to tell it to me. She always told it the same way.

"World War Two was over," she'd begin. Then …

"'My name is Haya,' the woman whispered. 'I'm working with an organization trying to trace the families of those who've survived and are living in transit camps.'

"'I'm on my way out of here,' Shuli said. 'I'm waiting for papers, and I'm in a hurry.'"

Haya told Shuli that I had no name, that she wanted to find me a temporary home, just for the weekend, because the transit camp was infested with lice, because there was no one in the camp to look after me. Shuli took me. She told me that when she closed the door of the room she was living in and put me down, I scrambled away from her, wouldn't let her come near me. Two days went by, she told me. I wouldn't come out from under the table, just stared at her, Shuli said, dirty hair hanging over my "haunted gray eyes." I wouldn't let her change me. I puddled on her straw rug, the one she said she loved because it had a star woven into the center. She left food for me in my safe place under the table, but I wouldn't eat it, she said, until she turned her back. At the end of the weekend, Haya came back; Shuli saw that she wasn't tall, had curly brown hair and serious eyes beneath a woolen cap. I was still under the table, clutching the blanket that Shuli had thrown over me, that I wouldn't let her take from me, which was smelly, she said, from my pee. Shuli wouldn't give me up. "I'm keeping her," she said. "Her name will be Orit." Shuli became my ima.

I was three years old, I remember, here, in Israel. I had a white dress like a bride, like Shuli, my mother, exactly like her. Shuli was getting married. We got ready at the same time; I putting on my new socks as she pulled on her stockings. I checked her dress at the back, making sure it looked good. She bent down so I could straighten her veil; she buckled my shoes.

"What color ribbon do you want?" she asked. I couldn't make up my mind, so she tied my hair up in yellow, pink, and blue, all intertwined. "Stop jumping up and down," she laughed. But I couldn't so she gave up on the bow.

"Hurry," I kept telling her. "We'll be late."

She was putting lipstick on for the first time ever. "How does it look?" she asked me. She was so beautiful with the lipstick.

"Can I have some?" She put lipstick on me too. "Hurry," I said. "He'll think we're not coming."

Shuli was hugging me. She was laughing instead of getting ready.

"He'll not wait for us," I told her, jumping up and down. "We'll miss the wedding."

People were sitting in rows on either side of us. Shuli was carrying me up the aisle to marry my aba—his name was Yehuda—with me holding the bouquet. A man in a hat and a white scarf read stuff and sang.

"That's the rabbi," Shuli whispered, tickling my ear with her breath. "He's performing the ceremony." My aba put his arms around Shuli after the ceremony, so I was squashed between them, in the warm lavender smell of their embrace, he kissing me with the side of his mouth while staring into my ima's dark blue eyes, at the paleness of her skin, at her shiny black hair that she'd curled, just for that day, beneath her veil.

I was four and a half when Ruti was born. "Don't climb into the crib with your shoes on, Ority. It's new! Don't pick up the baby!" My parents hovered over me, sure that I meant to hurt my new baby sister. I would have never hurt my sister.

RATIBA

1966

Ibrahim is away from home when Orit turns up. Still, I'm furious
with her. What if he were home?

"Ruti, stop pacing," Orit tells me. "You're making me nervous."

What does she want me to do? I'm fidgety. I can't keep still.
"For starters," I tell her, "don't call me Ruti. Even when we're on
our own." I have to call Samah, my sister-in-law, tell her not to
come over. Orit is standing in my kitchen, a Star of David 'round
her neck, wearing an outrageously short skirt. I do what I have
to do, what I should have already done: "Don't ever visit me here
again," I say.

"What?"

"You heard me."

She plops onto my kitchen chair, speechless.

"You can come," I concede, "dressed as you did before my wedding, like one of us."

Orit walks out of my front door. For a moment, I think she's going to leave. I even feel guilty, wanting to go after her; but no, she wanders around the stubble, then sits on my front doorstep, lights a cigarette as though I have all the time in the world, as though Ibrahim is not likely to come home at any moment and find her here. I pace on the step above her, at the doorway.

"Ruti," she says, flicking ash onto the stubble. "This nonsense has gone on too long."

"Exactly what nonsense are you referring to?" I ask. "My marriage?" Orit can be impossible sometimes.

"You have to put a stop to this, Ruti. Now," she says, ignoring my question.

"Ority," I say, still pacing. "I've no time to talk, so I'm going to tell you this, one time only: I'm no longer Ruti. I'm Ratiba. I've been Ratiba since I moved to Jerusalem and registered at the Hebrew University, since I first found a job at my Arab newspaper and wanted to try Ratiba on for size. You've known this all along."

My voice is perfectly level, but I'm angry. I point my head away from her, tilting my chin upward in the way she hates.

"Don't act as though I'm not here," she snaps at me.

I give in then, sit on the step above her, stare straight into her pained, gray eyes that make me feel I've done something wrong.

"Ority," I plead. "Don't do this to me. Ibrahim will know I've lied to him, that we've both lied. His father will know, and that will be worse. They'll say I betrayed them. God knows how Kasim will react. Why won't you wait until I come to Jerusalem?"

"Because I'm your sister," she says. "Because I shouldn't have to, because you're the only family I have left, because I'm only fifteen miles from you." She smothers her cigarette into the earth. "Ruti," she says, making me feel like shit, making me angry again because she won't call me Ratiba, "this is a ridiculous situation. It's not a game anymore. If you love your husband, you owe it to him to tell him the truth. He'll understand. There's no reason for you to lie."

"Easy for you to say."

What am I supposed to do? I go back inside, dump our coffee glasses in the sink. "Where was all this advice before the wedding?" I'm talking to myself, stifling my voice, scared to call out to my sister on the front step for fear Ibrahim, who is miles away at work, will hear me. "You were happy enough then to dress up and play the part." I spray water over the dregs of coffee, trying to chase them down the drain. "And how about before, when you put on that whole 'nice little Arab woman' act to charm Kasim?" I squirt soap over the glasses. "We talked about it then," I tell my dishcloth. "You promised you'd help me."

Orit has come in behind me.

"I made a mistake," she says.

"Well, this is nice. Here I am, married—and you made a mistake."

"I didn't think you'd keep this charade going forever."

"Charade? This is my marriage you're talking about."

Orit says she feels awful. She's sitting on my wooden chair, rocking, wrapping her arms around her stomach. "How do you do it?" she moans, moans as though this is her problem, and I lose my temper.

"Do what?" I'm still whispering as though Ibrahim is walking up the path. My hands are itching to shake sense into her. "Live with the man I married? Why is that such a surprise to you? You've always known how much I wanted Ibrahim; you've known from the beginning the price I'd have to pay."

"Ruti," she says, trying I can see to stay calm, "you'll be pregnant soon. When you give birth I'll be an aunt, not a make-believe Muslim one with no clear identity and no known address, but a Jewish one who wants to talk to her niece or nephew in Hebrew and celebrate the holidays in her own home with whoever it turns out to be. I'll want your children to sleep over and do jigsaw puzzles with me on my kitchen table. Will they be permitted to visit me? Will I be able to visit them? Will they even know of my existence?" She always could argue better than I.

"I told you," I answer. "Only if you come as Raula."

"Are you insane? That's not my name. No more than Ratiba is yours. Aba nicknamed us Ratiba and Raula as a game, nothing more, used those names as a stupid exercise when he taught us Arabic so we'd take his lessons seriously."

"Do you think he was playing when he taught us Arabic?" I ask. "Why do you think I started wearing a *hijab* at university? No one wears *hijabs* anymore, Orit. I was the only one. The Arab students thought I was some crazy radical who hadn't quite made it into the twentieth century. I wore it because I wanted to see what it felt like. I was taking Aba's teachings to their logical conclusion."

"As usual, you overshot your mark," Orit tells me, like she really knows. "Obviously, if Arab women don't wear them, you have no idea how they feel." Then she asks me how I could do this to our mother's memory, which is a dirty thing of her to do. I decide not to fall for it. As cool as rainwater, as our mother herself would have said, I answer, "Ima had her life journey, Orit. I have mine." She tells me that the Arab sister who danced at my wedding, meaning her, is dead, and that the Jewish one, meaning her again, wants to be part of my life. Her voice is trembling. I ignore it. Instead, I give her what she deserves: "Get this straight," I tell her. "I'm not Ruti. I'm Ratiba, and I don't know any Orit."

ORIT

I've lost my sister. For a while there, I thought I'd actually go insane. I called her home, so many times, at the edge of that stone Arab hill, but she'd changed and privatized her number. For a month, I stalked her neighborhood dressed as Raula, hoping to talk to her as she left her home in the morning, waiting to apologize as she returned in the afternoon hours, frightened to leave a note for fear Ibrahim might find it.

It was early morning in October, Saturday, I think, and it was cold. I—or rather Raula—was standing at the corner of my sister's house, rubbing my arms and hopping up and down to keep warm. Not a person in sight. I was just about to light my first cigarette of the day, when Ratiba's back door opened. "Ratiba," I called. "Stop. Talk to me." But I was greeted by a black-eyed glare, by the willful toss of her dark curls, so typical of my sister, and a view of her back as she distanced herself pigheadedly into a group of mothers and their kids, the mothers and kids having appeared, like magic, the moment Ratiba showed up.

I still ask myself, *what is wrong with her? How could she have done this to me?* I'm still mad, though not as mad as I was then. But I refused to give up. *Not yet,* I said. I felt phony dressed in the clothes of a make-believe person. *To hell with artifice,* I decided, stomping my cigarette out with my shoe, *next time I'll confront her head on, woman to woman, one human being to another, the way we all should in this insane part of the world.*

So I went back the following Thursday, though I really did have other things to take care of. I was waiting on the corner near the back entrance to my sister's house, wearing my regular mini skirt and my butterfly t-shirt, my Star of David suspended resolutely from my neck, when Ruti emerged with Ibrahim. *Damn.* I froze. Didn't know where to put myself. Luckily, he didn't see me, but Ruti, who's always sharp, she saw.

"Ibrahim, I left the stove on." My sister actually pushed her husband back inside. *That's it,* I said, lighting my second cigarette before the sun was even up, controlling myself from calling out loud there and then to Ibrahim and his neighbors that his wife is a liar. *I've had it with her. I hope she has a good marriage because I'm never going to be there for her again when she needs me. Never. Not ever.*

I struggled for a while after that to prevent myself from going to that rocky Arab mountainside, going anyway, hoping to talk with my sister, waiting to ask her forgiveness, to tell her that of course I'd be there for her whenever she needed me, as a sister should; but Ratiba was never there. Finally, after three weeks of traveling by bus to her village and back, I thought, *I have to stop doing this; this is not a life,* so I moved away. I took the bus north this time, and rented a small house on the edge of the Mediterranean, the house I live in now.

My life changed after that. Every morning, I walked, as I do now, along the beach. On my evenings off work, I'd carry my omelet between two slices of bread to the shore, and stare at the sunset.

The Six-Day War erupted, then settled our country into a new reality. All the while, I was imagining Ratiba living with her new family, writing her articles for her Arab newspaper, feeling, I had no doubt, as though her entire life was a waiting room outside that moment in the future when she'd drop her mask and be reunited with me, her only sister. *As far as she knows* I told myself, *I am still living in the city, only twenty miles from her village. What is she thinking?* I exploded, I still explode today, every time. *She no doubt has a baby, a child, by now. Perhaps twins? I have never even met her babies!*

I threw myself into my work at the theater, became obsessed with my acting, with the characters I was playing. There was never a moment, day or night, that they didn't run through my mind or test my heart. I examined each of them in excruciating detail, till one silent dawn while walking along the beach, I arrived with clarity at the conclusion that remorse is the single most painful and most permanent of human emotions. *The fateful year that transforms a human into an adult,* I proclaimed out loud, relishing my bitterness, allowing the rocks to hurt the soles of my feet, *the year the gods send their first in a series of warnings to a woman's hips, that's the year remorse moves like lead into her heart and never leaves.* I didn't care that I wasn't making sense.

I missed my parents.

I longed for my sister, my only living relative.

It was a Saturday evening. The sun hung in a giant red ball over the darkening sea. I was sitting on the far end of the sand dune when a mutt with a scarred face and calculating eyes made a dash in my direction. When she reached me, she hunkered down with such decisiveness; I flattered myself that I must have been her goal from the start. Yet without so much as a lick or a sniff in my direction, she twisted her body, pretzel-like, away from me and, with total and utter abandon, dedicated every last fiber of her being to a sand-flying, hair-shedding, grunting, and snarling struggle against whatever pest was squatting in her rump. Then, manifesting the same ability to focus with which she launched the attack, she abandoned it, wagged her tail, smiled, and sniffed my face for food and good will. Total commitment to the present moment. No lingering resentment. No looking back. No hankering to regroup and go back for more. Nothing. Her character was inspirational. I invested half my omelet in furthering our acquaintance. She followed me home. I named her Pretzel.

I had a home, with a dog, near the beach. I had work. Life was fine.

Oody is an actor I worked with: average height, green eyes, oozing charm. Until then, I'd kept my distance from him because his magnetism scared me. I was playing Hedda Gabler opposite his Lovborg. I'd always taken for granted that Lovborg is a broad man with an old-fashioned, deep voice, and romantic curls, that is, until I found myself working on stage with Oody, who was like vintage wine waiting to happen. Every night, at some point or other on stage, and each night at a different point so I could never anticipate the moment, he walked in my direction, his eyes holding mine in a trance. Every night I waited for him, my heartbeats drumming in my throat. He always came. He'd lean his tanned face close to mine, way too close for comfort, every night on stage, gaze into my eyes with his own dangerous green ones, so that my face, my neck, my whole being responded to him, and I was incapable of moving away. Every night, at the very moment Hedda or I, or whichever one of us it was, was about to succumb to his spell, he walked upstage, away from me. He'd pass his hand over mousy Thea Elvsted's luxurious hair. Every night, he left me like a racehorse at the gate. Was I Hedda, or was I myself? I couldn't tell. For weeks after the end of the run, I was unable to separate myself from the character I'd been destined to play.

So, that's the way it is now. Oody comes to my house after work. He doesn't invite me to his place because he has an uncle staying with him, he says, who's been disfigured in a car accident, who is sensitive, who needs his undivided attention. Instead, he stays with me three times a week. I no longer sit around watching the sea. No longer take naps or stretch out on the lawn chair outside with a magazine or a cup of coffee on holiday afternoons. I no longer lie alone, worrying in soapsuds, on my hours off work.

I no longer listen to the news. Oody won't let me. "The news is ugly, Orit," he insists. "It sorts people into batches and boxes, with different labels and separate destinations. We should create our own story. One that starts anew each morning and vanishes with dusk."

"Come, my gray-eyed loved one"—that's what he calls me— "I'll chase you to the end of the beach." Every morning, we race along the shore toward the Arab village and back. Sometimes, he runs farther than I and brings home a fresh-caught breakfast from the fishermen. Until two weeks ago when there was a package on our side of the beach and the bomb-squad people came to neutralize it. We jogged in the opposite direction for a week after that, as though terrorists don't know about the other side of the beach. He makes the best crepes ever, at any time of day or night, serves them to me in bed, calls me in the softest of voices his precious one and only loved one. And when he bends his face to mine, my body tingles.

"How can you rehearse indoors ?" he challenged me, three days after moving his stuff into my house, "It's confining indoors. We need space. We need to feel part of the universe."

That's the way he talks. Like that.

"I do fine here . Besides, it's late. What's the matter with you? It's eleven thirty at night."

"Come, my love, we're going to the beach. We'll rehearse underwater, with the sea urchins and the jellyfish." So we went.

The next night he started in again. I stopped resisting him. Every evening, now, we go to the beach.

Monday morning, he said, "Let's focus our attention on time, catch it, the way American Indians catch their dreams. For just a moment, we'll watch as it slips past us into history. Then we'll work through *The Cherry Orchard* with a bottle of wine."

But after a day of living the unrequited longings and the loneliness of Chekhov's achingly myopic and isolated souls, my energy was depleted.

"You're nuts," I said, "Please, Oody, I have to sleep."

I'm crazy about him. He's a walking exaggeration, but he's alive, fully alive. He has a talent that is irresistible, a way of making me feel beautiful, wanted. He sneaks up behind me while I'm in the garden trying to coax my avocado tree to live just until the end of the season. He cradles me from behind, kisses me on the nape of my neck, sending squirrels down my spine. How can I not love such attention? He strokes my arms and plays with my hair at any time of day or night, regardless of where we are, while buying Jerusalem artichokes at the souk or barefaced in front of my students as I'm trying to teach them how to listen. What's more, his behavior is affecting my acting. It's allowing me to reach into the dark places that have eluded me until now; before my eyes, my characters are becoming hungrier, feistier, more death-defying, spontaneous human beings.

1970

One summer night, performing a mixed-cast experimental play dealing with our eternal Arab/Israeli problems, I get a standing ovation. Not as part of the cast. Me! Alone! An oversized man is standing in front of the stage when we come out for curtain call, clapping and hooting as though I've just jumped down from a trapeze, his legs splayed as though he owns the theater, elbows held high, staring directly into my face. I nod *thank you* at him, professionally, in my opinion, curtailing my gratitude. As the features of my admirer gather from the fog of the orchestra into recognizable form, I think, *He looks familiar. Where have I seen that mustache before?*

He's not waiting for me in front, as friends and family do. *An admirer*, I think, and spend the rest of the evening going over our performance in my head, relishing my special moments

The next night, immediately after curtain call, as the house-lights are coming up but when the audience is still applauding from their seats, readying themselves with purses and shawls for their departure, I see him again. He's not applauding now; rather he's slinking away, bending forward in his effort to propel the bulk of his body up the aisle to the exit door, rushing after another man, the other man obviously with no time to spare. Something about the delicate frame, the bend of the other man's head, also reminds me of someone, but the applause is dying down now, and we need to get off stage.

There they are, near the litter and the garbage cans, outside the back stage door: Of course! Ibrahim, my sister's husband, and the singing uncle I met at his wedding. My first instinct is to rush back into the theater, to hide until they leave. But catastrophic thoughts are pounding with my blood into my head. "What's wrong?" I ask him. "Has something happened to Ruti?"

Ibrahim steps forward, proffering his hand in a hostile greeting. "Salaam alaikum," he says, then, "Shalom," in Hebrew. "How are you?"

"Why are you here?" I repeat. "Is Ratiba hurt?"

"She's fine." And with a mean curl of his upper lip, he says, "I didn't know you were proficient in the Hebrew language," and my sister's messy identity surges into focus.

"Ratiba told me you were in the United States," he says.

"I'm leaving."

"No," he answers, uncharacteristically stern. "We need to talk."

"It's not me you need to talk to." I fish a used envelope from my purse. "Here, talk to your wife." I thrust my address at him and race like mountain fire to my car.

Every day I wait to greet the mailman, sure that now that Ibrahim has discovered Ruti's identity I will receive a letter, some note of reconciliation. Time passes. Not a word. I go about my business seething with rejection. Everything seems different now. The food I eat tastes like dust. Daily chores irritate me. What have I done to my sister that she should cut me off like this?

RATIBA

Some days, as I'm writing my articles or lugging groceries up the hill, I can feel Orit calling to me in my head. Sunday morning, I wake with a new approach. *Enough*, I tell myself. *I'll go see her.* Ibrahim smiles at me, pecks me on the forehead as I come out of the shower.

"Nice to hear you singing," he says.

"I always sing."

"No, you don't."

Visiting Orit is the solution, I realize, celebrating my private thought. The moment Ibrahim leaves, I pack goat cheese, figs, some olives, and take the bus to Jerusalem. *Why hasn't this occurred to me before?*

Nothing is as exhilarating as autumn mornings: air tingles against my body like a mountain pool, leaves crunch beneath my feet, rolling ahead of me like spirit-children at play. I walk the five blocks from the central bus stop to Orit's rented room, excitement bubbling in my throat as I near her house until I'm no longer able to contain myself, and I break into a run. My bag of gifts is banging against my knees, hurting me, actually. I don't care. I'm running toward my sister's rented room. I reach her place, double over, wheezing, trying to catch my breath, totally winded. Finally, I straighten up and open the latch on my sister's gate. The windows are boarded up. A "for rent" sign is hanging over the gate. I test the front door anyway, shaking it in case the sign is mistaken, ringing the bell. The door is locked. No one is there. Leaves are cowering in the corner, near a metal box, the kind used by the food delivery people . It's empty, covered in dust, a layer of earth and scraps of paper on the inside.

"Damn it!" I shout, kicking at the door. "Damn it! Damn it to hell! Why didn't she tell me she moved?" I stomp back to the station. "Damn it! Damn it! Damn it to hell and back!" bursting out of me, like Tourette's syndrome, along the way. I take the bus home, not stopping in a coffeehouse, not even a store. *It's Orit's fault,* I tell myself. *If she wanted me, she'd have come to my house. She knows where I live.*

"Hi," Ibrahim says, when he gets home. "How was your day?"
"Good."
"Anything interesting happen?"
"No. Just the usual."

ORIT

I begin noticing the way other women behave in Oody's company, as though they've taken drugs. My close companions perk up by several noticeable decimeters when he walks into my living room. Oody does nothing more than rest his fingers on the back of a woman's, any woman's, neck as he passes her on his way to the kitchen. He does nothing more than stare for the briefest second directly into her eyes with his own river-bed ones, and she's a cuckoo bird bursting from its little wooden door.

"Why do they behave like that?" I ask Elisheva when I meet her later at the coffeehouse. My cousin heaves that knowing sigh of hers.

"Oody's a woman magnet," she says, sliding sweetener into her mug. "Your friends are as helpless against his masculinity as you are."

"I'm not helpless."

Elisheva laughs at me.

"He'll never change," she insists, ignoring my protest. "It's in his blood."

My friend from the theater, for example, who acts with Oody and me on a regular basis: I watch her body regroup whenever it senses that Oody is in the vicinity; watch her fold herself over in a total body-stretch, as she does when preparing for a part, until she's nothing more than a human paper clip. Hers is a proprietary relationship. Her rights to him predate mine. Without fail, my Oody focuses his calculating glance on her and strokes her cheek. I can't believe the assurance with which she plants her own personal ownership smack on the fullness of his mouth. I can't believe how intimately he folds her into his warmth, how, honest-to-God, she purrs.

Oody lives in a chocolate box, each juicy center wriggling out of its wrapping, his for the choosing. My next-door neighbor is transformed overnight from a fellow walker and semi-confidante to a stalker. She lies in wait for Oody with homemade casseroles and cakes. When I come home alone, she casts a rueful look in my direction as though I've hidden a prize she should have won and returns her casserole to its paper bag, to try again when Oody comes home. One night, before rehearsal, we invite her to eat with us. She sits at our kitchen table the entire meal by Oody's side, stroking his back and shoulders as though women at tables are meant to behave like that.

It's my birthday. Oody turns down an acting job and paints my living room gold. Bright gold. He invites all of my friends for dinner and makes flapjacks, crepes, omelets. He buys the most delicious berries and all of my favorite cheeses. He uses all my pots, all my seasonings. He tosses the pans, whips the sauces like a professional Italian chef, leaving my kitchen exhausted, vanquished, running in the blood of my homegrown tomatoes. I lean against the doorjamb, watching him, my heart suddenly aching for my sister. He picks bougainvillea and hibiscus from the street so that every surface of our room is a celebration of color. For dessert, he's baked cupcakes with pink candies perched on the top, with "Happy

Birthday, Sweetness" on cards speared in the center, on tiny, sharp swords. He dims the lights, sets candles round the room. He picks my sexiest dress from the closet, the one with the bare back and the scooped hem. Deliciously kissing the exposed area of my spine, deliciously sending lizards scurrying down my back, he directs me to take center stage.

"Sit," he orders. "You're the birthday girl."

One of my students is setting the table with Oody. I don't want to spoil Oody's orchestration, so I sit on the couch, like a puppet on its shelf, as she oozes around the table, her hip stuck, perhaps unconsciously, but definitely provocatively, against Oody's. I mean really stuck, walking round the table, from place setting to place setting, sliding the paper napkins under the forks with an exaggerated elegance at the very moment Oody puts them on the table. Every stop, every plate, provokes a little body jolt followed by an almost imperceptible rubbing of shoulders: the two butts and then the two shoulders talking to each other, telling each other at every stop, "Hey. We're here. Aren't we cute?" And perhaps even: "What now?"

Or is that my problem?

By this time, other guests are arriving, friends who deliver me from my sitting station to have fun. We eat; we tell stories. Oody has compiled a list of couple-questions: What's the movie he has to walk out of? Her secret pastime? What makes him excited? Makes her grumpy? Of course, it's the answers that have us rolling with laughter. Oody's turn: You've enjoyed a wonderful marriage when you discover that your spouse is having an affair. How do you react? Oody answers, "I'd ask myself what I've been doing wrong." *Wow*, I think, humbled.

We drink too much; we dance, knocking into each other as we navigate the furniture. We listen to Puccini, I sitting on the floor, Oody on the couch above me, hugging me with his knees, his bare feet pressing against my own. My heart is full, grateful. I turn my head to thank him, the dark form of his face outlined against our wall that is newly gold and luminescent, muted and flickering in the candlelight. One hand is enmeshed in my neighbor's hair; with the other, he's massaging my student's naked foot. *How would my sister react to this?* I wonder. Ruti, who has turned her back on her life, on all of us, for the man she loves.

What is it about Oody and women? Even Pretzel, the nine-year-old dog that followed me home from the beach, runs around in circles, rolls over on her back, and turns on her charm when Oody comes home.

RATIBA

I worry about Orit. Why did she change her address? Where did she go? *She must have met someone,* I think, *must have moved in with someone.* Then I think, *she could be married. She wouldn't get married without letting me know. Would she? Perhaps something has happened to her. Bad things happen all the time. She could be sick, could have contracted some dreadful disease. Would she tell me if she had? Why would she tell me?* I agonize, stuffing my fingernails into my mouth. I sent her away.

Samah comes over to pickle olives. "Is there anything wrong?" she asks.

"No. Why?"

"Because you seem preoccupied. More than usual, even."

Sunday is Ibrahim's heaviest day at work. He leaves early, doesn't return till late. I start going into Jerusalem on Sundays, dressed each time in a short skirt and mauve t-shirt I haven't worn since before I was married, removing my tights when I get to the city, in the smelly toilet stall at the bus stop, my hair piled efficiently, I think, to the back of my head. I'm buying newspapers, looking through the ads for news of Orit. I go to the supermarket near her old home, knowing how futile that is, searching the corkboard for word of my sister. One Sunday, as I am boarding the bus after having examined every street sign on Orit's side of the city, I see a poster plastered to the station wall. Orit Maimon, it tells me, is performing in some play, in Jerusalem.

"Sorry, sorry, sorry," I say, turning around, fighting my way through the people lining up behind me, resisting the urge to hug them all, resisting, as always, the pull of the herd. I pace the sidewalk with no destination in mind, squeezing my knuckles till they hurt with joy.

It's 3.30. I'm famished. Haven't eaten since last night. I step into a coffee house, order one of their twenty-four-hour breakfasts: eggs, salad, and on a whim, a celebratory glass of tequila. "Will anyone be joining you?" the waiter asks.

He's lean and gray, obviously a family man, old enough to be my father. "No," I say, smiling up at him, "I just want to drink." He brings me my eggs, my tequila.

"Want to join me?"

"I'm working," he says, and rushes off to wait on parents with kids.

I raise my glass, refusing for now to think of my Muslim husband, denying the pangs of disloyalty that are tugging at my stomach because of my secrets, my sister, the alcohol: "A toast," I whisper. "To my sister, my infuriating Jewish sister." But I'm really not a drinker. The liquor explodes in my mouth, setting fire to my tongue, my throat, making me spit it out noisily all over my eggs. I drain my water glass of its contents, splattering into it, spilling half on the tablecloth, down the side, in a puddle underneath. The waiter is glaring at me from the family table, his hand holding on to the back of the mother's chair for security; the kids at that table, a girl of about six and what must be an older brother, both giggling and pointing at me. Fortunately, the coffee house is empty other than for them, a couple of students way too preoccupied with their own issues to bother about me, and a middle-aged woman turned away from me in the corner, reading a book. I'm on the floor now—trust me, it's not clean—mopping up the spill. "No problem," I call, sticking my head out from underneath the table-cloth, waving my napkin at my waiter, stretching my face into the widest, possible grin. "I'll get it."

I'm shoveling up breadcrumbs, butter wrappers, and parsley leaves that predate my spill by several lunches, sitting cross-legged on the floor, hidden from view by the tablecloth. "Thank you God or Allah," I whisper in my coffee house tent, tears running for no reason whatsoever down my face. "My sister is alive, obviously not sick, acting, no doubt ecstatically happy."

On my way out, I pass the table of the woman and her book; the woman is disturbingly familiar.

"Hi," she calls to me, "Aren't you? You must be one of Shuli Maimon's girls, no?"

It's Mrs. Gabon from Herzliyah. "No," I say. "You must be mistaken."

"I don't think so, I'm ... " and she stands up, pushing her chair back, extending her arms.

I bang the door behind me and run for my bus. Why didn't I tell her who I am and where I live? Who I married? Because I can't. I can't. It's way too complicated.

I cook lamb and rice, Ibrahim's favorite food, when I get home, relinquishing forever the vegan days of my childhood. Commitment, I tell myself. That is what I need. I light a candle, pluck a geranium from my planter, set it on the table. His favorite music is playing as he walks in the door. My lights are dimmed.

"What's going on?" he asks.

"A celebration."

"Of what?"

"Of life. Of you, because you're a good man, and I love you."

ORIT

Our theater is dark. We've just completed a season of *Peer Gynt*. It'll be two months before we start our next show. One morning, after a particularly luxurious evening on the beach, I'm wakened by a pounding on my door. Oody went back to his own house in the early hours, and I'm grateful for the chance to sleep. So I turn over, yank at the pillow, and squirm deeper under my blanket. I inhale deeply, deliciously drawing Oody's salty body odor into my lungs, sigh, settle in for more.

There it is again, someone banging on the darned door. It's 6:00 a.m. Nobody is worth talking to at this hour. "Go away," I yell, but now whoever it is has decided to ring the bell.

"Come back later. I don't speak to anyone at this time of day."

"You'll want to speak to me."

I don't know that voice.

"What makes you so sure?" I'm already in the middle of a conversation. "What do you want?" I ask, squinting like a drunk (which I'm not) into the daylight.

"I've come to introduce myself."

"Why? Who are you?" And now I see a little boy attached to the woman with the voice.

"I'm Oody's wife," she says. "And this is Micky, his son."

It's evening, and I'm still in bed. I can't remember how this morning's meeting ended or how that awful woman and her little boy went away. I do remember my knees buckling under me. I remember sliding down what must have been the side of the door until I was in a sitting position, in my bathrobe, on the ground. But I can't remember how I got back into bed.

I'm staying in bed. Twice, Oody's been by. Twice, he knocked on the door and called to me from the gathering dusk.

"We need to talk," he shouted, loud enough for the neighbors to hear, "I'm sorry." I'd locked the door on the inside, and the window shade was down, so he went away.

I didn't cry, though I stayed in bed for the whole of last night— and I'm still in bed now. This morning, they called me from the theater, I told the manager I have a cold, won't be coming back.

"I'm sorry," he said. He asked if I'll be back next week. I said I'm not coming back. He said, "What, never?" I yanked the phone out of the socket.

I can't stand the stench of Oody on my sheets, so I crawl out of bed and throw them into the machine. I lie on the bare mattress for three more days watching inane American talk shows with Hebrew subtitles, eating oatmeal. What is it about Americans that they smile all the time? I dump the dishes into my sink. Each time I become hungry, I use a different bowl. Before long, I've used up all my bowls and all my oatmeal, and the sink looks pretty cruddy. I remember a cake in the freezer left over from my last cast rehearsal, fish it out from behind the cave of frost, climb back into bed, and eat the whole thing without waiting for it to thaw. I can't tell whether it's chocolate or carrot.

It's early morning, the sun won't withdraw its magnifying glass from the dust on the dresser and the mountain of soiled sweat suits that has erupted in the corner of my room. I gather the few worthless objects that Oody has left in my place—nothing more, really, than some plays, his dirty laundry, and his wallet. I throw them, unpacked, onto the patch of grass in front of my door, but not before I've pulled his I.D. picture from its pocket, and I tape a note to them: "Your wife and I are moving in together. I wouldn't come back if I were you." I swear to be celibate for the rest of my life.

I hate myself for my stupidity. It's not as though the signs weren't there—foghorns out at sea, neon poster boards over my life. I'm an actor, for goodness sake. My career depends on my seeing beneath the text.

I need my sister, Ruti.

I long for my parents.

The summer passes.

It's September first. I'm due back at work. Pretzel, who has taken to walking by herself to the beach, is scratching at my door. I let her in and bend down to pick up the newspaper. An explosion. Wounded. Then, "Oody Charlap, actor, killed in car bomb." After that, there's a quote from someone who's seen him, "He was in my store two minutes earlier. Had just bought bread rolls for his wife and son."

I hide behind my shutters, refuse to open my door. My cousin, Elisheva, arrives. I stare into Pretzel's eyes begging her not to bark, not to even whimper. She doesn't. She whines so quietly next to me on the bed, only I can hear her. Elishy walks around and around the outside of my house, calling my name, looking for a way in. Naama, my friend, arrives with her husband. They bang on my door, walk around the back, and sit in my frontyard for two whole hours, waiting for me to come home.

Pretzel and I see Naama's green shirt and red-rimmed glasses through the slits of our window shade. We wait until they leave. I take in the mail, pin a note to the door saying I've gone up north, asking the mailman to keep my deliveries at the post office. In any case, I reason, all I get is bills. No one writes anymore. No one's interested in authentic human correspondence, and brine from the deepest, most subterranean part of me gushes unbidden and painfully down my face, like I'm some biblical stone being beaten.

I lie like an unborn in the fetal position on my bed, thinking of Oody's wife and child. I can't remember their names. Perhaps I should pay them a condolence call. I don't, of course. After a while, I start worrying that my bones might melt, so I decide to walk. I don't want to bump into the mailman or the neighbor, so I walk at night along the beach. I feel weak, like an invalid, like the time I had my appendix out.

I'm allowed to be devastated, I tell myself, moving really slowly.

I'm not alone. Bunches of people are exercising their dogs or jogging. Who knew? Nightlife on the sand! They nod hello. I ignore them.

"Why did I send him back," I ask myself out loud, "into harm's way?" I don't care anymore that he was an adulterer or that salt water is gushing from my eyes, the windows to my soul now nothing more than burning faucets. Strangers are jogging by me, smudges of color through my tears. *You think I'm okay?* I think at them. *Just because I'm not howling on the sand, kicking my legs in the air? I'm not. I'm not okay.*

Oody. A tiny, evil being tugs at the inside of my throat every time I think his name. We jogged together, Oody and I. Every morning. We played here, right here. Every night, we'd watch the sun turn into a giant, raw hen's egg, the kind without a shell that Shuli, my Ima, used to pull from the entrails of the chicken. Every night, we'd watch it fall into the sea. As it was falling, Oody'd put his arm around my shoulders and draw me close to him, and I'd watch his face, the side of his face, because I was next to him. I'd nuzzle my nose against his bristly skin, skin that smelled of nothing in the whole world but itself, himself, warm and tough and salty. The kind of smell you want to climb inside of, can't get enough of, so finally you stop trying. Skin as safe as a Boobie blanket.

Until it's taken away.

By now the beach is dark. Most of the joggers have left. I'm uncharacteristically out of breath. I drag my body home as if it were someone else's, as if I were doing some strange, heavy woman a favor. *Why should I care?* I ask myself. *He was an adulterer, a liar.* I can barely breathe. If I hadn't sent him home, he'd be here, alive, with me. I climb back into bed and cry myself to sleep, the evil being not so tiny now, still kicking and tugging on the inside of my throat.

The next day, I receive an envelope in the mail. Inside is a clipping of a newspaper article with a picture of Oody and me kissing in a previous play. The caption beneath says: "Oody Charlap with Orit Maimon, his long-time lover." There is a note inside. "I'm sorry for your loss," it says. "Can we meet?" It's signed, "Ibrahim, your brother-in-law."

For two weeks, a month, perhaps even six weeks, I live like a convalescent, sleeping a lot, eating soft-boiled eggs, crawling each evening like an ancient person to the end of my road and back.

I carry Oody's picture with me in my heart, in my mind's eye, in the pocket of my jeans.

I send a thank-you note to Ibrahim. "We can't meet till you talk to Ratiba," I write. "Tell her that you know. Please. Bring me back into your lives." I mail it to the post office number on the back of his note.

I call my cousin. "Elisheva, are you home?" I stay at her house for a week.

ELISHEVA

We're sitting on leather couches near the window—Orit; my husband, Dovy; and I—in the best coffeehouse in town. "How about a salad?" I coax. She can't hear me. The coffeehouse is crowded—music, noise, sexy waitresses serving elegant customers out for fun.

"Ority," I mouth across the table, respecting her grief, I think, while needing to make her hear me. "What will you have?" She looks at the menu like a broken bird. Doesn't answer. "Ority, sweetness," I urge, furious with myself for having brought her here. "They have the best desserts in town. Want one?" She doesn't answer. Tears are raining down her face. My chest burns watching her.

"This is not the right place," Dovy whispers, tugging at my skirt beneath the table. "It's too much for her."

I know, I howl inside me, telling her, "I thought this might perk you up."

Perk her up? What is the matter with me?

"Want to go home?" I ask. She nods. "Want to walk?" She nods, tears raining down her face.

Dovy drives the car home. Orit and I walk.

"Would it help to talk?"

She shrugs. "If I hadn't sent him home," she says, "he'd be alive today."

I thrust my arm through hers. We walk all the way, in silence.

"Here," I say, when we get home. "I've made hot chocolate. Drink."

She sits next to it, ignoring it as old woman skin forms on the top.

"Do you want to hear folk songs?" I ask. "Remember this?" and I put a record on that used to be her favorite. She slumps on the couch, the music drifting through the house like smoke through a burned out village. I switch it off. Tears are forming pathways down her face.

"Ority," I call from the kitchen. "I'm making soup for tomorrow. Want to cut the vegetables?"

She peels potatoes, carrots, leeks.

"It's all right," I tell her. "You don't have to talk."

At 11:30, Dovy switches off the news. "Goodnight." He sighs, stroking Orit's head. She stands up and hugs him. "I'm so sorry," he mumbles into her hair.

"Ority," I ask, aware of how much better I am with the sick at the hospital than the needy at home, "want to soak in the tub? I have bubble bath." An hour and a half later, I knock on the bathroom door. "Sweetness. Are you okay?"

"Please, Elishy, go to sleep. I'll be out soon."

Forty-five minutes later she opens the bathroom door.

"Good night," I call from the living room, pretending to read.

She kneels by my armchair, lays her pale face on my shoulder. "I'll be fine, honest," she says. "I came for silence." A week passes. She packs her tote bag. "Thank you," she says so low we can barely hear her and wanders off, alone, down our driveway.

ALISON–ELISHEVA

1955

The ball rolled into a ditch beneath a parked car. I followed it, emerging caked in grease and fuel but triumphant, directly into the smile of Uncle David, my father's handsome cousin who had grooves on either side of his face and a pipe that dangled permanently from his mouth. Uncle David had a habit of appearing in the Midlands every few months, bringing with him an aura of the outside world where things I was terrified of, but wanted to know about anyway, happened.

He lived in the East End of London where my father was born. My grandparents had died in London when my father was two years old, he said, of the 1918 flu epidemic, after having survived the pogroms of Europe and the horrors of the First World War. The idea of dying of influenza scared me out of my wits.

"What if my dad dies like that too?"

"You don't inherit the flu," he reassured me. "You catch it from the weather."

As a child, during his visits from London, I sat on Uncle David's knee while he turned newspaper comics into fighter planes.

1956

"Send as many of your belongings ahead of you as you can," they cautioned—"they" being the voices on the other end of the line. "Bring your treasured objects. Fill your crate with linens, with instant coffee, soaps. Stuff like that."

When we moved, Alison, my English name, was discarded. I was given my real name, Elisheva, the name that was my grandmother's, inherited at birth but kept in mothballs, so to speak, or in tissue paper like some favored crystal goblet, wrapped and unused in the shared closet of my parents' minds. My brother, Norman, became Noam.

It's October. We arrive under the roar and the hot wind of jet engines and helicopter propellers into a blue-black curtain of magic night, night that smells of fuel, of orange trees, of light and unfamiliar breezes and strangely, vaguely, of urine. I am twelve.

"What if we are different from the Israelis?" I ask my mother.

"You'll grow to be like them," she says.

"What if I don't want to?"

"Don't worry, Elishy," she says. "In time you will."

It doesn't register that there are neither women nor children, nor even any old people in the night airport. It doesn't seem strange that the man who meets my aba at the actual steps of the plane is in uniform and that, in fact, all the other men are too. I've never arrived at an airport before. I take it for granted that this is how it should be. I don't know then that the man who shakes each of our hands—even Noam's and mine—and says "welcome home" to each of us in turn, who hugs our father with such gusto as we cluster together on the airplane steps that both of them almost topple on to the runway, that man is suggesting to Aba that he take us back to England on the final chance plane from which we have just disembarked. I don't know that at the very moment we pick up our suitcases to start our trek across the dark and suddenly silent asphalt, we are at war.

We are bundled into a car by the man who has greeted our father. My dad converses softly with the driver as he sits beside him. The car rolls with almost no engine sound. Covered army trucks lumber along the night road in the opposite direction, rumbling slightly on the incline. There are no other vehicles. Our only guides are the almost inaudible bulk in the driver's seat and the twin orange headlights as they clear a wavering path before us. Occasionally, and for no apparent reason, the car swerves, delighting my brother and me with our first-ever images of oranges hanging heavily, sensually, aromatically close to our open windows from their protective parent branches.

We climb in silence up the mountainside to the city built of stone, waiting in the unblinking blackness of night for a war that is already raging in the southern Sinai desert. The ascent is steep and mysteriously isolated. Our car chugs slowly, lurching in spurts, as though it's having difficulty breathing. Ima holds my hand and Noam's.

"If I forget thee, O Jerusalem," my aba sings, "let my right hand forget its cunning. Let my tongue cleave to my mouth if I do not remember thee."

What is missing from the picture when we finally reach the city is definitely people and lights. Jerusalem is ringed with olive trees, silver branches reaching out for us like fingers with their promise of the new and the ancient. Noam and I lean out the window in our effort to stroke the tips of the branches as we pass. Our parents whisper into the darkness, "Blessed art thou ... who has ... brought us to this moment." The car tips into a ditch, our driver swears, "Merde,"—he's from Morocco—" and we have a flat tire."

"Plant an olive tree," our neighbors tell us, after the war. "Olive trees are harbingers of peace." I can't think of another country where people talk so much about peace. "Shalom," they say when you meet them on the street. "Peace," when they come to your front door. Even when you are about to fight with them, for example, when they bang their car into your wall or when you call up a repair man to tell him the lights still don't work, knowing he won't come back, you preface your argument with "peace." Arabs greet and part from each other, in the same way. Using the same word. "Salaam," they say. "Salaam Alaikum."

Peace, I realize, is used here the way one refers to water in a desert. Way back in the Roman Period, I learn, Herod wanted to display his wealth. He did so by building bathhouses and extravagant waterfalls in a land chronically short of rain.

Our new town is small. I wander round its streets infatuated by the iron-work along the sides of buildings, in love with the antiquity of its stone, riveted to the spot by the iridescent light, by the sun that teases shade on the pink-white surfaces of the houses. I lean against an olive tree, certain that it and I are kindred spirits. I am startled suddenly by a man walking too near me, lugging a bundle with him across the empty lot, leering, mumbling under his breath at me, coughing up phlegm.

I board a bus in the center of town, empty at first. I sit near the window. Other kids get on and off along the way, everyone except me with a destination. After one or two stops, the bus drives by the *souk* and becomes insanely overcrowded. Mothers clamber up the steps with groceries, jostling ahead of them three or four children apiece while at the same time carrying infants at their breasts. Matriarchs, swathed in black, squeeze their way through the doorway, sweat dripping in dusty rivulets down their reality-bound faces, chickens squawking from their uncompromising grip. A man with baggy pants and a moustache lowers himself into the seat next to mine, smelling of sweat, of garlic, demanding space for his sacks of potatoes and flour. I climb over him to reach the aisle, practically falling on his lap with the effort.

"Please," I urge the woman nearest me, "take my seat."

"Thank you, sweetness," she assures me. "I'm not pregnant, just fat."

People are crammed into their places, their purchases solidly on their laps and on the seats next to them. I sway with the latecomers, clutching the metal pole, too short to reach the leather overhead straps. A hot, gravelly wind is blowing through the windows, bringing no relief from the squawking of the chickens or the smells of the humans. Some are smoking; others are cracking pumpkin and sunflower seeds between their teeth.

"Here, take," says the man with the potatoes and the flour, thrusting a fistful of seeds at me, spitting the shells onto the already thick carpet of vegetation that is mingling with cigarette butts at our feet. All this, despite signs clearly posted in every area of the bus in Arabic, Hebrew, and English forbidding smoking and spitting on the bus. I love it. I simply love it. I revel in this new country of ours.

I cannot go indoors. I sit alone as the sun goes down on the grassy hill at the bottom of Keren Hayesod Street, relishing for the first time the twin waves of cool and warm breezes, air that wafts, I tell myself, like the softest muslin scarves over the city or like undercurrents in a changing ocean tide.

My mother hugs me whenever I walk through the door. "Here comes my Dream Walking," she laughs. I know that this Jerusalem air will be the thing I'll most anticipate every fall, way after I've grown old and practical. Noam might be feeling the same about our newly adopted city. But he's a boy. No way can I talk to him about such things.

Our neighborhoods are shaded by carob trees, their tasteless fruit hanging ugly, sticky, and forlorn, and at the very same time by the pomegranate, breathtaking in her shameless, sensual splendor.

Sights such as these that my family has never seen in our pale, western lives hug the central streets of the city, the foul-smelling alleyways, the cinema square where Noam and I buy falafel; where vendors stand in puddles under the winter rains over their fiery red coals, calling, "Hot corn! Sweet hot corn! Only five groosh"; where we buy steaming donuts with raspberry jam burning our lips, trickling down, sticking to our chins.

RATIBA

It is summer.

"We don't do fun things anymore," I complained.

"What do you want to do?"

"Something fun."

That was last week. Yesterday, Ibrahim came home and announced, "Okay, I've taken tomorrow off. We'll go to the beach."

"The beach?"

"Yes. You wanted to do something fun."

"That's not fun."

"Why not? You used to love the beach."

"Because we used to swim. We used to be two human beings swimming in the sea like everyone else."

"And now?"

"Never mind," I said, not wanting to upset him. "Let's go."

So we drive north to the beach. It's hot. My face is puffed up from the sunscreen. We've brought deck chairs from home, the kind with the dwarf-sized legs that sink into the sand, leaving no room for your legs. We've brought fruit, cheese, and bottles of water, like old people. Ibrahim is sitting on his chair in his dark pants and short-sleeved shirt. I'm draped in fabric from head to toe. We are watching the Jews in their bikinis and their tans, free as minnows in the waves.

"You see?" I tell him. "I told you it wouldn't be fun."

Ibrahim is unwrapping his sandwich.

"We're not the only ones who are modest," he says. "Orthodox Jews are modest too."

"Right," I say. "That's a comfort."

I sprinkle water over my face. As I do so, a memory comes to me: Orit, my parents, and me, playing with a ball at the beach. There were other kids too.

"Join us," my aba called to them, throwing the ball to a girl of about Orit's age. The girl's name was Moriah. She kept throwing the ball to Orit. Never to me.

"Throw to my sister," Orit instructed her.

"Who's that?"

"Ruti. She's standing next to you."

"She's your sister? She doesn't look like your sister."

"How would you know what my sister looks like?"

After that, I refused to play, and Moriah moved on to another group of kids.

"Let's bury ourselves up to our necks," Orit said. "Let's put mud on our faces so we'll look alike."

Four heads were lined up on the beach. We asked a stranger to take a picture: the Maimon family.

I watch Ibrahim munch on his sandwich. I'm aching with remorse.

"You're so good to me," I say, reaching for him. "I love you ."

"Come," he says. "Let's walk."

We abandon our stuff to the beach and climb the dune to the shady area among the trees.

ELISHEVA

1956

We are living in a hotel until we find a house. My room is monastic: tiled floor, a narrow bed with a white cover, a dresser with a mirror perched over it, a wooden closet. A bullet hole glares at me, an eye in the wall immediately over my bed. It's the first thing I see when I open the door. There is another one at exactly the same height in the closet door opposite the wall; that's the one I fixate on as I'm falling asleep. Our two-story hotel belongs to five Hungarian men and a Mrs. Harari.

"Where are the other wives?" I ask on arrival, proud of my virgin Hebrew.

My mother is horrified. "Don't ask that," she mouths at me, her eyes wide, signaling to me behind Mrs. Harari's back.

Mrs. Harari disappears down the hallway.

"Why? What did I say wrong?"

"Don't ask strangers about their lives, Elisheva," my mother says. "You never know what they've lived through."

"It was just a question."

"Mr. Hanan and Mrs Harari are a couple," my brother whispers, as we lug our bags up to our rooms.

"Who's Mr. Hanan?"

"One of the five men. Their sons, Raffy and Binyamin, have been drafted."

The hotel is built of golden-white stone. The bathroom with the cement walls is at the end of the hallway with a sign on the door that says "Please knock," though I put my ear against the door and hear gargling or whatever sounds are going on, from the old couple in 2B, for example. They carry their spectacles, all their books, and newspapers with them into the bathroom, and we can hear them read to each other in the tub. They're in there too long, and a line of hotel guests bang on the door, demanding that they stop wasting water. "They are sucking liquid into their skin," my brother tells me. "Like camels."

They plan to move to the Negev after the war, to devote their lives to making the desert bloom.

"Hi, kids."

Noam and I pester the young married couple, to use our mother's terminology, in the room beneath ours by knocking on their door and sprawling on their bed. The wife, Bella, who has a coil of black hair hanging down her back, silver discs dangling from her ear lobes, and a negligee such as is seen only on the big screen, teaches us to roll dice. She reads cards and tells each of us our fortune. "You will grow to be a wise and gentle man," she tells Noam. "Many women will love you, but one of them will break your heart."

I look at my brother with his apple head and his straw-like hair.

"I don't think so," I say. Noam is puffed, like a pigeon, with pride.

Her forecast for me is less specific. "You could be another Golda Meir, if you want to, Elisheva," she says, but she's not looking at my cards. "All girls have that potential." She doesn't seem worried about the status of my heart.

I lie on Bella's bed and watch her brush her teeth in the middle of the day.

"They're on their honeymoon," whispers Noam.

"Who?"

"Bella and her husband. Who do you think?"

"But he's never here, even at night time," I whisper back.

"That's because he's a reporter. He's in the Sinai desert trying to get an edge on which side will win the war."

"Isn't that dangerous?"

"He's in the direct line of fire."

Bella has finished with her teeth.

"We will win the war, won't we?" I ask her.

"I pray that we will."

Praying doesn't seem enough, at this moment. "Can't you read it on your cards?" I ask.

The adults argue with each other about the war, about the past, and about their hopes for the country. We eat salads three times a day, no cereal, no hot dogs, just eggs and olives, until one day when Noam and I come back from a trip to the north, at the opposite end of the country from the war. We see the tables empty, mirrors and pictures draped in sheets, the five men and Mrs. Harari sitting on stools close to the floor, their shirts ripped, their eyes like tadpoles in murky pools, everyone else gathered around them, not talking. Raffy, Mrs. Harari's only son, has been brought back dead from the desert.

My ima steps into the kitchen.

Two days later, the war ends. "Reserve troops are still in the Negev," my aba tells us, "but the fighting has stopped." The mirrors of our hotel are shrouded in white. The couple from 2B celebrates in the bathtub. Mrs. Harari is holed up in the war-blackened room,

room 1D, that she shares with Mr. Hanan, her windows still taped, her sorrow seeping like fungus through the walls, making everyone else tiptoe down the corridors. The war reporter comes home. Bella yelps with joy through her open window. Noam and I race down the stairs to greet him. They won't open their door. "Shoo," our ima orders, as though we were geese. "Find something else to do."

Bella takes us to Arad, now that the war is over. Her job: to determine how they'd irrigated the region in biblical times. "The ancients knew how to preserve rain water," she tells us. The sun is melting into a hazy sheet, stretching colorless and forever to meet the edges of the sand. It doesn't seem to me that anything will grow here,

"What we're doing," Bella tells us, "is nothing short of alchemy."

"What's that?"

"It's when you turn the desert into gold."

I think of Raffy, killed on the sand.

"He wasn't her first son," Noam tells me. I never ask my brother how he knows things. He just does.

"Where's her first son?"

"He and her husband, killed in the camps."

I don't like taking food up to Mrs. Harari. She still has war tape on her windows, and, as though that's not enough, she's draped black sheets over them.

"What kind of store sells black sheets?" I ask Noam.

"A funeral store. Where do you think Ima bought her hat?"

"That's not funny," I tell him.

Even at noon, it takes a while for me to find her in her enormous armchair in the dark. I stay for one minute. Two, tops. "Talk to her, Elishy," my ima tells me when she hands me the tray. "Tell her about your day."

What am I going to tell her? That I don't understand what the teachers are saying? What the kids are talking about? That I don't get their jokes? Mrs. Harari has far more awful things to worry about. Besides, she never asks. Doesn't talk to anyone anymore.

"Can I open the windows?" I try. "Let some air in?" Because her room makes me gag. She doesn't respond, and I don't want to disturb her, so I leave things the way they are.

One morning in the darkness, as I'm setting Mrs. Harari's breakfast tray on her side table, something in the corner clatters to the floor. I lift it up, apologizing. I'm holding a gun—an army rifle—in my hand. I glare at Mrs. Harari, asleep in her chair.

"It's Binyamin's, Mr. Hanan's son's," she says, her eyes still closed. "He's home on leave."

Oh, I think, propping the gun back in its place, *she can talk.*

What kind of place is this? Did my parents know it would be this way? Wars? People's sons getting killed? People we know? Grieving parents secluding themselves in blackened hotel rooms? Refusing to come out? To talk? Army guns falling over breakfast trays? Propped like fern branches in the corners in the gloom?

It's the middle of the night. Everybody's asleep. A shot goes off. Not a large noise. More like a really angry pop. I've never heard a gun shot before, yet I know what this is. Lights flash on all over the hotel. Naked feet rush to room 1D. There's screaming, wailing, sobbing. Mrs. Harari has shot herself.

Again, the five men who own our hotel are sitting on the floor, their shirts ripped in mourning. This time, there's no woman. I can't bear to see them. As they sit, crews of people with rubber gloves, masks, wash cloths, and pails climb up and down the stairs, closing the door marked 1D behind them every time.

Thank God I have school. I like not understanding in school. *Let them talk,* I think, and I keep to myself. I can't bear the thought of going back to the hotel. Instead, I climb the hills of Jerusalem when classes are over, until my legs won't carry me anymore, knowing I should have told others about the gun. Then I ride the buses. I stay on each bus, through the streets of downtown, to the suburbs, to the hills around the city, swaying for dear life, as my mother would say, through the crowded areas. I ride until the buses empty out, hearing gunshots at every stop, until the drivers see that

I've been there too long, ask where I'm going, where my parents are, knowing I'm a criminal. I go back to my room then. It doesn't feel like a hotel room anymore. Hotels are fun. I hide under my sheets.

"There's nothing anyone could have done," my aba says, tiptoeing into my room, not wanting to disturb me, but wanting to make things okay. "She didn't want to live without her children."

"I could have opened Mrs. Harari's windows," I weep into my pillow. "I could have pulled down those awful black drapes, could have talked to her about my day. I could have told you, Aba, about the gun."

The next morning, we move to our own home. Zalman is a much older boy who lives on our street. He and his buddy, Srulick—a lanky, cross-eyed, big guy—help us move our stuff into our house. "Hi," they call, as I take out the garbage. They smile and wave.

"Thank God, we're out of that awful hotel, haunted with its death and its darkness."

"What do you think?" says Noam. "That death exists only in that hotel?"

I don't listen to him. *Our new house is a perfect place*, I tell myself, *with neighbors who laugh at nothing, who whistle when they walk down the road.* Our second day, just as I walk out the door, Zalman zooms up on his moped, "Hop on, Elisheva," he says. "I'll drive you to school." I do. We're friends.

School.

"It's not the friends. I'm making friends," I tell my mother.

"Then what is it?"

"It's the language. I don't speak it. It's the schoolwork. I can't understand it. It's the radio, the news—and worst, the songs, which everyone sings incessantly, from the garbage collectors and the vendors in the souk to every one of my friends. I can't catch the words!"

"Perhaps they can tell you what the songs mean."

"To hell with the meaning! I can see the words are only too fraught with meaning! I'm just trying to join in!"

The gray stone building that houses my school is down the street from the Orgil where they play war movies and Indian love stories. The kiosk, where we buy our raspberry soda water, is in the corner of the building used for political speeches. That is where, during the war, we hear news blasted by loudspeakers every fifteen minutes into the street.

It's stuffy in our classroom. The windows are shut and, apart from the oranges peeled beneath the desks and the egg and pickle sandwiches in their greasy paper wraps that make their rounds throughout the day, there is nothing but the flea-bitten dog tugging on his chain in the auto mechanic's yard to hold my attention. No one asks me if I understand.

"Don't vorry," says Ramy, the boy next to me, showing off his English. "I help." When tests come around, he writes the answers on the inside of his hand.

"Read," he whispers. "Write." But there's a sweat mark down the center of his palm, and the teacher is looking in our direction.

"I'm not dumb, you know," I say. He stares at me before turning back to the questions on the desk, not willing, it seems, to commit himself either way, leaving me wondering whether, in fact, I am. "In England, I was smart," I mumble. He's busy writing.

The principal instructed me to come late for my first day at school, at the end of the morning sessions. I came dressed in a blue dress with lace round the collar. Until the moment I walked into the classroom with its stone floor littered with schoolbags, sweaters, and crumpled balls of paper, until that moment when I was first hit by the pervasive smell of oranges, lead pencils and sweat, when everyone, boys and girls alike, most dressed in blue pants and khaki shirts, a few—I guess to be different—in khaki pants and Russian peasant blouses, turned their heads to stare at me as I stood alone in the doorway. Until that moment, I'd thought my dress beautiful.

"This is Elisheva," the teacher told the class, in English, as though to say, "Exhibit number one. Observe." How embarrassing is that? He could have as easily hung a sign around my neck: "Alien. Beware." He pointed to a space in the middle of a bench full of kids. I bumped past everyone's knees, all eyes on me, a deathly hush. The girl next to me smiled through everyone's silence. I thought she was asking me how my peace was, which means *how are you* in Hebrew. I answered, "My peace is good," which, it turns out, is archaic Hebrew, never used in Israel, and the class burst into laughter.

"No," she corrected me, in English. "I mean, vat are your name?"

This is how my classmates talk. "Good afternoon, my teacher. How is he today? Would he like me to collect the homework?" Or, even worse: "Would he excuse me for the last class of the day, as I have a doctor's appointment?" Who, in God's name, are they talking to? Some of the boys—for sure not the brightest in the class, the brightest are serious and soft spoken—they pay no attention to me. The dumber ones ambled over to me in the schoolyard, that first day, during break.

"Are you American?"

"No," I answered. "She's English." The dumber boys laughed so hard they had to double over and run around the playground, holding their stomachs. When they finally calmed down, they seemed disappointed I wasn't American. They kept asking me: "Have you seen Elizabeth Taylor? Do you know Sammy Davis?"

"Yes," I said, thinking they'd stop pestering me if I was from Hollywood.

They didn't call me Elisheva. They called me Ginger, because of my hair, my freckles.

Then, there was the issue of English manners, my parents' fault.

"Want an orange?"

"Yes, please."

"You don't spell that word with an aleph. It's spelled with an ayin."

"Thank you."

This didn't make the dumber boys laugh. It made them stare at me, in silence.

Of course, the ultimate embarrassment is my parents. Nobody's parents look like mine. My father is tall, elegant more by nature than by tailoring, and my mother is petite and slim, with the appearance and the gait of a young girl.

I wish my mom wouldn't wear makeup; that she had thicker ankles; that my father would wear khaki pants or at least sandals; that they'd blend better with the war-torn parents of the friends I've managed to make in this still vividly foreign land, who I'm certain never sing in the bathtub.

ORIT

I'm back at work, rehearsing *Medea*. Each time I attempt to understand a mother capable of murdering her children, a weight, like those ankle weights in the gym, only larger, like a whole body weight, drapes itself over my side, dragging it down so I can no longer move.

I lie on the floor, encouraging myself to meditate. The weight on my left side is growing heavier. I know it's my birth mother, hanging over me.

"Ella," I whisper in the darkened room, hoping the other actors can't hear me—"Ella" being the name that popped into my head one day when I was still a child—"please, let me do this." No change. "I know you are no Medea," I beg. "This is not about you." Nothing moves. "Mother," I insist, "I have to do this. I have to understand." Then again, a few moments later, "I beg of you, let me go." Ever so slowly, the mass floats above me, melts like a mist from my body. "Finally," I breathe into the silence.

Still, I am incapable of understanding Medea. Even regular aspects of motherhood elude me. *Sisterhood,* I think. *That's an emotion I could explore. I'll start with that,* and a memory comes to me:

It was the end of the school day. Most of the kids had already left for home. I stopped outside Ruti's classroom. The only person remaining, it seemed, was a large girl with an embroidered blouse, munching on a banana.

"Is my sister here?"

Who's your sister?"

"Ruti Maimon."

"She's your sister? She doesn't look like you."

Ella, my birth mother, slipped into my head. In those days, she spoke to me a lot. *Don't let this kid make you feel bad,* she told me. *She's got bad skin. She's two years younger than you are.*

Ruti's head popped up behind her desk.

"You can't be real sisters," the kid insisted. "You don't look alike."

Ruti marched over to her. With all her might, she thrust her fists into the girl's chest. The banana peel flew across the room. The girl toppled backward, like a painted Russian doll, flat out on the floor.

"She's my real sister," Ruti growled—growled like an animal through clenched teeth. "We have a blood-bond. Never say that again."

Families, Ella whispers, as I lie now on the theater floor. *We protect each other from pain.*

That's nuts, I think back at her. *What kind of crazy spirit mother are you?*

I resign from *Medea.*

"Why?" the director asks me.

"I can't understand her," I say.

ELISHEVA

"It's a shame we don't live near each other," I tell my cousins.

"You'd never be able to live in Herzliyah," Ruti says.

"Why not?"

"You need the hills and trees of Jerusalem."

"Why?"

"Because Jerusalem has spiritual stuff draped all over it. Your family needs that stuff."

"And Herzliyah?"

"Herzliyah is open and fun."

Our cavernous house is a single-story building built of the pink-gold stone native to Jerusalem. It has airy rooms and gnarled pads of stone beneath the windows, forming perfect reading nooks on those winter days when the air is pungent with the smell of the earth, when the iron-gray heavens groan, when torrential rains pelt against the glass, drenching the shrubs into weeping submission. I love it.

Our garden is in need of weeding; tomato plants and scallions spring up of their own volition, expecting, I tell myself, to be picked by their previous owners. In the center, an ancient olive tree is poised like a biblical matriarch. Honeysuckle and passionflowers infuse the air with such heady perfumes that my soul sings in the night air. I'd never tell Ruti that—or Orit.

When the '48 hostilities began, the Salami family joined their cousins in Saudi Arabia, or perhaps it just makes me feel better to believe they did. Our house is empty and very still. I feel the spirits of the Salamis waft from room to room. I see them sitting close to the floor; I smell the roasted lamb, the spiced rice dishes their family and guests enjoyed. Just as a whiff of honeysuckle reaches me through the window, I hear their babies cry. I hear red-and-gold glasses filled with tea clink as they celebrate the wealth, health, and comfort of my Arab ghosts.

Our house is full and buzzing with movement. My parents' guests sit on whatever furniture they can find and spill over in circles on cushions on the floor. My mother makes me hand around nuts and orange rinds in chocolate coating as they talk about our history, about the state that is still so new, and their plans for its moral and social makeup.

"The children will return to their borders," they sing, quoting from the Bible. "Baab-el Waad," I sing with them, naming the spot in which the Palmach fighters fell. "Forever remember our names." I know they are referring to the burned out tanks that lie rusting on the side of the road. I vow to remember forever the names of Mrs. Harari, who shot herself in her hotel room, of Raffy, her son, killed in the desert.

I love when Orit and Ruti visit. I take them with me to my youth movement meetings, showing off that I too have cousins.

"Who were the Palmach?" I ask.

"Zen Buddhists who came to live in Israel," Ruti tells me, biting into an apple. Ruti is always eating. Jerusalem bores her.

"They were not."

"For God's sake, Ruti," Orit orders. "Go buy yourself a falafel or something."

"Okay," she says and saunters off.

"They were Israeli fighters, not Buddhists," Orit tells me.

"I'm not stupid."

"You're smart," she says, "but this is what you are here for, to learn."

I love Orit.

We're sitting in a circle, Orit beside me, watching the shadows, watching the sun slide down the wall of our clubhouse.

The students on my parents' living room floor sing of soldiers killed in the war.

> In the plains of the desert
> The dew glistens.
> In the plains of the desert
> A man on watch has fallen.
> There, the youth fell.
> There, his heart stopped,
> The wisp of his hair
> Blown by the wind.

"Raffy Harari," I whisper.

The mystics say there are two Jerusalems, an earthly and a heavenly one. Climbing the hills, walking down the potholed streets, always without fail I am suspended between the two, finding it hard to believe that the heavenly is not right here in the patch of sun that blinks beneath the trees; aslant on the shadow of the gray stone building; in the brown palm that hands me my donut; in the light, always, always and forever, in the light. *To hell with Ruti*, I think. *Let her keep her Herzliyah.*

The first time blood gushes like Niagara Falls from my nether parts, a disgusting event that necessitates my staying in bed for a week, my mother takes charge.

"Congratulations," she says.

"Why?"

"Because now you're a woman."

I look at my angular body and my empty, nut-like face in the mirror. "I'm not a woman." I turn my concentration for a moment to the way I feel. I look at my mother, at the softness of her arms, the curve of her breasts and hips, at the beautiful hollows of her cheeks. "I'm not a woman," I repeat, "not by a long shot. Why is bleeding the indicator of womanhood?"

I'm not happy. "What does it mean to be a woman, anyway?" I ask.

"Well," she says, then hesitates, taken off-guard by my question, "it means you're old enough to make your own choices, your own mistakes."

"Because I'm bleeding? Does bleeding make you smart? Or dumb?"

"No," says my ima, in the appeasing tone she uses when she's being out-gunned. "Bleeding means you're old enough to be a mother." My mother says things like that, things that make no sense.

She pecks me on the cheek after that, ruffles my hair, as though I've just lost a milk tooth or I'm not already two inches taller than she, as though Raffy, Mrs. Harari's son, wasn't killed in the desert and Mrs. Harari didn't shoot herself through the stomach in room 1D because I hadn't told anyone about the gun.

"In the long run, you'll see," my mother says, tucking in the covers of my bed. "It will transform you into an adult." I roll my eyes. Blood. I can't see any connection between this blunder of nature, my out-of-control body, and my mother who is an adult, contained and controlled in everything she does.

"Please God, when you marry," she continues, "you'll go to the mikvah when you bleed."

"Why?"

"To prepare yourself."

"Prepare myself for what?"

"For adulthood."

ORIT

One day, I promise myself, *my sister's children will come looking for me.*

When Ruti and I were kids, my mother, Shuli, told me to light my memorial candle on the ninth of Av.

"Why then?"

"That's when we mourn those who were lost in the war."

"No," I said. "I want to light my parents' candle in the middle of spring, before the wildflowers dry out."

"Sweetness," Shuli responded, "it's your candle and your parents. Light them whenever you like."

The first time I lit my candle, I felt my parents breathing in our living room.

"If they're your parents," Ruti asked, "what are my mother and father to you? What am I?"

"You are my family for this lifetime," I told her. "They are for the next."

"How do you know there will be a next life?"

"Because my parents are waiting," I said. Then I added, "If we want, we could choose to come back as sisters in the next life too."

"Yes," Ruti squealed, hugging me round the waist. "That's what we'll do."

We linked fingers and took an oath.

"We're bound by an oath," I whisper to my sister now, as I walk to the mailbox. Every day I whisper the same words, hoping they'll reach her on the wings of our childhood. On this particular day I've schemed a way of cheating fate, of trying to cheat fate. Experience has taught me that no note will be there from Ruti if I go to the mailbox specifically for that purpose, so I'm circumventing the forces that be by sidling up to the mailbox as though I don't really mean it.

It doesn't work. The box is stuffed with junk. Why does my sister not contact me? Did Ibrahim not tell her of our meeting? Why did he come to the theater with Fahhid? Not with Ruti, his wife? And I realize, Ibrahim came alone because he hadn't told Ruti, had no intention of telling her. He intended to guard my sister's secret, I realize, in the privacy of his spiteful heart.

I don't even know if they have children. Ibrahim never told me. I spend my early mornings pacing the beach, imagining how many children my sister has. Are they girls? Boys? I invent faces for them, complexions. Each day, I change their genders, their names.

"One day," I promise my sister, seething with anger, "your children will sit in my kitchen. I will woo them from you. That's how I'll avenge your broken vow."

ELISHEVA

Our whistle soars like a pigeon from Naama's lips to my window.
Naama is my best friend. I stick my head out.

"What?"

"Elishy, come sleep over at my house tonight."

Naama, with her talent for telling jokes and the energy that
keeps her dancing round the camp fire until late at night, Naama
would make the perfect poster girl for the new Jewish State. But
there are two faces to Naama. One of sparkle and charm for the
outer world, and the one she sinks into at home.

It is early afternoon when I get there. She's lying three flights
up on the asphalt, her radio drowning out the stillness of her home.
Workmen are whistling, hammering from their scaffold on the
opposite roof. Children's squabbles bubble up from the sidewalks.

Naama's skin is burnished gold. When I look at her eyes, I
think of night rides on lonely roads, when the only things you see
on either side of you are fields waiting for dawn.

The fall of their son in the army has broken Naama's parents the way stone crushes grapes. Her father hides his thoughts in his books now, seldom looking up, never completing a sentence. Her mother's body is bloated beyond recognition, the defining angles of her face blurred by anguish.

She is sitting in Naama's bedroom, on the second bed—her cotton housecoat, her feet hanging swollen in their slippers, the soft expanse of her hand, the turn of her neck when we tease her. We tease her.

Naama and I read songs of the poet Rachel, Bialik, and stories of Shai Agnon together. We lean out of Naama's bedroom window, wave to Tova, the neighbor from the fourth floor, as she comes home.

"Will you help us with our homework?"

"Sure, what is it?" She never refuses.

Tova has an excitable body. She writes erotic poetry, detailed fantasies about herself and her husband naked in ways that send my adolescent mind into a skid, always out in the open somewhere, in the park or on the roof or in the sea. "The sensation of sun, the breath of cool or warm breezes, the lick of water on the naked skin, in the private places of the body, all those kinds of things," says Tova, "are essential for the arousal of the senses. So is food." Who would have thought? Food? Fruit? Berries? Wine? And people? Always people around them, she says, people walking past, unseeing and unaware, but essential to the fanning of passion that rages in these poems between Tova and her fantasized version of Mr. Rosensveig.

"A man cannot make love to a woman by bringing her flowers," she lectures.

I hide from her that my father brings my mother flowers every Friday, from the *souk*.

"The human body, in its entirety, is a vehicle for love," she pontificates. "It is created by God to be caressed, every inch of it, stroked, kissed, teased into the rich life of the senses, a life that otherwise lies dormant, wasted, mourning its unrealized existence."

"Oh."

I have never heard of people eating naked, and as for wine? Wine, in our house, is used as a sacramental greeting for the Sabbath. In our home, we eat fully dressed, sitting at a table that in some way represents the blending of our gratitude with God's bounty. In our home gratitude and bounty differ so vastly in nature from those of our friend from Naama's fourth floor that both Naama and I are left speechless, our mouths open like goldfish dumped suddenly from their bowl into an unplugged sink. Of course, what we are really thinking is how much we want to *be* Tova. How Tova is actually a being from another sphere, another planet. It is obvious. We can see that now. Tova is one of the sirens that we read about in her mythology books. Different. More dangerously, sinfully, wonderfully different than anyone we have ever met.

But my mind cannot hold on for long to this image. It wanders into the gray areas, imagining against my better inclination Mr. Rosensveig caressing Tova's curvaceous body. Mr. Rosensveig with his bad leg, his musty smell, the hair that sprouts like tobacco in discolored tufts from his nose and ears. My adolescent mind refuses to contemplate Mr. Rosensveig in the way Tova wants him.

"Never marry a sweet man," Tova instructs us, sadly looking at her poetry. "He will make your life dull."

Mrs. Harari, I think, would have relished the dull life with her first husband and son. She would have gratefully shared it in Mr. Hanan's airless hotel room, so long as her Raffy were alive. Naama's family too—they would be thrilled.

Still, we can see the corroding effects of Tova's dull life in the poetry she reads us round her kitchen table when her boys aren't home—poetry that turns our faces scarlet, that makes our skin tingle.

Tova introduces us to mythology, a world of alternate realities, mysterious and strange. After many evenings washing mocha wafers down with fruit punch on the cushions of her kitchen, we discover that though her worlds differ in the external details—*au fond,* as the French (or Tova) would say—beneath it all, all worlds are constructed equally along principles of longing and suffering.

Despite their different answers, despite the loveable, amoral gods and goddesses of Mount Olympus, the beasts of darkest Europe, the goblins of Africa, human questioning—our desperate human search for meaning—is agonizingly, awe-inspiringly the same.

I relish the stories Tova gives us, stories of how the world was created, of the great flood, the irreversible fall, gigantic animals riding to a better world on the back of a turtle, sacrifices needed to deliver winter, death, and fear, from darkness, stories aimed at placating the anger of the gods so they'll bring back life.

Tova sunbathes naked on the roof. She's gone back to school after having raised her sons. She rushes from the building and her husband each morning with gusto, her curls bobbing defiantly around her freckled face, to meet a lover half her age.

"Tova," I ask, after Naama told me, "do you have a boyfriend?"

"Yes," she answers, kissing my cheek. "I'm running backward, sweetness. Just for a while. I'm not ready yet to accept the alternative."

Tova celebrates our adolescence.

We leave her, race to the center of town to meet the figments of our imaginations, fantasies of ourselves as sirens of the deep, lustful and sylph-like with languid bodies and liquid eyes, of ourselves as women of the world who speak many tongues and only in poetic form.

We round the corner, and I skid to a halt. My dad is sitting on our porch, sweetly reading Lamentations. Today is the ninth day of Av, our fast day, our national day of mourning, the day our ancient Temple burned to the ground.

Summer: We are working in our kibbutz in the south, living in huts naked of furnishing but our own narrow cots. We wake at four each morning, and, after breakfasting on chocolate milk and cheese, we ride on the back of pick-up trucks singing from the Song of Songs to the waking fields. "I went down to the garden of the hazelnuts to see the stream in its fullness; to see whether the vine had flowered, whether the pomegranates had put forth buds."

Yes, I sing in my heart. *This is why my parents brought us here, not for the killings and the pain.*

Mornings, we fill crate after crate with grapes we pick from the vine or peaches from their curly overhead branches. Afternoons, we work our way down rows of sunflowers, plants that grow higher than ourselves, and, using scythes that remind me of Ruth from the Bible, we sing as we hack off their giant yellow heads.

"You are such a strange person, Elishy," Naama laughs. "Everything reminds you of the Bible."

Evenings, we dance around the campfire, more exhilarating by far on the kibbutz than in the city. Sergey holds me by the waist in the darkness, the air cooling around us. He twirls me around. "Follow me," he instructs, moving barefoot like no one has ever moved before. I dance, in love with the shadows, with the smells of henhouse, hay, and sweat; in love with Sergey, praying, *God, forgive me that I held my heart from Mrs. Harari. Please God,* I pray, *give me a second chance.*

Ruti visits on the last night of our work month. She walks with me to the village, her hair swinging in a rope down her back, to bring the ritual slaughterer, miniscule in his Yemenite robe. The knife that hangs from his waist is razor sharp; he tests it by drawing the blade along his tongue.

"Yuk," squeals Ruti. "That's disgusting." He walks back through the fields with us to the kibbutz, Ruti practicing her Arabic on him as we go. I can see he doesn't want to speak Arabic. He answers her in Hebrew.

The moment we reach the henhouse, the slaughterer draws his knife, commences to slit the throats of seven chickens, methodically, one after the other, a gift to us from the kibbutz for our yearly labor of love.

"No!" screams Ruti, who has never in her life eaten a living creature. "Stop!" She's jumping up and down, her face flushed, dashing like a mad chicken herself from victim to victim, trying to stop the carnage. "Don't do that! Stop! Can't you hear me?" In truth, the slaughterer doesn't seem to hear, for he continues murdering as though she's not there.

"Ruti," I reason, pulling on her sleeve. "What did you think he was going to do?" Ruti never thinks. She rips away from us through the long grasses. Tears streaming down her face, she flees into the fields.

The slaughterer and I wait for the jumping, headless fowls to grow still; I'm feeling sick, aware that I'll not be able to look at a chicken, let alone eat one, for many years. We hand them to others to pluck, salt, and roast over the fire that they ignite in a hollow of the ground. The slaughterer walks back to his home. *I should find Ruti*, I think, as I sing, *make sure she's okay*. But I'm not nice enough to leave the fire. For her part, I hear later, Ruti vomits in the field from the violence we've perpetrated on living creatures.

Late at night, in our little wooden hut, I ask her, "Why did you run away?"—as though I don't know.

"I traveled three hours in blistering heat," she says, "for a party, not a killing." She leaves in the morning on the first bus.

ORIT

It was the High Holidays. My family and I were in Jerusalem. Elisheva didn't take Ruti and me to the synagogue her parents attended, but to the shed used by her youth movement for meetings. The boys swayed melodiously, shirtsleeves stiff as cardboard, folded white above their elbows.

"Mmm, tanned arms—sexy," Ruti purred and winked at us. No respect. I flipped through the book trying to understand. Most of the writings were about ancient times, the temple, prophets.

Ruti grew bored. "See you later," she said and went for a walk. Drops of sunlight were sprinkled over the wall. They were singing, "He that makes peace in His high places, may He bring peace over us," when she left, Elisheva standing by the doorway, singing with the fullness of her heart. Elisheva is such a romantic. I wish I were like her. They sang until the birds chirped back at them, until the courtyard reverberated with prayer.

Ruti's face appeared on the other side of the window, back from her walk, her nose squashed against the glass, squinting at me, making funny faces, struggling to get her mouth around a mammoth cheese and tomato sandwich.

"I brought it with me in case of an emergency," she mimed at me, pointing like a clown through the pane at her brown paper bag. She rapped on the glass at Elisheva. "Enough already, Elishy," she whined. "Let's go."

After services, we helped Elisheva's mother set the table with caramelized noodle puddings and those round honey cakes that are meant to usher in a sweet new year. We sat around the table. They sang some more. They were always singing. They drove Ruti crazy with their singing.

ELISHEVA

1959.

I take the two-hour bus ride from Jerusalem to my cousins' home
at the beginning of the school break.

Bougainvillea and hibiscus bushes surround the Maimon's
house. Beyond the cypresses stretch fields rich in the aroma of
damp earth. And then, of course, the sea: the great Mediterranean
with its salt smells, its myriad life forms agitating, recreating, being
devoured live by other species in need beneath the surface.

Uncle Yehuda sits on the floor with his hairy legs crossed, play-
ing his accordion. He has music playing from the moment we
wake up until we collapse on our beds at night, anything from
Mozart and Beethoven to Israeli and Arab music, African drums,
Irish ballads. We sit with him, against the living room wall, and
listen to operas: *Carmen, The Magic Flute.* My favorite is *Nebucco.*
We follow the music with our own, translated scores. Sacred time.
Any delivery person or neighbor who arrives while we are listening

to opera can either to go back where they came from or step inside the Maimon's open door and listen.

Uncle Yehuda has chocolate eyes and peppery hair. He wears shorts and sloppy t-shirts. His study, the enclosed verandah, spills over with books. "Join us," he urges, when he sees me in the doorway. Aunt Shuli never sits in the cool living room, which has plenty of empty space, or in either of the sparsely furnished bedrooms; rather, she squeezes herself cross-legged among the mess of her husband's literature; knits woolen scarves as her husband works, despite the heat and humidity; and hums to herself in Yiddish what I think must have been her own childhood tune. "Come in," she says, clearing space next to her on the floor.

"No thanks," I say. I walk away, their union in this space too intimate to spoil.

"She looks more like an Egyptian slave woman than an aunt," I tell Orit.

"Who?"

"Shuli. Your ima."

"Yes," Orit smiles. "It's her hair, her bangs."

"It's the way she appears before us when we least expect it, offering up a tray of artichokes or okra on a cracker," I say.

Orit laughs. "You don't eat like that in your house?"

"Are you kidding? The only thing she lacks, Ority, is a straw fan."

Orit laughs again. "I'll get her one," she says.

No animal, nothing that has ever breathed, is served or eaten in Aunt Shuli's home. All her food is finger food. No need to sit at the table and say grace. By day, she is calm and sweet, though distant.

The first night I'm there, I wake in terror. "What's that?"

"Go back to sleep," says Ruti. "It's my ima,"

It's Shuli, screaming like a banshee through her dreams.

Uncle Yehuda drills Orit and Ruti in Arabic until their dialect has just the right lilt.

"We will never be friends with our neighbors," he tells us, "until we speak their language." Once a month, he invites his students home, Arabs and Jews. They sit on couches and on the window-sills, drink tea with herbs plucked from the garden, read obscure medieval texts. It is that easy. "Peace shouldn't be difficult," he says.

Summer, 1961.

I am here again.

Adolph Eichman. The pages of the newspapers are filled with his image: Eichman, calm and controlled before his accusers; Eichman, unperturbed as broken human beings recount, with excruciating details, the atrocities he committed; Eichman, cool and collected as tears stream down the faces of Holocaust victims, convinced, as a civil servant who was merely following orders, of his innocence, despite the testimonies, the torture, the horror.

Except for debates that rage incessantly around the subject of the trial, this is a season of national silence. The country—too horrified to talk. Every subject pales before the images of the Nazi in his specially constructed glass cage.

"Elisheva, don't leave the paper hanging around," Uncle Yehuda tells me.

"Where shall I put it?"

"Anywhere that your Aunt Shuli won't see it."

"Of course. I'm sorry."

"No problem. It's just that she can't handle the images. The stories."

I wake several times during the night. Each time, I hear Aunt Shuli pounding the floors like a caged cat from the kitchen to the living room to the outside balcony. Cigarette smoke is seeping through the walls, penetrating the fiber of the rugs and the cushions as she stalks. I smell it rising from the heating ducts in the room in which I sleep.

At noon, Uncle Yehuda's fellows come over, among them an exchange student from France. They bring their own newspaper with them, spread it on the kitchen table to talk.

Aunt Shuli's been in her room with the shades down since early morning.

"I wish the case were over," says Orit, "that they'd put the bastard to death, that we could get on with our lives."

She's pacing too, as she talks, running her fingernails through her hair. Bitten down to the quick.

I watch Orit pace, remembering what Ruti told me, that Orit's birth mother had walked from her bunk to the liberating soldiers at the gate of their concentration camp, had died at the moment she reached them, her baby toppling from her outstretched arm.

Ruti told me that Orit has communicated with her birth mother since childhood, that from the moment the name Ella popped into her head, as a child of five, her spirit mother has taken care of her. We hear her mumbling in the bedroom, see her walking toward us from the bus stop, her gray eyes glowing with intensity, obviously in the company of her spirit mother.

"My Ella mother loved poetry," she told Shuli when she was just a child. "She loved the sea, loved pretty things." Then, "I've picked flowers," she'd say, but Shuli knew they were for Ella.

"By nine," Shuli told me, "Orit could recite poetry by heart. 'Please, Ima,' she begged. 'Take me to the beach.' When we got there," Shuli said, "Orit never swam. Just sat on the sand facing the water, chanting songs of loss she'd heard on the radio."

"Did that make you feel bad?" I asked, sounding like my mother.

"Not as bad as when Ella wasn't there," she said. "Sometimes, when Orit was small, Ella failed to appear. That was when Orit lay on the floor and screamed. She screamed until I came home and picked her up, until Ella, her spirit mother, hovered over the both of us, whispered in Orit's ear, calmed her down."

Ruti raises her face from the article she's reading, breaking through my thoughts.

"You think they'll give Eichmann the death penalty?"

"What else could they do?" says Uncle Yehuda's student.

"That's not the kind of state we want."

"No," he responds, "and we didn't want the Holocaust either, or the wars against the Arabs."

"What would you like us to do, Ruti?" Orit asks. "Send him to the Galilee on vacation?"

And Ruti snaps back, "Don't be facetious. He could get life imprisonment."

"He's an abomination," says Uncle Yehuda's fellow.

Orit doesn't hear him. "Do you think I believe in the death penalty?" she demands, her forehead pushed up against her sister's face, her voice low, focused. "I don't believe in it any more than you do, but this, this," and she jabs at the newspaper with her pen, grinding the tip ferociously round and round until Eichmann's face is a gaping black hole. "This," she says, "is a monster from hell."

"Look what it says here," says Ruti, backing away, pretending not to care. "It says the government has sent six psychiatrists to evaluate Eichmann. They claim there is nothing wrong with him. They claim he is more normal than most people."

"That's not a defense, Ruti."

"I don't know," says the exchange student in a comfortable, intellectual tone. "I don't think your government can afford to give him the death sentence. I don't think they'd dare."

A pall.

"I guess this is a family affair," says Orit, her voice hanging over us like lead from a crane. "We shouldn't be discussing it with strangers."

How can we govern out of passion? I think. *How can we govern without it?*

RATIBA

My sister in law, Samah, and I are milking our mamma goat, when a memory floods through me.

Avi and Nurit Sayag, my father's friends, were originally from Tunis. They knew how strongly my aba wanted Orit and me to learn Arabic, so they invited us to their home, took us with them on outings, spoke Arabic with us.

Avi was thin, had a soft voice; his skin, shiny brown; his eyes, round like marbles, and though he only had two fingers on his right hand, he cooked with Nurit and repaired most of the things that broke around the house. He played the flute. He and Nurit worked in a home for retarded children. Curls bobbed around Nurit's head. Her body was round, feminine, with slender limbs, tiny wrists, ankles that were permanently in motion. It was a beautiful spring day, I remember, the first time we went to their home.

"I have mint, garlic, couscous," Nurit purred. "Help me make magic." Then, pulling me by my arm out the back of her house, she said, "Come feast with us, Ruti, on our shaggy dog."

"Shaggy dog?"

"Our yard. Haven't you seen it?" And she was already picking carrots and basil, thrusting them at us, the vegetables spitting earth from their roots.

"Take," she said. "Eat it the way God meant us to."

"Phew, Nurit," I said, coughing up dirt. "It tastes of dog doo."

But by this time, she was on to some other thing.

"Let's dance."

"That's not dancing!"

Nurit, constantly in need of motion, was spiraling back through her house, stirring her mixing bowl as she went. She loved food, music. Most of all, she loved Avi. She'd hang her arms around his neck, I remember, kiss his eyelids or jump on top of him from behind, riding him like a horse, her legs clinging around his waist. *Why can't I love Ibrahim freely, the way she loved Avi?* I ask myself now, as I remember them.

Again, it was spring. All our associations with them seem to have been in springtime. We were sitting on Nurit's plant-choked patio chatting, though anyone could see she was unable to take her eyes off Avi's face. He felt her stare, stopped talking without even turning in her direction, let out a deep, private chuckle, one that made us girls blush but which caused Nurit to jump on top of him, roll with him, both quite hysterical with laughter, over the rocks and the long grasses in their garden. *Poor Ibrahim,* I think. *I've grown so dour.*

Avi knew the medicinal properties of every herb. He took us to the mountains, taught us which plants to pick, made teas from their dried out husks. We spent the afternoon driving around Mt. Tabor.

"This is where the story of Barak and Debora took place," Elisheva said, all turned on. "He refused to go to battle without Debora by his side." Elisheva was always spouting the Bible.

"I guess that makes her the hero," Orit said.

"Who cares?" I moaned, munching on Nurit's cheeses. I was different then. I was curled snugly beneath a grassy knoll, my hair loose, shoes kicked off, comfortable. "Although, come to think of it," I added, "I like that our patriarchal society depended on a prophetess. I like having her as part of my heritage."

"I don't," Nurit said.

"Why not?"

"Debora was famous as a fighter, not as a mother."

"Why should she have been famous as a mother? What's so special about that?"

"Fighters destroy life; mothers nurture it."

Avi and Nurit took us into the private places of the mountains where we came across sheep and goats. We surprised a mother goat at the moment of her giving birth, the herd clustered and worriedly bleating around her. The baby fell on the path in front of us, the mother refusing to budge from the spot until she'd licked her baby clean, coaxed it into standing on its own spindly legs. Nurit lifted gifts of fruit out of her linen pouch for the Bedouin shepherd.

"Are the grasses good here?" Avi asked. "Did we get enough rain?"

The shepherd told him about the grazing, about the health of his flock.

We climbed up the mountain ridge.

"This is where Goliath challenged the Hebrews," Elisheva told us, reading from a plaque on the rock. We read the story of how David delivered his people from the Philistines. We made a fire, coffee. Nurit drew salt cheeses and pita bread from her bags. We ate, waiting for the moon to rise. We took turns reading poetry to each other. Orit, who never missed an opportunity, stood at the highest point, her body moving seductively, her gray eyes turned inward, to the rhythm of the verse. She quoted verbatim from the most sensual passages of the Song of Songs.

"It's an allegory," Elisheva told us, getting on my nerves. "It's about God's love for His people."

"I don't think so," I said and burst out laughing. "You are such a little nun, Elishy."

"Hardly," said Elisheva. But I could tell she was hurt.

"I don't know about the allegory thing," Orit said, still dancing.

I grew tired of Orit's dramatizations, teased her, added connotations of my own. Orit collapsed then, in a heap, laughing hysterically on the rocks that were glowing white and iridescent in the moonlight. We grew quiet, talked about more serious things.

"Our longing for the Messiah is our hunger for a world free from suffering," said Avi. "It's up to us," he told us, "to repair the damage done to our world."

Yes, I thought, then. *When I'm an adult, I won't stand by. I'll work. I'll repair.*

"What's the matter with you?" says my sister-in-law, breaking through my thoughts as I finish milking my goat. "We've been working for thirty-five minutes, and you haven't said a word."

"Samah, I'm sorry, I—"

She's gone. Stomped away from me, into her apartment. *Here I am,* I think. *Despite everything, I'm standing by, not repairing.* As I do the things I do, I long for the people of my childhood.

ELISHEVA

1961

Before the holidays, as the seasons are changing, we are awakened in the night by the phone. The geraniums are pungent in the ink blue sky. I can smell them because the night breeze is blowing the curtain ever so gently as the phone rings. A bird calls, alone in the night. I pick up the phone.

Orit's voice. "My father is in the hospital," it says.

I have never been in a hospital ward. A tight-lipped assistant nurse in clogs draws a curtain revealing a stranger with oversized scabs all over his skin. No gray curls, just a leaf of sweat-dampened white plastered to his brow and bloodshot eyes. An ancient spaniel, I tell myself, repressing the waves of saliva that are pooling in my mouth, repressing the lurching of my stomach. The loveable, bear-like form that is him has disappeared beneath gray sheets, a half visible bedpan, tubes extended into his limbs from stainless steel branches. The smell, most of all, the smell: we are standing in this cubicle, my aba, ima, Noam, and I, staring at my Uncle Yehuda and the stench of death. Shuli is holding her husband's hand. Ruti has stepped out on an errand. Orit arrives, takes one look at her father, darts like a frightened rabbit from the ward, crumples in a faint on the corridor floor.

I know as I watch—terrified, fighting to hold back my tears, unable to utter a word of comfort—that a lid is closing on my childhood, on a box bound for my family attic. *This is the adult reality,* I tell myself, *one in which the songs of birds on the night air, the perfumes of the outdoors will no longer shape my comings and my goings.* I know, as I watch, that despite the nurses, the relatives, the life-giving support, my beloved Uncle Yehuda will struggle from this time on, silent and alone, against his maker.

RATIBA

For weeks, I sat by my father's hospital bed praying that he come out of his coma. Amar, the nurse who tended him, was an Arab from Tayibe. I watched him turn and bathe my aba, place a sheet screen between himself and us, thrust his hands into the entrails of my father's lifeless body, remove impacted feces. *If there is such a thing as God's work,* I told myself, recognizing the modesty with which he did what he did, *it's this.*

"Tell me what to do," I said when we were alone. "I feel useless just watching him."

"Talk to him. He's your father."

"He's in a coma."

"Does he like to sing?"

"He used to hum as he walked around the house," I said. "He would mumble tunes to himself as he sat on the balcony and watched the sun go down."

"Sing to him now. Talk to him."

I didn't.

"Well?"

"I will. When I'm alone with him."

Amar was obviously not going anywhere, so I sang anyway, a little off-key, with a frog in my throat because I was irritated at Amar's lack of tact.

"That's how you sing?"

"I don't sing in front of strangers."

"Why not?"

"I don't know. Perhaps because I'm modest."

"But this is for your father."

I turned the back of my metal chair toward Amar and sang again, louder this time, to my aba.

"Much better. I knew you'd have a good voice." Amar lifted my father's wrist, held it between his thumb and his forefinger.

"Don't you think you're a little intrusive?"

Not one bit daunted, he answered, "Well, on your first try, you nearly drove your father into the next world."

The smile on Amar's face caught me off guard; my irritation melted.

"Feel his pulse," he told me. "Look at the monitor. See? Your father's heart rate has changed. Feel how strong it's become."

"Wow."

"Your father is responding to your voice."

"Does it change when you talk to him?"

"You know the answer to that. It is your voice. Knowing that you're here keeps him on this side of the divide."

From then on, Amar and I included my aba in all our conversations.

There were several times when neither my ima nor Orit was at the hospital. It was then that I learned to work with Amar at my father's bedside, sponging his stiffened limbs, wiping his face.

Until that time, my relationship with my aba had been that of the youngest daughter to her father, not much more than that.

Now I drew closer to him. I was grateful for that. I sang to him the songs he had hummed as he'd walked around the neighborhood. One Monday morning, I arrived earlier than usual, entering out of the gloom of predawn through the emergency room. Amar was waiting for me.

"Your mother and sister have fallen asleep," he said. "We need to wake them. Your father wants to say good-bye."

"No." I panicked. "There must be something we can do."

"There is." Amar was gentle but firm. "We can let him go."

ELISHEVA

I'm here. We're all here. We gather with my cousins and watch as illness robs us of my life-loving Uncle Yehuda; watch as my Aunt Shuli crawls on to her husband's naked bed, smelling of death; watch as she follows him into the next world.

"After my army service," I tell my family, blind to the ways in which our lives will erupt, "I will become a nurse."

BOOK TWO

ISRAELA

I'm small. Tiny, actually, compared to those who live in my neighbor-hood. My eyes are brown. Tresses hang low over my shoulders hugging my frame in different shades of greens, browns, reds. I am delicate, but I am surrounded by giants who desire and hate me, who grab at parts of me, who want to cut me up into separate halves, like the women with the baby in Solomon's proverbial tale. They want to possess me, annihilate me, rename me. I am long waisted, narrow. Looking at me, then, you'd think I was fragile. And I'm really rather shy. Yet people have been shouting over me since my birth, which was a long, long time ago. They've fought each other to the death, killing each other, over and over, in my name. For centuries, they've built me up, torn me down, serenaded me, adored me, even. They've mauled me, scorched my skin and my hair. They've dug into my deepest entrails, hiding things there, only to dig them up again later, which by all accounts is abuse of the worst kind. Then, over and over, when I least expect it, because it usu-ally happens after a particularly painful struggle, they decorate me in flags, celebrate my existence, dance and sing around me as though I were still a young bride, which I'm not. Abusive husbands are like that. One moment they're beating you up until you are nothing but a bunch of crushed bones, the next they're making love to you, begging you to forgive them, to feed them, not to leave them. As though I had some place else to go. You'd think I'd have learned to expect this kind of treatment by now. But, no, it always catches me by surprise.

Today, more than ever, they pour casts over my stomach, ugly casts that feel like iron braces over my still-fertile womb, casts that are expanding at an alarming rate, threatening to cut off my circulation, so I can barely breathe, so now I'm nothing more than an old woman in a chastity belt. So far I've survived that too.

People claim they have God-given rights over me, which makes me feel that, despite my age and the many beatings I've taken, I must still be quite beautiful or desirable or even rich in some unique way. Still, I never asked for this attention. I wish, I pray to God, my God, Elokim, my companion and lover, I pray that my suitors—those that desire and those that hate me—will leave me in peace.

RATIBA

Fall 1965

We met at the Hebrew University. Ibrahim was completing his degree in Middle Eastern studies; I was studying journalism and Arabic and Hebrew literature. He spent most of his spare time with other Arab students on campus. I came each day from my rented room; a ten-minute's bus ride from Jerusalem.

"Why are you studying Hebrew writings?" he challenged, before he even knew my name. "Arabic is our language."

"I study to understand," I told him, "as should you."

And so it was, that in the very first class we had together, we fell into a heated debate over the meaning of Arab culture, the relationship of the Arab people to Israel, and the essence of the Arab/Israeli dilemma. The more we talked, the more overwhelmed I felt, drawn—hypnotized even—by the warmth and depth of his amber eyes. He had a scar on his upper lip. It gave him a harsh, almost violent look, at odds with the softness of his eyes. Strangely enough, I liked it.

I asked him if he knew the Jewish story about the angel. He didn't. I said my father had told it me when I was a child, that according to the story, children are born with all the knowledge they'll need in this world, but the angel touches their lips at birth so they forget, so they have to learn it again, their own way, as they make their journey through life. Ibrahim said that's nice, but why was I telling him a Jewish story? I told him because it fits, because the angel must have been extra forceful with him when he touched him on his lip, which means he has a particularly urgent mission to look at things as though for the first time. He wanted to know where my father found a Jewish story, and I said, "Ibrahim, you're not listening to me. It doesn't matter where the story comes from. My father read a lot. Collected stories from around the world."

Ibrahim thought I approached boundaries in my mind head on, the way a two-year-old approaches a railway crossing. He said he loved what he called the "husky tone of my voice." He told me he liked the way I squashed my nose with the tips of my fingers when I concentrated. He said it drove him crazy when I refused to compromise.

"But it's a short drive, Ibrahim," I teased. I didn't know I do those things, but now that I did, I liked it. Relished my newly discovered feminine power.

Sometimes, I knew I'd gone too far because Ibrahim is a conservative. I could see him thinking, *Why does Ratiba exaggerate? What is it about her? Why does she try so hard to provoke?* I saw him look at me as I came into class wearing American jeans I'd bought in Jerusalem, my butterfly t-shirt, dangly earrings. I actually saw him think: *The way she dresses, I'd hardly know she's Arab.*

All right. I'll change my earrings, I told myself. Yet I could see he wasn't able to keep away from me. In the middle of class, in the middle of a heated argument, Ibrahim leaned precariously backward on his metal chair, from his desk to mine, whispered, "How sweet and soft your speech is. What is it about you that so fascinates me?" I loved that. He said he found my look, my entire manner, challenging, disturbing, exciting.

He walked into class: I blushed.

Our debates continued after class. We agreed to meet outside of school for further discussion. Started eating lunches together, spent our free periods rambling over hillsides and reading Arabic poetry as we sunned ourselves on the whitewashed wall that encircles the campus.

He wanted me to tell him about my parents. I told him they were no longer alive. He asked me when they passed on; I told him just a couple of years ago, that my abee had a tumor in his liver.

We arrived at our spot beneath the wall, took our lunches from our book bags.

"We watched him getting sicker and sicker," I told him. "When my ommy was done washing him, changing his linens, and combing his hair, when she had run out of things to do, she'd sit at the end of his bed, massage his swollen feet and sing to him. My sister and I would bring her food, pray for him to get better, and go out into the hospital corridor, which was lined with sleepovers like ourselves in crumpled, sweat-stained clothes and uncombed hair, waiting for their relatives to die, praying for them to get well. We'd step out into the enclosed courtyard and smoke, dumping the ash into the flowerpots. We'd stalk the depressing green hallways and wish the janitors would use a less toxic-smelling detergent when they washed the floors. There was nothing we could do to help him."

We sat for a while in silence.

"After his funeral," I told him, "my ommy climbed onto his bed like a loyal puppy or an Indian widow and refused to budge from there."

"They must have loved each other a lot," Ibrahim said. I told him my abee was my mother's whole life. He wanted to know how long she'd mourned him like that. I told him until she made herself sick too, which in any case is what she'd wanted.

"What do you mean?"

I said my father was the only person my ommy ever really loved, that it wouldn't have occurred to her to stay alive for my sister and me. I told him how eventually she'd developed the pneumonia she'd waited for and how, within a couple of weeks, it had carried her off, out of here, to be with my abee.

Another silence.

I glanced down. "Oops," I said, looking up again, directly into his strange, yellow eyes. Without realizing it, I'd taken Ibrahim's potato chips. I'd chomped down (as my mother would have said) the entire bag. Hadn't shared a single chip with him.

Ibrahim leaned toward me and laughed, played for just a moment with my hair, held his hand over mine as it rested on the stubble of the grass.

"What a romantic story," he said. I told him it's romantic if she found him in the next world; it's a nasty, cosmic joke if she didn't.

I thought for a while of my ommy, her gentleness, the painful way she had of never being fully present. But I couldn't concentrate on that because he was running his forefinger down my arm. I confided in him how sometimes, when I was immersed in an article or writing an essay for class, I'd break out in a sweat because I could see her wandering around the clouds of the next world as lost there as she was here.

Ibrahim kissed me, and I knew I'd crossed over.

He asked me what other family I had. I told him my parents' families lived in Jordan, though all I could think of was the warmth of his skin. We were lying against the wall, our faces in the shade, his arm around my shoulder. *He's so easy to talk to,* I thought. *I really shouldn't be lying to him,* but I had to concentrate on what I was saying because he was playing again with a strand of my hair. "You have to meet my sister," I told him. "She's one powerful woman. Are you listening to me?" But then I was sorry I'd asked him that because he dropped the hair strand and concentrated.

"How is it you are so unorthodox in your approach?" he asked, more interested now in the conversation than in me. "Did your parents allow you to dress and talk the way you do? And how about your sister; does she approve?"

I said, "Wait till you meet Raula. I'm nothing next to her."

He wanted to know if our parents brought us up this way. I told him my mother never talked that much; that he shouldn't get me wrong, she wasn't a bad mother, but she'd had a hard childhood; that she believed life is short and cruel, that everybody should just do their duty while they are here and wait till the game is over. I couldn't believe I was telling him all this.

"My father encouraged us to assess things for ourselves," I said, "not to be prejudiced by what went before, which is the way I want to bring up my children."

Ibrahim lifted my hand close to his eyes, examined it, inspecting it, I thought, for a lifeline. "What about loyalty to our values?" he asked. "Why should this country belong to the Jews?"

And now I overshot my mark. Said things that didn't make sense. "Being loyal to our interests shouldn't blind us to reality, to the prospect of living with them in Israel."

"What?" He actually moved away from me, at least two feet away, his face contorted. You'd think he'd just discovered something really awful—maggots in his parents' bed.

"Why would that be so terrible? Jews have lived under Muslim rule."

My hand was dropped.

"You'd be willing to give up on us as Arabs?"

"Of course not. Not completely."

"You would. You would be quite happy living under Israeli rule."

"Give me time, Ibrahim. I'm trying to work things through, same as you."

I drew from my mouth the blade of dry grass I'd been sucking on, propped myself on my elbows and said, "Well, no, not forever. Eventually, of course, we'll have our independence."

He wanted to know when that "eventually" would be, and when I was silent, with the sun glaring directly into my eyes, he told me I was dreaming of our people's suicide.

That was the end of our lunch. I dumped my sandwich in the plastic-lined trashcan at the corner of "our" wall, munched instead, compulsively, on a bag of almonds I'd discovered in my pocket. Ibrahim rewrapped his lunch angrily in its wax paper, stuffed it back into his backpack.

"It's going to fall off inside your bag," I warned. "The paper. Your tomatoes are going to get squashed."

He was too frustrated to hear me.

To hell with it, I thought. *Let them squash.* We climbed back up the hill without uttering a word. Ibrahim started in again:

"We live comfortable lives," he said. "But how long can we sit here in the State of Israel, of all things, without coming to grips with our dilemma? My grandfather planted olive trees on this land. How—and which parts of it—will belong to us?"

"The Jews lived in Europe, in North Africa, in the Middle and Near Eastern countries for centuries." My voice refused to raise itself above a whisper. "They planted trees too. They don't claim a right to those places."

"That's because those countries were never politically theirs."

"Whether we like it or not, Israel was never politically ours. We were given Trans Jordan. They were promised Israel."

"You talk like a Jew." Red bumps were swelling over his forehead, his nose, his chin.

"What's the point in our studying this if we can't put ourselves in their shoes?"

"Because we're not in their shoes. Because we need to stand firmly in our shoes and look after our own needs."

Then, in a measured voice:

"My father is a wise, forward-looking man, Ratiba. He's also a Muslim. You're a woman. You're gullible, headstrong. He never would have sent you to study among the Jews. When you meet him, you'll have to modify your talk and your dress. I want him to like you."

"What about you, Ibrahim?" I drew my scarf protectively across my face, a curtain against a desert storm, so my voice was muffled. I felt my eyes flash across our path at him. I was angry, hurt. "Must I modify my talk for you too? How about my thoughts, should I change them to suit you? Should I dress differently so you'll like me?"

Ibrahim kept his head down, scuffed at the pebbles at his feet.

"We're living in a period of dangerous transition," he said. "Don't push me too hard."

I was so mad. I couldn't bear to look at him. Patronizing. Rigid. Sexist.

ELISHEVA

July 1982

Avrohm was wheeled into my ward during the Lebanese War. The wards were crammed with soldiers. I barely found time for civilians. Most of the wounded have gone home now, thank God.

Avrohm has a long face and a broad forehead, like a philosopher, I think. He and his wife, Yona, were our neighbors when we first came to this country. Originally from Russia, he married into an old, Jerusalemite family, he tells me. He is Zalman's father, motorbike Zalman, who'd helped us move our stuff into our home, who'd hung around our house with his buddy Srulick and the other big boys on our street.

Avrohm says they knew Orit's mother, Shuli, when Orit was two years old, that they had attended his family's Passover celebrations before Ruti was even born. He has a tumor. I don't think he'll be returning home.

He has too much time to brood.

"Tell me your life story," I coax.

"Nothing to tell."

"I don't believe that. Try me." It is almost midnight. The other patients are quiet. I sit by his bedside, and he talks.

"When I was ten," he says, "my mother died of a stroke. After the initial week of mourning, my father announced that we couldn't continue the way we were, never knowing when the next pogrom would hit, or whether we'd survive it. He wanted his children to be safe, he said, so he instructed my older sisters to take me to Palestine."

"How brave those people were."

"I didn't understand that, then," he says. "What did we do, I'd ask myself, that my father didn't want us?"

Avrohm is tired. *He's lived a long time with that particular sorrow,* I rationalize, and I switch off his overhead light.

RATIBA

1966

After that, Ibrahim and I kept our distance. But in class I found it impossible to engage in Israel/Palestinian debates without stabbing at him with my sarcasm.

Friday afternoon. The last class of the day. The room was quiet. *No need to participate,* I thought. Identical problems discussed, day in and day out. Always leading to the same dead-end. Insoluble. Irritating. Constant. Propelling themselves with a soporific hum through the afternoon hours like a car on a familiar road, bound for home, for a contentious, dysfunctional home, its heater flickering, holding close to the danger mark. A new answer must be found, I reasoned, a radical one if necessary, but one that would erase, forever, those onerous dividing lines.

A bee buzzed his way in through the open window, reminding me that it was spring; then, sensing that this atmosphere was not for him, he circled his way over our heads looking for the exit. *A little yellow man in a prison-striped suit,* I thought, *worrying his way over our heads, suspended, wanting out.* The flies that were landing on people's shoulders or rubbing their back legs together on the desks looking for food were immune to the subject matter. Someone was playing the piano in a nearby classroom, obviously not pleased with the outcome, because he kept repeating the same notes over and over with, I decided, no discernable improvement. A pair of cats in heat set up their wailing mating call under our side of the building, also not getting what they were after—or did they?—because before long, a cat voice rose from its sickly, honeyed sound to a ferocious howl. That, in turn, was followed by multiple cat voices setting up a cacophony of primal calls. I could feel the cat claws scratching at each other; I cringed at the fur being ripped from each other's throats, could practically smell their musty, deadly, savage cat odor. Yuck.

It was hot, obvious to me that, other than the cats, the outside world had fallen into a stupor, didn't give a damn what issues were being dealt with in our classroom.

Some students took notes; others leaned with their chins on their hands or scribbled cartoon figures on their notebooks, focusing on the class debate. There were only three male Israeli-Arabs in the class, of which Ibrahim was one, and only two Israeli-Arab women: Sarima, who'd just returned from a year of study in England, and me. We women sat together for solidarity. Not that Sarima needed support. She was almost violently patriotic and extremely verbal.

"Okay," announced the professor. "What do you have to say about Arab rights in an Israeli, democratic state?" Immediately, just as a second, bolder bee made his entrance, the debate surged into high gear. Everyone had his or her own angle to deal with, everyone tense, focused on the issue. Ibrahim was speaking. Ibrahim, who hated the spotlight and rarely said anything in class. This was important to him. But the others were talking over him, throwing legal points at him as he spoke, pros and cons, verbal tomatoes.

Then Ibrahim's argument shifted gear again, and for a moment he caught everyone's imagination, everyone's, that is, except mine, for apropos of absolutely nothing, just as he was driving into his own safety zone, I blurted out:

"How does it work in your family, Ibrahim? Do you allow your women to talk?"

He looked at me.

"Can we women express an opinion?" I said. Then, "Is what you're saying now your view or the one you've been spoon-fed since you were a child?"

Ibrahim charged noisily from his place three rows in front me, trying to bolt from the room. It wasn't easy. It was a small room, overcrowded with chairs, book bags, and students. I watched as Ibrahim weaved himself around and between the close-fitting desks, arching his body through narrow passes to avoid crashing into things. His sweater got entangled on someone's backpack, letting out a rip like a gasp of pain as he yanked it free. The books he was carrying banged into the door handle as he turned, falling with a thud from his arms. The room was silent. Other than the desperate noises of Ibrahim's flight for freedom, you could hear a pin drop.

Ibrahim was mortified. He slammed the door behind him, leaving the books where they were, open and disheveled, on the speckled gray tiles of the floor.

Sarima lunged toward me: "What's the matter with you?" she hissed. The professor focused the full force of his attention on me and glowered. "I warned all of you to scrutinize your motivations before committing yourselves to a point of view," he said, "any point of view. I told you that until each of us drops our anger, until each of us really sees the other, there will never be peace in this region. Personal relationships are the same as politics, Ratiba, viewed through a narrower lens."

I was mortified. I wanted to rush from the room and throw my arms around Ibrahim, wanted to caress his shame away. Instead, I sat in my seat, staring glumly at the professor, saying nothing.

Ibrahim avoided me as though I were the devil, and in fact I did seem possessed. Ibrahim's silence, his back turned in my direction, the independence of his mood and tone: everything about him drove me insane. I couldn't leave him alone. Just couldn't let him be.

It was a Wednesday, again the last period of the day, a tired, dragging, uneventful day. The students were walking into the classroom. I called down the hallway to Ibrahim: "What about when your women want to think for themselves, Ibrahim? Do you let them?"

Ibrahim's face flushed. Only his scar turned white. "The women of my family both think and talk, but they do so carefully and cautiously," he said, "as should you." He turned away, bumped directly into the professor. Again, his books fell from his arms, but this time he picked them up and, without a single glance in my direction, walked ahead of me into the classroom. My cheeks burned as though he'd slapped me across the face. Still, the devil wouldn't let go of me. Lowering my voice, I aimed at him again: "You mean they think only what you allow them to."

The other students had had enough. Jumped into the fray. All of them. Everyone had something to say, a side to take, a criticism to launch, an anger to express. Chaos. It took the professor fifteen minutes to call his class to order. "This is what we are suffering from," he shouted at us, "fruitless conflict on a global level."

I was eating my lunches on my own. There was plenty room at my table. I enjoyed sharing ideas and jokes with the other students during lunch hour. When I came in the morning or left at night, classmates nodded a quick, wordless greeting, then rushed on ahead as though they were on their way to an important meeting. Only they weren't. I knew they weren't. Ibrahim was afforded a great deal more sympathy than I, though I couldn't for the life of me work out why. He stalked off every lunch hour into the surrounding hills to eat alone, too stubborn to share his troubles with others.

Three weeks passed in this manner. Despite everything, despite my ranting and raving, I missed him. Besides, I wasn't proud of the way I was behaving. I stopped speaking up in class, became quiet and withdrawn, left political disputes to others. Another couple of weeks went by. I longed to reconcile, but not for any force in the world would I let myself give in. The hours seemed weighted, like the books in my backpack, unable to rotate, as they should, into days. Finally, one morning after class, at the end of what seemed to me a year, but which was actually only a couple of months, I picked an iris from the field, waited for Ibrahim after class, and handed it to him.

"Sorry," I said. "I never should have spoken to you like that." I couldn't even remember why we'd quarreled.

So we started again, slowly, cautiously. At first, Ibrahim was withdrawn, overly polite, careful not to see me too often. He told me of his family, of his mother who'd died giving birth to his younger brother, of his father who'd refused to remarry.

The days grew longer. We started to meet again in the evenings after a full day of classes. Drove across the mountain ridge to the campus at Givat Ram, and then down the hillside to Ein Karem, where Christians claim John the Baptist walked two thousand years ago, arriving at one of the little outdoor cafés at dusk as the perfume of the grasses and wildflowers was at its most intense. I worked hard to repair our relationship. Agreed with him a lot. Laughed. Teased him. Before long, and despite his better judgment, I could see Ibrahim was again attracted to the peculiar combination that he insisted I exuded, of unorthodox curiosity and receptiveness. He was again attracted to what he called "the challenge of my mind." I loved that. How many men feel that way about their girlfriends? Because now I really was: his girlfriend. Attracted, he said, to my thoughts that scared him the way a roaring bonfire had scared him as a child on moonless nights. He was captivated, as before, he said so poetically, by the softness and smell of my skin, by the way the same rebellious forelock escaped from my headscarf every time I concentrated in class, bounced out, as though of its own volition, he said, in a quivering, ebony question mark, hung down the very center of my face, over my nose. "What kind of strange radical are you, anyway?" he asked. "Why have you started wearing a hijab? You didn't used to. Women don't wear head coverings anymore."

"When does my hair fall over my nose?"

"When you write."

He didn't seem able to make up his mind about me. Sometimes, a quizzical expression overcame him in the middle of my talking. "Are you sure you're a Muslim?" he asked. I laughed and ran away from him, down the hill. "I thought I was a 'strange radical,'" I said, pointing to my hijab, hoping it would convince him. "See? I'm the only authentic Muslim in class."

"You're a walking anachronism," he told me. "Women today don't wear hijabs."

I loved the almost intimate knowledge Ibrahim had of every plant and wildflower we passed. I loved that he could prepare four different cheese dishes in the time it took me to make a single salad.

ORIT

It was thirty days since Shuli, our ima, died. We were packing her things, hers and Aba's, into boxes. Most of it we were giving to the poor. It was a terrible job. Our parents' smell, touched with must, still clinging to their belongings.

"Ority, look," Ruti said, opening Shuli's enamel treasure box. Shuli's beads, the amethyst brooch that Yehuda had given her on their anniversary, her wedding ring.

"Which do you want?" Ruti asked.

"I want their photos."

"We'll have those too, of course, but which of these things do you want?"

"Don't take this the wrong way, Ruti," I said. "I was not their birth daughter. These things should be yours."

Ruti burst into tears, thrust the enamel treasure box deep into my tote bag, stuffed Shuli's brass candlesticks inside, stuck the china doll that sat on Shuli's dresser, over the top.

"We only have each other, now," she warned. "We're sisters. We either share—or throw the whole lot out."

ELISHEVA

July 1982

Avrohm's eyes are watering. I've given him pain medicine. He is uncomfortable today, more than usual. Zalman was here, singing to his father, telling him stories.

"Hey, Elishy," Zalman smiled, when he first saw me. "Let me look at you. Yes," he said, "you've grown into a beauty, just as you promised."

"You look good too," I said, averting my face, pretending to fix his father's drip.

He lowered his voice.

"I'm happy my father's in good hands."

He's just left, and Avrohm's eyes are watering.

"Tell me how you made it in this country," I ask. "Did you live with your sisters? Are they still with us?"

"We never lived together," Avrohm tells me, breathing heavily. "Out of respect for my parents, my sisters traveled south with me from the Haifa port"—he pauses, struggles to talk—"to deposit me at the seminary in Hebron." He stops. Then, "They left me there, made their windswept way to a kibbutz in the north."

"You have a way with words, Avrohm."

He grants me a bloodshot smile. "It was my sisters who told a good story," he says. "They wrote to me until the day I married, describing for me every detail of their lives."

RATIBA

1966

Lacking my mother for my prenuptial ritual, I celebrated my *henna* in the home of Samah, my sister-in-law, with my own sister, and the women of Ibrahim's village. I regarded our ceremony as more private, more fun than those Ibrahim attended. More a genuine ritual, I thought. The women brought me gifts: embroidery, dishes, linens. They listened to their favorite records and—laying me on a settee that they'd draped in a shiny, turquoise fabric with a dome of gold glitter stretched in an arc above me, so I felt like a character out of *A Thousand And One Nights*—with the help of a plastic kit containing the outline of ancient designs, they wove a web of filigree onto my hands and feet.

They filled in the outlines of the stencil with reds and browns, embellishing them further with glitter. Their own hands stroked, prodded, patted as though, I thought, they were braiding bread or their children's hair. The calloused hands of Ibrahim's aged neighbor worked firmly, confidently on my feet—"Please," I'd begged, "do my feet too"—scratching me slightly as they worked. The velvet hands of my sister-in-law smoothed my own as they painted. *Mothers' hands,* I thought, missing my own, *that from time immemorial have raised children, baked, woven family fabrics, tended their aged. Even laying out the dead for their final rest,* I told myself, conscious that my mind was roaming dangerously far afield.

As I lay like a sheet cake for the frosting in my turquoise tent, munching on fruit and *baklava,* the women joked about their husbands, spun their private problems into tales.

When the *henna* was complete, my extremities a web of designs, the women wished me well. "Here," they said, "now you are ready, ready for your husband."

ELISHEVA

July 1982

Again, it is past midnight. The ward is quiet.

"Do you want to talk?" I whisper to Avrohm, in the half-dark.

"Yes."

"Tell me about your sisters," I say, and I prop him up on pillows.

"Sarah, the eldest, was on kitchen duty," he tells me, moistening his lips with his tongue. He breathes for a while. Then, "She was the most serious, the most prone to daydreaming. God chose the exact moment that she reached for a soup pot, to find her a husband." He stops, difficulty breathing again. Then, "It slipped from her grasp," he says. "The pot, that is, threatening in the process to fall on her head. Pinhas caught it"—breathes—"and after the necessary period of night walks and poetry reading, he caught her too."

He is smiling, calmer now.

"Should we stop?"

"No," he whispers, his lips sticking to his teeth. He heaves in a lungful of air. Then, "Rivka's courtship was more complicated," he says. "She heard Koby sing around the campfire"—stops—"fell in love with him before she'd even seen his face." Rests. "But although he danced next to her in the circle, leaning into the flames as he did so until his face shone with their glow"—spits phlegm into his bowl, rests—"he didn't seem interested. He was a member of the Palmach, would disappear on military maneuvers." Here he stops altogether, closes his eyes, his hands falling open.

I am about to switch off his overhead light when he opens his eyes. "But my sister was a force to be reckoned with, Elisheva," he says. "It took her six months, working alongside him in the chicken coop, before he woke in the mornings needing the boost of her energy"—pause—"needing to hear her laugh."

"You are a natural bard," I whisper to Avrohm. "We'll continue tomorrow."

RATIBA

1966

Five a.m: The siren-like wail of the *muezzin* calls the men of the village to prayer. In my sleep I resist, whimpering, Ibrahim tells me, trying to hold onto someone in my dream as Ibrahim releases his arms, rolls away from me, shuffles from our bed in the gray not-yet-light to the bathroom, his eyes still closed. In my sleep I imagine his father and brother shuffling too, at the very same moment, to their bathrooms, in their separate apartments, in their still-darkened rooms. Community, I think, still mostly sleeping. Except for rainstorms or infrequent snow flurries, our windows remain open. Early-morning breezes brush my face as Ibrahim rubs sleep from his eyes as he, his brother, and his father perform their ablutions, prostrate themselves in the direction of Mecca in prayer.

Six thirty: I'm sitting up now, waiting for the last strands of dream to leave me: faces, voices, yearnings, regrets, Orit and me as children, picking poppies and yellow wildflowers from the empty lot near our house. I liked hers better than mine, but she wouldn't trade. "Those were the ones you chose, Ruti," she said. "Those are the ones you'll like best when you put them in water." Orit was four years older than I but she talked to me like an adult.

The men step, almost simultaneously, into the cool, white air of our respective balconies, relishing the still-cold touch of the tile beneath their naked feet, listening with me to the waking sounds of our village: the proprietary trumpeting; the strut and swagger of the free-roaming rooster and the satisfied chortle of his hens; the phlegm-filled spit of our elderly neighbor torpedoed each day at exactly six thirty-four onto the undeserving earth with a slap that cows birds into silence; a lone car purring down the side of the hill; the cough and sputter of other vehicles, trucks and pick-ups, older perhaps, or less cared for than the car, refusing to start until attention had been paid; the tentative tapping sounds of the early morning hammer as it tests for construction; and the cursed, bent-over widow, who neither stands nor sleeps, pouring slops into the earth from her already scrubbed floor, her body an ominous black hook against the white rock of our hillside. *Orit would have loved this,* I tell myself for the hundredth time.

Ibrahim and Latif drink sweet coffee strong enough, my mother would have said, to curl their hair, smoke their first cigarette of the day, and meet as they walk down between the thistles to the bus stop, their breath already on the stale side of the day.

My Ibrahim teaches Arabic at our local high school; his brother, also a university graduate but not as fortunate as Ibrahim, takes the bus each day to Jerusalem; takes it grudgingly because when he gets there he's trussed up in a purple hat and sash like a doll in a toy fairground, forced, he claims, to work as concierge at one of the hotels. Latif, whose most elegant outfit is blue cotton pants and a t-shirt. *Attitude,* I think, *people predicating their lives on attitude,* but I say nothing.

My father-in-law, like his own father before him, remains in his workshop beneath our building to hew the pink rock of our mountains into building blocks, curved tiers, rounded steps. I see him at work in there as I pass: head bent beneath the folds of his *kaffiyah,* half-empty glass of Turkish coffee, the butt of his cigarette smoldering in its ashtray. I would love to go in, despite the din, because his constant chipping and hammering with steel on stone fascinates me. But Kasim is a taciturn man. He dashes my confidence every time.

"Are you sure you want to do this?" he asked me, before I married Ibrahim. "Ratiba, think seriously. Would your parents have advised you to when they were alive?"

"Of course."

"Good," he concluded. "So long as you know that marriage is a commitment."

Why did he ask me that?

Our wedding was three months ago, today.

ELISHEVA

I'm talking to Orit about Avrohm. "Guess what I've done?"

"What?"

"It was his birthday. Zalman and his family celebrated with him, in his room. When they left, I gave him my present. A tape recorder. He loves it. He's like a very old kid with a fire engine. 'Let's not tell my children about this yet,' he said, smiling at me. 'Let this be my gift to them, after.'

"You should see him propped against pillows in his hospital cot, Orit, the recorder set on his food tray. He's weak, but he isn't going anywhere until he's finished with his toy. He keeps erasing sections, biting his lip with the effort, perspiring, expanding details as he speaks, wheezing because he's constantly out of breath. He gets so exhausted … I have to stop him. 'No,' he begs. 'This is important.'

"'It was a Monday evening in late spring,' he recorded, and he launched into this long story about how his third sister fell in love while on night duty, guarding their kibbutz from marauding Arabs. 'My sister, Leah, and a youth named Yair,' he said, 'simulated the call of the jackal and night creatures, sending coded messages in the darkness to other guards along the fence. Then, when the sky began to pale, when it became clear that another night—their night—had passed without incident, Yair bent toward my sister, drew his army blanket from his shoulder to hers, and kissed the pine-needles that were enmeshed in her hair.'

"By the time the machine snapped off, Orit, his breath was as calm as a baby's. "Avrohm," I told him, "you have a talent."

RATIBA

April 1967

I'm pregnant, and although we are all terrified of the possibility of approaching war, my immediate family are as mindlessly happy as though we lived on a distant island and the baby were theirs. Samah, my sister-in-law, knew before I even told her. She has some sixth sense when it comes to babies and pregnancies, can tell by the glow on my skin, she says. The morning after I tell Ibrahim, two minutes after he leaves for work, Samah charges into my apartment with five women from our village bearing cakes and jugs of tea. It's not even 8:00 a.m. I'm not dressed. We're having a party.

Ibrahim smiles all the time now. He strokes my stomach whenever he's within reach, chatting to it as he opens the refrigerator door, asking our unborn child if he prefers pickles to cookies, juice to milk.

"How do you know he's a boy?" I ask. "He could be a girl."

"True," he says, giving the issue serious consideration. Again directing his query at my stomach, he asks, "Sweetness. Do you prefer cars to dolls?"

"That's just sexist." I laugh.

"True," he says, and he continues his conversation with my stomach about the heat, the neighbors, politics.

He has Arabic music playing all the time because he wants our child to know where he comes from. Every night, he makes love to me, slowly, deliberately, sweetly, because the doctor told us it was safe. He tells me he loves me all the time.

Samah says there's a box of baby blankets, diapers, and rattles in our storage shed.

"Check them out when you have time," she tells me. "You'll know the box. It's marked. Don't touch Kasim's stuff, though," she warns. "He's private that way."

I nod to Kasim as I pass his workshop, remove the key from its overhead hook, open the shed door at the back of our apartment. This is where we store things, all the families, that is, that live in our building. It's been a while, I think, since anyone's been in here. Cobwebs everywhere. Spiders very much alive, well, angry at the intrusion of light. I close the door, allowing my eyes to grow accustomed to the half-dark. A metal box, she said. I find it, pushed against a corner next to what must be Kasim's stuff, between the old-fashioned European valise that was my mother's, which Ibrahim must have stored in here when I first arrived, and a wooden trunk with worn leather strips across the top.

Ibrahim's household tools are all over the place. I yank the metal box from its spot on the cement floor, dirt dropping off it like a scarf, then coiling up again into the air, reluctant to relinquish its bed. I'll open the box in the apartment. It's too dirty in here. I bump my knee on the wooden chest as I try to navigate past it. Such an interesting chest, metal knobs, straps, the works. The kind you'd expect pirates with hidden treasure to use.

The chest is even older than my mother's valise. There are mice droppings all over it. Rust has spread over the hinges and the locks like a skin disease, even over parts of the leather—or is that mildew? Obviously hasn't been used in years. I struggle with it for a while, till it startles me by jumping open of its own volition. Brown paper. Then some gray tissue paper that rips as I touch it. Wow. A dress, an old Arab wedding dress, rich in embroidery, dark, musty-smelling. I forgot about this. My mother-in-law Fatima's wedding dress, the one I was meant to wear, that Kasim kept from me on my wedding day. The fabric is soft, sad looking. *Poor Fatima*, I think. I bury my face in its folds, in its musty, ashen smell. *You didn't even live to see Ibrahim's second birthday; died while giving birth to Latif, neither son remembering your voice, your touch, expressions unique to your face alone.* I'm glad to be here in the shed with my mother-in-law, holding her dress, fingering the veil with its decorative coins dangling from its edges. "I'm sorry," I whisper to her, "sorry you never watched your sons grow."

The paper is so friable; it rips as I attempt to rewrap the robe. There's more paper beneath it though, in the chest. I lift some of that—there's something beneath the dress. My God. What is this? My hands start to tremble, to shake violently. I can feel my chest thump beneath my blouse because what I'm holding is a prayer shawl. A Jewish prayer shawl. What is it doing in this place? In this wooden box? In my home? My Arab home? I lift the prayer shawl from its ancient wrapping. It's not large—a boy's perhaps, the white of the silk yellowed. As the prayer shawl drops open, I see a massive stain across its center, obviously washed, but clearly there: an ugly, faded bloodstain.

"My God," I whisper into the dim light of my family's tool shed. This is someone's secret. Someone else's secret.

It's hot in the shed. Clammy. The smell of mice droppings is making me gag. As quickly as I'm able, I lay the prayer shawl back in its hiding place.

I shouldn't be here, I tell myself, unable to move, suddenly terrified that someone will see me leave the shed or that they'll come in and discover me in this place, with this buried secret in my hands. I dump the wedding dress as best I can over the prayer shawl, shove the tissue paper, even the brown outer wrapping, over it all, the tissue clinging to the sweat of my palms like a baby begging to be held as I try to push it down. I hear a footstep, a muffled cough outside the door and freeze. Kasim, I think. I hide in the darkness, petrified, my heart thumping loud enough, I'm sure, for my father-in-law to hear it outside.

What is this bloodstained prayer shawl doing in Kasim's trunk? With his dead wife's wedding dress? A few moments of silence. I lower the lid and run from that place.

ELISHEVA

July 1982

Orit and I have developed a ritual around Avrohm's tapes. When I don't have the late shift at the hospital, we sit on my balcony munching grapes, drinking coffee spiked with Kahlua.

Today Avrohm's voice is clear. "A rabbi wandered on to my sisters' kibbutz," it is saying, "By that time, they'd been living happily for almost a year, like most of the other women, in their sweet-smelling wooden huts, with their lovers. He was a young man with a bushy beard and friendly eyes. A purple skullcap was pinned to his curls. 'Call me Zvi,' he said. 'Pleased to meet you. What are your names? Nice, nice names. I've been traveling for a while, stopping at almost every village or settlement from Jerusalem to here. I needed to see the country with my own eyes—so beautiful. God has blessed us.'"

Orit giggles at Avrohm's style. "A little precious, don't you think?"

"They ate," continues Avrohm. "'How many members are there here? How safe are your borders? Why don't you marry?' he asked them. "'We don't believe in marriage.'

"'And your parents? Are they still alive?'

"So before that Tuesday of late summer was over," Avrohm continues, in a voice so weak, I almost miss it, and he tells me how the rabbi married twelve couples with the single ring that had been his mother's. I turn the tape over.

"The rabbi left," it says. "As he walked, he sang. 'Thank you, O Lord, our God and God of our fathers,' he sang, 'for the loves we feel for our children; loves that children have for their parents; for the pleasures men and women draw from each other; for the astounding beauty of the young. Thank you for allowing me to sanctify the union of these vibrant souls. Thank you for their well-being, for my wife's wellbeing, for my own. Thank you for making sure that I am no beauty, that I'm married to a woman who will brook no nonsense. Thank you for this country that is spread before me now like the splendor of splendors. Thank you for giving me the leisure to walk the length and breadth of it, for the freedom to thank you along the way. Thank you for allowing me to witness our return to the land and for the peace that we're enjoying at this moment, that comes to us in dribs and drabs like water from some leaky celestial faucet. Oh, Lord, God, and God of our fathers, protect us from harm, bring peace into our hearts and into those of our neighbors so that we live in harmony with each other, for that must surely be your challenge to us at this time.' The rabbi continued his prayer as he descended the hill into the gentle village of the Druze and their goats."

The tape snaps to a close. The next day, between patients, I go into his ward.

"Avrohm," I ask, "how could you know what the rabbi prayed?"

"Because that's what I pray too." He smiles.

RATIBA

I carry Ibrahim's coffee out to the balcony. He's reading the paper, missing the sun as it sinks opposite us in a navy sky.

"What does your father keep back there, in the shed?" I ask.

"Don't touch his stuff, sweetness. He's private that way."

"I was wondering what he stores in there, inside that fancy trunk with the brass knobs."

"I've no idea. What business is it of ours? He told us he doesn't want us fiddling with his stuff, so we don't."

I bring cookies.

"You never know," I say. "He could be hiding things in there."

Ibrahim lowers his paper, glares at me. "What did you say?"

"You never know."

"What would he be hiding?"

"I don't know."

I take my coffee mug back to the kitchen. *This is ridiculous,* I think. *I'm not a kid.* So I fill a bucket with detergent, carry rags and brooms out into the evening air. The light is on in Kasim's workhouse.

"Hi," he says, turning off his lathe. "Where are you going with that?"

"I thought I'd clean out the shed."

"Why?"

"It's filthy. Full of mice droppings and cobwebs."

My father-in-law scrapes his chair back, emerges from his cave, eases my bucket and my broom from my hands. Without a word, he walks them back to my apartment, leaving me to trail behind him, like a kid. Ibrahim is right there, in the kitchen.

"Ratiba," Kasim is saying, emptying my bucket water in my sink, Ibrahim pretending to read the paper, "every family has its way of doing things. In ours, we let things be."

"You don't want me to clean?"

"No. I want you to let things be."

Kasim walks back to his cave. My husband is behind his paper. "I told you," he says.

ELISHEVA

July 1982

I'm in the nurse's lounge, replaying one of Avrohm's recordings when I feel someone listening with me.

"Are you Elisheva?'

I nod.

"Is the story you're listening to about Avrohm's family?"

"Yes. Did you know them?"

"My wife is Avrohm's cousin."

"And you are?"

"I'm Amram, the new orderly. I've been transferred to your unit."

I bake muffins. Orit brings beer. Amram, our orderly, makes coffee. For the first time, we've managed to get Avrohm to talk about himself.

"In 1929, as my sisters, now barelegged and suntanned, were singing their pioneer songs in the Galilee," he records, "Arabs attacked my seminary in Hebron. With blood-curdling yelps, they burst into my yeshiva slashing, wounding indiscriminately with their short knives and their semi circular scythes. Blood gushed in every direction, on the holy books of learning, the tables where the students learned, and on the Torah scrolls themselves. They ran from house to house in the neighborhood where we yeshiva boys lodged, slashing the mattresses, pulling boys out from under their beds, from behind the closets, from beneath the coats, to stab them in the chest or back or to slit their throats. They poured blood over sinks and toilet bowls, killed and irreversibly maimed old men and boys, none of whom had ever held a weapon.

"I hid, frozen with fear, behind my bedroom door. I was short for my age, thin. My voice had not yet started to change. It is not clear how Mohammed got into my room, but suddenly my arm was grabbed from behind. I was pulled from my room up a narrow alleyway, down the neighboring street to a nearby home. The stranger stood at his door with his axe raised. 'You can't take this one,' he told the mob. 'This one is too young.' The mob passed by the doorway as the angel of death had passed by the bloodstained doorposts of Israelites in ancient Egypt. A hush fell over the Arab's house. 'My name is Mohammed,' said the man, in Arabic and sign language. 'Don't be frightened.' He threw a sweater over my shoulders, even though it was a hot day, because I was shaking. The Arab made me a glass of tea with sugar cubes and mint leaves. 'Come,' he coaxed. 'Sit. Drink.' But I cowered mutely in the corner between the table and the stone kitchen counter, staring at the breadcrumbs and the tiny piece of cheese that had fallen from the Arab's breakfast, watching the army of ants that was making its way from the doorway to the cheese, wondering where the man's family was, unable even to raise my eyes from the floor. Finally, the violence abated, the sporadic pounding of feet, the heavy breathing of men and women running from danger came to an end. 'Come,' said my Arab. He took my hand in his own giant, calloused one.

"'Now,' he said, this time in Hebrew, 'I'll take you back to your people.'

"Dead and wounded were being carried onto ambulances. The plaster on the stucco building of my yeshiva was bruised, splattered with blood, caked in dirt. Buses were chugging smoke and smog at the front door. Mohammed watched with me from the corner, men and boys helping the victims onto buses, the younger ones weeping, carrying for their charges, under their arms, their books and bags of clothing. Others were rushing Torah scrolls away from that defiled house of learning. Mohammed released my hand.

"'Go,' he said. 'They're waiting for you.' I couldn't move.

"'Go,' urged Mohammed, a second time. 'May God be with you.'

"'Mister,' I murmured, but boys from Jerusalem were already running toward me, their arms outstretched. Mohammed had turned away."

Avrohm's story plays through my mind as I work. A few days later, I ask him, "Why didn't you live with your sisters, after the riots?"

"Nobody asked me," he says. "It never occurred to them that I might want to work the fields as they did. So I was left in the Holy City, after the riots, in the laundry-shrouded streets of the Bucharen Quarter."

"Near the girls' school?"

"Yes. I'd take a shortcut through the empty lot on my way home," he says. "I could hear snatches of female play, girls singing, someone playing the piano. I wondered what went on behind the wall of that fortress. Occasionally, I'd see Ms. Hannah, the principal, a sturdy, thick-legged, no-nonsense matron, her headscarf pulled to her eyebrows. *Not her,* I'd tell myself. *She can't be female.*" Avrohm laughs weakly, but with a glint still behind his cataract. "I didn't know then," he says, "that Hannah and her girls' school were etched into my lifeline."

"What do you mean?"

"One day, walking from my boarding room to the seminary, I became embroiled in an anti-British demonstration. A crowd had gathered in front of the girls' school, an angry crowd.

"Before I knew what was happening, a British soldier with a furiously red face and whiskers, blustered his way through the protesters, his cudgel raised above his head, blindly clobbering everyone in sight. 'You,' the whiskers hollered at me, 'where d'ye think yer going?' A blow to my head rendered me unconscious but gained me entry into the hallowed halls of female education. Four neighborhood boys carried me into one of the inner rooms and left me there, mumbling to each other as I revived about how some guys get all the luck. Women attended to my wound. Bandaged my head. Placed me on a narrow cot with sheets that smelled divinely of soap and a pillow. For two days, I was unable to open my eyes, but I heard female voices. "Don't move," they said, "It will hurt you. Drink this," they said, or, "Eat, it will give you strength." Female hands tended to my needs. I heard music. A piano. Someone was playing Chopin (though I didn't know it was Chopin at the time). On the third day, I opened my eyes. 'Thank you for your kindness,' I mumbled to the two middle-aged women who were knitting at my bedside. They returned my bundle of books to me, and I resumed my walk."

I can't stop thinking of Avrohm and his stories. Three days later, between patients, I again set his recorder on his bed. "Tell me more," I say.

"I was passing the girls' school again one day during my twenty-first year," he records, "at the corner where the shade tree grew, the one with the twisted trunk that seemed uncertain, at any given time, whether to stretch toward the street of the prophets or that of the rabbinical sage. There, right at that spot, I was accosted by the heart-wrenching sounds of Brahms. I stood there for as long as the invisible musician played and thereafter made a point of passing that corner every day at the same time. Sometimes, it was Chopin, sometimes Mendelssohn. Always, it pulled at my heartstrings. Eventually, by clinging to the drainpipe and hoisting myself up, I caught a glimpse of a pale girl sitting at her piano. Her face was broad and feline with wide set, serious eyes aslant beneath a cap of brown curls.

"I walked back to my seminary, told my rebbe that I'd met my beshert. He asked me how I knew. I said because I'd recognized her. She was my beshert, I insisted, the one assigned to me at birth as my soul mate.

"Inquiries, introductions, and arrangements were made, and I married my Yona."

Later that evening, I tell Orit Avrohm's stories. "Listen to this," I tell her. "Over thirty years later, at the end of the sixty-seven Six Day War, Jerusalem was reunited; Hebron was again part of Israel. Avrohm packed gifts of wine, fruit, imported cheeses, and preserves. He'd remembered all this time. 'Come,' he said to his adult son. 'We must go to Hebron to look for Mohammed, to thank him.'"

"Wow!"

"Yes. Only Mohammed was nowhere to be found."

RATIBA

January 1970

Monday. Ibrahim's been aloof all day, quieter than usual. Then, just as I'm setting the table for dinner, his cousin Fahhid turns up, and Ibrahim announces that they're going out.

"Where to?" I demand, surprised. Fahhid hasn't been in our home since the day he sang at our wedding. "Salaam Alaikum," he says, looking at the dirt on his sneakers, shifting his enormous bulk uncomfortably from one foot to the other, not even asking us how we are. My girls stare at him from their baby chairs as they slurp their *labaneh*. No cooing sounds from them. No hello from him. Nothing.

"Where are you going?" I ask again. Ibrahim never goes out in the evening without me.

"Out," he says again, and he closes the door behind them. For a flicker of a moment, not trusting Fahhid, the woman's fear flashes into my head. *No,* I tell myself, knowing my husband. *Ibrahim wouldn't cheat.*

"Abee!" Daifa calls, reaching for the closed door.

"He has business to attend to," I tell her, as though I'm talking to an adult, and I force myself to make light of it as I mash up her banana.

It's Tuesday. Ibrahim is in a worse mood.

"What's the matter with you?" I whisper, risking everything, panic surging into my head, my chest. "Have I done anything wrong?"

"I don't know. Have you?"

"Ibrahim, do you have anything to tell me?"

He turns away then. "Sorry," he says. "I didn't mean to hurt you. My students are giving me a hard time, that's all. More invested in conflict than in life." He takes his coffee out to the balcony to read.

A gulp, a sob of relief torpedoes from my chest. For a moment, I was sure he'd discovered my secret.

Nighttime. He's lying with his back to me, already slipping into sleep. I fold my arms around him. *Perhaps it would be better if he did find out,* I tell myself, my face pressed against his back. Then I could end this tortuous charade, could get my sister back. I can see her hands in my mind's eye, soft, tiny dimples over the knuckles. Paws, I used to call them. She never liked that. I can see her looking at me, at Ibrahim and me, in the darkness. Her haunted gray eyes. I can't remember what her nose looks like. Her skin. I can't remember her mouth. *What is she doing?* I wonder. She could be married for all I know. I hope she is. I hope she's not alone. *Like death,* I tell myself, *she's fading away from me. I've killed my sister.*

I get out of bed, pad around our apartment in the dark. I watch my babies as they sleep. Wadha's arm is hanging through the slats of her crib. She must have fallen asleep reaching for something. Daifa is sucking on her thumb.

"I'll want them to sleep over at my place," Orit said, the night we fought, "to play jigsaw puzzles on my kitchen table." Only Orit thinks in such detail. What have I done? I cry to myself, stuffing my hair, all my fingernails, into my mouth. What terrible thing have I done?

Morning. I open my eyes, an anemic, colorless morning. Ibrahim is on the bed, fully dressed, staring at me.

"Hi," I croak, my voice not awake yet.

"Sweetness," he says, "your sister is the only relative you have left of your original family. Why don't you write to her?"

"I do," I argue, getting out of bed. From the safety of the bathroom, I call, "Why do you care? What is she to you?"

I come back to the bedroom. He's left for work.

ORIT

The bus slows at the curb, emitting burps of air as it deflates. No university in sight. Demonstrators are marching down the center of the road, headed in our direction, their picket signs, like drunken idols, waving in the air.

"Israel, get out of Palestine," they tell us. "Abolish the road blocks." "Jerusalem for the Arabs." They'd probably be more effective, I think, if they'd pick a single gripe, and run with it.

"No way to get past them," the driver says. "You'll have to walk from here." I'm the only person trudging up the hill.

I find Ibrahim in his empty classroom, peering through his window.

"What are you doing here?" he asks, "on this, of all days? On any day, for that matter?"

I choose to avoid his question.

"Where are your students?" Though I know the answer.

"Embroiled in one of their interminable protests."

I join him at the windowsill. He's watching the demonstrators march away from us, into town.

"I saw it on the news."

"So why did you come?"

"I knew you'd be available."

"Demonstrations," he moans. "They refuse to come into the building, let alone attend lectures."

"Why aren't you with them?"

"The students? Because they're wild. Because they throw lethally sharp rocks. Because I don't want to. I want to teach."

"How long will it last?"

"Until they become rambunctious. They always do. Until the police and the foreign press arrive. They always do. They won't stop until at least five students are detained."

The mark over Ibrahim's lip is white. Then, "Okay," he says, turning from the window. "What do you want?"

"I've been waiting to hear from you. You were going to tell my sister you know about me. About her."

He lowers himself into his metal chair, his head in his hands, on his desk. Then, "I don't understand her," he says, looking directly at me, a child's whiny tone to his voice, as though begging me for an answer. "I thought we had the perfect relationship. I thought Ratiba was perfect. Now I find out, she's not even Ratiba."

"Why didn't you tell her?"

His voice hardens. "Your sister married me under false pretenses. She lied to me, to my father."

"So why don't you tell her?"

"This is the path she has chosen," he says. "She's going to have to live with it."

"What, forever?"

"Until she tells me the truth."

"But I want my sister back."

"I'm sorry."

I scribble on his desk with some chalk.

"Don't," he says. "That's school property."

"Ibrahim." I lay my hand over his. I tell him what I've really come for. "Give me your children."

"What?"

"Let them know who I am. Tell them about me, in a kind way. Send them to me."

Ibrahim's voice is flat. "That decision is in your sister's hands. When she talks to me truthfully, I'll get my wife back, and you'll have two nieces. When she comes openly. Not before."

RATIBA

1975

We have two beautiful daughters, but no matter how much we try, I can't fall pregnant again. Samah says my womb has closed. She talks like that sometimes, like some crone on a hill. In the privacy of my heart, I know the reason: the prayer shawl in the tool shed is casting its shadow over us.

I look like a witch in the mornings, my hair springing all over the place like the snakes on Medusa. I do my best to capture it against my head as I pad across the tiles, toothpaste dripping on my t-shirt, my yellow brush still jutting out between my teeth. I've not yet wakened my girls, but I'm watering my geraniums because I love them, because if I don't water them now, I'll forget, and the sun will cremate them as it's cremated everything else we see from our window. I remove from its hook over the sink the muslin of milk and diced garlic that has curdled into labaneh overnight, put hummus up to boil, taking comfort in the thought that my sister-in-law, Samah, is doing the very same things at the very same time for her girls downstairs. Family, I insist, stubbornly, the familiar ache pulling at my heart. My family.

My girls toddle into the kitchen one after the other, scruffy little rag dolls. Wadha's head, a mass of curls, her eyes liquid dark, like mine, whimpering a little, still clutching her one-eyed lamb with the pink fleece; Daifa silent, her narrow face paler than her sister's, a mark across her lip, not as pronounced as that of her father, but there just the same. Her arms are raised in a proprietary manner so I'll pick her up, claiming her special moment near my heart before I walk them to school. Delicious. Daifa smells like crushed herbs, Wadha, like cotton candy. Has since the day she was born.

A memory comes to me as I bury my face in Daifa's hair: my father walking Orit and me to nursery school, holding Orit's hand, talking to her because she was big. I, running behind them, trying to catch up.

"He's not really your aba," I whispered, when I reached them, whispered so my father wouldn't hear.

My sister-in-law, Samah, and I haggle over fresh-picked olives with the keen-eyed boys of the neighborhood. We milk the four mommy goats that nibble on the hillside grasses at the back of our house, taking care that they neither kick nor, heaven forbid, overturn the bucket. We prepare the leftover milk for cheese. As I work, I think. I have daughters no one but I can see. I appeal, in my mind, to my sister. *Look at the life-affirming things I do*, I call. My life has no witness.

ELISHEVA

July 1982

Avrohm is drawing a crowd. When they see me walk toward his ward with his recorder, patients, orderlies, even doctors gather in his doorway, or they shuffle in and sit on the second bed. Everyone seems to be abiding by one unspoken rule: if they talk, they will be asked to leave.

Among Avrohm's audience is an elderly Arab called Wahid, with an ulcer. One day, he calls me, as I'm about to leave his room. "Elisheva," he says. "I have a story."

"You do?" What I'm really thinking is how out of control this whole story telling thing is getting. I'm meant to be nursing here.

"Please," Wahid begs, "bring the recorder."

So late that night, I do.

"Mohammed," he tells me, "was my father's closest friend. Before Mohammed died, he told my father how he'd rescued a Jewish boy named Avrohm during the 1929 riots of Hebron. He said he'd taken him back to the yeshiva after the fighting ended, had sent him back to Jerusalem on the Haganah bus. I have a note, written in Mohammed's hand before his death, that gives some of the story. Only, it's torn, so I haven't got all of it. Let me read what I have, Elisheva, into the recorder, so it will be preserved."

Here is the voice of Mohammed.

"I waited on the corner where the yeshiva stood, watching, unable to pull myself from that spot until every last child had boarded. The ambulances left. The buses rolled mournfully away. Alone. Not a person on the streets. Not a single Arab other than myself. I walked through the splintered door of the seminary, noticing the handle lying, like the broken head of a doll, in the grass. Shattered windows, shards of glass everywhere, over the floor, the overturned chairs, the butchered podium. The ark, where the Jews kept their holy Torah scrolls, was open, its curtain ripped, suspended by a cord, splattered with blood. Books of learning lay open, strewn together with blood-soaked prayer shawls on the floor of the central room, defiled with vomit, with urine.

"I turned away, closing the door behind me. I wandered through the streets not knowing where to go, what to do next, streets silent as the end of days, until I recognized the home from which I'd rescued little Avrohm, the door of that house, also open, also hanging broken from its hinge. I stepped over the threshold. A broken yet constant drone, like the low bellow of suffering cattle, pervaded the air, accompanied by an unbearable stench of excrement. 'Salaam Alaikum,' I whispered. 'Shalom,' I tried then. No answer. The room was in a shambles: shattered plates everywhere, an overturned bed, filthy sheets pulled across the floor, blood, bread rolls, a table with one of its legs hacked away, a badly battered urn, coffee bleeding dark and dry from its spout, an open suitcase in which a ritual wine cup had been thrown over a jumbled mess of phylacteries and clothes, evidence, I realized, of an attempt at flight.

"In the corner, slumped between the walls, half hidden beneath the filthy bedclothes, shrouded in the still pervasive moan, the awful smell, was a woman, dead, her eyes open like glass, bubbles of spittle and blood congealing from her mouth across her clothes to the floor. Beneath her hand—what looked like the hacked off handle of a broom."

Wahid snaps off the recorder. He shows me the yellowed paper he'd been reading. It is frayed, crumbling at the edges. The paper is torn away, lost after "broom," Wahid's last recorded word.

"Where is the rest of it?"

"I don't know."

"How do you have it with you, here in the hospital?"

"I heard Avrohm's story. I asked my daughter to bring it from home."

"What will you do with it?" I ask.

"The recording is for you," he says. "The note I will keep where it has been since Mohammed's death, in the copper box used by my father to store his treasures."

I am overwhelmed. This hospital, I tell myself, is a living archive. These people under my care—I need to record their every living breath.

RATIBA

1979

Who am I kidding? I write so few newspaper articles I don't even consider myself employed. I accept a teaching position at our village school, the school my girls attend. I'm a bit anxious about that. Surprisingly, it doesn't seem to bother them. The kids are sweet, all of them, eager to learn.

It's cold in the classroom. The winter sun can't penetrate the thickness of the walls. "Want to learn outside for a while?" I ask my students. They clatter their pads of paper and their pens outside, happy to study on the scraggly patch of grass that passes for a lawn. "Write an essay," I tell them. "Imagine you are missing someone really badly. Write them a letter."

The moment the children settle down, a bulldozer screeches its way up our hill, out of the silence, dumps a mountain of rocks on the building site at the side of our school, wails its way down the road and up again. It comes again, over and over. Out of nowhere, workmen start to yell instructions, goading the bulldozer on, I guess. The dog belonging to the house opposite us won't stop yapping, won't let up protecting his family from harm. *Bad decision,* I tell myself, *bringing them outside.* I'm amazed at how impervious children are to noise.

They don't write for long. My neighbor's son hands his essay to me.

"I wouldn't write a letter if I missed anyone," he tells me. "I'd go see them."

"What if they were living in another country?" asks my Daifa.

"If I really missed them, I'd save up money and go to them."

"My aunt lives in America," she persists. "My mother never writes to her."

"Don't you miss her, Ms. Ratiba?"

"I do. A great deal."

"Then why don't you write?"

"My aunt never writes to us, either," Wadha says.

"That's weird," says the boy. "That's not family."

When we get home, the girls tell their father about their essay. He turns his quizzical look at me. As though he's never mentioned the subject before, he asks, "Why does your sister never write?"

Why does my family torment me like this? They never even knew Orit.

ELISHEVA

July 1982

Amram, my orderly, whispers behind our patients' backs that he has a surprise, and I know he means a tape. Our wards are overcrowded. It is a while before we get to it. It's about Zalman, Amram tells me. His wife, Zalman's cousin, recorded it.

I bring Amram coffee and a pastry from the cafeteria. I drag the only armchair we have in our department into our nurse's room, make him sit on it.

It was a week before Zalman's bar mitzvah, the tape tells us. His mother was out of control, pacing round the kitchen, swatting at flies with her dishtowel, dragging the chairs from their appointed places at the table, clucking with her tongue as she did so to indicate that someone other than herself had left them in the wrong position, then shoving them squeakily back to the exact same spot; moving the salt and pepper shakers two inches to the right, two inches to the left, then, in frustration banishing them altogether to the dark interior of the kitchen cabinet, all the while berating her husband for being a *caliker*. What kind of husband does she have, she wanted to know, answering her own question, who could invite guests for the wrong date? Avrohm said he was sorry, that he'd looked up the date on the wrong calendar, one of many pinned as samples to the printer's wall; Yona demanded to see the calendar. When he showed it her, she started over, berating him that they had already sent out the invitations, and how could they change things at the last minute, once they were booked?

And so it was that Zalman was ushered into the bar mitzvah suit, made especially large to allow him room for growth, and escorted to the synagogue by a host of relatives, friends, and neighbors the week before his bar mitzvah. Zalman learned by heart and beautifully recited the portion of the law that was not his bar mitzvah portion. He rose from his seat and gave a perfectly presentable speech about the lesson of the week, received good wishes and, after the Sabbath, wrapped fountain pens and shavers.

The following week being Zalman's actual bar mitzvah, his father again sat at the scratched kitchen table and drummed the weekly Torah portion into him until he could recite it in the synagogue without shaming his parents. Again, he was pulled into his especially large suit, and again escorted to the synagogue by the same joyous crowd of well-wishers.

Only this time, Zalman improvised. In their excitement over the duality of their son's rite of passage, his parents had overlooked the necessity of a second speech. At the appointed moment, Zalman rose from his seat of honor. With clarity and understanding, he repeated word for word the lesson learned from the previous week's portions that had been so well received at that time. Then, in a moment of added inspiration, he closed with: "Now that the people of Israel are in their own land, may it be your will, O Lord, our God, and God of our fathers, that bar mitzvah boys from this moment on will discard the cumbersome dark suits of the ghettoes and don in exchange the khaki pants and the short-sleeved shirts of our brave new world." A second of silence. Yona turned her face to the rabbi as though pleading for a dispensation. Zalman added, "And may the Lord God and God of our fathers give us strength to beat the shit out of our enemies, and may we and our children and our children's children live in peace and harmony with our neighbors. Amen." He hastily retreated from the podium.

A second moment of silence, and the synagogue burst into side-splitting laughter. Men crowded round Zalman, clapped him on the shoulder, and burst into song. They lifted his chair above their shoulders, dancing in ever-spiraling circles around the synagogue hall. Women wept into their handkerchiefs, as their mothers had done since the beginning of time, and threw boiled sweets at his head. Eleven and twelve-year-old girls secretly assessed his shiny mop of curls and recognized with a thrill the nascent devil in his eyes. Finally Zalman was escorted up the gravel road to his home, a man for all the world to see.

I click the machine off. "A happy one!" I exclaim. "Amram, we have our first happy tape!" I want to hug him. I don't. He's a religious man. He might faint.

A memory comes to me: We'd lived in the country for less than a year. I was on an errand for my mother in the Bucharen market when I saw Zalman sauntering down the street ahead of me, his hands in his pockets, whistling. Near me, on the shabbiest end of the Street of the Prophets, he saw a government notice posted on the wall: "College for Telecommunications," it said. "Sign up today."

I pulled at his sleeve. "Hi."

"Hey, kiddo, what's up?" his mind obviously somewhere else. Then, on a whim, "See this notice?" he said. "Come with me."

He charged up five floors, two stone steps at a time, with me racing behind him. A metal desk, a chair, and a man with a checkered shirt greet us. The man had rolled up sleeves and a pencil behind his ear.

Zalman came straight to the point. "I've come to register."

"Do you have money for tuition?"

"First register me. I'll bring the fees."

"Don't you need to discuss this with your family?"

"Mister," Zalman told him, "at my age, I make my own decisions." Then, looking at me, he .winked. "Worlds have changed, kiddo, since my parents gave up on me." And I remembered what his friend Srulick had told me, how hard it was for Zalman, when he was small, to stay in the classroom, how he would wander around the streets, find Arab donkeys, clamber on their backs by first standing on wooden crates he'd dragged from beneath the rotten onions and potatoes behind the market stall and ride home on them, clutching to the bristly tufts of the donkeys' hair with his undersized fists. Srulick told me how, instead of writing tests, Zalman hung around the stalls in the *souk* listening with his wide-eyed stare to the transactions, the wheeling and dealing of adults. By his twelfth birthday, Zalman was bartering, working as a matchmaker between boys two or three years older than himself and Zena, the willing woman in the shack behind the post-office. The bigger boys would tell him to offer Zena five lira. He did, reveling in the novelty that he could sell the same merchandise over and over, while each item at the *souk* was sold one time only. *What the heck,* Zalman thought. *I'm just working here.* And he was, Srulick said, until one day, when Zalman's friend Yankel gave him five lira.

My brother and I would watch Zalman with the other big guys of our neighborhood, perched on mopeds at the curbside, revving the engines, showing off. He was never rude to his parents; it wasn't till years later that his face lost its angelic look. His voice, I realize now—as Avrohm dozes next to me, his head against the hospital wall, his mouth open, snoring—has maintained its warmth. He couldn't stay home. Girls from all over town, women, I thought, gravitated to Zalman. He took them with him to the empty city lots. My friends and I would see him there, flirting, charming, when we picked flowers. Sometimes, he said no to those women, played soccer instead on Friday nights with the moped-riding boys, their leather jackets, their cigarettes.

Our little adventure at the technical school and the man with the pencil behind his ear created a bond between Zalman and me. Whenever he'd pass my house, he'd dismount from his metal horse, run up my front steps, leave a wrapped lollipop on the mat. "For kiddo," the wrapping said.

I was taking out the garbage.

"How about I take you to the games, Elishy?"

"You know I can't. They are on the Sabbath."

"You won't have to do anything wrong," he promised. "We'll climb over the wall."

I shouldn't have. I transgressed. I definitely transgressed by telling my parents I was at a friend's home that Saturday, but I was flattered that Zalman wanted to spend time with me. I'd had enough of being good. Zalman was the most fun boy in town, and he was big. What other big guy bothered with kids my age? The women he went out with would have sold their baby sisters—would have sold me—to be with him. Besides, I'd watched him when he thought he was alone, and I knew. He wasn't nearly as cool as he made out.

We went, me all dressed up in a Sabbath skirt, a white blouse, sandals. One leap, and he was on top of the wall, the crowd cheering at the game on the other side. "Give me your hand," he ordered, and he yanked at my arm until I thought it would pop from its socket. While he was up there, he pulled another kid over too. I would have been more help, should definitely have used my other arm, but what I was really worrying about was keeping my skirt down so strangers in the passing cars, whom I was never likely to meet, wouldn't see my underwear. We were doing this climbing-over in plain view of everyone. We weren't even the only ones climbing. As I said, there were others. No one cared that we were doing something illegal.

We squeezed along the bleachers, over everyone's knees, until we found a space between a burly sandwich-munching man and a man so short he had to jump up and down to see the action.

It was so much fun! In every direction, the obsessive crack-ing of sunflower seeds, a carpet of shells thickening by the sec-ond, like dirty snow, beneath the seats. Apart from the occasional renegade progeny of a religious home, like Zalman and I, who'd succumbed to temptation, the audience was comprised of secu-lar Jews for whom Saturday was merely a much-needed day off work. Nevertheless, nothing was sold on the Sabbath, no candies, no popcorn, neither hot dogs nor drinks. But sunflower seeds, the shelling and spitting-out of husks, that was the national pastime of our extremely nervous people. Salted seeds were brought into the stadium from home, in deep pockets, by the bushel.

Zalman was ecstatic. "Look at this, Elishy," he screamed over the crowd. "Isn't this terrific?" He spotted his buddy five rows above us, looking for a seat. "Srulick," he yelled. "Over here!" So Srulick folded himself next to us, behind the tiny man hopping up and down.

"No problem," said the little man. "There's plenty of room," and the four of us shouted and jumped, the sandwich-munching man on the far side joining in as we rooted for "our" team—I not having the faintest idea which team that was. More than anything else, Zalman said, he loved the power, the rancid smells, the sweat of the crowd as three thousand strangers rose time after time united in the brotherhood of one mighty roar, united in their passion for a game and for a man named Chodrov, whom Zalman said was their master-player. A few moments and I stopped even trying to understand the game. The smells of sweat and salt, the camarade-rie, the joy—everyone's 100 percent commitment to that particular moment, that place—that was what I loved.

I<small>SRAELA</small>

163

"Where do you go on Saturday afternoons?" Avrohm asked when he got home. Zalman didn't answer.

"I tried everything," Avrohm tells me, when he wakes from his hospital nap, "from praise and bribery to threats, and worse, to the kind of chilling silences from which there is no return."

I became a regular member of Zalman's family. Like the rest of the neighborhood, I regarded their open front door as a standing invitation. People wandered in at any time—in the summer the door remained open until dawn—lowered their bodies onto the divan and unburdened themselves of life's pains.

Itzik was the skinniest man I'd ever seen. His hair was plastered to his brow with brilliantine bartered from UN officers; his pants, mustard green, were glued to his bony legs; the metal buckle of his belt was way too big for his body; and his shoes, pointed at the toes, were especially adjusted for tap dancing. We would look up and see him in Yona's open doorway, his knees prancing up and down like a pony rearing to go, then tap dancing into the living room, round the table, skirting the chairs, out through the narrow kitchen door to the thickly treed back of the house, around and in again through the front door. Anyone he happened to meet as he moved lyrically through the house—me, Zalman, or even Yona in her tired feet and housecoat—was born aloft by the sheer force of his good will.

"Itzik," I yelled at him, gagging at the oniony surface of his cheek and his breath that smelled of garlic, "put me down." He planted himself solidly on the music stool then, legs splayed at either end of the piano, his home-glued tapping toes pointed outward. With the forefinger of each hand, as though he had just learned how to type, he played our favorite songs. "A small girl with gray eyes gazed out at the sea," or "I walked alone, I saw beside me, a young rider astride a horse." Yona took him into her kitchen, fed him eggs and salad. She fed him eggs and salad every time he came.

The word around the neighborhood, though nobody knew why, was that Itzik was a crook. One day, without warning, he disappeared. After a month or so, one of his older brothers sidled into Yona's living room, leaned his back against her whitewashed wall and said, "Yona, I have bad news."

"What? What happened?"

"Itzik. He's in jail."

Lilith lived across the empty lot at the back of Zalman's house. By sixteen, she'd learned that nice things come from fraternizing with men, and that for those nice things she was willing to tolerate an occasional bruise, beating, or verbal abuse. The boys of the neighborhood craned their heads out their bedroom windows, watched her skip down her steps in the evenings dressed in high-heeled shoes and low-cut dresses, smoking cigarettes, hanging on the arms of UN peace-keeping officers. Even if the boys didn't see her, they always knew when she was "going out" because of the nervous laugh and the perfume that trailed behind her on the otherwise drab, provincial air.

"There goes the lady of the night, playing her part in the peace effort." Zalman laughed.

"Sour grapes," I told him.

Siesta time. Lilith sat at the bottom of the hill, on the patch of bald earth that constituted the hangout of our neighborhood, her back against the Eucalyptus tree, her naked legs up against the public bench. She propped the chocolate box she'd received from her UN escort against her knees and waited till Zalman, Srulik, and his other buddies saw she was there. When they were gathered around her just the way she liked it, she pulled the ribbon ever so slowly from its bow, pursing her scarlet lips and raising her head the way, she said, she'd seen real women do on the big screen. The boys held their breath as Lilith dropped the coveted morsel into her mouth and swallowed.

"Wow," they sighed in unison. Ceremoniously, in absolute silence, she passed the chocolates around her circle of admirers. From my watch, against the olive tree near Mr. Rozenzweig's grocery store, I saw them sniff the skin on her arms and behind her ears as she leaned in to them.

Within half an hour, the sun had moved above them, piercing through the Eucalyptus, melting Lilith's make-up, smudging her eyeliner, leaving her skin in its natural state, pink and blotchy. Lilith tucked her legs under her then, transformed herself into a regular brown-haired sixteen-year-old, like any other girl on the block. Almost. She shared her cigarettes with the boys, listened as they told her their dreams, the troubles they were having with their girlfriends, told her what they really wanted.

Suddenly, like the weather between the seasons, her mood clouded over. Abandoning her chocolates to the dead leaves and the ants, she stomped back to her room.

"Dumb guys," she said, passing by me on her way, "they're all the same." Her shoulders slumped, her head down, kicking moodily at the pebbles as she walked, her plastic shoes dangling pink, strappy, and forgotten from her fingers.

Lilith's parents lived in the one-room apartment above their daughter's. Her mother, Mara, was beaten by her husband, Zalman told me, bullied and browbeaten in plain view of the neighbors, despite their many warnings. Lilith told her mother to leave the bastard, talking about her own father. She said her mother should move in with her, downstairs, but Mara didn't like the way her daughter lived. "How can I stay with you?" she said. Lilith told her to suit herself.

One morning, just as I arrived at Zalman's house, Lilith returned to her apartment on the other side of the empty lot with a gaping wound down the left side of her face, her cotton dress torn, blood dripping scarlet on the stone as she climbed her stairs. Avrohm took her to the hospital.

Lilith's mother's only escape from the misery of her life was to shuffle through Yona's open door, sink onto the divan, and smoke.

Zalman told me he was working hard, saving to leave for the United States.

"Why?" I asked, my body stiffening, panic surging through me. "Why do you want to leave?"

"I can't stay here if I'm unable to serve my country."

"You served your country in the early days," I said. "Srulik told me you'd wait till the British were playing football, when they'd stacked their guns in a pile, like a teepee, he said. He said that you'd steal them—the guns, that is—when the British weren't watching, that you'd run to give them to the Etzel fighters."

"Yes," said Zalman. "The Etzel men were permanently short of arms. Once a week, the British would play football with us neighborhood kids. My aba never knew what was so important that I'd sneak away from his Sabbath table and his singing."

"My brother told me you served during the War of Independence."

"I was just a kid, kiddo."

"What did you do in the war?"

Zalman hoisted himself onto our front wall. This is what he told me:

"It was May ninety forty-eight, way before you arrived in this country, kiddo. Israel declared her independence. In the middle of the dancing, the songs, the crazed with excitement waving of flags, war broke out. Jerusalem was under siege.

"Fifty neighbors brought their sleeping bags, blankets, and pillows to the courtyard shelter that functioned in peacetime as the storage room. I was eleven at the outbreak of the fighting. Nothing could keep me in that cramped, foul-smelling foxhole for more than a few minutes at a time. Uninhibited by the proximity of the neighbors, my mother yelled at me not to dare leave. 'I'm not a kid anymore,' I begged. 'I can't breathe in here, there's no air.'

"The moment my mother's attention was diverted, I escaped by means of the blackened bathroom window into the courtyard and from there to the world of war and action. I ran to Mahane Yehudah, the outdoor market, in the early hours of the morning to see whether the convoys from the coastal towns had managed to get through the Arab barrage at the mountain pass. I jumped onto the hooded wagons with other boys my age, pulled potatoes from beneath the canvas. The drivers from the coast stood around the lorries, their rifles hanging limply at their sides, relieved on the few occasions that the entire convoy had been successful, or grieving in silence at the murder of their comrades, exchanging reports of survival and disaster with the market vendors who clapped them lovingly and roughly on the back, hugged them; then rushed to unload the goods, to hand them to us, envoys of our families. The heroes from the convoys that ruffled our hair, I remember, gave us sacks of potatoes, canned meats, boiled sweets to take home to our families. I always tried to bring some goodie back for little Orit, your cousin, who shared our bunker with her mother. Orit sat in the corner, her gray eyes wide as a cat's, her thumb and the corner of her grubby blanket stuffed into her mouth, refusing to cry, listening to the gunshots, the explosions and the endless sounds of soldiers' feet padding like a platoon of hungry tigers over the roof above us.

"Twice, while we hid in our shelter, the building above us changed hands. At first, Israeli forces fought from our rooftop, then Arab fighters took up position, chasing the Israelis away. Then, again, it was the Arabs' turn to run. All the while, we residents were stifling from a lack of oxygen, down in the shelter.

"The cemetery of Sanhedria, so populated today with the headstones of neighbors and friends of that generation, was then for the most part an empty lot situated at the closest point to East Jerusalem. Israeli soldiers prostrated themselves in the parched bed of future graves, their rifles strained toward Arab fire. I was big, much older looking than other kids my age. I could run fast, could easily dodge enemy bullets. So when word came that the previous runner was killed en route, I told them I was fourteen, picked up the food packets for the soldiers, and ran. 'Come back,' they yelled at me. 'You're too young!' But they were short of men, and I was already running. From that point on, I dodged the bullets twice daily from the Bucharen neighborhood to Sanhedria and back, bringing sandwiches and canteens of water to our heroes at the front.

"During the fighting, burials could not take place. The deceased had to be stored in the small morgue at the back of Bikur Holim hospital. The neighborhood longed for a ceasefire, if for no other reason than to bury our dead, for the stench of putrefying bodies permeated the area.

"Arabs stood on the hilltops, their guns aimed at the inhabitants of Jerusalem, picking us off one at a time. Jaffo, King George, and Mamilla Streets were silent except for the occasional prowling teenager wending his way from food suppliers to home to soldiers.

"My friends and I learned quickly that to survive the barrage of Arab fire, we had to run zigzag fashion between the shots. One extremely hot day, I came across the body of a man at the bottom of Mamilla road. Other than the two of us, the street was deserted. I tried to hoist him over my shoulders, but he was way too heavy to lift. In the end, I dragged him up Jaffo Road by his feet, his face ashen gray, blood caked in his hair, sticking to the dirt. I have never pulled anything that heavy. The stench of his death has never left me.

"When I reached the foul-smelling structure at the back of Bikur Holim, I heaved the body with all my might, and, with the help of two Chasidic watchmen, I laid my burden on a metal table already full to overflowing with corpses. Once my corpse was in place, the first Chasid resumed his job of covering exposed body parts, his side-curls swinging waves of sadness over the dead. The second went back to his corner, back to weeping over the worn book of psalms he was holding in his hand. I was overpowered by the stench, kiddo. I ran from that place, my stomach a wrenching, empty cavity."

Zalman stopped talking. We were perched on my wall, I swinging my feet back and forth, Zalman, absorbed by his memories.

"So you see, kiddo?" he said. "That was that."

"What was that? You haven't finished."

"Another time," he said.

The next time he drove down our street between jobs, I caught him. "Please," I begged. "You promised." So I hoisted myself back on the wall, with Zalman beside me.

"My two friends and I lived around the same courtyard," he began. "Meyer Sweetser was a thin, fair-skinned Polish boy with a slight squint and a lock of blond hair that hung daredevil fashion over his left eye. He never sat down if he didn't have to, and when he did his right leg twitched violently, impatient at its forced captivity. He lived with his parents and a pretty blue-eyed sister named Haya in the top, right-hand corner of the building. 'One day, with God's help, in the not too distant future,' my mother, Yona, would say, 'Haya will make a good match for our Zalman.' During the war, the Sweetser family stayed in the shelter on the other side of the road where Mrs. Sweetser, who was extremely pious, squabbled constantly with her husband, who wasn't. My second friend was Binyamin Lubayof, whose great-grandparents had wandered into the promised land from Uzbekistan a hundred years earlier.

"Binyamin lived with his grandparents, his parents, and his three good-natured brothers beneath the building. The neighbors agreed that the Lubayof's basement apartment was safer than any community designated shelter.

"When any one of us friends escaped the confines of our shelter, we would crouch behind the low wall of sandbags at the southwest corner of our building facing the Arab neighborhood of Sheik Gharah and warble a low, bird-like whistle. Within minutes, the other two would appear.

"On this particular day, Meyer, the eldest, took a packet of Turkish cigarettes from his pocket, lit one, drew the smoke into his lungs as though he'd been smoking his whole life and handed it to me. He said he needed us to go with him the next day, to the morgue. I passed the cigarette to Binyamin, told Meyer to count me out, that I wouldn't go to the morgue again if my life depended on it. Binyamin wanted to know why. He thought maybe I'd found another corpse.

"Meyer said the bodies needed to be lanced, that the doctor from apartment five told him they were swelling up from the heat and from infection or something, that they needed to be punctured, like balloons, to release the inflammation. Binyamin started walking away. He wanted to throw up, he said. He wasn't going to touch any dead bodies. Anyway, it was against Jewish law to tamper with the dead; it was forbidden even to keep them unburied like that in the morgue, his dad said so.

"I asked Meyer what would happen if we refused. He said we could have an epidemic on our hands, an outbreak of some awful disease. The doctor had been doing it by himself until then, but he had guard duty the next day. There was no one to do it but us.

"By this time, kiddo, we were all smoking. Meyer picked up some pebbles from the patch of earth beneath us and threw them one after the other across the street. Shots were fired from Sheik Gharah. We paid no attention.

"Meyer said we'd have to do the lancing with ice picks, that the doctor had left them for us in the morgue, that we'd have to continue doing it until the war was over or until there was a ceasefire. Binyamin said he was fourteen, old enough to enlist. He didn't care what his mother said, he told us. He was going to join the Etzel fighters and kill those lousy bastards.

"So you see, kiddo, my two buddies and I defiled the bodies of the dead to spare the living.

"We did it in the early mornings, sneaking wordlessly from our bathroom windows and dashing zigzag fashion up Jaffo Road, shouting curses at the Arabs as we ran. We tied our mothers' scarves around our mouths and noses and uttered brief but—trust me—ardent prayers before entering the house of the dead. The ice picks were waiting. By the time we emerged again, the sky had turned from the gray of early dawn to the clearest blue. Birds chirped between the gunshots. The stench has never left me. When one of us got hold of a cigarette, we shared it with the others on our way home. Pretty macabre stuff, hey kiddo? I've never told this to anyone else. I'm telling you because you're like my little sister. I can't say no to you.

"By the end of the third week, our little routine was interrupted by a ceasefire, a truce celebrated by ritual burials. Our men were short of soldiers. Meyer and Binyamin joined the Etzel. They wouldn't take me; I was still too young. They were dispatched one Friday night to a fighting unit somewhere near Deir Yassin. No one knew what had happened to them until the war ended, when their bodies were found in a pit at the entrance to the Arab village, swollen beyond recognition.

"In two periods of truce and three bouts of war, kiddo, we lost East Jerusalem with the Temple Mount and the Wailing Wall, the only surviving vestiges of our ancient Jewish temple. But against all odds, we chased the Egyptians down through the desert from which they had come and turned the tide on the invading Syrians, the Lebanese, and the Iraqi armies. Cynics say that wars end not because of goals realized, but when neither side has energy to continue. And so it was. Despite our enormous losses, Israel, as a state and as a home for the Jews, had survived. For this, there were thanks. Bitter thanks, kiddo, uttered in the synagogues, in the bedrooms, in the deepest recesses of the heart. Then both sides of our holy city folded in upon themselves like jackals turning their backs on their rotten prey to lick their bloodstained jaws, to sit in the houses of mourning, to weep. To do nothing but weep, with dull minds and empty hearts, kiddo, or rejecting the low chairs of mourning, desperately to pace the pain away.

"Then came the final walk from the house of sorrow to the village of the dead, after which came the obligation to start again, to separate the two sides of the city, to patch the wounds in the treacherous stone, to seal the roofs and mend the cracks in the windows, Arabs on their side of the city, we on ours. Yet, still, in the hearts of mourning mothers, in the broken hearts of the Lubayofs and the Sweetzers, whom I could no longer bear to see, was the pain."

The evening was cool. Zalman's words were being forced out of him like rubber bullets, muted and hard, his breath wheezing between sentences, his face drenched in sweat. By now, he seemed to be talking more to himself than to me.

"Most of the Jerusalem Arabs had fled," he was saying, "leaving spacious homes behind them. I tried to persuade my family to move from our tiny apartment beneath the girls' school into one of the empty villas, but my father said, 'No. We didn't fight with the soldiers. We haven't earned it.' In fact, now that the war was over, the empty homes were divided up among families like your friend Naama and her parents, whose houses had been burned down by rockets fired from Sheik Gharah. They moved into a single home with several other families, which meant dividing the only bathroom and kitchen into conflicting schedules.

"Alliances and feuds were formed between families, kiddo. Children played ball together one day and fought bitterly the next over their right to use the courtyard. Mothers, who had not known each other until the war ended, economized on their use of water by bathing their babies together in the kitchen sink, only to squabble the next morning over pots gone missing. Balding husbands ate their evening meals with their families, then sat on the wooden bench on the communal verandah, staring longingly at the younger wives of their neighbors. Nighttime, there was a weary shuffle to and from the bathroom. Mr. Cohen worked as a night watchman across town. Mr. Kimchi would slip out of Mrs. Cohen's room every morning at four. It was a mess.

"And yet, on midsummer night, exactly at midnight, Naama's parents held her in their arms, gathered in their pajamas with their neighbors in the overgrown lot that served as their garden. For the single night that it was fated to live, kiddo, the residents gazed in awe at a particular flower's white trumpet and at the iridescent light it cast against the blackness of the sky."

We sat for a while in silence. Zalman was having difficulty breathing.

"Food was still rationed. For some time women and children continued picking cilantro, parsnip roots, and berries in the fields; Arab women on their side of the border, Jewish women on ours. Women were transforming chicory into coffee, eggplants into chicken livers, turnips into ice cream, while the bereaved mothers wept.

"The mothers mourned, kiddo. My mother, Yona, cooked her okra stews and cleaned her floors for some time, sitting with her knitting by her open window, overlooking other women's children at play. In the privacy of their homes, kiddo, parents and siblings— they wept.

"Eventually, a year or more after the declaration of Israeli independence and the outbreak of war, the dusty days of summer shortened, bringing the High Holidays and the Jewish New Year in their wake. The rains came. One by one, my mother's students came back. The velvet drapes were removed from her two sleeping pianos, sounds emerged, rusty and awkward at first, slow and unsure. Music started to course once more, kiddo, from the children's hesitant fingers to the world outside. Our city was shaking herself from her dead. The bereaved still wept."

Zalman stopped talking. We were sitting in the dark, a warm breeze, the sky studded with stars, Zalman leaning forward, his face in his handkerchief; the handkerchief spread open in his hands. After a while, he lifted his head and said, "From the start of the '47 hostilities to the end of the '48 war, seven hundred and fifty thousand Arabs left Israel, some willingly, others by force.

Between eight hundred thousand and a million Jews were banished from Arab countries because of our declaration of independence." He drew himself up and winked at me. "How strange is history, hey kiddo?" Then, "Your parents will be worrying about you." He drew a wrapped lollipop from his pocket, handed it to me, and drove away.

RATIBA

1981

I don't know what's happening to my girls. Daifa takes Wadha's clothes without asking. Wadha acts like it's the end of the world. Wadha is developing breasts. Daifa says she's ugly.

"Stop squabbling," I chide. "Why can't you be nice to each other?"

"What's the big deal?" Daifa's voice, devoid suddenly of anger, drops by several octaves. She wraps turquoise fabric round her face, playing with me, and says, "It's natural for siblings to hate each other."

A memory: My first day at junior high. I was edging behind the other kids as they crowded toward the classroom, everyone except me laughing, fooling around, feeling comfortable. I was the only kid transferring from another school. I was invisible, pushed along anonymously with the adolescent stream of bodies. Suddenly, hands clamped over my eyes. "Guess who?" said a gruff, man's voice. It was Orit, acting. Only she could be convincing as a man. "Hey, hold up!" she hollered. The entire class load of kids came to a halt. All talking stopped. "This is Ruti, my sister," Orit announced, standing on tiptoe and pointing downwards at my head with the finger of one hand, while wrapping my shoulders with the other. "Be extra nice to her because, from this day on, she's the smartest, nicest, most beautiful girl in our school, and you'll want to be her friend."

"What did you say?" I ask my daughter.

"You hate your sister."

"No, I don't."

The gossip on our hillside is that I have a sister, whom I keep from my daughters, whom I've banished from our home because I hate her.

"Then why don't you write to her?"

"I do."

"Yes," Wadha says, nibbling on a cucumber. "And you also taught us not to lie."

"Why do you never call her? Daifa challenges. "We have a phone, you know."

"Yeah!"

All it has taken for Wadha to side with her sister was one word from me.

"Why did she leave you then, without saying good-bye?"

"She didn't just leave me," I tell them. "She left all of us."

"What did *we* do? We were not born yet."

Ibrahim wants a son so badly.

ELISHEVA

July 1982

I walk Avrohm down the corridor as often as I can. He's growing weaker. I help him out of bed whenever I find the time, sit with him near the window, his knees wrapped in a blanket. His mind is riveted on the past. I want to pull him out of his gloom.

"Tell me about your Zalman," I say.

"He lives in the US."

"You must miss him," I say, and he tells me that when Zalman grew big he and his wife sent him away.

A memory comes to me.

Zalman and I were sitting on my wall again with me sucking on one of his lollipops, dangling my legs. I asked him why he couldn't serve his country, he said because they'd denied his army registration. I asked him why. He said because he had a murmur in his heart.

"I didn't believe it myself, kiddo, when they first told me; I argued with the medic, asking him again what was denied. The medic said I couldn't expect to be accepted into the Israeli military with a murmur in my heart. Again, I asked what murmur? He said I had a dysfunction in my heart, probably since birth, and why was I arguing with him. He was an officer, after all. I went to a cardiologist at Bikur Holim hospital. Yes, they told me, I did have a heart valve problem, but it could be corrected.

"The night before surgery, kiddo, after I'd completed all the necessary medical tests, when I was lying between hospital sheets sure that the following day would be my last, while my surgeon, I felt certain, was at home, washing down his last crust of apple pie with his after dinner tea, my ima, her felt hat no doubt squashed to her head with her most uncompromising of hatpins, rapped on Dr. Kalovski's door and informed him that she was Yona P., my mother, and that she wanted to consult with him. Dr. Kalovski, my ima told me, seemed put out. He told her that he had no time at that moment, but that he'd see her after rounds the following day.

"Undaunted, my ima ducked under the doctor's arm into his living room, telling him that she wished to discuss my surgery at that precise moment. Dr. Kalovski muttered to himself, pulled a pile of papers from his desk drawer, told her that, other than my heart murmur, I was perfectly healthy and that though the pro- cedure he'd be performing was still in the experimental stages, he was sure it would be a success. He added that of course, there are always a percentage of patients who don't react well to surgery, that there are those who have difficulty with the anesthetic, that they could only pray all would go well.

"Kiddo," Zalman asked me, "have you ever seen a bea- ver's teeth? Ever seen it build a dam? That's how unstoppa- ble my ima is. She informed the doctor that, while it was true I was, thank God, a healthy young man, she surely didn't need to consult a doctor about matters of prayer. He, no doubt, she said, had his own issues. If she had listened to the doctor at the time of my birth, I would have long ago been left to die. Then she warned Dr. Kalovski flat out if he operated on me the following morning and the operation was successful, she would be the first to thank him; if, on the other hand, he didn't succeed, I would be the last patient he operated on, ever. My ima let herself out the surgeon's front door. Dr. Kalovski canceled my operation."

Zalman and I sat on my wall for a while after that, with Zalman picking at his teeth. Then, "You see, kiddo," he said, "my maternal family has lived in this country for eight generations. I was raised in an Etzel family. What kind of a man can't defend his country?"

He told me he was having difficulty sleeping, that he'd stopped concentrating on his studies even though his matriculating exams were due in just a couple of months. He suffered from excruciating headaches, he said. Lethargy had descended over him, leaving him unable to work or study at all.

His mother pleaded with him that there was a whole world of people beyond our borders, people who never go to war. She begged him to take his savings, start a new life in the US, free of Israel and its battles. She told him that, with God's help, we would have peace in a couple of years, that he'd come home then, a self-made man.

Many times, I sit with Avrohm on our plastic hospital chairs, shafts of light from the window bathing his handsome brow. "My Zalman left the country," he tells me, with a backpack over his shoulder and fifty dollars in his pocket." Avrohm's eyes are watering.

I see a twelve-year-old girl, with red curly hair and freckles, tears streaming down her face. I hear her sob. "Don't go. Don't leave. We're friends."

RATIBA

July 30, 1982

"Samah!" I screech, not giving a thought to who might hear me. I race to my sister-in-law's apartment. "Samah!" I scream, pounding on her door. "I'm pregnant!" It's years since I've given up on having more children. Ibrahim and I have been married for almost fifteen years—and I'm pregnant. Samah says she's been praying for me. I don't know what power she calls on or what kind of a sorcerer she is—but she's out-gunned Kasim's prayer shawl. Samah doesn't know about the prayer shawl. Still, she tells me not to make too much fuss with this pregnancy.

"Don't tempt fate," she warns.

ELISHEVA

August 29, 1982

It's thirty days since Avrohm passed gently in his sleep. Orit, Amram, and I are in the nursing station about to listen to his final tape. Amram has brought a cake. This is an auspicious occasion. It's chocolate raspberry with icing. Orit has brought wine, and we are ready.

"To Avrohm," I toast. "May your soul rest in peace."

"To hell with the 'rest in peace' part," says Orit. She raises her glass. "To our dear friend, Avrohm," she says. "May you be blessed with wellbeing wherever your soul resides."

Except for the constant bleeping of monitors and the occasional emergency light, our floor is sleeping. It is 2:00 a.m.

"I was diagnosed with a brain tumor," says Avrohm's voice. "My Yona ran around our apartment shouting, 'His childhood injury has come back. His injury has returned.'

"It's not a guest," I said. "It's an illness."

"'It's the bang on your head the bloody British gave you.'

"The doctors don't think so," I told her.

"'I don't care what those doctors think it is, the wound you received when the British clobbered you on the head—it's come back.'

"I fell sick during the Lebanon War. Hospital beds throughout the city were filled with the wounded. My Yona nursed me at home for as long as she could. Finally, she brought me here. So I am under your care now, Elisheva. Thank you for that. Thank you also for bringing me this wonderful recording machine, which is gathering my life around me like a comforting scarf, when I need it most."

Click. The machine shuts off.

"That's it, Elisheva?" Orit says. "That's all we have?"

"Zalman came again from the United States to sit by his father's bedside," I tell her. "He arrived on a Friday. Avrohm was wheezing, a lifetime of oceans, grit, and gravel churning in his chest. Zalman lit candles by his father's bedside. 'Relax, Aba,' he soothed, as he stroked Avrohm's beautiful, broad brow. 'It's the day of rest.' He hummed his father's Sabbath song:

Come in peace,
Angels of Peace,
Angels from above.
Bless us for peace,
Angels of Peace,
Angels from above.
Go in peace, Angels of Peace…

"I was watching from the doorway. 'Go home,' I urged Zalman. 'He needs to sleep.' Zalman left his father's ward, his shoulders hunched forward, unable to hide his grief. The moment his son left the room, Ority, Avrohm journeyed on."

RATIBA

March 1983

We have a baby boy, Hamzah. Ibrahim is celebrating with his father; his brother, Latif; and his cousin, Fahhid, who has the most wicked of glints in his eye and the thickest, most spread-eagle moustache imaginable. Fahhid chews tobacco, which he spits out on the ground heartily as he walks. He comes alone. Cousin Kamal, who is the skinniest man I have ever seen, arrives with his fat wife and five children very much in tow. He leaves them to wait for him in the yard with a bag of plastic rattles and pink, coconut-covered candy for the kids of our neighbors propped between his wife's mountainous knees. Cousin Kamal never goes anywhere without bringing his wife, his kids, and a bag of pink, coconut-covered candies.

The men of the village come too, a few at a time, in dribs and drabs, until Kasim's apartment is full to bursting. The wives, who are simultaneously congregating in the yard, have come for their own good time. It's hot. Some of the older women rest on stone benches near the walls, swiping perspiration from their foreheads with the backs of their hands as they chat; others help the younger ones carry out platters of watermelon, mint tea, and almond pastries.

Upstairs, Latif, my brother-in-law, thumps away on his little clay drum while the others tap the floor to tunes they carry in their heads. We hear them through the window. Cousin Fahhid stands in the middle of the room, his legs splayed as wide as humanly possible, the feathers of his chest puffed, and his arms akimbo, holding on to his hips. He sings Kasim's favorite love songs. The men join in sentimental spurts, each one adding the bit he remembers the best or loves the most, drawing out the languid sounds for as long as he can, recalling perhaps how things were when he was young. "Ibrahim," they call, "come dance with us," but Ibrahim escapes down the back stairs to me.

"Come, watch them," he tells me, pulling me out of the kitchen.

I stand in the doorway, holding my baby. The men get so carried away, they link arms, weave their bodies between the table and the cushions in an exaggeratedly high-stepping, butt-swaying chain, encircling us, leaning on each other's shoulders, chanting as they move. The more hardened sit crustily, like liveried lackeys, on the firm couch and the high-backed chairs against the walls of the living room. They smoke, puff on their *nargillas.*

Latif places music on the record player, pipes it through loud speakers that he's hooked up in the yard. Four of Samal's five children leave their baby brother crawling at their mother's feet, climb up the drainpipe and the berry tree so they can look in at the men. Fahhid and Kamal catch them at it, draw them through the open window, shouting directions, laughing as they pull the kids from the tree, allowing them to stay, stuff themselves on pastries and raspberry syrup, enjoy the fun.

There are neighbors who were not brought by their husbands to wish us well. I see them in the darkened frames of their windows, breathing into their lungs the aroma of our roasting lamb, watching as Samah sets stuffed fig leaves and *baklava* on the tables of our yard. One neighbor is holding a glass of coffee in her hand. She doesn't have children. The other, whose sons are celebrating with us, at their father's side, is leaning on her windowsill, her head in her hands, listening to the wailing strains of our favorite oldies—alone and happy, or alone and grieving? We don't share such thoughts.

"Your baby's not so keen to come into this world," the doctor told me, two weeks after my due date. "We'll have to help him."

My Hamzah is a perfect Caesarian baby, gentle, undemanding. He has Ibrahim's olive skin, my father's chocolate eyes, and a broad brow all of his own, making him look, I think, like a tiny philosopher.

"Where am I?" I laugh.

"Wait," says the doctor. "In time you'll find yourself in him."

I'm terrified of the bloodstained prayer shawl in the shed. I do everything in my power, other than blurting my thoughts out loud, to prevent Kasim from holding my baby.

BOOK THREE

ISRAELA

I watch contentedly, purring like a well-fed cat from my place in the sun, my green-and-gold, fertile place in the sun among rows of corn, of sunflowers and potatoes, food that grows firm and proud in my newly turned fields. I've been lying here since early spring, my body brown, rich with moisture. For so many centuries I lay blind in the desert. Today my many eyes twinkle in pools, even in waterfalls, but most often in blessed puddles of water formed by the farmers and their sophisticated systems of irrigation. The sun warms me as I listen for my seeds, my still-blind seeds. I drape my body over them, watching, feeling them turn slowly, slowly open, revolve mutely in their dance, a dance particular to germinating life, to life waiting to happen.

Elokim and I are lovers. He chose me above all others, so no one has God-given rights over me but Him. I, He says, am His loyal Eastern bride. We meet at the beginnings and the ends of time. We lie together at the very moment worlds are being created, in early morning, just as the sun is toasting my fields so I know my fruits will sprout on their trees, grasses will grow, blossoms will burst from the tight fists of still bare branches, and lambs will drop, healthy and bleating from their mothers' wombs. Elokim holds me in His arms as oceans lap over the sands, licking the rocks with their greedy tongues, teasing them, looking for love. We kiss in the warm, pink places of early dawn, or under a blanket spun from mist, especially for me. We wake where the sea meets the sky to the sweetness of His rainbow, as hope first opens her eyes.

ORIT

1967

The Six Day War is over. Elisheva is waving at me from the other side of the bus station. "Hey, Orit!"

"Elishy!"

I have come to Jerusalem to stay with Elisheva, to witness the reunification of the city; to jostle my way through the crowd, a crowd crazed with excitement; to kiss the ancient wall; to walk down the central streets of Jerusalem and mingle with smiling Arabs, Jews, Turks, Abyssinian monks, diplomats, and journalists from all over the world, all openly greeting each other, clapping each other on the back, happy, enthusiastic, filled with the excitement of new tidings, filled with hope. I go again, just a few months later. Can't keep away. By this time, the excitement of the Old City has spilled over to West Jerusalem.

Every morning, I wake to the sounds of banging, hammering, whistling, men at work calling to each other. Since childhood I've associated "explosion," yelled by builders under the houses, with cool breezes and wellbeing. My youngest self, even before my mother moved with me to Herzliyah and married my father, was infused with feelings of peace when construction workers dynamited rocks into the air, feeling that our world was being built again around us after the war and that it was good.

I get up early, just as the day is waking on the other side of Elisheva's open windows. Every morning, I rush to stand at the top of Elisheva's street, watch the sunrise over the hills of Judea. I roam the city, poking my nose into every hole, nook, and cobwebbed corner. I go to the Western Wall, and, though I don't utter traditional prayers, I press the stones with the palms of my hands and with my naked lips, revel in the smell of antiquity against my skin.

"I don't know what the future has in store for us," I tell Elisheva, "but at this moment, with the birds singing on both sides of the streets—right now, I'm happy as I've never been before." Elisheva hugs me.

I develop such a fascination for the archeological digs that for a while I'm determined to purchase a shovel and a rubber pail and move here. I don't. Oody is waiting for me back home. Besides, it is the people and the mystical, the ancient buildings, and the haunting alleyways of the Old City that most intrigue me.

Dear Elishy, I write when I leave.

I passed faces framed in arches, carved in rock. I saw robes over men and women behind veils. Heat was shimmering off them as they lurched toward me in the haze, reaching me, as though through time, hiding their eyes. Urchins were rolling dice in the shadows of their doors. Round the narrow streets and domes, traffic barked at me, like camels through a sandstorm belching, burping. There were little boys with dirty faces, Elishy, knocking at car windows, surrounded by buses smoking at the lights, hawking hand cream and Coke.

When the sun slipped down to nest in its pocket beyond the hills, and evening breezes rose, this entire ancient heart began to spread, like the widest angels' wings. Vendors spirited away their goods and scurried into darkness. Jackals prowled around the hills and wailed. I heard them. Bats darted their ink-black bodies silently up against the falling night, Elishy, and newborn prayers—like ancient babies—rose in smoke and sound over olive trees and rivers long run dry. Psalms were whispered in the dusk. I heard them. Wrinkled palms caressed the Wall just as prayers were mumbled on the other side, where we can't see, merging with figures prostrate in the Dome. Prayers, newborn and instantly ancient, Elishy, rolled over the dice, tossed in the shadow of the young boys' doors.

In short, I had a blast. Thank you.

ELISHEVA

History is being made. Orit and I are here to witness it. Before the war, kibbutz settlers in the north of the country spent all their nights and much of their days down in the bunkers, sheltering their children and themselves from Syrian fire. The children's houses were under constant guard. Around the country, terrorist attacks: Fatah was attacking along our borders, primarily from Jordan and Lebanon. In '65, we were attacked thirty-five times; in '66, forty-one. In the four months of this year alone, thirty-seven times.

Syria launched regular skirmishes, attacking our farmers and our fishing boats, shelling Israel from the Golan Heights because they objected to our National Water Carrier system by which we are now transporting water from the north, to the southern desert of our country. Jerusalem was a gunshot away from the Jordanian watchtowers, and a constant target. In March '65, Nasser, prime minister of Egypt, proclaimed, "We shall not enter Palestine (meaning the Jewish state), with its soil covered in sand. We shall enter it with its soil saturated in blood." He threatened that he intended to bring about "the perfection of Arab military might." His national aim, he claimed, was, "the eradication of Israel." He cut off our access to the Straits of Tiran, and amassed his army on both sides of the Suez Canal. A chorus of leaders from Syria, Jordan, and Iraq added their threats to Nasser's. President Abdur Rahman Aref of Iraq declared, "The existence of Israel is an error which must be rectified. This is our opportunity to wipe out the ignominy that has been with us since 1948. Our goal is clear—to wipe Israel off the map."

The Soviets provided military and economic aid to Syria and Egypt to use against us. UN Secretary General U Thant cleared the path for their attack by recalling its peacekeeping forces. Legend has it that Golda Meir, our foreign minister, went to Jordan dressed as an old Arab woman, suing for peace. Whether that is so or not, our government did promise to protect Jordan and their political interests if they remained neutral. Jordan refused. Our government appealed to the international powers, to Britain, France, and the US. "Wait," they kept telling us, "wait," as Arab forces gathered on our borders, in the hundreds of thousands.

Naomi Shemer, our poet laureate, quoted from the Bible, "Take your son, your only son, the one you love," she sang. "Offer him, as a sacrifice, on one of the mountains which I will tell you. / And a great cry went up. / Here is the fire, and here is the wood, / But where is the lamb for the offering?"

Those words trembled on everyone's heart. The streets of our cities—silent with fear.

In these six days of war, our boys captured the Golan Heights from Syria, and the Sinai Peninsula, from Egypt.

Nine thousand mortars pounded Jerusalem and the then eight-mile-wide waist of our country, from Jordanian's superior strategic positions on the hills above us, positions that will provide us with security, a buffer zone against our enemies from now on because those hill are ours, recaptured in battle. We recognize these areas as biblical Judea and Samaria, the land that had been conquered from us by Jordan during our 1948 War of Independence. The rest of the world calls them the "West Bank of Jordan," and "occupied territory."

In six days, our boys took back the Old City of Jerusalem with what remains of our ancient temple, over which, in the seventh century, Caliph Omar built his mosque. That's what we are like over here. Orit says we're two teams in a mechanical game, programmed for all eternity to stomp on each other's heads. "We'll not stomp," I tell her. "Wait. You'll see."

This is Orit's third visit to Jerusalem since our military victory. Tourists, pilgrims, politicians, we all walk round the streets in wonder. One really hot day at noon, we walk bang into a celebration. Communities around the world, wanting to feel part of the excitement, are competing with each other, I guess, over the reconstruction of the bullet-riddled gates of our ancient city. Here we are, standing witness as tourists fix a bronze scroll to the archway. As always, we are witnessing singing. "Jerusalem of gold," they chant, with us joining in, "of copper and of light. For all your songs, I will be your instrument."

Of course, the United Nations' Security Council is opposed to the expansion of Jerusalem, claiming that, as "occupied territory," it should be left untouched. But nothing will stop us.

Orit spends her visit with me in a state of euphoria. We leave my apartment before dawn, Orit wandering around the streets and alleyways of the city beside me like a disembodied waif, a being with no physical needs, no need to drink, to pee, to sit, or rest. We return after dark, I to plunge into a warm tub, she to gaze at the moon over the Judean hills like a girl smitten by first love, while her first great love, Oody, is waiting for her in their home, up north.

Orit is fluent in Arabic. We pace the streets of our united city with her saying "Salaam alaikum," and a whole lot more to our Arab neighbors, shaking them by the hand, patting the heads of the children, inviting them to sit with us in coffeehouses, which they do, perched at the edge of smudged formica tables and smiling at us. I sit with them, unable to say a word because I know no Arabic, ashamed of my ignorance and resolute that a shared future necessitates a shared language. I smile, mutely, mopping up the milkshake spilled by the children, making a big show of how happy I am merely to drink my coffee and not to understand, to totally miss this once-in-a-lifetime, historical moment. I watch, enviously, as Orit plans a future in a shared city of peace.

We explore streets so narrow the overhanging balconies kiss in mid-air. Arab merchants grin at us, offer us tea in thin, clear glasses, coffee in tiny cups; offer us stools to sit on. They shake our hands, introduce us, in a language that most of us cannot understand, to the many children who smile and cling to their parents' thighs.

"What is it like on your side?" they ask.

"Come," we reply, "shut up your shops. Come see what we have over there."

We rush back to our side of town. Our streets are crammed with Arabs and Jews laughing, trailing wives and kids in their wake, like kings, or jackals, down the very center of the road. All the stores are open. Music is blasting from every open doorway. Everyone walking in and out of all the shops, Jews too, as though for the first time, as though they have not already lived in this town their entire lives and are not bored by these stores. Arabs and Jews, seeing the same things, for the first time, together.

"Hold on, Orit," I gasp. "You're walking too fast. I can't keep up."

Orit laughs her infectious laugh,

"You're right," she says. "Let's not rush. Let's walk slowly, very slowly. Let's take really long strides, like people must have done during the fat years of the Bible. Let's pretend we're not excited, that we're used to this, that we're cool."

But we are excited. And we are not one bit cool. This is the most momentous thing our people have witnessed in two thousand years.

Now I know. The realization arrests me in mid-step. I know the answer to the question that pestered me as a child when I'd watch my father bind himself in his devotions. "Blessed is He who spoke," he'd whisper "and the world came into being." I knew then. I could see, always, that my father was an integral link in our long chain of history. How did he get to be like that? I'd wonder, and more to the point, why wasn't I like that? Because it was eminently clear, at all times, that I was just a girl, a regular red-headed whiff of a thing, with no claim whatsoever over time. I couldn't even run down our street without wandering off course. At this specific moment, walking down the center of Ben Yehudah Street, I know.

"For the sake of my brothers and friends," I declaim aloud, relishing my father's prayer, "I will talk of peace in your midst. For the sake of God's house, I will seek goodness for you."

This is the moment that gives birth to our unblemished white dove, to the dove that will fly in our dreams and from the balconies of our apartment buildings, always loyal to the clear blue sky of its poster backing, the dove that will sail across our country on the backs of bicycles, will fly on bumper stickers, our depository of dreams, across the world, ready, always ready with the olive branch, her gift, her most prized possession.

"Next year, we will sit on our veranda," we sing.

"And count birds as they wander by.

"We shall yet see how good it will be.

"How good it will be,

"Next year."

We have our moment. It is now: our one, irretrievable moment—ours for the holding, the keeping, the sharing.

The keys and safekeeping of the Mosque of Omar, built so long ago above our own Temple Mount, are handed over to the Jordanian Wafq as a gesture of goodwill. Arab areas of East Jerusalem, dilapidated under Jordanian rule, are rebuilt and considerably extended. Running water and electricity are installed in Arab villages. Anxious to include his new Arab population in the fabric of Jerusalem, the mayor encourages public servants in East Jerusalem to maintain their positions on the administration. For others, new jobs are created. The majority of them accept, only to be intimidated by the more radical factions among them, and resign, coerced to close their shops by their own politicians. At first, they participate in municipal elections; soon they withdraw their cooperation.

Our excitement lasts, though the tea parties have ended. Fundamentalist Arabs don't hold back for long, a Jewish Jerusalem, inclusive or otherwise, is not their party; 1968 heralds an era of fatal explosions, car and bus bombings, and lethal packages left around the city. We become cautious, suspicious, watchful of bundles and paper bags left unguarded on cinema seats, on the sides of the road, in trashcans.

1968

A year has passed. It is siesta time on a lazy day. Spring and summer fuse in a pale pink haze. A car purrs down the road, not yet aroused from its rest.

"Elisheva, how are you?"

It is Ruti. I haven't heard from her for two years, since before she married and became Ratiba.

"I'll be in Jerusalem next week," she says, typically, without a word of introduction. "Take me to the Old City?"

"Why?"

"Because I've never been there. Please. We'll spend the day together, like old times. We'll have fun."

Ruti arrives in a t-shirt and jeans, with no head covering, without a trace of her Ratiba existence. In three sentences, she informs me that she is happy, that she's in love with her husband, that she's pregnant with her second child. Other than that, we don't mention a word about her life in her Arab village. She won't let me mention Orit.

"What's the matter with you?" I argue. "She's your sister."

"I don't care," she throws back at me. "You talk about her—I leave." I refuse to call her Ratiba.

We walk to the *souk*.

"Have you brought money?"

"It's not much, but whatever I have, I brought."

"Good. We'll buy a dress, a long, colorful robe, the kind that the Arab women wear."

Yes, I think to myself in my own secret language, *we'll pluck it as an orange from a tree, sunned and tempting from the colors hanging over the stall.*

We slip into the narrow streets of the Arab *souk,* carefree, chanting, as always, "Jerusalem of Gold." I take a picture of us both standing with our backs against the ancient stone, our self-conscious smiles, Ruti with her unruly, black curls caught by the camera in mid-bounce; me, with my red hair, my freckles, and my skin that has turned flame-red.

Noise. Music. The monotonous wail of peddlers hawking their wares. Aromatic Turkish coffee born aloft on silver trays, lowered and poured into porcelain cups by barefoot urchins to the old men crouched in the doorways, at the entrances to their stores, or in the darkened arches of the ever-receding alleys. The alleyways are permeated with the smells of ripening meat and stale bodies, of figs, guavas, and urine, but most of all, the odor of ancient, dust-worn stone. Ruti adopts a proprietary attitude; this, after all, is her world now, not mine. But I know she's just putting on an act. She's as excited, as bowled over as I am, as I always am when I come here, by the sounds and the smells. Ruti prods the figs knowingly with her fingers. "They're better in my village," she tells me, biting into one. "Juicier, plumper." She buys a bag of almonds and shares them with me as we descend farther into the alley of the meats.

Naked sheep, cows, and woolly oxen-heads are strung high and swooning above the stalls, swathed in flies, flies unmoving and unstill. Trays of baklava lie oozing in the heat. Old men squat on the stone stilled like aging whiskey, their eyes mindless extensions of their pipes and smoke jars. Kids scamper round corners, worming their way into business deals.

The vendors are happy, smiling. "Come, come buy," they coax, selling wooden camels, sand from the Holy Land, scarlet headdresses laden with coins, bartering with the tourists, their colors, their mini skirts, their loud voices. Heavy, robed women, veiled and dark, glide through the archways.

Tourists call to each other, the shrillness of their voices jarring against the steady buzz of movement, of bartering and selling. The smell of dust fuses all—the heat, the colors, the bustle, and the eternal buzzing stillness of the flies.

The dress we pick is orange and red. It is crushed and smells of smoke and spices, spun of the very fabric of our minds. The man who sells it is surly and abrupt, but his father smiles a toothless grin.

"You're a hot one," the old man whispers to Ruti, and pinches her on her rear.

"Regardless of whether I'm hot or not, father," Ruti responds in perfect Arabic, "I'm probably the age of your granddaughter."

Ruti goes back to her village, to her Ratiba life. She won't give me her phone number.

RATIBA

Friday, three strange men in leather jackets come brooding from the mosque. "Life is good here," they tell us, smiling, looking round my apartment, thanking me for the coffee I offer them, turning round to check that the couch is behind them, before they sit. "We're prospering." When they've drunk their coffee and admired my daughters, they say, "Yet look what has happened. Israelis own the country."

"They've owned it since 'forty-eight," Ibrahim tells them. "Don't worry. Life isn't bad for Israeli Arabs."

"We're not Israeli Arabs," says the one with the scar over his brow. "You and us all, we're Palestinian Israelis."

Well, that's new, I think, pulling my mind away, *semantics. Wars are fought over semantics.*

When they've eaten my cookies, they say, "The day the Jews were thrown out of Europe was a dark day for the Arabs."

"Palestine was promised to the Jews before the Holocaust," I mutter. I can't help myself.

Ibrahim lowers his brows. His eyes grow dark. The scar over his lip whitens.

"Sweetness," he says, turning away from the men so they can't hear him, "how can I talk to you? You have no sympathy left for our people."

"That's not true," I whisper. "I love our people. I love you. I'm just being objective."

"Don't be objective," he tells me. "Be Arab."

A new mall opened in Jerusalem. My sister-in-law, Samah, and I take my girls into town. I hardly recognize the neighborhoods, can barely find my way around, it's changed so much.

The supermarket is vast: aisles laden with goods. They have everything here, fruits they never had before: canned lychees, cherries, passion fruit. There's a deli with roasted meats and salads, even ready-made hummus.

"What's the matter with these people?" Samah asks. "Don't they know how to cook?" There is a separate section for aluminum pots, curling irons, waffle-makers. On the top shelves, they have electric heaters. They sell the prettiest cups, gift baskets all made up with crackers, exotic cheeses—and clothes. There are tables laden with shirts, pajamas, even underwear. Daifa stretches from Samah's arms toward a pair of panties, pink and lacy. Samah lifts it for her by the tips of her fingers, as though it's soiled.

"What are we doing here?" she says. "These people have no shame."

"No one made you come," I tell her. "Now that we're here, we might as well have fun."

My Daifa copies Samah. "No thame," she says, crumpling her nose, her voice an exact replica of my sister-in-law's. An actor, I think, like Orit.

Daifa starts to whine, "Wanna go home."

"You wanted to come," says Wadha, acting the grownup. "Now you have to stay."

"Go home!" And Daifa starts to cry.

Wadha is in baby-shopper's heaven: an entire aisle of pretty bottles: shampoos, body lotions. I'm picking toiletries from the shelf, relishing their scent, the prettiness of the containers—everything floral and pastel. Every time I open a tube, Wadha sticks her little nose in to smell it with me.

"Home," Daifa cries, and she topples containers from the bottom shelf. I open a familiar-looking bottle. A whiff of lavender attacks me, my mother's lavender lotion that stood on her bathroom shelf until the day she died.

"Ommy," Wadha says, "why are you crying?"

"I'm not, sweetness."

"Yes, you are," says Samah. "What made you cry?"

"Nothing made my anything, and I'm not crying. D'you want to buy stuff or what?

"Why Ommy cwying?" Daifa wails, clinging to my knees.

"I wanna go home," Wadha says, whimpering herself. "This place is bad for Ommy."

In the end, I'm the only one to get anything: ten plastic bottles of lavender lotion, an entire box.

ELISHEVA

Orit has been here six times in the last year and a half. She can't keep away. I love her zeal, her idealism. I love her presence in my apartment: her will, her wonderful huge heart pushes my walls apart, creates more space, wider vistas for me to breathe in. Of course, we argue constantly about the newly conquered land west of the Jordan.

The rains have come early this year. It is 1968, November, yet we are fully entrenched in winter. It was only drizzling when Orit and I left the house, but now it's really coming down, the skies blessing us with a vengeance. The trees are hiding their heads among their leaves, the leaves whipping frantically in the wind like the few people we see running to the bus stop, hunkering down against the morning in their coats and scarves. Orit and I are stomping up the long hill in the direction of the university because we've been sitting too long, drinking too much coffee. We need to exercise. So we are taking a hike, in the rain, in the direction of the university.

"Orit," I bark into the cold, "those areas are bordered and inhabited by Arabs, resentful Arabs. It is the best and the brightest among us who are settling there."

"They shouldn't. It won't work."

"Why do you think the settlers are moving to those arid areas? Moving there with their families, with small babies, with parents?"

She doesn't reply. Steam puffs from her nostrils. I know I'm getting on her nerves. She hates it when I lecture her. But I can't stop.

"They're going to have to build homes there, Ority, make the soil fertile, lay an infrastructure, build schools, community centers, synagogues. Someone has to build communities on those new buffer zones."

"Why?"

"You know why, to protect our populated areas from enemy rockets."

"It is neither in our nature, nor in our interests, to be occupiers," she says, and stops for a moment to breathe.

"Nor is it in our interest to be at war, Orit. The settlers' only intention is to guard the territories and live in peace with our neighbors."

No one in this post-Six-Day-War era listens to reason. I can tell that Orit is only half-heartedly repeating the voices that warn against our occupation: give the territories and their citizens back to Jordan, they insist; occupation will never work; it will erode our moral fiber, our integrity, our compassion. Most of us believe we can do it, that we should do it, as a safeguard against war.

"Whoever recognizes our right to exist in our land," I say, "will live in peace. The others will have to be watched."

"Aye," she quotes, "there's the rub."

We walk in silence, struggling against the wind.

"Honestly," she says, "you'd think you were standing on a soap box, Elishy, or talking through a megaphone as a representative of the ruling party."

I'm out of shape, too short of breath for political debate. Besides, Orit is obtuse, impossible to deal with.

But she persists. She's always like that, picks at scabs like a tourist in mosquito season.

"Palestinians resented living under Jordanian rule, Elishy, and Jordanians are their brothers. Now, they'll be subordinated to us, a Jewish government—Jews who have been an anathema to the Arab people since the time of Abraham."

Things are changing. Irrevocably. Since the establishment of the state, we've boasted that we'd never hire foreigners or minorities to perform our manual labor, and so it has been. With the sudden inclusion into the country of thousands of skilled Arab workers hungry for employment, we've shed that reality. I guess, at the beginning, hiring Arab labor was good both for them and for us, but by now it has become the very source of bitterness and recriminations that was predicted. The right-wingers call the settlers "patriots," while the leftists regard them as "colonialists." We call the area "the West Bank" (of the Jordan.) The rest of the world calls it "occupied territory." Perspective. Wars are waged over perspectives.

Shame on us. Shame on the Arabs and the Jews: our dove has faded from her azure background, separated herself from the bumper stickers and the backs of bicycles, our current repository of dreams. It has flown from our grasp, disappeared beneath the smog and the gathering clouds. Our moment is lost, our olive branch snatched away, dropped again down the sand-clogged drain of time.

Orit is right, I think, swayed as always by opposing arguments. *Who are we to think we can govern history? History laughs at us. Our function is not to govern but to live.*

1972

Dovy and I go almost every Thursday evening with Naama and Asher to Mazal, a Yemenite restaurant not far from our home. Our babies come too, our neighbors, and our neighbors' babies. That's the kind of place it is, a place everyone loves to hang out in, as though we are all going to our own mother's kitchen. We ask Orit to join us. It is over a year since Oody was murdered. Naama and I keep watch over her. We talk to her almost every day, worrying that she might sink back into her depression. She refuses to date, to "get involved," as she calls it, but she does visit me often. She meets us, periodically, at Mazal's.

By eight or nine every night of the week, the place is packed: construction builders on their way home from work, teachers at the nearby high school escaping the heat of their own kitchens, pious Jews with skull caps and Talmuds fresh from their evening prayers, courting couples, weary parents with their over-stimulated kids, and members of the Knesset, the parliament, seeking a moment of genuine camaraderie. All pass hot sauce or a pitcher of water from one table to the next. All haggle over politics.

There's no need for the music that weaves its way through the eatery air, merging as a background in a richly patterned tapestry with the pungent aroma of roasting steaks, skewered *kebabs* and *kubbeh*. Nothing can compete with the sound of voices calling across the room to greet a friend, argue over elections, or call for a glass of wine or an extra plate of *baklava*.

The chef knows all of her customers by name. The stained door swings open, and Mazal emerges dramatically from her kitchen, the sweet smell of boiling rice billowing in clouds of steam around her and her daughters, all of whom follow in her wake, all three of whom are thinner replicas of herself, all laden with trays of hot *malawa, couscous,* salads, *kubbeh,* meats, bottles of dark malt beer, and steaming glasses of mint tea—the works. She sits next to us for a while as we eat before moving on to sit with others, favorites we like to think, like ourselves, telling us about her grandchildren, gesturing with pride at her three sons who are manning the open grill and the cash register alongside her husband, Koby.

The restaurant walls are plastered with pictures of past presidents, members of the Knesset and other dignitaries, all smiling, all posing with their arms around Mazal and Koby, all of whom have, at some time or another, rooted for their team as they watched "the game" on the TV suspended from the ceiling, all of whom have quarreled in this restaurant during election time, all of whom have enjoyed Mazal's food. Mazal tells us that her parents came to Israel on the "magic carpet."

"Where did they get that name?" I ask her.

"That was not the official name," Mazal answers. "The official name was Operation Wings of Eagles. Eat, Elisheva, take some hot sauce with that; it will enhance the flavor."

As she passes the salads from person to person, she tells us, "In the early days, almost a million Jews fled to Israel from Arab countries: Jews from Iraq, Tunisia, and Morocco. In 'forty-nine, British and American planes flew a quarter million Yemenite Jews on four hundred different flights from Aden to Israel, most of them children who had themselves reached the Yemenite capital by arduous routes, many of them contracting malaria and other diseases on the way. In the month of October 'forty-nine alone, nearly twelve thousand 'lost Jews,' as they were called, were flown to Israel from Yemen. In all, almost fifty thousand Yemenite Jews were airlifted directly into Israel after a two-thousand-year wait, on nothing less than magic carpets."

"How do you know all these details?" Naama asks.

"Hey," answers Mazal, "these details are my story." And she continues.

"Ten thousand Yemenite Jews were waiting in Camp Geula—Camp Redemption—the Israeli-run transit camp in Aden, ready to leave," she says. "Many of them were sick or exhausted from their journey to Aden, but none of them had ever seen an airplane. When the planes swooped from the sky, roaring like vengeful agents from another sphere onto the dusty, earth-packed runway, the Jews shrieked in terror, scattered in all directions and refused to embark. So the rabbis quoted passages from the Bible, first from Exodus, 'You yourselves have seen what I did to Egypt, and how I bore you on wings of eagles and brought you to Myself'; and then from Isaiah, 'But those who hope in the Lord ... will soar on wings, like eagles. They will run and not grow weary, they will walk and not be faint.' That did it," says Mazal, calling her daughters over to replenish our empty plates. "It was the Bible that brought us here."

None of us are eating.

"The project was so risky it was undertaken in complete secrecy. Fuel was scarce. Flying over Arab territory was dangerous. The planes were frequently shot at. The runway in Tel Aviv was constantly being bombed. The operation was accomplished in secrecy, without a single loss of life."

No one talks. Then, "At first," Mazal says, " we were placed in tent cities and army barracks; later, we were moved to transit camps. The economy of the new state of Israel, such as it was, almost collapsed under the burden."

I free my youngest from her high chair. "These stories," I tell her, kissing the avocado on her face, "they are your legacy."

1973

Egyptians attack on Yom Kippur, along the Suez Canal. Around the country, men run from the synagogues, still fasting, to the front. "In the name of the tankists, the parachuters, and the commanders," they sing, "I promise you, my little girl, this will be our last war." Each soldier is singing to his little girl and to my baby with the trusting eyes and the avocado on her face.

"God laughs," the cynics say, "as man makes his plans."

ORIT

1975

It's four years since Oody was murdered. I live on my own now. I enjoy living on my own, near the beach, spending my walking, bathing, eating time talking in my head to Oody's ghost. I've made peace with him. I talk to Ruti too, my absent sister. I haven't made peace with her. The reality is I can no longer conceive of making peace with her. What would I say? What could she possibly say? It's better this way.

Thursday morning. I receive a note from Ibrahim. "Can we talk?" After all this time. I arrange to meet him in a Tel Aviv coffeehouse. He's already there when I arrive, slouched in a corner booth, smoking, looking sadder, softer, his hair thinner than I remember.

"What is it?" I ask, hoping he's ready for me to meet his children.

"I wanted to talk to you."

"So I see."

The waiter approaches. I order coffee and a pastry. He orders the same, though I'm sure he doesn't know what that is.

"I'm a patient man," he says.

I consider it appropriate to wait. He sucks smoke into his lungs.

"I get up every morning," he says. "Every morning, I tell myself, *Today she'll tell me.* For years, I've been following the same schedule: washing, praying, drinking my morning coffee... telling myself that today will be the day. It never comes."

"Why don't you tell her you know?" I ask.

"She's a good woman."

I hold my tongue.

"A good wife."

"So?"

"You're her sister," he pleads. "I thought you could tell me how she's capable of living the way she does, making my food, sharing my bed, bearing my children... loving me, behaving all the time as though she cares, yet guarding her identity from me, as from an enemy."

"You've never told her you know?"

He shakes his head.

"Why not?"

The waiter brings our coffee.

I want to shake Ibrahim. "Tell her already," I hiss at him. "Then get the hell on with your lives."

"How will we be able to get on with our lives with Ratiba knowing I knew all along? How will our girls deal with such a story? Their mother never telling them, never telling me she's Jewish. Ratiba's a proud woman. She'll not be able to live with the shame."

"What do you want from me, Ibrahim?" I ask, my fingers drumming on the tabletop, the way they always do when I'm mad. "If you can't, you can't. Do what most people do—muddle through as best you can, and good luck to you."

"I'm waiting for her to tell me the truth."

"How would that be better than you telling her?"

"Telling me the truth would redeem her."

"Bullshit."

He snuffs his cigarette in his saucer, leaves some money next to his coffee, now cold, scrapes his chair back.

"What about your children?" I ask. "Can I see them?"

"There's nothing left for us to say to each other," he says, though that is not what I've asked him. His upper lip is trembling.

"Do I get to see your children?"

The glass door closes between us. I watch as he slouches against the plastic siding of the bus stop, hunched inside his windbreaker, already lighting another smoke. "There he goes," I say out loud. "Another living, breathing person walking out of my life."

RATIBA

I watch as Fatin and Samah sway down the hill toward us, canvas bags of garlic, potatoes, and herbs swinging rhythmically, like bulbous udders from their wrists, their children tugging at their sleeves, crying for candy.

No one is listening to the children.

"My aunt waited for two hours at the checkpoint yesterday," Fatin is saying, "before those bastards let them through. Her children were bored and crying and getting into trouble, and her ninety-year-old father peed in his pants on the backseat of their car because he couldn't wait any longer." Fatin is sweating from the walk, from the late afternoon sun, from her grocery bags. She sets the bags on the ground, heaves a couple of breaths, starts up again, walking, swaying, talking. "D'you think the Israelis cared? Not a bit. They're heartless, those people. My uncle said the lines were so long, the kids were choking from the car fumes, screaming over the honking of the traffic just to be heard by their own brothers and sisters." Stops again. "Not to mention the dripping Coke bottles and cookie crumbs messing up the new upholstery…and they'd just had breakfast, my uncle said. People were bribing those who waited ahead of them to exchange passes. My aunt says the Israelis are inhuman. They are."

I'm leaning against the stone wall. "I don't know," I say, when they reach me. "Ibrahim's cousins sat on our cushions for three agonizing hours last week, stuffing themselves on salads and pita, smoking, dropping ash and sunflower shells all over our furniture. The children were dashing 'round my apartment like it was a merry-go-round, going into my closets, even dressing up in my clothes without asking permission. Not for one moment did their parents stop criticizing. Criticizing *us*. I can't take them any longer."

"What's wrong with you? Entertaining them for an afternoon is the least we can do."

I've no patience for Fatin. She's too radical. "They never stop complaining," I tell her. "They're constantly whining about how the Israelis treat them like inanimate objects, gorging themselves all the while on the cakes I've baked especially for their visits. You'd think, just once, they'd thank me for having taken the trouble. 'We would never move here, to your nice, white houses,' they say, 'even if we could.' Right. We're meant to believe that…and I watch as they shower crumbs on the sofa. I can't stand the way they make Ibrahim feel guilty. Why should he? He's an honest man. He does everything in his power to get them work passes when they ask him to, and we always let them sleep over at our house when they sneak illegally over the green line."

Samah sits on the top step, fumbles absent-mindedly in her shopping bag, drawing out a cluster of grapes, purple and plump, covered in dust. "Want some?" she offers, popping three into her mouth. She imitates the sorry voices of her Palestinian guests. "Why should *we* suffer? We don't set off explosives."

Samah ties her toddler's shoelace, tousles his hair.

"We should be more supportive," Fatin insists, peeling a banana, dividing it between her children. "Their lives are hard. We're letting them fight our fight for us."

Fatin's two boys have stopped begging for candy. They're listening to every word. *God knows*, I think, *what they're learning from all of this.*

We pick our way farther through the market. Aminah, our neighbor, is squeezing tomatoes on one of the stalls, searching for the soft places. She scoops dried beans from the barrel before she sees us.

"Look at her," Samah whispers. "Tell me she's not pregnant," and I say, "I can't see anything," and Samah says, "I can. I can tell that look anywhere."

"How long?" Samah extends her arm in a knowing gesture, prodding the circumference of Aminah's seemingly regular stomach familiarly, as though it is an eggplant she's examining for ripeness with the palm of her hand. "Three months already, right?" Aminah lets a gurgling sound fall from her throat, low and content, half chuckle, half sigh.

"Right," she says. "Life is good."

This village, Ority, I call in my heart, *where you visited me on the slope of the mountain range; this is where I live.*

BOOK FOUR

ISRAELA

We fight. When He turns His face away, we fight. When He weeps over the violent nature of the human, a nature that He created and which He refuses to control; over the suffering that our children cause each other, over the harm they cause me. We fight when I beg Him to intercede. When He doesn't, He makes me tremble with rage and frustration. When He scowls and allows His children, my children, to suffer, we fight. I struggle against Him when I am left alone for decades, for centuries, deserted, reduced to sand, to dust.

I have good friends; for this, I am blessed. They are my looking glass. They claim to know what it is about me, what it has always been over time, that others find so appealing. It is they who are talking here, who have been expressing their feelings about themselves and about me. They love to talk, my friends, to find solutions to our problems—the single, non-existent, solution that will cure everything. They will, no doubt, talk more, vociferously and often. Still, it is my spirit that speaks beneath their voices, my experience that guides this story. My pain, my endurance, has earned me that right.

ORIT

1997

It is late one windy afternoon. A boy knocks on my door asking for a job.

"What kind of a job?"

"I'm a gardener."

"As you see, I don't have a garden; nothing to speak of, that is."

"I can fix almost anything around the house."

He seems nice.

"Leave your address with me," I tell him. "I'll ask around. Maybe one of my neighbors will need you."

"Oh."

"Not good?"

"Not really."

"Why?"

"I was hoping you could teach me to act. I wanted to trade my skills for yours."

This I don't like. The boy has done his homework. "Sorry," I say. "I'm too busy for that." I'm about to close my door when he says, "The truth is, we're family."

"I don't think so," I say, and I see his eyes—round, chocolate, like my aba's. "I'm Hamzah," he says.

"Who?"

"Your nephew."

RATIBA

We're adding a fourth story onto our building, constructing three apartments for our children, for when, *Inshala,* as Ibrahim says, they get married. Nothing about my life goes according to plan. My girls should have been married, should be looking after their own children by now. They've refused every offer. Other than that, life is easy. Houses are being built along the range of our hilltop, as far as the eye can see.

My girls are thrilled. Wadha is planning to paint her walls cream. She wants cream organza drapes, she says, low cream cushions and cream rugs. "My home will be a place of repose," she says.

Daifa has already started painting her walls. "The construction is unfinished," I warn. "It's too dusty to paint." I don't stop her though. It's her apartment, and she's an adult. Lime green. Her entire apartment will be green, she informs us, with pale blue drapes, blue-and-gold cushions, a blue couch.

I laugh. It sounds awful.

"Cool," she pronounces. "My home will be cool."

Hamzah doesn't care. "It's a woman thing," he says. He's fifteen, the closest of all of us to his father's heart. Since his very first steps, he's traipsed after his father, going wherever his father goes, holding his hand, asking him questions, repeating his opinions, making them his own.

I rarely think of my sister nowadays. I'm too busy. It's been so long. Our lives have taken their separate ways. I sit on the unfinished floor of my daughters' apartments, surrounded by drops of drying cement, spatulas, half-wrapped workmen's sandwiches. The smell of wet stone is everywhere. I watch my girls as they dream. My mother's voice pops into my brain: "Nieces and nephews," she says, as she had in the old days, "the gift of joy." Wadha: beautiful with her coffee-colored skin and her still trusting face. Daifa: slender limbs, her olive skin paler than Wadha's, that honeyed voice of hers, the quickness of her wit. Hamzah: with my father's eyes and that anomalous, broad brow. I think of the proverbial tree in the forest—my only sister, unaware of my children's existence.

A terrible thing has happened. Over a period of several months, Hamzah, my sweet son, Hamzah, has grown morose, withdrawn, impossible to talk to. I came home one evening to hear Ibrahim and him screaming at each other in the shed. Ibrahim never shouts. Hamzah had never raised his voice to his father. I had never seen them in the shed before. For a moment, I panicked. *The prayer shawl*, I thought. *They must have found it.* But no, everything in the shed was just as it always was.

"What's the matter?" I asked my husband.

"Nothing."

Hamzah started to tell me something. Ibrahim glared at him, his eyes hard as granite, his scar white over his lip.

"No," he commanded. "Do not talk. I forbid you ever to speak of this."

"What was the problem?" I asked later that night.

"He's a teenager, that's what."

"What were you doing in the shed?"

"It was cool in there."

The next morning, Hamzah disappeared. We combed the neighborhood. We asked our friends. We put anonymous notices up in the post office, in the supermarket. We even told the police, though Ibrahim keeps telling me he's not in trouble.

"He's a competent guy," he tells me.

"He's fifteen!"

"He's always been self-sufficient."

Yes, I think. *And he's always been here with us.*

Every night, we drive around the neighborhood, round the city, through all the neighborhoods of Jerusalem. Hamzah never goes into Jerusalem. We've swallowed our pride, have asked Hamzah's friends where he might be. They're on the lookout for him now, knowing we are terrible parents.

Kasim, my father-in-law, is devastated. He walks the streets looking for him, neglecting his work, leaving early in the morning, not returning until dark, going from store to store asking if they've seen his grandson, refusing to talk to us.

Every day, every night, we drive through the streets, searching. Every night I cry myself to sleep, when I sleep.

I don't sleep. I pad the floor of our apartment. I sit outside in the ink-black air and smoke. This is what it must have been like for Shuli, my ima, I think, remembering the way she'd pad the floors of our home.

"What did you do?" I scream at Ibrahim. Scream. I have never screamed at my husband before.

ORIT

I realize he must be hungry, so I warm some soup, make him a sandwich. I don't have any cookies to give him.

"I remember you," he says.

"What?"

"Yes. I remember going to the theater years ago, with a friend. It was a big deal for me because I'd never been to the theater before. You were terrific. I didn't know you were my aunt."

We sit at my table drinking tea. I am completely unnerved by the presence in my kitchen of my sister's child. *Years of fantasizing this very scene,* I tell myself, *have paid off. I have him. My nephew. In my kitchen.*

He tells me how Ibrahim pestered him to cut the long grasses around their house, how he went into his family's shed to get the lawn mower. He hadn't been in there since he was little. The shed was musty, he says, filled with old and interesting looking stuff. He walked around, looking, picking things up: mostly obsolete machines, broken parts of appliances, suitcases. On a shelf, he found a tin can with keys, torn newspaper clippings, some loose cigarettes, a wallet. He opened the wallet. Inside, he found a note to his father. "We can't meet till you talk to Ratiba," it said. "Tell her that you know. Please. Bring me back into your lives." The words "Orit Maimon" and my address were scribbled on the back.

"How could parents of mine behave like that?" he asks, twisting his paper napkin into a point, fraying it at the edges. "The note was from before I was born. I couldn't believe it. They lied to us, to my sisters and me. All these years, they let us believe our ommy had a sister in the US. You had begged my abee to bring you back into our lives, begged him! In all these years, nobody had been brought back. "

"How did you know it was me?"

"My Abee caught me with his things, in the shed. I confronted him. He told me it was my aunt, Orit, whom he'd always referred to as 'Raula.' You were a legend in our home. My abee was constantly asking my mother why Raula never writes. 'You have to tell Ommy,' I yelled at him. We had our first fight. 'I have my reasons,' he said, and I yelled at him again. 'You're living a lie. We all are. We're all living a lie.'

"'One word of this to your mother,' my abee threatened, 'and you are no son of mine.'

"So I left.

"Here," Hamzah says. "This belongs to you."

It's the twin to the newspaper clipping Ibrahim sent me years ago, of me kissing Oody in some play.

Tomorrow, I tell myself, *I'll buy him stuff that kids like: Coke, CDs, ice cream.*

RATIBA

Hamzah sent us a note. "I'm fine," it said. "No need to worry about me. I have a good place to live. I have work." No address, no telephone number. Ibrahim is so sad he can't talk.

Years ago, when I lay in the maternity ward, my newborn boy at my breast, I was filled with pity for Ibrahim because he wasn't able to bring forth life, to suckle or nurse. The telephone was by my bedside. Ibrahim had not yet arrived for his daily visit. I itched to call Orit. I wanted to call her each time we took our babies home from the hospital, after the first baby steps, the first teeth, and the birthdays, especially the birthdays. Instead, I was forced to lie, to respond to Ibrahim's incessant questions with "I already told you, Ibrahim, she lives in the US. I do write to her. Yes," I told him again. "I always send your love when I write." Later, my story changed, telling him that my sister, whom he still thought of as Raula, was in the US to search for her real family, that we had fought before she'd left for the US because I hadn't wanted her to leave.

Ibrahim is a good man who loves me. I have healthy, beautiful children and an extended family that, though they are not perhaps as close as they might be, is nevertheless good to me. But now I sorely miss the mother I've never allowed myself to mourn, I ache for my sister. My heart yearns for my son. I don't sleep.

Throughout those special times that create memories, the words of my childhood kept popping, unbidden, into my mind: "If I forget thee, Oh Jerusalem," though I don't even believe in that stuff. My right hand had lost its cunning.

Now that Ibrahim no longer bends his spine proudly backward in an exaggerated gesture to get a better look at me, when he no longer calls me "my beautiful one" during our intimate moments, when his time at home is spent hidden behind a newspaper, now that even my daughters are starting to go their separate ways, a loneliness, an aching sense of loss descends over me, an anchor dropped in polluted waters with such weight it can no longer be ignored.

"The girls still need you, Ratiba, even though they're grown," Ibrahim tells me.

"You don't have to humor me."

"Hamzah is okay. He said so. He needs time, that's all. You have to get on with your own life," Ibrahim says, though clearly he's not getting on with his.

"My life is like water down a drain."

"You've raised two unusually thoughtful daughters and a son who's fine. He says so. That's not water down the drain."

"What should I do now? I'm too young to spend my days making cheese."

"You're a teacher. A journalist. You write articles. That's important."

"You don't even agree with my articles."

"There. That's a challenge for you, then. Be more convincing."

I tell him I want to visit my roommate from our student days, to catch up on old times. He says, "Sure, do whatever you want."

He doesn't care where I go. *It's the prayer shawl,* I tell myself, *Kasim's prayer shawl, again hanging over our lives.*

ORIT

"My name is Orit Maimon. I'm here to see Dr. Falk, Ruhama Falk."

Ruhama is an old classmate of mine.

"You'll have to wait. She's with a patient." Ruhama's assistant, Lilith, a woman with fading hair and chapped hands, would be pretty were it not for a scar that runs down the left side of her face. She opens up a little when I tell her I am a friend of the doctor.

"The doctor treated me when I needed her," Lilith says. "Now she's teaching me to treat others."

Dr. Ruhama, as Lilith calls her, embraces me. She lifts her files from the chair. "Sit," she says. "I have a minute before my next patient." Lilith brings us tea and a saucer of cookies. The clinic is white as a sugar cube.

"I'm looking for an Ethiopian dancer, named Moshe," I say, "for a play I'm directing. Elisheva told me you treat members of his community here." Ruhama remembers Moshe, a musician who visited her in the past.

Moshe welcomes me into his trailer: a bed, a card table, two folding chairs, and a welcome mat. He pours tea, drops a disk into his stereo, and despite his limp and his lack of space, demonstrates with grace the dances that his troupe performs. "Moshe," I beg. "Come outside so I can learn them too."

We step onto the earth behind his trailer, empty of people at this hour. We dance, slowly at first, gaining momentum. Moshe is holding his balance forward, folding his knees and his lean, tight body low over the soil, like a bulrush in the wind. He's thumping at mother earth with his feet as though trying to wake her, as though reminding her that he's here, that we are both here. I move at his side testing the rhythm, testing Moshe's sense of gravity until I get it. Then I relax. Moving into my own space, I allow my body to do its thing. My scarf, color of fire, the one Elisheva says is my trademark, sinks like a sigh to the ground. As we move, Moshe's limp all but disappears. Dance has freed his movements into grace and rhythm. The shyness between us melts.

"Tell me about yourself," I say, collapsing finally on the ground.

"What do you want me to tell you?" Without music, Moshe is more formal than I.

"About your people, your history."

"Where should I start?"

"At the beginning, I guess."

"We're an old people." He giggles, realizing how heavy that sounds. "Some believe that our ancestors left Egypt with the rest of the Hebrew slaves. Instead of walking with them to the Holy Land, they walked to Ethiopia."

"Did they not want to come to the Holy Land?"

"They did. I think they lost their way." A laugh.

How unaffected, I think. "And you?"

"I haven't lost my way, yet." He smiles.

"How did you know about Jerusalem? You were so far away, Until thirty years ago, no one here knew of your existence."

"The same way European Jews knew, I guess. My grandmother told me about it, and before that, her grandmother told her, and before that, the grandmother of my grandmother."

"What did she tell you?"

I have my back against his fig tree. He is sitting opposite me, cross-legged in the sun.

"She gathered the children around her as she stirred her pot. There were many, because my grandmother said all the children of our village were *Beta Yisrael,* the House of Israel. 'In Jerusalem,' she'd say, throwing her sagging arms into the air, arms that protected us from our childhood fears, 'nothing bad happens.' She'd turn her face to the sky and wrinkle her eyes, kissing the tips of her fingers, stretching them out to God. To us, it looked as though she was touching the heavens. 'In Jerusalem,' she'd say, 'our troubles will disappear.'"

Moshe excuses himself, then brings out a plate of dates and sets it on the ground.

"Once a year," Moshe says, "we'd put on our most fine clothes, all white. We'd climb to the top of our mountain and sing in the direction of Jerusalem. This was *Sig'd,* the holiday on which we pined for the Holy City."

"Were you not happy in Ethiopia?"

"No. Ethiopians called us 'falashim,' foreigners, because we were not like them. They beat us up."

"I thought anti-Semitism was invented in Europe."

He smiles. "When I was small," he says, "a wide boy shouted at me because I was a falashe. The wide boy took an iron rod and stomped it into my toe. See, that is why I walk like this."

Later, Ruhama tells me not to be fooled by Moshe's limp. "His people upped and walked to Jerusalem," she says, "or, at least, to what they thought was Jerusalem, which turned out to be the Sudan. He was seven. He walked for four months with thousands of Ethiopian Jews, till our government flew them here, to their promised land."

"Wow."

"Yes. It was their Exodus," Ruhama says, sipping her tea. "It was their great march to freedom. We called it Operation Moses."

I'm preparing to leave Ruhama's office. "I'll walk you to your car," she says and adds, "Moshe watched as his father prepared for their trek. Knowing how anxious he was to travel light, he asked him why he was taking a shovel. His father told him it was to bury those of them who would die along the way. Five thousand of them died, Orit," Ruhama tells me, "en route."

She bangs my car door shut.

"Moshe served in our military," she says, leaning on my window. "He insisted. He served, limping, through the treacherous alleyways of Gaza, Ramallah and Jenin."

I drive back to Moshe's trailer. He laughs when he sees me on his welcome mat.

"I need to ask you more," I say.

"Do you know what was the greatest surprise for us?" he asks, still smiling.

"What?"

"It was seeing white Jews like you. We didn't know there was such a thing as a white Jew."

"I doubt I'm good enough," I say. "As a representative of white Judaism, that is." He giggles. I've never seen a man giggle. *Yes*, I think, *he's a sweet man.*

We're leaning against a fig tree outside Moshe's trailer. It is a hot, late summer afternoon. "You should have heard our women sing as we started our journey, Orit," he says. "When illness and hunger came, they sang us through them, when they were able. They sang through blistering heat and winds until their mouths were caked with dust. They sang through the rains that blinded us to everything in our path, their voices reaching us in rasping whispers. When we could no longer hear them, we knew they were singing, that their song was for us.

"We welcomed the rains when they first came. We drank from the puddles, from leaves, from water we cupped in our hands. We opened our mouths, inviting the rain to fall directly into our throats. Plate-sized drops. If the rains had stopped at that, it would have been a blessing. Instead, they beat down on us with a fury that was as cruel as the sun had been. The noise of the rain deafened us. It separated us from each other, forcing us to battle alone, under the darkened sky. It persisted for days; the skies were close and hostile. It was clear that the rains didn't want us to reach our destination. I was small, up to my knees in mud.

"Every utensil, every article of clothing, was submerged in mud. The women sang in whispers, one cluster of women after another, one group taking over when the breath of the previous faded, and so on and on, in a chain of melody. Until the rains stopped, they sang, Orit. Then the sun beat down, mercilessly on our heads, our faces, our arms. The sun didn't want us to reach Jerusalem either. The trek was too hard. We rested during the hot hours, walked by night. The calls of animals, of spirits in the bush, terrified us. The women sang on many of those walks too, when they could. I'd clutch the skirt of my grandma and follow her rear through the dark.

"My people died without a whimper. They'd wander off, one at a time, to die beneath a shrub, or we'd find them lying ahead of us or behind us when we went back to look for them. We'd watch our elders cover the corpses in shallow graves, graves we knew would never protect them from animals. We got used to the dying, stepped over them, continued walking.

"Babies died, many babies. Their mothers would squat on the ground and keen over them, lacking the voice to cry. Often, the women refused to walk after the loss of their children. Madness descended over them. I remember one mother clutching her dead baby to her bosom, a creased bosom, like a prune. She was pushing her baby's dead face up against her nipple, clucking, coaxing him to nurse. When one of the elders tried to take the baby from her, she clawed at him with her nails, scratching his shrunken face till blood ran from it. That woman took her corpse-baby and limped into the bush, turning and hissing at us as she backed into the trees. The elder walked after her.

"He returned alone. Before long, the wounds she'd inflicted on him became infected, so he died too. There were those who walked into the bush because they were too hungry to go on. They wanted to meet their maker in private. Others died on the path, while walking.

"We could tell who would be next by the flies, by the pus encrusted at the corners of the mouths, by the death in their eyes. The old ones went first, grateful to be part of our march.

"In the Sudan, we were interned in camps. We didn't know whether we'd be allowed to leave. Orit, when the Israeli birds swooped from the sky to carry us to Jerusalem, then we sang.

"The plane was still hovering over the ocean when the Israelis taught us your song. "Jerusalem of Gold,' we sang, as the plane landed. You should have heard us then."

I look at Moshe. A light is glowing beneath his skin.

"Our old people, those who had survived, kissed the earth. Babies who could barely crawl crouched next to them, their little bums sticking up in the air, copying everything they did. We danced at the airport, Orit, with the Israelis who came to greet us. They brought us flowers, blankets, diapers for the children. They gave us keys for the homes that would be ours from that day on."

Moshe has stopped talking. Tears pool in his eyes, forbidden to fall. I don't tell him that I know his story, that we all do. His hand is resting on the earth next to mine. I want to hold it. I don't.

"But your government didn't know what to do with us. We were sent to live so far south or north, most of us have never seen Jerusalem."

"Our cities were congested," I tell him. "Our government thought you'd prefer the rural areas."

"You're right. But we came to live among you, as one nation, not on the peripheries, like aliens."

Moshe gives the saddest smile. I can't think of a thing to say.

He chews on a pine needle. "In Ethiopia," he continues, "our culture was predicated on the respect the young had for their elders. Here, in the promised land, the young make up their own minds about everything, what they want to learn, how they want to work, even whom they should marry. So our old people sit in their houses, waiting to die. And our youth? They chase the local way of life in the streets, hoping to adopt the confidence of the Israelis by osmosis. Many of our children have lost their lives in suicide bombs or in military service. Still, we're different. For two thousand years my people have been characterized by their patient temperaments. Now we've attained our dream, we've become bitter. I too am bitter, Orit, bitter and angry."

I think of the Ethiopians I see in the streets carrying groceries from the *souk,* the women erect in their robes, babies bound in fabric to their backs. I think of the kids walking to school with their Israeli counterparts. Do they feel foreign? I recall a soldier I saw at the station, waiting for a train. A group of soldiers were relaxing, smoking, joking with each other. An Ethiopian immigrant, also a soldier, was sitting apart from them on the concrete, near the top of a flight of steps. His head was in his hands, I remember, and his face was wrought with pain. I remember thinking he must have lost a loved one. Now I wonder whether he felt excluded.

Moshe says, "If we don't do something soon, my people will despair."

Until today, I've regarded our government as a parent body stretching its resources to cover immigration, defense, infrastructure, medical care, social welfare, education, and so on. Now I worry whether our government is elitist after all, whether it doesn't care to invest in the Ethiopians. I remember the accusations made by the Moroccan immigrants of the fifties and early sixties, who'd also come with little education, with little knowledge of western culture.

How can these people be separated from their Jerusalem, I ask myself, *from the culture they were so eager to embrace?* I realize what Moshe has kept from me: that we've not protected his people from isolation, illiteracy, or the ravages of poverty; that the elders of his community have taken that failure upon themselves.

A week has passed. A morning swept by mist. Moshe is sitting outside his trailer, slicing cucumbers, so I ask for a knife, and we finish them together. We talk about his dance group, the songs that tell of their experiences in Ethiopia, of the way they felt when they first arrived. Again, we become embroiled in the difficulties that Ethiopians face.

"Orit," Moshe says, challenging himself to say what is on his mind. "You assume that your ways are the best, that in order to survive among you, others must relinquish the way of life that has served them for centuries, must become mirrors, parrots of yourselves."

"You're right, but Moshe ..."

"You are too busy 'making it' in your own world, a world that is falling prey to disparate ideologies, conflict and war."

"Moshe ..."

But Moshe won't stop: "You've no time to glean from the wisdom of others, to wait until our cultures blend."

"I know. I'm sorry. Moshe, your Hebrew. I never realized how good your Hebrew is."

"It has to be good, or Israelis will think us stupid."

I can't talk.

"My dear friend," he says, "there's a kind of bird. She doesn't fly away when confronted by a predator, pretends she can't see the danger, busies herself instead with her feathers. That's what you are doing, Orit. You are refusing to recognize a fear you can't handle."

I feel like a kid.

"This country is that bird," he says. "In the army, I served in Gaza. The Palestinians were smuggling explosives and armament through underground tunnels from Egypt into Israel, beneath people's homes. Our job was to drive around in tanks, to explode those tunnels, to warn the residents that their houses—the houses above the tunnels—would be destroyed. Gaza was nothing but rubble, dust-choking clouds and devastation, the roar of tanks, the smell of disaster. No work. No infrastructure. Little food. Less water. The Arabs hated us. Their hatred crackled in the air, shot at us like bullets from their eyes. Every corner was a turn into death. All that the women and children understood of their misery was that we, the soldiers in Israeli uniforms, were the devil. We were there to destroy their lives. Little babies who could barely walk, couldn't yet talk in sentences, knew whom to hate.

"'Whom do you hate?' their mothers would hiss, stopping deliberately in front of our tanks, refusing to move away. 'The Israelis,' they lisped, lisped, before they could even pronounce the letter S."

"I need to go," I say, biting my nails. "It's late."

"You want to know what I think now, Orit? I think the Israelis hate the Arabs the way Ethiopians hated us. I'm no longer sure that what is happening here is good."

"Moshe!" I'm rocking back and forth, trying to stop myself from crying, my arms wrapped around my body. "How can you not see the difference? You didn't send snipers or suicide bombers against the Ethiopians. You didn't smuggle explosives into their country. You never refused to recognize Ethiopia as a state of its own. What you were suffering from was segregation, racism, pure and simple. If you think the Israelis hate the Arabs, it's a temporary hatred, born of war, of a self-declared enemy living in our midst. Killing in our midst. We've made mistakes," I say, "but we are not racists."

"Yes," he nods, not listening to the end of my outburst. "We've made mistakes. The grandmother I adored, whose arms protected me from my every childhood fear, is gone, and her prediction was wrong. Our troubles didn't evaporate with our arrival; pain is felt acutely in the promised land. Injustice is as at home on the streets of Jerusalem, as on the streets of ancient Babel."

"I'll call you," I say and run to my car.

When I get home, my kettle is boiling. Music is playing. Hamzah, my comfort, is sitting at our table, studying for his exams.

RATIBA

I've just come home from school. I was asked to teach the kids about Nakba, the Palestinian day of catastrophe, a day of demonstrations against Israeli independence. I didn't do a good job.

"What are they commemorating?" I asked my students.

"Israel," they yelled, all with one voice. "The Jewish state is our catastrophe."

"Not ours," I said. "We're citizens." They stared at me.

"My abee said you're not a good teacher," Fahhid's son said. He's my least favorite student. "He said you have no loyalty."

"We have citizenship here," I told him again, wanting to cry like a child. "We are Israeli Arabs."

"We're Palestinian Israelis," he said, throwing the words back at me. "We mustn't forget our brothers. My abee says so."

The children asked too many questions after that, that I couldn't answer. It was worse when they didn't ask.

At home, Wadha is doing her schoolwork at the kitchen table. I lift squash from the basket to peel when I feel Wadha staring at me.

"What?" I ask.

"Mom, why aren't you happy?"

"I don't know where my son is."

"Why weren't you happy before?"

"I was! How can you even ask that?"

"You were happy a lot of the time," she says, softly. "A lot of the time, you were hidden behind a mask."

ELISHEVA

It's summertime. Zalman's old bike-riding buddy is admitted to my ward.

"Srulik, remember me? I'm Elisheva, Zalman's friend."

"Look at you!" he says. "I never would have recognized you!" He seems to think that's a complement.

Srulik's a large, pensive man, prone to bouts of silence, but more frequently to storytelling and the spinning of one-liners, trying to cheer up the patient in the other bed. During the Six Day War, after Zalman had left the country, Srulick was a soldier serving on the closest point to the border that ran in those days between the east and west sides of Jerusalem. He was in charge of relocating the inhabitants to a safer part of the city.

Neighbors clustered on the corner of Naama's street clutching bundles, suitcases, and, though pets were a luxury in those days, the occasional dog or parakeet. I was staying over at Naama's that day, so I was evacuated with them. Old people hugged their shawls around them, more for comfort, I think, than cold. It was a warm night. Every now and then, someone would go missing, delaying our departure until the soldiers found him. All in all, despite the barrage of fire that came, like Morse code, in steady bursts from the other side of the city, the operation went smoothly.

Srulik and his unit had searched every home, backyard, barn, and outhouse. All of the inhabitants, except for us—the group sitting in the final truck, had been driven to safety. The lights were off in the houses. Our headlights were dimmed and covered with tape, a tarpaulin pulled over our heads. Srulik was in the driver's seat, keys in hand, reaching for the ignition, when, responding to some impulse, he jumped from his perch, ran to a house on the opposite side of the road, entered, and opened the closet door to the right of the hallway.

There, crouched on the floor, was a child, nine or ten years old, her skinny knees protruding from her dress. The child's eyes, he later told us, were closed; her fingers jammed into her ears. She wasn't making a sound, he said; snot and dirt were smeared on her cheeks. Srulik slid down the wall of the closet, until he was sitting next to her, his head buried in the hem of an abandoned coat. "Your family is waiting," he told her. "They've sent me to take you to your new home." The little girl turned her face toward him. She had the biggest, darkest eyes, he said, he'd ever seen.

Srulik introduces me to his wife, a woman with a curvaceous body and wavy hair. Remember that night?" he asks. "Sit, Elishy. I'll tell you a story."

What is it about these people, that they think I have no work?

"Ten years later," Srulik tells me. "1977. I was running down the steps of my apartment on one of those Jerusalem days when the air is cellophane clear, the blue of the sky and the green of the trees picture perfect. I was whistling as I walked. A girl approached me.

"'Hi, Srulik,' she said.

"As you know, Elishy, I've lived in this neighborhood my entire life. I know most of the people of the city, from the clients of my business endeavors to the, shall I say, more colorful types. But I couldn't place that girl. That was a girl one doesn't forget. I asked her if I could help her in any way. She said she'd been looking for me. I asked whether I knew her, she said yes.

"Believe me, Elisheva. I'd outgrown by several years those glorious few months when men believe God has set aside one particularly ravishing girl, dog-eared her, so to speak, just for them. In my heyday my looks never exactly drew girls into the streets looking for me. My shoulders sloped, as they do now, and my hair was already receding. To top it off, I was wearing plaid shorts, an orange shirt, sandals—and socks.

"The girl had the deepest eyes," Srulik said, continuing his story. "I asked what I could do for her. She told me she'd come to marry me. She was serious. I grinned, wrapped one leg around the other, the way I still do when I'm nervous, and muttered into the sunlight that this must be my lucky day.

"'Mine too,' she said. That's what she said, Elishy. Straight out." Srulik coughs again into his basin.

Watching him, listening to him, I marvel, as I always do when my patients tell me their stories, at their ability to heal.

"I asked her who she was," Srulik says, emotion stripping him, for a moment, of his story-telling powers. "She told me she was Tanya, that ten years earlier I'd saved her from the closet in Abu Tor; that she'd come to marry me."

Srulick slaps his hospital sheet, coughs again. "We married shortly after that," he says. "We've lived like a couple of doves ever since, haven't we, sweetness?" His wife smiles. "You know what's most wonderful?" he asks me. "She makes me laugh." His wife nods again, enjoying the story, stroking his hand. "We jog together in the mornings before work, folk-dance every Sunday and Thursday evening."

Srulick tells me that Tanya sings in the shower and while painting watercolors on her easel. He plays the guitar on their veranda, between the pickle cans that have been converted into geranium pots and the crates of produce that don't fit in the kitchen. Sometimes they shout at each other. Sometimes they sulk. At times they slam doors and fight till the neighbors gather at their windows. Always, he tells me, they love. Twins, a son with wavy hair and a daughter with deep, dark eyes and a gift for spinning yarns have already flown, he says, from their nest.

"Srulick," I say. "You're living the perfect story."

"Then how, for the love of God, do I get a heart attack?"

RATIBA

"You keep telling me you want to visit your roommate," says Ibrahim, "but you don't. What's holding you?"

"I hate to leave you." Silence. "Okay. This time I'll go."

"Don't go on my behalf."

I walk out of our apartment, determined this time, to do something. My heart is aching. I knock on Kasim's door.

"Salaam," he says. He considers smiling a waste of time. "What can I do for you?"

"I've brought you a cake," I say, trying to sound casual. I have never brought him a cake before. "I baked two, thought you'd like the other one." He brings the coffee to a boil. I cut a slice of my cake.

"Abee, do you speak Hebrew?"

"A little."

"Where were you brought up?"

"Here," he answers. "Where else?"

I try to ask him about the prayer shawl. I really do. The words won't come out of my mouth. We drink in silence, sitting at opposite ends of his table.

"Is there anything you want to talk about?" he asks.

"No."

"You're sure?"

I don't answer.

"You came to bring me cake."

"Yes. Well," I say, "I'd better go back."

I'm about to close his door when he lays his hand on my arm. "I've watched you hold Hamzah from me over the years, Ratiba. It hasn't worked. Your boy"—and his voice is all choked up—"he's the sweetness in my life."

Yes, I think, *but what about your bloodstained prayer shawl?*

"I'll be here," he says, "if ever you need to talk."

ORIT

My original Pretzel companion is long gone. Today I walk to the beach with her granddog, Pretzel the Third.

"Orit Maimon?"

A strange sight greets us when we return from the beach.

"Good afternoon, ma'am. How are you? Wonderful, wonderful, yes, thank God, we're fine. We've just repaired the roof down the road from you. There, on the fourth house at the end of the street, no, on the other side, beyond that bush. Do you know them? Nice people. I imagine you must have the same view as they. May God always be good to you. We couldn't help but notice, while working up there, that your roof needs work. Yes, ma'am. It's in bad shape. There's no way it will hold up against the rains."

Itzik, his wife, and their daughter form a strange work force as they plod from house to house on what must be the hottest day of summer. Kalanit and Shira, both of whom have their own weight to take into consideration, are encumbered and heavily perspiring in the voluminous skirts, the sleeves and the stockings of the righteous. Kalanit's Yemenite face gleams with sweat and determination beneath the wig, worn for generation upon generation by women in their European *shtetls*. Itzik leads his work group down the road. His hair is gray, his dark clothes are absorbing every last ray of the sun, and the fringes of his undergarment are swinging from either sides of his pants. The three plod down the center of the road bearing buckets, brushes, and drop cloths round their necks, from their shoulders, and suspended with string, painfully from their fingers. "We work with a material manufactured especially for flat roofs," Itzik assures me. "It will make your roof smooth as a mirror."

How can I not employ them? If nothing else, I want the women to set their buckets down and drink a glass of water.

"Truth be told," Itzik tells us on his third workday, the roof not one bit smoother or more mirror-like, "when I landed in jail over twenty years ago I hadn't much hope left for any kind of life." I wonder whether my roofer is this outgoing with all his clients, or whether it's Hamzah he's really talking to. Hamzah finds him fascinating. He leaves his schoolbooks and his friends, because now he has school friends, to hear his stories.

"God in His goodness caused me to be born to a family of eleven children," Itzik says. "My father was a tired old man by the time I was born, and while my parents were well meaning, they couldn't afford to raise either me or my siblings." Itzik accepts the glass of water Hamzah offers, mutters the appropriate blessing, sits on a closed tub of tar. For a while, the only sounds on the rooftop are emanating from the birds, enjoying their afternoon siesta, and from Itzik's wife and daughter, wordlessly sweeping their special substance with their brooms. "I've struggled to keep myself alive ever since I can remember," Itzik is saying, "so that, may God be blessed, I was relieved when they hauled me off to jail. I would have been happy to die in there. I never thought I'd make it to see Kalanit again. But, boy, did I miss her."

Hamzah falls into the trap. He always does. "How long have you been married?" he asks.

"I met Kalanit when I was eighteen. She was two years younger than I. Wow, was she beautiful. A stunner. You'd never believe it looking at her now." He paused. "She's had it hard," he said.

Itzik offers me a cigarette, lights one for himself, winks at Hamzah. "She was still living at the orphanage when I saw her searching through the want ads at the grocery store. We went out for one month. Then we thought, *What the heck?* If you'll pardon the expression, and we got married. She said she loved me because of my 'charm.' In those days I had a way with the ladies." Itzik puffs on his cigarette. "I was young and dumb," he says.

I look over at the women in my roofer's life, the sun directly over their heads.

"Right now," I tell him, "I'm more worried about them than about your story." He isn't listening. Hamzah rolls his eyes at me and smiles.

"I realized I wasn't going to die in the slammer," Itzik says. "As my mother used to say, you don't die that easy. Kalanit was threatening not to be there for me when I got out. I couldn't see myself making it without her."

Finally, Kalanit and Shira move to the shade to drink from the pitcher I've provided. Even there, it's almost a hundred degrees. Perspiration is streaming like tears from the women's every pore. Itzik is still talking.

"I didn't make conversation with the other inmates," he's saying. "I was harmless enough, so they left me alone. I didn't want to use the barbells in the jail's so-called gym. I've never been a reader, and I ate little of the little they gave me. I lay on my cot and slept most of the day, getting up only to use the 'facilities,' or when forced to go out into the yard by the guards.

"There were nights when I simply couldn't sleep, when the guards yelled at me to lie down. One morning, after pacing through the night, I woke to find a rabbi sitting on my cot.

"'Hi. I've brought you music.'

"'I don't want any.'

"'I'll leave it anyway.'

"'I don't have a player.'

"'I'll leave you mine.'

"'Why?'

"'Because your soul needs nourishing.'

"'Get out of here. I don't have a soul.'

"'We all have a soul.'

"'Much good it's done me.'

"'You've not listened to it.'

"'Oh, yeah?'

"'It can't do you any harm,' and the rabbi left.

"The rabbi came back every day. The music he brought was un-cool and disturbing, multiple male voices straining with all their might, both their vocal chords and their emotions, expressing something I couldn't even begin to understand: love songs to God.

"'Why can't you bring me love songs about men and women?' I asked him.

"'Learn how to love God, yourself, and the world around you,' he said. 'Then, you'll be ready for the love of a woman.'

"I asked him what the hell he knew about the love of a woman, anyway. He said he had a good wife. I wanted to goad him, so I asked him in a crude way, a way I would never use today, if he would bring me those songs when I'd learned all of that, and he said by that time I wouldn't need his music because I'd be making my own.

"His records sang of their love of the Messiah, of all things, which is the last thing I cared about, but which the rabbi said meant a world of peace and perfection, and then they sang, with real longing, of the end of days, which seemed at the time more to the point.

"The boys who formed the choirs, whom I could tell by the cover were no more than kids, sang about life, that it was only a narrow bridge to the next world. Insane stuff like that. Yet when the words made the least sense and the melody was at its least cool, I found myself getting choked up over nothing. I was in a bad way. I was going to have to stop listening to this stuff.

"Among the most raucous songs, for which I had little patience, songs that went with the picture of the manic, black-garbed boys dancing in circles, their side-curls spiraling outward, among those there were beautiful tunes, which the rabbi said were psalms: 'I will lift up my eyes unto the hills from whence cometh my help.' I liked that, though I knew it was corny. Through the bars of my cell, I could see the barbed wire surrounding the fences and gates of my jail. Beyond the ugly streets of wherever it was I was serving time, I saw the blue-pink mountains, remote and peaceful. The rabbi said King David wrote those psalms when he was in trouble, that he had lived at the foot of a valley in Jerusalem where three rivers meet to this day, that King David used to look upward at the ring of mountains on which his son, years later, would build the temple, and find solace. 'Solace,' he said, 'means peace.' I liked that word.

"'King David wasn't always successful in life,' my rabbi said. 'Many times, he lived in fear of his life.'

"'Why? What did he do?'

"'He sinned.'

"The rabbi said that the real heroes are those who've had hard lives and are willing to start over. He said the Hebrew word for soul is the same as for breath. 'When we listen to our soul,' he said, 'we are listening to the breath with which God created the world; our breath is God's soul.'

"'Get out of here,' I said.

"When he talked like that, I have to tell you, I thought the guy was crazy. He said we could tell by the translucence of a grape, how perfect God's world is; that the horrible things happening around us are the consequence of our need to destroy each other, that in as much as we are more developed than other creatures, it is our duty to protect them.

"The rabbi told me everything had turned around for him from the moment he'd learned those things. God caused me to make up with Kalanit. She visited me regularly at the jail, waited for me till I got out.

"We had a daughter, and my rabbi brought all of his students to dance at her naming. We called her Shira, 'cause—hey, she is our song."

"Strange man," Hamzah later tells me, preparing salad on our kitchen counter.

Hamzah is called to the army. In reality, he volunteers.

"You don't need to. Your father is Arab."

"I am an Israeli. I need to." Hamzah fills out forms, undergoes a stream of interviews. He has me sign as his mother, Rut Maimon.

"Are you sure you want to do this?" I ask, panicking. Then I rationalize: if Ruti had let me into her life, all these years, I wouldn't be doing this. Even if I wrote to her, I tell myself, she wouldn't answer. So I fill out the form.

Hamzah is called up. I don't know where he's serving. He calls me every few days, like a son. I'm working in a Russian theater in Lod, performing with immigrants, for immigrants.

"On your next leave," I tell him, "I'll take you to my theater. Wait till you see our audiences cry, Hamzah. See them laugh. People of heart, who know no Hebrew."

He laughs at me. Always laughs when I'm excited. When he comes home on weekends, he brings a massive bag of laundry. "Mount Hamzah," I call it. I'm a regular ima.

ELISHEVA

Dovy and I moved to Haifa. I work in the emergency room at the Rambam Hospital. Dovy was brought into the hospital under my watch when I was still in Jerusalem. That's how I met him. There was a huge hullabaloo when he arrived because he was so badly wounded, because he was a major in the army with a future all laid out for him. He'd stepped on a mine. His leg was blown off, so he was obliged to stay for a long period of treatment in the hospital. I got to know him as he fought his pain, fought to walk on an artificial leg, fought me. He was fighting to give up, fighting to live.

That was years ago. He's as fine today as anyone can be with an artificial leg, can walk fast, climb stairs. He can remove his prosthesis whenever he wants and swim. I call him my "golden boy" because of his round head and cropped hair.

"You are my Roman general," I tell him, remembering illustrations in my old schoolbooks.

"I'd rather be your Israeli general." He grunts.

ORIT

After half a century of hostilities between Israel and her cousins, both sides are, we believe, on the brink of peace. I produce Athol Fugard's South African play depicting characters that struggle through the night with their differences, their guilt. My actors are an Israeli named Baruch and a Palestinian named Youssouf.

It is an intimate space, the house full for the duration of the run. On opening night, Baruch brings his wife. Youssouf comes with his mother from Sheik Gharah. Hamzah watches from the third row. "You do good work, Orit," he tells me, making me feel that I've won an Oscar. Fugard's play is a success. The run draws to an end. The stage is dimmed, props are carted away, my actors and I disappear into our lives.

Off stage, the play between Israel and our neighbors continues. Hard-liners hold from the beginning to their warning that Israel not compromise on territory, though most hurl themselves into the euphoria that is sweeping the country. Negotiations are what we need. Compromise will buy us peace. Land for peace. But in 2000, when Arafat walks away from the table, we all, all of us, sink into despair. Idealists harden. War is all they want, we say. There will never be peace in this region.

I no longer think of my sister.

Three months later, my actor calls me.

"My mother died."

"Youssouf, I'm sorry. Was she sick?"

"She felt bad a week ago. After a couple of days I took her to the hospital because her fever was high. The fever never abated. A virus had attacked her heart."

"Is there anything I can do?"

"Can you recommend a rabbi in Jerusalem?"

I don't need to tell him that rabbis in Jerusalem are like prayer books in a synagogue.

"Why would you want a rabbi?"

"My mother was Jewish."

"And your father?"

"A Muslim. He's buried in the Muslim cemetery in East Jerusalem."

"And you're not burying your mother next to your father?"

"No."

Youssouf told me that his mother, Frieda, was born in Berlin in 1911 to Jewish parents. In the late 1920s, he said, they left Berlin for the Holy Land. Frieda fell in love with the tawny hills of Palestine, with the shepherds still swathed at that time in tunics and headdresses. More significantly, she fell in love with As'ad Falladi, an Arab from East Jerusalem. Youssouf does not know why, only that his mother's parents returned to Europe in 1930 and perished there. He said that in '48, when East Jerusalem fell to Jordan, Frieda and As'ad, his parents, lived in Jordan. In '67, East Jerusalem reverted to the State of Israel. From country to country, their home remained the same stone structure in the suburb of Sheik Gharah, with iron latticework painted Jerusalem blue to ward off the evil eye, iron that As'ad had forged in his workshop, labor of love for his Jewish bride. From Palestine under the British, to Jordan, to Israel, their living room retained its washed floors, faded rugs, jugs filled with thistles. And with books, books most of all, in Hebrew, German, and Arabic.

Youssouf finds his own rabbi. He opens his mother's door to Hamzah and me, dressed as never before in tie and jacket. His face is covered with the stubble of the Jewish mourner, and on his head, a cantorial skullcap.

"You look like a rabbi," I whisper.

"Thank you for coming," answers Youssouf, ignoring the flippancy of my remark. A candle flickers on the coffee table. I am calmed by the blend of Middle Eastern and European tastes. Youssouf introduces us to his friends, Saloma and Fatima, who work with him on the Palestinian newspaper, and to Shoshana, who studied with him years ago at the Hebrew University. Next to Shoshana sits her husband, Oshri, wearing the knitted skullcap of the traditional Jew. The only other person in the apartment is the second actor from Fugard's play. Shuli's voice plays through my brain. "Everyone who comes into your life," she'd say, "comes with something to teach."

"Make yourselves comfortable," mutters Youssouf. "I'll be back," and he disappears out the door.

Saloma and Fatima hand round pastries, prepared by Youssouf. No one, other than my sweet Hamzah, wants to desecrate the atmosphere by eating, so we settle instead into a discussion about Youssouf, Hamzah munching and sipping throughout. Forty minutes later, our friend returns, ushering ahead of him into the place of mourning, a rabbi with a beard and a long coat. Close on the rabbi's heel comes his son in identical garb, curls swinging from the sides of his head. The father stands, the son stands next to him; the father sits, the son sits as though glued to his father's thigh. An expectant hush falls on the room.

"Dear friends," Youssouf says, "thank you for coming. It has given me great happiness to return my mother to her people." Then, "Welcome, Rabbi. We have laid my mother's body to rest. Please tell me: Where, according to tradition, is my mother's soul? What is my function now, as her son?"

Panic rises in my throat. What about Ruti? What if Hamzah never sees her again?

"Your mother is journeying to her resting place," says the rabbi. "Your function is to help her find peace by means of prayer. Dear friends, Youssef's mother possessed a unique ability for love. Rarely have I encountered such a son. With respect for the life his mother chose at her husband's side, for the love that existed between his Jewish mother and his Muslim father, Yosef has brought his mother home. May her memory be for a blessing. Dear Yosef, please accept this copy of the Ethics of our Fathers."

And so it is that Yosef gets his name.

Yosef pumps his mentor's hand. He opens a folder, reads aloud poems he has composed in his mother's honor: his mother bringing a drink to his sick-bed, releasing an insect trapped in a glass. I am overwhelmed by his tenderness. Yosef depicts a woman of humor, of steadfast character, a life-guide for a child of mixed birth and vulnerable identity. As he reads, the candle blinks on the coffee table, an ethereal light contented in this friend-filled room of mourning.

"Interesting man," Hamzah mutters, our arms linked, as we walk back out into the night.

BOOK FIVE

ISRAELA

For centuries, I was barren, used only as a desert track for dreamers to cling to, for prophets to get lost in and find their vision, for nomads to wander through on their way to some better place; used as a meeting point for smugglers and thieves.

Today, I hear agents of violence, and I remember the future. I rumble with fear. In my heart, I call to their mothers, "Take your sons to your houses. Bind them to your chairs; gag them, blindfold them if necessary until they grow calm. Then teach them, for they have forgotten, about peace, about the blessed life, about a future—a present—without pain."

Beneath their prayers, in their morning cups of coffee, beneath their love-making and their child-rearing, and in their sorrow, especially in their sorrow when burying their dead, I hear the simmering of heating souls, I smell the charge of armies, of lives exploding uselessly into smithereens. I sit in mourning over a disaster still to come.

RATIBA

2000

I'm longing to call Orit. I call Elisheva instead.

"Ruti?" she shrieks.

"How did you know it was me?"

Elisheva laughs at me. "If I didn't hear from you for a hundred years, which I actually haven't, and if you were at the other side of the world, which you might as well be, I'd recognize your voice. How are you?"

"Good. I'm good."

"How's that man of yours treating you?"

"He's terrific; you know that, Elishy. Are you busy?"

"No more nor less than usual. I'm always busy, but I still live. Why?"

"Because I need to visit you."

"Are you okay?"

"Yes. I'm fine. I'm missing you."

"Oh, Ruti. We've missed you too, all of us, so much. Come. We have an extra room. You can stay for as long as you like. You can stay forever."

"Well, maybe not forever. Soon. For a few days. Wait, Elisheva, don't hang up."

"What is it?"

"Nothing. We'll talk when we see each other."

"Ruti," she says again, sensing I think, that something is wrong, "what is it?"

"Just wanted to ask how that man of yours is."

"He's a love. Wait till you meet him."

I wait too long.

Bus Explodes in Haifa
Bomb in Jerusalem
Children Killed on Way to School
Pizzeria Bombed
Coffeehouse Blows up
Car Bomb
Explosion in Netanya Market, in Hadera Market
Train Station Blows up in Binyamina
Family Murdered on Way to Daughter's Wedding
Woman Stabbed
Suicide Bombs Hit Tel-Aviv and Jerusalem
Three Bombs explode on Ben Yehudah Street
Bomb Explodes in Mahaneh Yehudah

I go into Jerusalem more and more frequently to buy an Israeli newspaper where I'll not be seen. I read it and then stuff it in the trashcan near the bus stop.

These are the violent years following the failed Camp David Accord. Every place that the Fatah or the Islamic Jihad can reach bursts into flame. The boys of our village sharpen rocks, pelt them down the hillside to the cars on the highway, feeling like heroes.

"Why do you do that?" I ask my kids at school. "We are Israelis, like them."

"We're not," they yell, all at once. "We're Arab."

"The Israelis are evil, wicked, dumb," they tell me, throwing words out one after the other, like pebbles. "They don't belong here."

"How many of you want to live in peace with our neighbors?" I ask.

"I do," whispers Rauma, my favorite student.

"How do you think we can achieve that?"

Two of my neighbor's kids start to giggle. "Miss," they call out, bouncing up and down. "We achieve it. We play football with the neighbors on our street, peacefully, every day."

Rauma says, "My parents are glad we're in Israel. They say our lives are good here."

Rauma quenches my fears. That's why she's my favorite. Other students stare at me glumly, bored by the topic. They're kids. They need to play.

"I'm not talking about the people on our streets," I say. "I'm referring to others who share this country with us."

"You mean the Jews?" Mahmoud, Fahhid's son, is talking. "We don't want peace with them."

"Why not?"

All the students scream at me at once. "Because they don't share the country. They own it."

"Arafat will give this country to us," Mahmoud says. "He'll make Jerusalem our capital." Silence. Then, "My abee says so. Why should the Jews own Jerusalem? Why shouldn't we?"

"When you own this country," I ask so sad I can barely breathe, "will you share it with the Jews?"

"Hell no" says Jamal's boy. "Let them go back to wherever they came from."

"Jews have lived in this region for thousands of years," I say, ignoring his language.

"That's a myth. My abee says so."

I'm the enemy now. The kids are lined up against me.

"This country is ours," they yell.

I open my front door, faint from fatigue.

Daifa has heard. "Why did you do that?"

"Because I want our kids to think," I say.

I receive a call from the principal. "What did you do?" he barks at me. "I've been receiving complaints all afternoon."

How do those I have abandoned feel, I ask myself, *as they leave their homes for work or school, not knowing whether they'll see their loved ones again.* Our village is quiet. *Where is Hamzah?* I worry. He and Orit haunt my every waking hour.

I read about Zalman's cousin in yesterday's paper. Zalman was Elisheva's friend when we were kids. His parents have been dead for years, but two of his aunts, Avrohm's sisters, both in their mideighties, are still living in the north. This is what I read:

Yesterday, at 7:00 a.m., a suicide bomber walked up the path of the Shlomi settlement. He could no doubt hear the drone of the tractors; smell the fertilizer newly laid over the earth. Rivka Yahalomi's daughter, Orna, a woman in her fifties, was riding her bicycle to the road as the bomber neared the entrance. He must have panicked as she came close because he detonated his explosive on an otherwise empty path. Orna's body was blown to pieces, strewn over the area. The bomber's head was found today, two fields over.

We received a note today from Hamzah. The same as the others. "I'm well," it says. "I'm working. I have friends. I'll contact you when I'm ready." He mailed it from an untraceable address.

"Ratiba," Ibrahim asks, "why won't you eat?"

"I don't see you eating either."

During the worst period of my depression, Wadha takes the bus to Jerusalem. Ibrahim and I keep to the safety of our neighborhood and worry about her. On the most violent days, I stay in my room, refusing to watch the images on TV. I tell Ibrahim I'm sick, refuse his offer to take me to a doctor.

Jerusalem is a tinderbox.

"You don't have a fever, Ratiba. Why won't you eat?"

"Bring me back my son, and I'll eat."

When a suicide bomber sets off an explosion in the university cafeteria, killing both Jewish and Arab students and cafeteria workers, Ibrahim puts his foot down. "You're to stay home, Wadha," he tells her, "until things calm down." Wadha stays home. My depression persists.

Ibrahim lowers himself onto my side of the bed, his voice finally cracking. "We can't go on like this, Ratiba," he sobs. I have never seen him sob before. "We must talk." I turn my face to the wall. You'd think he was the one with the secret.

I've never left Ibrahim before. I've always returned by nightfall. The night before I'm due to leave for my visit to Elisheva, we lie in bed as always, only this night we're both pretending to sleep. I should have told Ibrahim about the prayer shawl in the shed. I should tell him now. I don't. He is too aloof. Besides, with the Intifada and with Hamzah gone, it hardly seems important. Lately, he's been spending his spare time away from home, drinking coffee on the corner with the men of our village. When he is home, he sits for hours on our veranda, gazing at the houses that have clustered around us over the years like a herd of goats on the slope of the hill, mirroring his gaze.

Two days ago, he came home with men I'd never met, Palestinians who sneaked over the border from Gaza. Polite, I thought, but with a hungry undercurrent, like a river full of grit, of sudden, uncalculated depth, of whirling, stinging, living parts. Ibrahim pulled me into the kitchen.

"Where are the girls?"

"Why?"

"Because these men want to meet them. They want to make a match between them and their sons."

Ibrahim wasn't looking me in the eye, was talking as though that's the way we do things in our house.

"Our girls don't know their sons," I said, looking past him through the doorway at the men sitting on my tidy white sofa with their dusty jeans, with the hungry eyes of men with a cause, one of them with a tear in the sleeve of his leather jacket; the other, a large man with a paunch, with hair growing low over his forehead.

"That's the point," my husband said. "That's why they need to meet them."

I took my husband's face in my hand, turned it toward me.

"Why are you looking at me like that?" he asked, still averting his eyes. "We won't force them to marry, but, sweetness," his voice achingly devoid of love, "if they like the men, why not? This is the one way we have of helping our people."

"How?"

"By getting them to settle here legally."

"I thought they looked down on us for living with the Israelis, for having sold out to them? I thought they didn't want to kowtow to the Jewish State."

"Right, Ratiba, they don't. If Palestinians marry our daughters, they can turn the Jewish State, by virtue of numbers, into a Palestinian one."

"I see," I said.

"So where are they?"

"Who?"

"The girls!"

I returned the cookies to their canister.

"Out," I said, and I succumbed to the sirens screeching in my brain.

Every day, Ibrahim begs me to talk to him. "Share your thoughts with me," he says. "Tell me what's going on inside your head!"

Yesterday morning, as Daifa was coming out of her room, before she'd even combed her hair, Ibrahim told her that a Palestinian friend of his had been in our home looking for her.

"He wants to bring his son to see you this evening," he said.

And my daughter, my feisty, strong-willed daughter who has always refused to be "matched up," poured herself a mug of coffee and said, "Sure, why not?"

"Why not? That's it? Daifa, this will be no casual acquaintance," I squawked. "The man wants you to marry his son."

"Yes, Ommy. I've met his son. Abee introduced me to him last month when you were collecting your paycheck in Jerusalem."

"Daifa, it's not you this man wants. He's a member of the Palestinian Liberation Organization. He has an agenda. He doesn't have citizenship."

"If I marry him, he will. If I were to marry him I could work with him. Be part of something larger than myself."

Wadha was standing in the doorway sewing a button on her shirt, watching our scene play itself out. Ibrahim was hiding behind the newspaper, my newspaper, the one I write for. *Bastard,* I thought, *he's not going to help me here, not say a word. He's going to eat his omelet, while I breakfast on heartburn.*

"Can you hear what you are saying?" I said, trampling the feta cheese over my bread with my fingers, forcing my voice to remain in a regular key. "These men are angry, dangerous even. You are a woman, Daifa, with human being needs, women's needs, not a political pawn."

"Ommy, why are you so worked up? I know what I'm doing. I told you, I've met him. He's nice. Besides, where is the 'think for yourselves, make your own decisions' mother that brought us up? The one we've always been so proud of? Just words, right? When push comes to shove, parents never mean what they say."

"I always mean what I say, Daifa. I want you to choose a life of love, of joy, not violence, not danger."

"Other mothers would be proud to have a daughter who wants to help our people. If I marry that man, that's what I'll be doing. Helping."

I pulled my windbreaker from the hall closet, banged the door behind me, picked my way through the early morning mist to Adiva, our sweet, aging mama goat. I sat on a rock near her as she lay in her stall, as she ruminated on her straw.

What have I done? I paced the stubble 'round and 'round my mamma goat's bed till I was sure I'd made her dizzy. I tried to force my brain to work out what it was I'd done, but I couldn't. *What have I done to my children?* My brain, like an automaton, refusing to punch out its message. I tried to think what I should do from this point on, but no, nothing would come out of me but, *What have I done to my children?* Adiva was no help. She'd given up on me way back, when I gave away her first litter; when I first started stealing her milk for cheese. Despite my efforts to be different from the way my mother parented me, despite the pride I'd taken in the example I thought I was setting, I'd failed my children, had guided them to the brink of disaster.

I can't appeal to Ibrahim, I thought. *So much I can't tell him. A giant mound of desert sand has grown between us, a Middle Eastern Becket play. Huge. Smelling of feuds, daggers, camels. There's no way I can move around it,* I told myself. *Sand in the bathroom, in the kitchen, in the food I eat, invisible, but there just the same. Taboo. Observed by both of us, like vultures hunched on a tree, waiting.* I couldn't hold another thought in my aching head.

I fell in love with Ibrahim while discussing politics, challenging differences. *Now,* I thought, *all we have to talk about is the weather, or what time he'll come home at night. God or Allah or Pan or whoever it is that supplies married couples with words, didn't give us enough, not the right kind, not the gentle, wise kind.* All I can think of is my absent son and the dark secret in the shed. Orit hardly pops into my mind. *Why is my father-in-law hiding a bloodstained prayer shawl? A Jewish prayer shawl! What evil thing did he do?*

Quite apart from the secret, I thought of the unspoken tug-of-war that has developed over the years between us, with regard to our children. Ibrahim and I—I realized—transformed into King Solomon's mothers, wrenching our babies apart.

I went inside. Daifa and Wadha had gone off somewhere, to their own lives. I watched my husband sit like a stranger, alone in his chair. I watched his body, softer than it once was, vulnerable in his t-shirt. *Why doesn't he share his thoughts with me? Does he know about the prayer shawl in the shed? Does he know about his father? Why am I not brave enough to ask him? What am I frightened to lose?* I felt an impulse to caress the soft parts of my husband's stomach, to love him the way I had once loved him, confidently, aggressively. *This,* I thought, *is my sin: marrying a kind man, then letting him putter around our apartment in the isolation of his head. Me too,* I confessed. *I am also wilting in the privacy of my mind. I miss my past. I yearn for the father I loved so much, who made life so simple.*

Last night, in bed, I thought, *I'm growing old. That's why he doesn't talk to me,* my mind babbling into nonsense, frightened to encroach on the enormity of my secret for fear it might gobble me alive. I lay with my back curled away from Ibrahim. *How paradoxical life is,* I told myself. *A woman grows old and is rendered invisible. Like when I went with Daifa to have my eyes tested, the way the admissions people saw only Daifa, though I was the patient, and I was standing right there in front of them, damn it, like a vase of plastic flowers on the counter, gathering dust; because Daifa is beautiful, because beauty is fickle, refusing to rest in one place, and old Arab women fade into nothing right in front of people, like water stains on paper.*

I hate myself when my head patters off into those useless places. *Where is my son? Where did Kasim get that prayer shawl? Why the bloodstain?* From some hiding-place in the folds of his dream, Ibrahim turned, wrapped himself around me.

I love the smell of his body. Love the feel of his skin against mine. I love the way he snores in his sleep, the way his girth has spread over the years.

Snowflakes fell, an icy host during the night, all the way from heaven. A few must have lost their parent body as they reached our atmosphere because Ibrahim and I wake to see them wandering in through our open window, watch them land on our wooden chair, melting into nothing at all.

"I'm canceling my trip to Haifa."

"Why?"

"Because it's snowing."

"It'll have stopped by the time we're dressed."

"Still. I'm not going."

ORIT

It's Independence Day. As Hamzah's registered mother, I'm invited to a military gala held in an amphitheater in Jerusalem, the army's way of thanking its soldiers. I've ironed Hamzah's uniform, starched his shirt. I'm wearing a spanking new dress in his honor, smoky blue and silky. He is so handsome.

"Come," I say, jumping up and down, pulling at his arm. "Run down to the beach with me before we leave, just to see."

He chuckles, caught for a moment in my excitement. "I should have registered you as my kid sister, not my ommy."

Fairy lights have been strung over the sand, canvas chairs are set up, some still stacked, waiting for us to take them. Musicians are handing out song sheets, setting up their equipment on the planks of wood that constitute their stage. Iceboxes dot the area. Comedians are already acting silly because people are streaming down to the beach in groups, chatting, calling to each other, some already singing, Our neighbors, a young couple with twins in a stroller walk over to us, leave the stroller to their parents, encircle Hamzah approvingly in broad, exaggerated gestures, patting him on the back, on the top of his head, making noises, like Pashas.

"Handsome!" they croon. Then dropping the dramatics and hugging him, they say, "Congratulations. Today, we celebrate you."

Sweat is glistening on Hamzah's brow as we drive toward the city, his knuckles clenched white against the steering wheel. He's smoking. I remember the last time he came home on leave; he was smoking then too.

"What's the matter?"

He pretends not to hear me. *Like a teenager,* I think, *a soldier, but still a kid.* We reach the stadium, park.

"I'm trying to work out whether my mother would have approved of this."

"She should."

"My abee wouldn't." He heaves an old man's sigh. "Palestinians celebrate Nakba," he says.

"Your abee is not a Palestinian. He's an Israeli Arab."

Hamzah shrugs. Doesn't seem convinced.

I lean against the wall, my energy spent. *What am I doing?* I ask myself. *What evil game am I playing here?*

We've arrived. We're part of an ocean of soldiers and their loved ones surging into the stadium. *The entire world in the military,* I think, *nobody left for the parks or the beaches.* Hamzah, who is now taller than I am, plants a kiss on my forehead. *Like a son,* I tell myself for the second time this evening. He stubs his cigarette out with his foot, walks away from me to the section at the front of the stadium reserved for soldiers, looking stiff, alone. I watch other parents, real parents, as I edge myself into my seat, parents like Ruti and Ibrahim, who, though they might be screwed up and mean-spirited, are authentic. Poor bastards. A lump is clogging my windpipe. They don't even know their son is in the army.

The band starts up. I am one of two thousand parents rising from their seats, singing our national anthem. I look at the faces of the people near me: worn, determined, more than anything else proud of their warrior children. As people resume their seats, as the first speaker walks to the podium, bristling in his military insignias, dizziness overwhelms me.

"Are you all right?" asks the mother next to me.

"I'm fine," I mumble, trying to smile. The moment she looks away, I leave.

Three hours later, after the best performers in the country have sung, joked, danced, when the carefully crafted speeches, which I'm unable to hear, are done, I'm here, where I have been since I first sneaked out, at the exit to the stadium, waiting for my hero.

We find my car.

"I've sinned against my parents," Hamzah says.

We drive home in silence. Long after I'm in bed, long after the lights in my house are switched off, the singing continues on the beach. Everyone but Hamzah, me and the Arabs, I think, singing until the morning light.

I snap my light on. "Hamzah!" I scream. "Hamzah! Wake up!" I storm downstairs, barefoot, in my nightdress.

"What?" He's in the kitchen, fully dressed.

"D'you hear what they're singing? It's Ehud Manor's song. Sing it with me."

As the dawn lightens outside my kitchen door, Hamzah and I add our voices to the revelers' on the beach:

> If only a rainbow would come down to us from a cloud.
> If only there'd be a repair for this world.
> If only our gift would not be lost forever.
> If only the desert would grow grass, a lawn.
> If only we could still sit in the shade of the fig tree.
> If only we could not hurt
> And each would love his brother.
> If only they would reopen the gates of Eden.
> If only East and West would merge.
> If only our days here would be renewed as of old.

If only one nation wouldn't lift its sword against another.
If only we wouldn't abandon the path of hope.
If only man could be merciful till evening.
If only we had a single possibility of love.

"You need to go home," I tell Hamzah.
"Yes," he says. "As soon as I finish my military service."

ELISHEVA

I'm in Jerusalem. My superior told me not to leave my hospital at this time, that I'm needed there. But it's quiet in Haifa now; the explosions have been coming with such frequency in Jerusalem, I couldn't stay away. So I'm here, walking up Ben Yehudah Street.

The majority of stores remain doggedly in business though several are closed, and those that are open are empty. The street has a ghost-like feeling to it. I am the only pedestrian in the center of town. I pass placards nailed to doors: "Closed For the Intifada," they say. "See You When It's Over." The message makes me shudder.

I turn into King George and walk to Yaffo Street; more of the same: scraps of paper swirling about in the gutter. I go to Mahaneh Yehudah, the market that has been bombed many times, each vendor manning his stand, refusing to give up. The air of the market is thick with hovering souls, as is the bus stop where students and children waited on the fateful Monday morning of this week for their ride to school.

I stop at that bus stop. The debris has been cleared away. Voices of the murdered children, of adults who were going to work, reverberate in my mind. That's what it's like now all over the country, people listening to dead voices, breathing prayers. "Our Father…grant us grace because we mean no wrong." That is the hit song, this year, played in the coffee shops, the empty restaurants I pass, and on the bus I take out of town.

"Don't worry," the driver tells me, "by tomorrow, the city will be full again."

This morning over breakfast, I saw an advertisement in the paper: a bistro-style table, china, and candles spitting wax from a candelabra being lugged up the stairs of an apartment building, delivering a catered meal to the safety of a customer's home. Storeowners are selling their goods online.

Dovy and I have come to a settlement in Samaria, Shomron, on the uppermost ridge of the mountain, for the marriage of Dovy's nephew.

Voices flutter across the hilltop as birds gather and hush in the shade tree, as the colors of sky and earth meld into night. The wedding canopy is on the crest of the highest peak overlooking the valley, a breathtaking panorama in the daylight, now a vista of the sleeping hills below. The bride sits in an enclave, close to the ground, candles glowing in bowls. Her friends sit around her, draped, like her, in gauze-like dresses, rings dangling from their ears and arms. They sway and sing to her, playing on their earthenware drums, on flutes; tunes sinking into the valley as new melodies begin their curled ascent.

Guests follow the groom into this enclave chanting, bearing candles. The groom approaches, a violinist playing at his side. The groom bends, raises the veil that covers his bride's face, whispers his commitment to her. The procession turns then and climbs, still chanting, still bearing candles, back up the mountain to the canopy. Dovy and I catch a glimpse of darkly clad men crawling up the mountain beneath the foliage, rifles extended, on the ready. They are members of the community. They are crouching and running as silently as mountain cats, following a routine, protecting the wedding group from snipers. Seven times, the bride walks around her groom. Blessings are recited, the marriage document is read, the groom places the ring on the forefinger of his bride, the glass is broken in memory of the destruction of the temple, and two hundred people sing "If I Forget Thee, Oh Jerusalem." As they sing, I hear the guards in the shadows, their guns on the ready, singing together with us our age-old allegiance.

Sabbath eve: The air cools. People turn indoors to bathe, the children to shine the family's shoes, husbands to take out the garbage. The bride has taken the family dog to the hilltop to watch the sun fade from the sky. Her brother hears the phone ringing from the shower. Neighbors have been calling all day, all week with blessings, good wishes for his sister and her groom. He waits for a while. Someone else will get it. Two rings. Three. No. They must be out. He pulls a towel from the rack and rushes soap and steam across the floor, around the kitchen counter laden with pies baked for the wedding week, to the phone. He skids as he reaches for the chair, stubs his toe, grabs the receiver in one hand, hops around with his foot clutched in the other. He gets entangled in the cord, is pulling at his towel as it falls to the floor. "Yes," he laughs into the phone, "Hallo! Don't hang up! I'm here!"

Meshulam, their friend, has been murdered, shot in the heart through the windshield. One hour ago. On his way home from a visit to his parents-in-law, informing them that his wife is pregnant. She is fighting for her life in the hospital. A widow. A pregnant widow.

Devora weeps with her son. Then, she raises her head and says, "This is your sister's wedding feast. We won't tell her of Meshulam's death until after the Sabbath." Family members keep their emotions close to their hearts throughout that evening and for the duration of the following day.

Guards make their rounds. As the evening descends on that second day and shadows lengthen across the flowers, while guests talk and children kick a ball around on the lawn, a silence descends over the village. The soundtrack of their lives has been tampered with. Devora sits by her son. Darkness falls. Mother and son take leave of their guests and of Devora's Sabbath truce. They leave for the cemetery.

It is the fourth day after Meshulam's funeral. We are sitting in the house of mourning.

"Palestinian kids keep stealing equipment out of my truck," says Meshulam's cousin.

"They wouldn't steal more than once from mine," says his brother.

"What do you mean?" I ask. Nobody answers. A shiver catches me.

I remember Yosef, Orit's actor friend, telling us that the settlers are evil. "They are cold," he said, "inhuman."

Evil is not a word I use lightly. I'd say that I reserve it for particularly infamous historical figures. Yosef's remark reminded me of the CNN report that told of Israelis destroying Arab olive trees. The report had filled me with shame. I had shut off the TV in horror at what was happening to us.

Two days before the wedding, my feelings changed.

We'd come to the wedding in a bus fortified against snipers and bullets, a routine form of travel on the steep road that winds up to the Shomron. From the interior of the bus, Dovy and I saw olive trees. "Oh," I told our driver, "these must be the Palestinian trees that the Israelis cut down."

"Yes," he said. "Arab snipers hide behind them on either side of the road. From there, they pick off civilians in their vehicles the way children shoot cardboard ducks in fairgrounds. But we've developed a strategy," he said. "Their trees are important to them. They shoot us, we take down their olive trees. They leave us in peace, we do the same for them."

Dovy and I need to find a home for our dog, Hummus, because we're planning a vacation. Dovy's nephew, Oory, lives with his family beyond the Green Line.

"They've always wanted a dog," Dovy tells me.

"What about the murders in the settlements?" I ask, ashamed of my cowardice. "I can just as easily find Hummus a place near us."

"The road to our village is safe, Elishy," Oory assures me over the phone. "We drive that road every day. No one has been killed on it."

The family lives in a trailer in a village south of Hebron. We have supper with them. They take us to a local fair.

The villagers are selling everything from crocheted blankets and clothes, to homemade honeys, cheeses, and olives, so similar to their enemies, sitting at this very moment on the reverse side of the mountain. The men wear skullcaps and allow the fringes of their garments, as prescribed in the scriptures, to dangle on the outside of their jeans. Children play around the booths; babies hang from the linen cloths that tie them to their mothers. The sun sets, men cluster together in prayer. An idyllic picture by all accounts, except for the pistols hanging from their belts.

"Where do they get their Zen-like equanimity?" I ask Dovy, "Don't they get anxious living here?" Dovy rolls his eyes at me.

On my daughter's refrigerator there's a saying that goes like this: "Serenity is achieved when your ideals and your way of life coalesce."

Oh, I think, *so that's what that's about.*

Hummus understands that we're leaving her. Without a whimper she climbs into the bed we've brought with us. Dovy and I leave for the city.

Next morning, I call to see how my dog is faring.

"She's fine," says Oory. "She walked the children and me to school this morning."

"Nice."

"We are planning a trip," says Oory, "but we won't be able to take Hummus with us. Our neighbor is a shepherd. He has dogs himself and knows how to treat them. Can we leave her with him while we are away?"

"Sure," I say, feeling put out.

That conversation is at 10:00 a.m. At noon, the shepherd, father of five children who has refused to carry a firearm because he believes in peaceful coexistence, who has gone into the fields with his sheep every morning for the last thirty years armed only with a Bible, that same shepherd is murdered. After the funeral, the media interviews a neighbor.

"I talked to him last week," she tells them. "He told me he was apprehensive because the Bedouins were no longer looking him in the eye. I told him to be careful, that perhaps he should carry a firearm. 'I can't do that,' he said. 'It's against everything I stand for.'"

Oory, Dovy's nephew, purchases firearms and moves with his wife and children, together with two other young families, to a trailer on the field in which their shepherd friend was murdered.

"You have babies. How can you put their lives in danger?"

"They're safe with us," Oory tells us. "I have firearms."

"What about when you leave for work?"

"Bat-Sheva also has a gun. She will use it if she has to."

"But why?"

"Because we're not about to let another murder occur on that field."

Naama and her children have zero sympathy for Dovy's relatives. Naama, my closest friend, is yelling at me.

"Tell them to get out of the territories," she says. "Tell them it is settlers like them who create our country's problems."

Dovy and I are trapped in the rift. What is the matter with me? Why don't I have an opinion?

"These were our country's problems way before we settled these areas," Oory and Bat-Sheva tell us. "We were sent here thirty years ago to defend these territories against aggression—aggression, thirty years ago!"

I can see they regard Dovy and me as "unreliable."

"We've been here for thirty years," Oory is saying. "We've lived under terrorism, have cultivated arable land into farms and orchards. We've erected guard posts, from which we can detect terrorists before they cross the border. Why are we the bad ones? Because the Palestinians don't want us here? They don't want us anywhere in the Middle East. Perhaps we should all pack our bags and leave? The last one out should do what Ephraim Kishon, the cartoonist, predicted years ago: switch the lights off behind him."

Worse things are happening. Some of the settlers argue, "If our government won't protect us, we'll take matters into our own hands." A group emerges among the settlers, frustrated at the amount of attacks they have to endure. They are accused of plotting revenge against their Arab neighbors, are brought to court, found guilty, sentenced.

We cannot talk to Naama about Oory and Bat-Sheva.

"Guarding the territories should not be part of military service," she tells us. "It's not right that our sons end up on the most isolated roads in the country, guarding civilians from their neighbors. We won't do it. Anyway," she says, "the settlers are fanatics, a threat to the Palestinians. Their very presence beyond the Green Line oppresses them. If they'd get out of there, the Arabs would leave us alone. We could live in peace."

Oory is taciturn. He won't be drawn into any more arguments on the left.

To my surprise, I find my voice. "We can't go on like this," I say. "It's essential that our country be run along principles of pluralism, not fear, in which Arabs and Jews can live in peace."

Oory stares at me, his mouth open.

"What a novel idea," he says. "Peace. How come no one else thought of that?"

"You don't need to get nasty."

"We do, Elisheva. That's the point. What if we give the Palestinians political independence in this country, as you say, if we give them control over half of Jerusalem as they are demanding? What happens if that fails as it did in Lebanon and Oslo, Elishy? If they again see concession as their ever-shifting starting point? If they demand more, as they've done on all of the previous times we've conceded land for peace? Will we have to start the cycle of wars over again? What if they become a majority and oust us from the region?"

Israelis go to funerals. And they go to weddings. They go to funerals out of need, to part from their loved ones. They go to weddings out of defiance, to share a moment of happiness. Naama's husband, Asher, attends weddings of people he doesn't even know, just to feel alive. He dances angrily until the summer stars pale and the invited guests go home.

My Dovy also goes to weddings. He sits at the table ignoring the food. He drinks too much, my friends tell me, belting out melodies at the top of his already loud voice. Women leave the table in twos and threes, they say, unable to hear each other over the boom of his voice. Others understand. Strangers remain at the table. They sing with Dovy until something inside him gives way and he falls quiet. He tells me later that some clap him on the shoulder, while others merely nod as he turns his back and drives back home to me.

My Dovy doesn't talk about his feelings. We drive to Caesarea one warm summer night, to the Roman theater. We sit on the ancient seats and listen to Yehuda Poliker sing.

> What do you think of in the dark
> When you can't calm down?
> At whom are you angry
> That there'll be no forgiveness?

I glance at Dovy in the darkness, at the face of my Roman general, awash with tears.

More than 40 percent of Israeli children in the territories are suffering from post-traumatic stress disorder. Our hospital staff is told to caution families not to listen to the news more than once a day. Bad for the morale, we are told. Foreign companies no longer invest in Israel. Businesses grind to a halt. Hospitals are overflowing with patients. Homeopathic healers tend to everything from backache and skin rashes, to shingles and neurological disorders. Cancer of every kind is on the rise. Our emergency room is understaffed. These are the thoughts that run through my mind as Poliker sings.

An ambulance carrying a pregnant woman to the hospital in Jerusalem is stopped by the border patrol. The woman is not pregnant. She has a belt of explosives under her dress.

A suicide bomber is sent into the heart of Tel Aviv on the Purim holiday. Her behavior seems suspicious. She is arrested.

"Why didn't you detonate your explosives?" they ask her.

"I walked around the streets," she says, "with my hand on the detonator. I saw children at play, men and women strolling along the streets and sitting in coffeehouses. I thought, *These aren't evil people.* They told me you were agents of the devil, but you don't seem bad to me."

A suicide bomber is sent into the heart of Tel Aviv on the Purim holiday. He detonates his explosives and murders mothers, fathers, and little children. Supermen, furry lions, and plastic bears are strewn over the street, over strollers drenched in blood.

An ambulance screams through the streets of Jenin, forging a path through the crossfire, carrying an Arab child with a severe illness to his doctor in Jerusalem. The following day, a suicide bomber murders that doctor and his daughter in a Jerusalem coffeehouse.

An elderly man is stoned to death in the Jordan valley.

A grandmother and her grandchild are murdered in their car.

A family is shot to death as they drive to their daughter's wedding.

Two security guards spot a suicide bomber. They converge on him, pushing him out of the coffeehouse. The bomber detonates his explosives, killing the guards. Six people are killed, scores maimed for life. If it were not for the guards, say the authorities, the casualties would have been worse.

A female suicide bomber murders a woman and three of her children on Jaffo Street, Jerusalem.

Children are blown up on the number eighteen bus on their way to school.

An explosive kills and injures shoppers in the outdoor Hadera market.

In the Jerusalem *souk*. In the *souk* in Netanya.

In a restaurant in Netanya, killing families who are celebrating Passover.

"God, my God," I beseech, as I leave work each night. "Please. Make it stop."

Palestinians complain about the hardships they suffer at the checkpoints. "We need employment," they say. "We have to wait forever before we're allowed to pass into Israel for work. Israeli soldiers are curt," they say, "insensitive. Israeli citizens have no problems crossing at the checkpoints, why should we?" Ambulances, even ambulances carrying sick patients and childbearing women are made to wait, forced to go through a process of search and investigation.

"It's racism," say the Palestinians. "That's what it is."

Sirens. We run the victims into crowded operating rooms, wards, the morgue, or simply rip from them, in the open hallways, the blood-soaked remnants of their clothes, remove from their hair the limbs and pieces of body parts that have been catapulted onto them from the bodies of strangers. I try to block from my consciousness the scream of ambulances as they storm again and again the open security doors rushing bodies from the gates of hell to the focused chaos of our medical crew.

We insert needles and drips into the dying and the wounded, not having the time to comfort them, knowing that shrapnel, nails, and twisted wire are embedded in these people's every organ. The air is heavy with the smell of burning flesh, urine, feces, blood, vomit. Babies are crying for their parents; parents, grandparents, and siblings rush from room to room, screaming the names of their loved ones.

Suicide bombers are a daily, sometimes a twice-daily, occurrence. This time it was a suicide bomber on a Haifa bus. We can see that many of the injured will die within the hour. Others will take a month or more. I don't tell them they'll leave the hospital in wheelchairs, having lost the use of their limbs. If these patients survive, they'll be obliged to endure excruciatingly tight bodysuits for the year it will take to heal their burns and longer, until they grow a new epidermis.

I know their lives and the lives of their loved ones are transformed forever. I've seen it before. Family members will quit their jobs to tend to their children, parents, siblings, and friends. Lovers who have pledged themselves to a life of romance and devotion will climb onto the hospital cot to be close to their partners, will caress whatever body part it is safe to touch, comb their hair and wash their bodies with sweet-smelling creams. They will massage their limbs, place ice chips between their lips, sing to them, bring them flowers, pictures, friends—anything to convince them of their devotion and of their own imminent recovery.

Although these lovers are the best hope the patients have of recovery, after a year perhaps—I have seen it so many times—they will give up, unnerved by the guilt they will carry with them for the rest of their lives that they no longer love in the way they had promised. Even if they persevere, the wounded will send them away, terrified by what they see in their lover's eyes, weighed down by the chores required for their most basic daily maintenance, by their own desperate longing for the life that was theirs and which is now lost.

The youth of South Tel Aviv were all dressed up, smelling of shampoo, wearing clean jeans, pretty blouses, lipstick in the most delicate shades of pink. Boys, their hair slicked back with water and a comb, their coolest t-shirts. They threw kisses at their parents, waved as they ran down the road last night to the disco on the beach.

They are lying by the sea now, bombed to death, forever dismembered. Remembered forever in our every waking moment.

I come home from the hospital overflowing with the cries of my patients. I no longer think of them as patients. I think of them as people, my people in pain. Dovy understands when I walk past him, as I trudge into our apartment, not even stopping to say hello. He knows that I need to shower, to let the water flood into my every pore, need to scrub the flesh till it's raw, to brush my teeth in the shower until they bleed as I'm letting shampoo drip down my head and into my open mouth. I don't care how it tastes as my tears flow. After I've rubbed my hair dry, after I've lain for the briefest of moments on the bed and tried unsuccessfully to rest, I need to move. I race up the hill to the park, round and round the crazy-making circular pathway, until my bones will no longer carry me, until I can no longer breathe. Only then do I come home, hang my arms around my Dovy's shoulders as he's working at the table, kiss him on the nape of his neck.

An Arab named Daud is sitting at a coffee shop drinking his first cup of coffee, enjoying his first cigarette of the day. He is only a block away from the bus as it explodes into the Haifa morning, darkening it forever. Instinctively, disregarding the warnings that civilians keep their distance because explosions come in clusters, he jumps into the vehicle still exuding flames, and, feeling his way through the wires, the still burning seats, the blood, he pulls from the wreck the first person he comes across with signs of life. With the help of the medics—and the Chasids already on the scene, already lifting the injured and the dead, already reclaiming body parts from the surrounding bushes—he loads her onto the gurney, watches in horror as she's whisked away.

Three days later, Daud, a bouquet of flowers clutched in his arms, pays a visit to his charge. Gita, mother of five, grandmother of fifteen children, lies on her hospital bed recovering from surgery. Her hair is bandaged, her face and body are swollen and badly bruised, some ribs are cracked, but the puncture in her lung has been repaired, and she is alive.

"Look at him, Elisheva," she says as the Arab enters her room at my side. "This man was God's emissary." She extends her arms, embraces, and blesses him and his descendants for all eternity. Her husband throws his arms around Daud. They weep on each other's shoulders.

One Friday, knowing I am home, and perhaps needing friendship more than usual, Orit comes over, pulls her books from her back-pack, sits to work at my table.

"Look, Elishy," she tells me, thrusting her mug of coffee aside and forcing me to sit with her. "Look at this. Gertrude greets Hamlet back to court just three months after the death of his father."

"Yes," I say, more to humor her than out of any intellectual interest, "doesn't leave him much time to mourn."

"But look. He is overwhelmed with grief. Read this."

"What, now?"

"Yes. Leave the dishes, for God's sake. You can do them later."

I do what I am told.

"Where shall I read? Here?"

"Yes. Go to where his mother tries to reason with him."

So I read the part of Gertrude: "Thou know'st 'tis common. All that lives must die, passing through nature to eternity."

And Orit reads Hamlet: "Ay, madam, it is common."

And I, Gertrude again: " … If it be / Why seems it so particular with thee?"

"D'you see what's happening here?" Orit asks, her eyes like opals in their sockets. "The audience is asked to journey from the general form of ritual, 'the trappings and the suits of woe,' to the personal suffering of Hamlet. Look, Lishy. Look at the significance of these lines."

I've never seen Orit so excited, but then again, I've never seen her work on a text before.

"Of course, 'tis common, all that lives must die," she says. "That's the equanimity we feel for the pain of others. Don't you see? When it is our own loved one, when the death is particular to ourselves, Lishy, we are catapulted into an experience of loss so painful, it defies the boundaries dividing this world from the next. If we could only experience the deaths of others with the same pain we have for our own dead and departed, we would not be able to tolerate violence. Don't you see? There would be a global forbidding of the shedding of blood. Human beings around the world would put a stop to it. Wars would be abolished—too much pain. The lion would lie down with the lamb."

Orit stops talking.

For a moment or two, neither of us says a word. The refrigerator purrs in its corner. Then, "You know," she says, her voice soft, self-effacing, almost shy, "I don't mean to sound grandiose or anything, Lishy, but that is the real task of the actor—to bring universal suffering home to the audience with the poignancy of the personal, to bring it to them, that is, with the unique gift that is Shakespeare."

I sit next to my friend, overwhelmed by her passion. I love her so much.

Ruti comes at last. Back for the holidays. "There's something I have to discuss with you," she whispers into the phone, time not having diminished her proclivity for drama.

"Have you seen your sister?" I ask. "Spoken with her?"

"If I did, I'd have to tell Ibrahim. You know that; the whole messy issue would explode in our faces."

"Perhaps that's what you need."

"What?"

"Are you happy the way things are?"

"Things are fine."

It's impossible to talk to her.

"There's something I must discuss with you," she tells me as I open the front door. She arrives with a bag of pomegranates, another of goat cheese, and a suitcase that has seen better days. Immediately, she goes to the room assigned her, changes into a dress with the price tag still hanging from the zipper, pulls from her tattered bag a scarf embossed with tiny gold disks, drapes it round her shoulders, rushes to join us in the living room.

My sons and their families are with us. My friend Naama arrives with Asher and their son, Ilan. We light the candles. "Please, God," we pray, "protect our sons, our families. Teach us to live in peace with our neighbors. God of our fathers," I pray, "cool the raging spirits."

Ruti stands beside me in the synagogue. At first her voice comes out rusty from her throat. Then, with several stops and starts, her voice forges a path through the grit, and, with an off-key lilt, she lurches into the melody of her childhood. "Oh, Lord," she prays, "open my lips that my mouth might sing your praise." Tears are streaming down her cheeks. I remember her face, years back, through the prayer house window, chomping on a sandwich.

"Enough, Ruti," I say. "Let's go."

We set the table. Together we dip apples in honey, praying against all odds for a sweet new beginning. Ruti is still singing. "And I will bring you to my Holy Mountain," she murmurs, swaying, clutching my prayer book close to her chest.

"You've changed," says Ruti.

Asher asks, "Yes. We've changed. How about you?"

"I was hoping we'd fool around like we used to."

"Do you fool around in your house?"

"Not that much. No. I guess not."

Nobody talks. Then, "I'd hoped you were still the way I remembered you." Ruti looks so sad—I want to cry.

"Violence has changed us," I say.

"As long as the army controls the Palestinian areas, there will not be peace in this country."

We turn in Ruti's direction, shocked at her nerve.

"Is that a threat?"

"What?"

"I said: is that a threat?"

Of all people, this is Dovy, who is constantly harping on our need to find an alternative to violence. He, my Dovy, is angry with Ruti. Livid.

"Calm down," I say. "We're family."

Ruti isn't listening to me.

"Why a threat? Can't I express an opinion?"

"Sure. Feel free." Dovy is not at all himself. "Make yourself at home, why don't you. Just let me point out, in case you don't get newspapers where you are, that unlike you people who live unharmed, protected even, in your Palestinian area, we've just lived through a year of bus bombings, car explosions, and any old crazy suicide bomber with hormonal problems who takes it into his fancy to blow himself up wherever he might find a crowd, just for fun, so he'll get virgins in whatever place he's headed to from here. But, sure, please feel free to express your opinion, and we'll remove all control from the Palestinian areas, why don't we? In fact, why don't we save them the trouble and blow ourselves up?"

"I'm not 'you people,'" Ruti says. "I don't live in Palestinian territory. I'm an Israeli Arab. I have Israeli citizenship."

Not a word is spoken

Out of the silence, Ilan's voice. "You're an Arab?"

What's left to say? My boys start to sing. "Merciful Father, have compassion over us, grant our hearts understanding…"

But Ilan won't let go. "Are you no longer an Israeli?"

"Of course I am. I'm an Israeli Arab. There is such a thing, you know. Where do you think I've been for the past thirty years?"

Listening to my sons sing, the words of the teacher come to me: "Don't call them your children; call them your builders."

When we wake in the morning, Ruti is gone. No note. No phone number. What about the issue she needed so badly to discuss? What if it is important? Then I see: she's taken colored pencils from my son's collection, drawn a picture, left it on the dresser. It looks like a scarf with a red stain in the middle of it, like blood. Above, in crayon, are the words: "A prayer shawl, Elishy, is hanging over my home." What is she talking about? She's so impossible. Which family isn't struggling today against fate? I stuff the drawing into three envelopes, one inside the other, hide it underneath my underwear so Dovy won't find it.

ORIT

Medea haunts me. For the second time, I've been asked to play her role. My theater is empty except for the technician hanging lights. Still, I'm having the hardest time, my body tense, trying to relax. I'm pulling my neck over to my right shoulder when two military guys walk into my rehearsal room. They are not happy.

"Can I help you?"

"We are sorry to inform you … Hamzah … your son … "

Someone is calling my name. There is a stench of metal, of sweat. It's Mike, the electrical guy, leaning over me, his face upside down, slapping my cheeks.

"Get up," he orders. "We must move."

"Is he alive?"

"He's on the critical list."

"Where are the men?"

"I told them I'd drive you. So sorry, I didn't know you had a son." As he talks, he runs to the far side of the room and back, bringing me my purse, my sweater. "They left this," he says.

"What is it?"

"The military report about your son. Wounded in the line of duty."

I race from the theater. "Wait!" he calls after me. "I'll get my keys!"

My car is already down the street.

I knock, though I can't see the number through my tears, and I can't stop my right leg from shaking. Ruti opens the door. After all these years, it's that simple.

"What?" Her face is already white with fear. "What happened?"

Before she can utter another word, before I turn and flee from that place, I thrust the army notice into her hand. She glances at it. No doubt realizes that I'd signed under her name. No doubt sees where Hamzah had forged his father's.

"It's Hamzah. He's hurt."

"Where?"

"On military duty. He's at the hospital in Haifa."

"He was in the army?"

I nod.

"You knew?"

I can't answer.

"Get away from my house." Her voice is focused, like the growl of a killer cat. With the full force of her being, she lunges at me, pushing me from her. I fall back, my head cracking on the asphalt. "Never come near me again."

Her voice hits me again like a hurled rock, as I peel myself from the gravel. "If you visit him at the hospital, even once," she snarls, "I'll have you arrested."

"Well," I pant, hobbling away, my breath wheezing between my tears, blood dripping down the side of my face, "at least now you have a reason." *There*, I tell myself. *I've said it.*

Where is my compassion? I grumble into the darkness as I stumble from my sister's closed door.

It is the morning after that awful day. Early morning. Nurses are gliding over Formica floors like robots in their rubber-soled shoes, in and out of cubicles; shafts of light, seriously delusional, forcing their way between the bars of the windows, landing on the bed covers, on the walls, expecting a cast party. Orderlies are rolling wagons of test tubes, blood, and pills into wards that smell of my aba's final days. The hospital is as quiet as a morgue. Hamzah is on the critical list. I'm edging down the corridor like a thief when a man in a brown suit approaches me.

"Orit Maimon?"

"Yes?"

He hands me an envelope. It's a restraining order. I am not allowed to go near Hamzah or the home of my sister under penalty of the law. Does she have no heart? I take the elevator back to the lobby, exit the sliding glass doors, cross the courtyard, lean over the railing, and sob. A stranger standing near me asks if I'm all right. "Do I look all right?" I snap. Then I clutch onto her still outstretched arm and let the tears do as they please.

They won't let me visit him. I pace the grounds of the hospital, biting my fingernails. I ask a visitor carrying flowers to tell Elisheva I'm here. I pace the lobby praying she'll send word.

The country is being torn to shreds, like a tapestry, like a family heirloom thrown to cats so they can sharpen their claws on it. My name, Orit, means light, yet I bring darkness to those I love; I am helpless against the many black days when lightning rips in zigzags across the sky, when thunder roars. Elisheva tells me to go home, that she'll call me when she has news. I drive home from the hospital, charge across the sand, skirting the jellyfish, kicking at Coca-Cola bottles, swearing in disgust at diapers spat back out by the waves. My face and hair are exposed to giant drops of rain; I watch the rainbow, God's promise that He will never again destroy the world as He did in the days of Noah. I watch, as the ocean turns green in shame.

I am at the bus station in Tel Aviv. The buses are parked, but the air is toxic with fumes. The windows on the front of the buses that usually tell their destination are blank, all of them, like the milky white eyes of the blind, of some blind people. I'm racing around the buses and between the passengers who are not going anywhere. "I've lost my purse," I'm crying, "the purse Ella gave me, so richly embroidered by Shuli."

I wake in a panic. It is 3:00 a.m. Hamzah is in intensive care.

ELISHEVA

I can't understand Hamzah's chart. It says his parents are Ruti and Ibrahim, that he was brought in by the military. His body is in traction, his face bandaged, his internal organs shot. According to his chart, he was wounded in a skirmish. The only number on his chart is Orit's. Why is Ruti and Ibrahim's number not here? Why Orit's, when she has had no contact with them since their marriage? I've called Orit umpteen times. She's never there. She doesn't return my messages. Why is there no contact number for Ruti?

My staff tells me that Orit is downstairs, pacing the floors of the hospital, waiting for word on Hamzah. They say she never goes home; that she's not allowed on the floor. Something about instructions given by the parents.

I'm connecting Hamzah's drip when Ruti and Ibrahim arrive. Ibrahim is unrecognizable. He looks sick. His face droops. Ruti has changed. A lot. Gray is seeping into her curls, her face creased beyond repair. I don't have time for such thoughts, however, because I'm embroiled, from the moment they see their son, in their pain. Why did they send Hamzah to the army? Why didn't Ruti tell me he'd enlisted? Arabs don't serve in the military.

I have learned to pray as families weep. I pray God to stop the bombings, to protect our children, our spouses, our soldiers, our friends. "Please, God," I whisper, as I change Hamzah's bandages, as I empty his sack of urine, "cool the raging spirits."

Hamzah is on the critical list. His parents can't even hold him.

Our outpatient unit is crowded with people suffering from post-traumatic stress.

For the second time, Orit has lost her sister. She refuses to talk about her. She sobs over Hamzah as though he were her biological child.

"What were you thinking?" I scold. "How could you have him live in your home for three years without telling me?" I don't touch the army issue.

Orit doesn't answer. Instead, she exposes herself, with scary abandon, to the news. Depression descends over her until she can no longer get out of bed.

"Where did we go wrong?" she asks herself out loud, as she lies on her crumpled sheets. For instance, she thinks, what would have happened if we'd never gone into Lebanon in '78? What would have happened if we'd let the Palestinians continue with their raids into the north of Israel? However bad it was then, it was better than it is now. But Orit isn't a politician, and I can see that her head is hurting.

"How could I have sent Hamzah to the army?" she wails into her pillow.

She's like one possessed. Did we have to launch an attack in the war of '82 and oust the Palestinians from Lebanon? So what if they were pounding our border with Katyushas? That situation was more containable than this?

In her frustration, Orit leaves that subject to gnaw on another, mulls in her mind, out loud, the stories of Israeli casualties. She can't keep the image of Hamzah's body, blown apart on the dirt, from her mind; mumbles into her pillow about mothers who were tired of war, wanting to bring their sons home alive, not wanting to wait for the body bags. Orit had voted for Ehud Barak because of his promise that he'd bring our boys back from Lebanon. "What was it like for him," she asks the walls of her room, "to bring our troops down from those hills alone, in the dead of night, without the consensus of the Syrians or the Lebanese, to load their ammunition onto trucks and drive out of there in the darkness, the way the ancient Hebrews left Egypt?" For a moment, she perks up, reliving the ecstasy we all felt when we saw our boys returning; then she sinks into the despair that came snapping at the heels of our joy, when the Palestinians regarded our withdrawal as a sign of weakness.

"I took my sister's child," she wails. "I sacrificed him on the mountain."

By now she's out of bed, pacing around her room, talking out loud to the spirits in her head. I'm crouched on my knees, on her wicker chair, biting my nails, trying to convince myself that it would be best to let her be, not to interrupt her craziness. I can see she has a fever. Her room is in a mess. When she stops ranting, I make her take a shower. She repeats her tirade under water.

"You know what our problem is, Elishy?" she asks, water dripping off her.

"What?"

"That we didn't listen to the Arabs in 'forty-eight. They told us straight out they didn't want an island of Jews within a continent of comfortable Arab land."

"First of all, Ority, the Arabs were never 'comfortable.' They were desert tribes, battling for centuries with lack of water, cattle, and each other—forever feuding among themselves; second, what did you expect us to do? Go away because they didn't want us? The Hebrews running from slavery didn't turn back to Egypt. They walked up to their necks in water before God parted the Red Sea.

Orit screws up her eyes at me. She stretches the palms of her hands to the ceiling.

"What is wrong with you, Elishy?" she says. "We're not living in biblical times. We're responsible for our own decisions, our own lives. Talk to me about today, about now. Help me."

I don't respond.

"Elisheva."

I have nothing to say.

"Elishy?"

Softly, she says, "Maybe if we'd gotten to know our neighbors a few at a time while shopping or riding on a donkey or a bus or perhaps if we'd invited them over for hummus and pita and a few boiled chickpeas as we sat on our balconies, perhaps that would have worked."

"Yes," I say. "That would have been good."

She leans her head on my shoulder and closes her eyes. "And Hamzah would be whole."

She's such a magical child, I think. Orit is drunk with fatigue.

"Or all of us could have gone into the streets," she continues, "like horses with blinders on and nuzzled around for each other in the dark."

"Orit, you're shivering. Put your robe on."

She can't hear me. She's falling asleep.

Then, "You know, Lishy…"

"Give it up, Orit. I can't take it anymore."

Orit raises her head, twists her hair into a rope between her hands, and squeezes until water pours onto the bed.

She persists, "Think for a moment of the surprise those merchants-cum-fighters on the west bank of the Jordan must have felt when they woke one morning in 'sixty-seven to find themselves within the State of Israel, a Jewish state. They. The Arabs. Why didn't we see? Even if we were living in your messianic times, Lishy, what were we thinking? That the Arabs would renege on their own allegiance, join in the fun of our Zionist melting pot and learn Talmud?"

By this time, I myself am wondering what our Arab cousins had thought, across whatever border they were living at the time, as we daydreamed in our classrooms. *What were they doing,* I ask myself, *as we bumped along in pick-up trucks to help immigrants in their transit camps? What did they feel as they watched our parents reclaim the Hula valley from the swamps, contracting malaria in the process? As they saw us transform the soil into agricultural communities and cities? Most important, as it now transpires, why didn't we ask these questions before? Why did Jordan and the other Arab emirates not invite their brothers to find a home in their countries? Why did the Palestinian authorities steal the money that poured into the Palestinian camps from around the world? Money they could have used to build themselves a home?*

Shivery bumps are covering Orit's skin. Her lips and her fingernails are turning blue. I don't tell her what I've just been thinking. Instead, I put my arm around her shoulder, "Orit, sweetness," I say, "why do you torture yourself like this?"

She's naked, except for the towel that is small and damp, her hair dripping over her. In the quietest voice imaginable, through teeth that rattle with cold, she pleads with me, "Because I can't sleep, Lishy, because I don't want war, because I sent Oody to his death and Hamzah into harm's way."

Hamzah is still on the critical list.

I'm driving along the coast with Naama and Asher to cheer Orit up on her birthday. My Dovy will meet us at Orit's with flowers and cake ready to make the day as festive as possible, but Naama, Asher, and I arrive late, quite late.

We're on the road to the town in which Orit lives, when a rock crashes through our windshield, missing Naama's head by a centimeter. In a flash, without even thinking, Asher stops the car and runs after our attackers. They're boys. No more than fourteen years old. When they realize that Asher is coming after them, they turn on their heels and run for cover. But Asher is strong. And he is determined. Naama says she's never seen him move that fast. He runs until he catches one of the kids by the back of his shirt, yanks him back to the car.

"Where do you live?" Asher growls. The kid pretends not to understand, but a liquid stain is running down his pants. "Where do you live?" Asher repeats, shoving the kid into the back, the smell of his sweat and other fluids engulfing me, Orit's happy birthday balloons between us on the seat. No answer. "I'm sure you'd rather I take you back to your house than to mine," says Asher. The boy nods his head in the direction of the Arab village. Asher drives. Naama sits silently next to him, the boy behind her, his knees violently shaking. When we arrive at the village, he points to his house. Asher parks the car, yanks the kid out, knocks on the door. A man opens, dressed in pajamas, his hair rumpled, a glass of coffee in his hand. On the table behind him, in a saucer, a cigarette is burning.

"Is this your son?"

"Yes."

"Do you want him to grow to be a man? Have a wife? Kids? A good life?"

"What has he done?"

"He was throwing rocks from the side of the highway. One of them shattered our window, barely missing my wife. You have to decide now what kind of future you want for your son."

The man doesn't answer.

"Look," Asher insists. "It might be too late for us, but what about our children? Don't you want them to live? In peace?"

The man in pajamas walks into the backroom and comes back with a belt. Without a word, in front of Asher, in front of me clinging for support to the front open door, he takes hold of his son, beats him mercilessly with the belt.

"If you do that again," the father says, "if you ever do that again, you're no son of mine."

Asher and I get back into the car. Naama is surrounded by broken glass. In her lap, a rock, sharpened on one end into a lethal point. For a while, the three of us sit without moving, without looking at each other. Then, Asher turns the key in the ignition. We start down the road toward Orit's house, to celebrate her birthday, three of her five smiley balloons still bobbing next to me on the backseat.

"Oshy," Naama whispers, "I need you to stop." Asher draws to the shoulder of the highway. Naama gets out of the car and vomits.

Nurses, doctors, and orderlies rush toward the wounded. A blood-drenched gurney speeds in my direction, skims across the floor toward me, propelled by a rabbi with a purple skullcap. I race the injured toward the operating room. For this patient, I realize, it might be too late. The shrapnel has exploded in her chest.

Then I see her face.

People are pulling at me, trying to force my arms apart. There is a noise like a bulldozer or maybe it's thunder or the ocean. I can't hear what the people are saying, but I know they're trying to make me do something I don't want to do. Somebody near me must be crying because I'm drenched in tears. Then, the noise stops. Silence. They've closed the door on the thunder, on the ocean. A man says my name. I have the feeling he's been calling it for some time, so I open my eyes. Nurit, my sweet, happy Nurit; Nurit who loves every human being on the face of the earth, who for years has carried olives and honey for the Bedouins she encounters in the mountains; Nurit who works in a home, caring for Israeli and

Arab children in need, who used to jump on her husband from behind and ride him like a horse; Nurit doesn't look anything like this ghost with the glass eyes and the cooling limbs in my arms, because she's womanly and beautiful. Her skin is warm; her eyes are rich with laughter. But this body is clutched, lifeless, to my chest, the front of my uniform, drenched in blood.

"No," I scream, as they pull her from me. "No! This one you can't have!"

The rabbi pries the corpse from my grasp.

"Let go, Elisheva," he urges. "Let her go home."

He rocks me like a daughter in his arms.

They won't let me go back to work. Every morning I take the bus to the hospital. I don't trust myself to drive. I stand like a beggar at the door to my department. "I need to tend to Hamzah," I say. They won't let me stay.

"You need a break," they say. "Take a vacation."

Hamzah is still on the critical list.

The first week of mourning is over. Avi and his children are sitting on stools, in their ripped shirts and unwashed hair. They won't get up. Won't talk. They don't want to eat. They won't open their blinds or let the daylight into their home. They ignore the supplies Dovy and I bring them, that their friends and neighbors bring them, a blockade of food in casserole dishes and soup pots on the counter, separating them from the world, wrapped in dishtowels.

Hamzah is on the critical list. They won't let me tend to him.

The first month of mourning is over. We go to the cemetery to set a headstone for Nurit. The crowd around the grave is as large as at the funeral. A rabbi reads the psalms. He looks familiar. He's wearing a purple skullcap. After the ceremony, he takes Nurit's family aside, sits with them on benches near the washing area and talks to them. I don't know what he says, but when they stand up,

Avi embraces him. Avi and his family don't talk. They nod and put their arms around us.

It is three months since Nurit was taken. Hamzah is out of critical care. Avi has gone back to working with the children at the home. He talks only to them. His own children keep to themselves as they go about their business. Occasionally, one of his daughters runs her fingers through her hair or raises her arms, clapping to a tune on the radio in that manner that was Nurit's. For that flash of a moment, Nurit is brought back into Avi's kitchen. For that moment, Avi is engulfed in the world he so much loved.

It's early morning. Dovy is buying vegetables at the *souk*. I'm standing in my kitchen in my bathrobe and slippers. My hair is uncombed, and I've not yet washed my face. I'm about to drop a tea bag into the trash when Naama walks in with a stranger.

"What's the matter with you? Don't you know how to knock?"

He's not a stranger. He is a man with gray hair and glasses. He is wearing a padded lumber jacket. He's wearing a purple scull-cap.

"This is Rav Zvi," says Naama. "I thought it might help if you talked to him."

"Why? Can he bring Nurit back?"

"Just talk to him." Naama is uncomfortable. She's maneuvered her body so she's standing in between the rabbi and me. She's rolling her eyes around and tightening her lip, signaling to me that I should be polite, trying as always to make things nice.

"I'm not ready," I say flat out in front of the rabbi. "You should have called." I don't care that I'm being rude. Rav Zvi doesn't seem to care either.

"That's the thing," he says, sure of himself. "We're seldom ready."

It's too early for debate.

Rav Zvi has seated himself in Dovy's armchair.

"Throughout my life," he's saying, "I was known as the marriage rabbi. I wandered around the country looking for happy occasions, happy people, people in love. I wasn't ready when the Intifada started. What choice do we have? Today, I spend my life at bombsites, hospitals, and graves."

Three more weeks, and my supervisor calls me from the hospital. "Hi, Elisheva, sweetness. How are you?"

"How is Hamzah?"

"He's fine. His tubes are out. He's learning to walk."

"I need to be there."

"Come, sweetness, we need you. We're short-staffed."

ORIT

It's evening. I'm back, sitting outside the hospital door, waiting for Elisheva to tell me how Hamzah is doing. I'm reading the paper, pretending that I'm not a wanted person. This is what I read:

> Fifty head of cattle munch on their regurgitated food breathing steam into the night, staring from their pens, the air pungent with dung. Five hundred people are moving up the hill. Only the sound of feet is heard trudging on the earth, the smell of dust ahead.

> For over fifty years, children from both sides of this sand road, an Arab village on one side, a Jewish one on the other, have played tag together. Adults visited each other on the patch of grass, sipping their glasses of tea, sharing their gifts of fruit. They talked about crops, about the changing of the seasons.

Wednesday. 11:10. p.m.

An elderly couple clears the last dishes from their meal: Two cups, two tea bags, two spoons of sugar measured from the can. Two slices of lemon cake on the plate.

11:16 p.m.

Gunshots: The pounding of feet; heavy, panting breath. In the black beyond the curtain, the elderly couple bleeds onto the floor. Lights blink on throughout the village. Voices call out. Forms rush through the gloom, across the grass, flitting through the silence.

11:26 p.m.

Gunshots: a mother and her boys, six and four, dead in their cot, a teddy bear smiling in their blood.

Lights spot on and off the surrounding hills, searching. It's cold. A sniper is hiding in one of the houses.

Ten minutes was all it took.

Five hundred people walk in silence along the path. Witness the bodies sinking into the grove. Chant the mourners' declaration of faith. Eucalyptus trees brush the skies, keening in silence.

Elisheva tells me that my court order is for real. I cannot see Hamzah. She says he's getting better. His tubes are coming out. I read the paper:

An Arab boy with a squashed-in nose, sad eyes, and pockmarked skin is caught sneaking over the border, explosives around his waist. The Israeli border patrol neutralizes his belt and arrests him. He is short for his age, he tells the soldiers, and ugly. He is fourteen already, he says, but only looks twelve. He couldn't find a girlfriend, and he has no friends. The bigger boys of his village told him he'd find girlfriends in the next world, he says, if he became a suicide bomber and killed Jews. His mother told him he'd be a martyr, that everyone would love him.

"Son," the arresting officer tells him, "those were no friends. And that is no mother."

Elisheva says Hamzah is out of danger. He's beginning to walk.

I take a trip to the Galilee to think, to get away from the people who add to my pain. One afternoon, on one of my hikes, I come across a synagogue that looks as though it hasn't been used in centuries. Thistles crowd round the stone. I wipe cobwebs from the window and see a room lit from within, a domed ceiling, and a rabbi sitting at a table, reading. I go inside. "My name is Orit," I say. The rabbi is young. He has a beautiful smile. He invites me to sit with him, pours us both some tea.

"What can I do for you?"

"Nothing. I was walking by. I've never seen this place before."

I wasn't wrong about his smile.

"You need to be looking for something, to find it," he says.

"We've been looking for peace for fifty years," I say, "and we've not found it."

"Perhaps we've not looked in the right place."

Arrogance, I think. I say, "Of course, you know where that place might be."

"I don't. It breaks my heart that God is hiding His face from us. Like everyone else, I ask myself, *what are we doing so wrong* or, *how can we make it right?*"

I had prejudged him.

"How can we believe in a God that hides His face when we most need Him?"

"That's what we are all asking," he says.

"If God loves us, why does He let us sin?" I ask, strangely certain that I am no longer author of my thoughts.

"We have free will."

I hate that answer. He says, "Perhaps He is waiting till we work things out ourselves," and I ask him how the God we believe in could be so heartless.

A glow is lighting up the window at the rear of the building. The rabbi asks me about my life. I launch into a description of my mother, Shuli, telling him about her sweetness, her scattered manner, her absence. Before I realize it, I'm talking to him about Ella, my birth mother, whom I've not mentioned to anyone since I was a child.

"Do you have brothers?" he asks me.

"No."

"Sisters?"

I don't tell him about Ruti, don't mention the heinous thing I have done to Hamzah, my sister's child, but my eyes are welling up. I can't stop them. "I know Ella and Shuli are interceding on our behalf," I say, and, still certain that I am not the author of my thoughts, I add, "God is the single, unifying force, right? In which case, why is everything in our lives so splintered?"

"He appears in many forms, and we are made in His image."

"In the image of the God we have shattered."

He is silent. It seems strange to be drinking tea in a synagogue, wrong to be talking about God in this place, in such unorthodox terms.

"No attempt to understand God is unorthodox," says the rabbi.

My head jerks upward. I am looking into his eyes, eyes that are speckled, like the eggs of small birds. He has read my mind. Yet he seems to have left me for his own thoughts because he says, "If you save a single life, it is as though you have saved the world."

"Yes," I say. "Arabs and Jews are destroying the world, over and over."

"And yet," he insists, "our purpose is to save lives."

"How?"

"With love."

The demon inside my brain pops out: "Perhaps we should take the suicide bombers into our homes and love them."

"That's the piece of the puzzle we're unable to see."

"Somebody has to intercede on our behalf," I mumble. "I want it to be Shuli."

The rabbi is staring so intensely at me that I blush.

"What do you do here?" I ask, more to break the intimacy of the moment than out of curiosity.

"I think. I drink tea. I bring the children and the old people of the neighborhood here in the evenings, to share God's joy with them."

"How can God be joyous while we are suffering?"

"I don't know."

"So this is what you do."

"Yes. This was my father's home, may God rest his soul. They called him the 'marriage rabbi.' The suicide bombings, the national mourning—they killed him."

Again, I want to cry. Again, he is staring.

"Your mothers' souls are heavy," he tells me. "Their mothers were heavy souls before them, and so on and on for as far back as we know. You are carrying a heavy burden."

"What about my father's soul?"

"You've learned from your father. Perhaps, you need to listen to your mothers."

I leave him. A mist clusters 'round me as I make my way to the bed and breakfast, my home for the night.

The next day, I return to that place. I have things to ask my rabbi, to share with him. The synagogue is empty. The door unlocked. The windows covered in cobwebs as though I had not, less than a day ago, cleared them away. A note is tied to the door with string: "House of Prayer Available. Needs Tending." I turn the note over. "Seek out your soul mate," it says. "God will help."

My heartache accelerates. My friends heal the victims of the Intifada. My mother, Shuli, had worked as a social worker, helping the wounded and the dead of her day. Naama, my closest friend since we were in high school together, is a doctor. Elisheva, my cousin: a nurse. Me? I destroy those I love. I delivered sweet Hamzah into the hands of our enemy.

I volunteer at the hospital. I ask Elisheva to show me how, and she does, but the wounded and the dying make me dizzy. What's more, though I am a dancer, though I move with alacrity on stage, I'm too clumsy in the hospital to be of any help. By the time I find the supplies, others have bandaged the wounded. I try to adapt myself to counseling, to driving an ambulance. I take courses in first aid intending to become an emergency medic. My intentions fizzle into nothing. I feel like shit.

A thirteen-year-old boy is standing with his back to me. He has blue pants and a starched white shirt on, like our flag. He wears sandals with two straps that we call Bible sandals. He's alone, his face against a wall, seeking comfort. A spade hangs from his hand. He can neither see nor hear me, but I know he is Hamzah. A fool's hat, the kind worn by pioneers in our more naïve days, is buried in the sand at his feet.

I wake from my dream. A melody is running through my head, the Yiddish song Shuli used to hum. "Ima," I moan, "I miss you so badly I can't breathe."

Shuli's melody continues. *How would she guide me?* I wonder, realizing that that was the problem I had during her lifetime. Shuli didn't give direction. The word *commonsense* pops into my mind. *Hardly an attribute I'd associate with Shuli,* I think. Then, frightened by the vibes permeating my room, I light a cigarette, pace, talk out loud.

"I'm spending too much time alone," I say. "I should do what the rabbi's note told me, give myself one more stab at a man friend," though I know I won't be able to bear the pain. My mother's tune persists. *I'll go for a walk,* I think. I don't. I hide under my covers, drawing from them whatever assurance I'm able that I'm sane, that this space is the room I call my own during daylight hours. *Comforter,* I think, hugging my blanket, *good word.*

Dawn seeps through my blinds. It's raining. I'm still obsessing over why Shuli would need common sense in heaven, when it's clearly not an attribute one associates with the afterlife. Suddenly, as loud as life, Shuli says, "Let go, Ority."

To hell with it, I think, praying immediately that hell is the wrong reference. I decide to address her directly.

"I want to help with the wounded, the dying, the families," I say. "I do. But I'm like a centipede, my legs, all hundred of them, popping out and getting in the way."

And Shuli answers me. "Perhaps yours is some other function."

"Like what?"

"Like maintaining the dream we started with, our vision of tolerance, pluralism, and peace."

"What we need is hands-on reality," I say, reclaiming my own commonsense. "People who can stop the very real blood from flowing, not dreams, not make-believe."

"Without those dreams," she says, "our country will go straight to hell."

This is Shuli's voice. Shuli, who floated through my childhood with never a word of advice, knitted woolen sweaters in the summer, screamed bloody murder in her sleep—in my sleep.

"Nothing is more violent than these years of Intifada," Shuli is saying. Has she forgotten about the Holocaust that coughed us up, each in our turn, spewed us out naked into the arms of strangers?

I wonder how experience presents itself to the dead. Is it stacked in chunks, one piece over the other like the jumbled pieces of a puzzle? Or in disconnected units, each piece of experience unrelated to the one that, in fact, does not even go before? Until now, I've assumed that humans are an integral part of one linear cosmic story. In fact, we might as easily be a myriad insane conjectures, volcanic embers left over from the Big Bang, yearning, inventing meaning, burning our way meaninglessly through time.

I go to the bathroom, close the window against the wind.

"You need to act," Shuli is saying when I climb back into bed. "Look around you. People are frightened to leave their homes for the grocery store but go to the theaters any day in the week—they're packed, and the plays are asking questions. Important questions."

I'm thinking how much easier our experience would be if actions didn't lead with such deadliness to their own conclusions, so we can never go back to settling for the life that seemed tragic enough at the time, but that now seems like a good compromise. The women of Israel, I think, would be happy, grateful to suffer the loss of an Oody to adultery. Not to death, of course—to adultery. If only we could be certain, I think, that the package waiting for us around the next corner will be safer than the one we are holding so precariously in our hands.

Shuli is still talking:

"We rely on our artists to tell us the truth," she says.

"Ima, is this you speaking to me?"

"Yes."

"What is the truth?"

Silence. I ask her again. I wait for three, four minutes. I ask her again. Silence.

"Ima?"

"Yes?"

"Do you care what's happening down here?"

"Of course. We all care."

I refrain from asking her who the "all" are. I mean, I think, is it her and Aba, or her and Ella, or her and Aba and Ella; or is it perhaps all the ancestors going back to Sarah and Abraham? It's heaven, after all. What about the ancestors of our enemies? Are they up there too, giving their own contradictory messages to their progeny? Do they share heaven with our ancestors, or do they have their own? Are they all at peace with each other in heaven? In which case, what the hell are we fighting for down here? Do the various heavens—because if there are two, there are surely more—do they fight with each other? Or would fighting negate the very nature of heaven? Or should I make the whole issue easy on myself and believe that all beings other than us are in the other place. Elisheva would tell me we don't believe in hell, only in a period of time in which to prepare for heaven. But perhaps she's wrong. Perhaps this land flowing with milk and honey and guns and threats and fear and blood is all there is, and the Shuli who is giving me such good advice is herself nothing more than a projection of my deepest need. Will God punish me for thinking these things?

"Ima," I say, "do you know about Ruti?"

No answer.

"Did you watch when I stole my sister's child?

Nothing.

"When I sent him like a sacrifice to the altar?"

Silence laughs at me.

"I've lost them both."

Nothing. Not even a melody. *Right*, I think. *They never respond to the real stuff.*

Returning to the legacy my mother is laying on me. I say, "Many thanks," and, clutching to my pillow as to a life jacket, I fall asleep on my cold, stone floor.

Four Druze soldiers are killed that night, guarding our country. Israel wakes in the morning to weep for them, to pray for the safety of their souls.

RATIBA

Hamzah is on the critical list.

We haven't had time to climb into bed and weep. We weep on the run, in the car, to and from the hospital. Most times, the weeping happens without us, tears running down by themselves, as we talk to the doctors, to Elisheva, wetting everything as we are trying to fill out forms. We sob as we talk to Hamzah, not at all sure that he can hear us behind his bandages, under his traction. Two bloodshot eyes are all we have of him. Ibrahim and I take turns at night, sleeping by Hamzah's bed, in the chair. On the nights that I'm home, I clean. I've scrubbed everything in sight, and still I clean. I can't stop. We neglect our daughters. They're suffering. I don't know how to comfort them.

My Ibrahim is aging. He doesn't seem able to stand upright. His hand shakes. He forgets to close the front door at night, leaves drawers open, leaves food on the table till the ants come. Last week, we needed to fill out some forms at the hospital. He'd left his ID, his entire wallet at home.

"Let me stay tonight," I beg him. "Go home. Get some sleep."

"No," he says. "I drove him away. I'll bring him back."

Ibrahim and I are petrified whenever Wadha goes to the city. But we've raised her to be independent, and she's decided, as she's not married, to go back to school. Ibrahim suggests that she go with him to the university in Bethlehem.

"I won't," she argues. "These are my graduate studies, I need to be in Jerusalem."

"The school year doesn't start for seven months," I say. "Inshala, by then, Hamzah will be better, the situation will have eased."

Kasim goads his son, looking past him into my face. "This is what comes from copying the Jews," he says. "Your women don't listen to you. You are no longer a man in your home."

I know he blames me for Hamzah. "If you only knew," I mumble under my breath, "what it's like to destroy your son's life."

Instead, I ask him, "What do you know about the Jews?"

"No more, nor less than you," is his answer.

Stubborn old man, I think, remembering the bloodstained prayer shawl, hoping that's all he is.

It is the end of the university year. Hamzah is in traction, but he's off the critical list. Our lives revolve around his hospital care. I'm home while he sleeps.

Wadha comes into the laundry room, pretending to fold the sheets.

"I need to talk to you."

"What's wrong?"

"Nothing. Why do you always assume something's wrong?"

"Wrong happened, Wadha."

Wadha crumbles onto the stool I use for folded underwear.

"I'm sorry, my love," I say. "What is it?"

"I shouldn't have brought it up now."

"He won't be better for a long time. You can't put your life off."

"You've put yours off."

"You children are my life."

She hugs me. "How could we have let this happen to him?" She sobs.

"I'm sorry, my baby," I say, smelling the sweetness in her hair. She was the closest to Hamzah before he disappeared.

"Tell me your news," I say. "I need to hear something other than pain."

Wadha closes the door, although she knows there is no one in the house but us.

"You're not to tell Abee. Not now. He won't be able to handle it."

"Are you in trouble?"

"No."

"Wadha, what is it?"

"I've met a Jewish man. I want to marry him, to adopt his faith."

Before I'm even aware, my question shoots from my throat. "Where would you live?" Wadha's mouth falls open.

She's gaping at me as at a demented person. "That's the problem?" she asks.

I refold the towels thinking, as I do so often these days, that the prayer shawl in the tool shed is taking its revenge. Time has passed. The prayer shawl issue seems unreal, a figment of my imagination, perhaps, yet who knows?

"I'm studying Kabalah. It's Jewish."

I don't respond.

"It's an ancient text that teaches how to behave according to the moral principles of the universe."

I fold underwear.

"Don't be angry with me."

I don't trust myself to speak.

"I shouldn't have said anything, but you taught us to think for ourselves. I thought you meant it."

"Wadha, my love," I say, "you know how I went to Haifa last fall to meet my old roommate?"

"Yes."

"This year, it's your time to go."

"What, with you?"

"No. I won't be going again."

"Why not?"

"It will be good for you to meet my friends alone."

"Are you trying to divert my attention from what I'm telling you?"

"No."

"Mom, I don't know that woman. She was your friend a hundred years ago. Besides, I'm talking to you about something else."

I put a load in the washing machine.

"That visit didn't do you any good, Ommy. You've been in a horrendous mood since you came home."

"Hamzah is reason enough for depression," I say. The detergent smells of chemicals. I must find a healthier brand.

"You were depressed before Hamzah disappeared," she says, her voice no louder than a whisper. "It was your depression that drove him away."

I clutch the ironing board, my back turned toward her. "If what you're saying is important to you, you'll go to Haifa this fall and visit my friend."

I can feel Wadha glaring at me. "Nobody's mother is as arbitrary as you," she says. "There is no reaching you."

"Will you go?"

"I'll think about it."

"Good. Now go put these socks in their drawer."

ELISHEVA

2005

My Dovy is appointed by the government to evacuate Jews from Gaza. The settlers are furious with him. "How can you betray us?" they demand. "How can you remove us from our homes, in our own country, from the land we've developed since childhood and grown to love?"

Devora, Dovy's sister, matriarch of the settlement on the Shomron and mother of the bride whose wedding we'd attended, refuses to speak to us. "Look what you are doing!" she hisses at Dovy. "Look at the schism you are causing in our family!"

We no longer share family celebrations. Our children are torn between two sets of relatives.

"Where is their Zen-like equanimity now?" I ask.

"The violence they live under is constant," Dovy tells me, eyes closed, his elbows propped on the table, holding up his balding head. "The only way they can tolerate it, is by creating a community for themselves that is homogeneous. No threat from within. I am that threat from within. I am shattering everything my family and friends stand for."

In the secrecy of my heart, not caring that I'm being a nag, I call, *Please, God, my God, calm the raging spirits.*

BOOK SIX

ISRAELA

I tell myself that Elokim is my companion and lover, that He would never abandon me.

Because mothers have forgotten their cunning, like a Jew forgetting Jerusalem, like an ocean choked with mountain stone and earth, like Medea, like gerbils that swallow their babies live when danger approaches.

"Stop!" I scream, but no one hears me.

If somebody were murdering your child in the next room with the door closed so he couldn't hear you, would you keep silent? Or would you pound as hard as you could on the soundproof door? I do. I pound on the barrier of sound, and I scream stop—knowing that no one can hear me. Make room! Elokim and I will rollover, will clear a space for Allah and his people. Only come in peace. Stay in peace. Learn to share in peace this place where God has set you down, Arab and Jew, for better or for worse.

All these changing of borders, this fighting, is the extent to which my personal comforts have been disregarded. What is it about humans, I ask myself, that they can't see this? What have I done over the centuries that I've spawned children who are envious, competitive over me?

It was not me who first separated Isaac and Ishmael, Jacob and Esau. That would be far beyond my abilities. Do the stories of their Bible not clearly warn them how not to behave? What not to repeat? Why don't they see that? It was not I who misinterpreted the Koran into an imperative for murder. Would Allah not have preferred his people to live in peace? Does Elokim, my God, want anything but peace for His children? Because that is where the real source of jealousy lies—there, in the humanly misinterpreted, father-son struggle between brothers.

Imagine if Elokim or Allah or Zeus or Shiva loved equally all the peoples of the world. Who would champion our cause?

So they have Allah and we have Elokim and we are at war.

ELISHEVA

Hamzah is out of danger.

"Just let me know when, Elishy. I'll take you."

Our daughter, Hila, is about to be married. Dovy and I drive to Jerusalem from the sands and the white apartment block of Hila's home in the south to see my brother, Noam. We've heard about my brother's mentor, the Kabalist of Safed, and want to make a pilgrimage to see him.

My brother drives. We arrive at the mountains around Safed late at night, begin our descent into the bottomless bowl, surely one of God's secret places, I suggest nervously, surely the deepest pit of God's netherworld, not to be visited by men, definitely never by women. We are driving to the burial sites of holy men and mystics. We step out of Noam's car into the darkest-of-dark dome of sky studded with stars, stars as low and large as chandeliers. Strangely, beneath the stars, we see nothing, only ominous forms, God's shoulders I think, settled for eternity, alone against the moonless sky.

Our senses grow accustomed to blackness bedecked with heavenly lights, to night alive with jackals, close yet off somewhere hidden in the hills, howling into the darkness. Wolves are out there, hungry and hunting, guarding God's private backyard against intruders.

We visit the caves of the mystics. We stand inside the burial sites with their grimy walls, their smell of rodent droppings and burning wax, caves saturated with the smell of the dead and the righteous.

A man appears out of the darkness. He will be our guide, he tells us. We light candles, scramble around in our pockets and in my purse for scraps of paper, transcribe our prayers into miniscule writing so we can ask for as much as possible, and leave them on the tombs—the men in the caves assigned to them; I in the one to which I am directed.

The palms of my hands are open, resting on the tomb. I wait. This is my time to pray. I close my eyes.

"Please God," I beg, "help Hamzah regain his life." That's it. That is my prayer. *Focus,* I tell myself, knowing there is so much more to ask for. Despite, or perhaps due to the lateness of the hour, there are other people around me. I feel them coming in and out as I am trying to pray, mumbling beneath their breath. *This is the time to open my heart, as those other women are doing,* I think, remembering the way I used to feel at exam time, even when I'd prepared.

Now, I tell myself. *Pray now.* A shopping list of wants comes into my head, smelling of cobwebs, my mind sizing me up as I try to pray. *Who was the mystic buried in this tomb? Who was he really? Or is he, in fact, a she?*

Then I start in with: *Who am I that this dead person would intercede for me in heaven? How do the custodians of these caves know where the dead are, anyway, or what they are able to do there? Is this superstition? Is it faith? Or is it a violation of a dead person's privacy?*

The men join me from their cave, their segregated place of prayer. We get back into our car, climb up and around the mountain path to the city of Safed. I am beyond devastated. My moment. My special moment—I've dropped it down the bottomless bowl of night.

The Kabalist begins seeing his clients at midnight. People are waiting on the benches ahead of us; so it is not until dawn that we are admitted into the room that seems to have absorbed the sweat and sorrow of the night. I am aware that the pilgrims waiting on these benches are burdened with heavier cares than Dovy's and mine.

The light is dim. The Kabalist is sitting at a table so worn with people's elbows it dips at odd places along the edges. A lamp casts a pool of light over the circumference of the desk, over a book, over a purple skullcap that rests headless beneath it.

He is a stooped man of medium height, soft voice, and a gentle manner. "What is it that brings you here?" he whispers.

I am redheaded, outgoing. I have an open, freckled face and a way of talking that is confident. But I am still reeling from the opportunity that I dropped down the black hole of what I am now certain is God's backyard.

Dovy speaks on my behalf.

"We would like a blessing for the wedding of our children," he says.

"It should be in a good hour," whispers the sage. "Is it your daughter or your son who is getting married?"

"Our daughter, our first."

"And the groom, do you know him well?"

"Yes." I've found my voice.

"What are their names?"

I'm not thinking straight.

"Hila and Andre," I say.

"No." The wise man shakes his head. "I need their Hebrew names."

"Of course. How silly of us," Dovy stutters. "Our daughter's name is Hila, daughter of Elisheva and Dov. Our son-in-law's name, well—we always call him Andre because he's originally from Belgium. Sweetness, what is his Hebrew name? Arie?"

"Yes," I say with conviction. "Arie, son of Binyamin."

"No," responds the Kabalist.

"No?"

"I'm sorry," says the sage in the gentlest voice imaginable. "Those names are not a match."

"What do you mean?"

"I'm sorry," he whispers. "I cannot bless this combination."

We leave. What about a blessing for Hamzah? We'd forgotten to ask.

No one speaks. The righteous dead would have slept well on our drive to Jerusalem. The following day, Dovy and I take the bus back to the glaring colors of the south. We don't utter a word to our children of our visit to Safed.

It's a week before our daughter's wedding. We're in a make-shift synagogue in the south, a community center during the week replete with scraggy corkboard announcements on the walls and a basketball hoop. We are sitting on benches. My body is limp from the heat, from our five-minute trek beneath the relentless sun. My dress, silk for this festive occasion, is sticking like wet tissue paper to my body; perspiration is seeping into my eyes, stinging them so I can barely see Dovy and his man-sized handkerchief, on the far side of the room, mopping sweat from his face, his neck, and as far beneath his open-necked shirt as it is appropriate in a synagogue. Suddenly, "Aharon son of Binyamin" is called up to read from the Torah. Simultaneously, from our separate seats, Dovy and I hear the name and watch as our son-in-law-to-be walks toward the podium, Dovy's handkerchief suspended, like Pavarotti, in mid-air, Pavarotti with a pale complexion and a limp.

We gave the wrong name to the Kabalist.

Some months before the birth of our granddaughter, we return to Jerusalem. Again, we ask Noam to take us to see the sage. This time we give him the correct names. This time, the righteous man blesses our children's marriage.

"Please," I ask the righteous man, and he prays that Hamzah be healed, body and soul.

People are seeking out seers and mystics, groping for blessings, for reassurance, looking for answers in a world that guarantees nothing.

Orit goes to a weekend seminar on laughter therapy. She calls me a week before it starts.

"Come with me," she begs. "Laughter creates endorphins or some such thing in your body that are good for you."

"What will we do there?"

"I don't know. What do people do when they need to laugh? We'll probably tell jokes, be forced to play tag, or hide-and-go-seek. Hey. I don't mind what we do so long as it gets us to relax. We can play spin the bottle and climb all over each other for all I care."

Naama goes to a psychic: A small room. Clean. No crystal ball. No cards. No heavy, turbaned medium. Just a modest, clean ante-room, a table, two chairs, and a woman in her late forties who smells as if she's been frying onions in the next room.

"Who is Adina?"

Naama is not about to give anything away.

"Why?" she asks

"Because she is thinking good thoughts about you from the next world."

"She was a good friend," Naama concedes. "It is a year today since she was killed in a car accident.

"Who is Moshe?"

"He was my father."

"Yes," says the psychic. "He is watching over your home."

Naama bursts into tears.

––––––––

Like the end of a child's tantrum, the heat of our summer is beginning to wane. I arrive from the north, my hair pulled beneath a hat, my skin beginning to crease, my step heavy. Last Thursday, I found my ima scratching, bareheaded, at the foot of her olive tree, the tree that twelve months from now will protect her on her cot from her last, wordless summer. I took her picture. It's the last picture I have of her.

"Hello, Alison."

She's not called me by my English name since before my twelfth birthday.

My mother is leaving me. She wanders 'round her home with the parched Japanese roses and the smell of decay, her face and form frail, netted in sunspots. She no longer sings in the kitchen or in the bathtub. Instead, she rages, her limbs trembling in an involuntary protest against a future into which she has been plummeted, and in which she wants no share.

During the day, she dusts what she can no longer see. In the evenings, scorning sleep, she sits at my father's desk with her lips pursed in concentration and her hand trembling from the effort; she writes way into the night, scribbling reams and reams that no one can decipher because she is writing in a language none of us understands. Creating order. Making sense, crumpled papers spilling around her on the floor.

My dad's desk: I remember myself, with the smell of my mother's lentil soup permeating our home, lurking in the doorway when my father worked. My father's feet turned toward each other beneath his desk, the brown of the carpet, the quiet, the sanity of it all.

"Ima, can you hear me? Do you want anything from the store?"

"Paper, more paper," is all she ever says.

I watch her at my father's desk, searching for her life.

My mother has forgotten my Hebrew name.

She won't let us open her blinds. On the other side of my mother's room, there's an olive tree, a pomegranate, people outside are walking to the market, still talking of trading land for peace. Newspapers she used to read are piled in the doorway of the music store; there are books in large print for aging eyes, books on tape for those who can no longer see, songs that can be turned up for those who can barely hear.

If my mother had taken this walk with me, she'd be coming back now. Neighbors would have been happy to greet her. Instead, they have to wait for the final ambulance to blanch in horror and say their last good-bye.

It is three in the morning. My mother is not in her bed. She's dusting, wielding her feathered wand in the gloom. "I will clean," she tells me, repeating what she'd declared that devastating day.

"Ima, it's the middle of the night."

"But I won't cook."

"You haven't cooked for a long time, Ima. It's okay."

"I cooked for him," she insists, meaning my father, who was present in the orderliness of this home, his chair, since the night he died. Eventually unable, I suppose, to handle her failing mind or the stench of approaching death, his spirit left us. I remember his presence that particular morning; by that afternoon he'd gone. Believe me, I do everything I can to coax my father's soul back into his home, but, no, he's gone, probably because my mother no longer remembers him.

My mother has forgotten my name.

I am at a memorial service for my parents.

My father: The rise and fall of his chest on the Friday evenings of my childhood, when he wrapped his arms around my brother and me. He'd read us the stories of Abraham, of the binding of Isaac; of Jacob, how God had promised them the land of Canaan for their children; of Sarah, who forced her husband to drive her handmaiden into the desert, together with her baby Ishmael; of how God told Abraham to listen to his wife because He would make Ishmael into the father of a nation too; of Rebecca, who protected her son from the wiles of his brother, conjuring up, in the process, wiles of her own. My father told us how Moses led his tribes through the desert to the promised land. He told us about little David, his willingness to stand alone in that valley, not far from Jerusalem, and risk his life against the Philistine.

As a child, I had failed to see how each of those characters made mistakes, probably because the juicy parts were edited from my version of the text, and that my generation was bound to repeat the pattern: divine direction versus human failing. Supreme Intelligence set against our own myopic grasp of history. Human nature getting in the way, inserting itself like water seeping into sand between our parents' vision of state-building and its execution. The result of our actions is our reality. It lies in our beds with unsheathed knives.

Weeknights, I begged my father to trade his stories for those of my Grimm's fairy tales. He skipped the scary parts, wanting to deliver us from the nightmares that sent me scurrying into my parents' room.

"I had a bad dream."

"What about?"

My father never gave in to that one moment more of sleep I allowed myself when I became a parent. The second I touched his shoulder he'd be up, fumbling around beneath the bed in his blue pajamas, feeling around among the lost shoes and the dust balls for his slippers.

"I dreamt of Hitler, that he was coming down the mountains to get us, that the Nazis were living in towns and villages around us, that we couldn't tell who they were or who we were."

My dad put his arm on my shoulder as he walked me back to my room. He tucked me back into bed and we said the *Shema* again:

"Listen and understand, O Israel, the Lord is our God, the Lord is One ... and you shall teach your children ... "

"That's who we are," he said, and I fell asleep.

I wonder now why loving God is a commandment and why to love your neighbor like yourself is the second most important principle of faith, a rule like not crossing the road on a red light. I wonder why protecting the stranger in our midst is almost as important in the scriptures as honoring our father and our mother, as not coveting our neighbor's wife. Is that because it is so hard to do? Because if the strangers in our midst were friendly, we would not need a commandment to protect them. Or is it because if we disregard them, our world will collapse into the shards of stone on which our creation was first recorded and disappear?

Will God not protect us if we disobey Him? I wonder. *If we don't love Him? I'd protect my children.*

As the melodies whirl around me, I remember the synagogue of my childhood. Worlds away, a domed structure smelling of dust and must, but mainly of wood and old books. The women, sitting in the gallery in their fruited and feathered hats, the older ones with dead foxes draped over their shoulders; my mother wearing fitted suits, standing erect in the front row, her chin stuck unnaturally forward because she was intimidated by the older women, those who were always telling her what to do.

"Why can't I play outside like the other kids?"

"Because I like having you with me."

I never minded my mom keeping me at her side. I enjoyed the repetition of the tunes, the rocking to and fro, the stillness.

Most of all I loved the melody the congregation sang as they rose from their seats at the end of the morning prayers. "Bring us back to you, O God," we'd pray. "Renew our days as of old." I'd picture myself living in biblical times, like King David in the desert or, more accurately, like the shepherds in the black-and-white pages of my Bible-book. Then, I'd ask myself whether I wanted to sacrifice animals in the temple. I'd think of Tabby, the cat that slept in the shed behind our house. No, I wasn't ready for that.

Now, as I listen to others chant, an echo rings in my ears: our temple; the wailing call of vendors; the bleating, blind panic of goats; the lowing of cows terrified in their final moment. I hear doves sighing out their last sweet sob, children running in and out of booths, psalms sung on the outer steps as the sun comes up over the hills tingeing the air with warmth, prayers, the call of the ram's horn, the play of the harp, of timbrels, drums. Yes, I can smell the spices too: incense, lavender and myrrh, the sick, sweet stench of freshly spilled blood, of dung, of death. Smells and sounds that served my people in their desperate need to communicate with God.

I never understood why the old ladies sobbed into their handkerchiefs at the prayer for the new month.

"May you grant us... a life of peace, of goodness, of blessing-From what I could tell, it was quite an okay prayer, better than most. Perhaps they confused it, I thought, with the ones we said in memory of fallen soldiers or civilians killed in the war or the prayers in which they asked for forgiveness on the High Holidays when almost all the old people cried. *I mean, look at them,* I would tell myself, *these musty old ladies with their bosoms and their pearls. What crimes could they have committed? Do people who do terrible things look like the rest of us? No one's going to rob a bank, kill someone, or covet someone else's wife, and then come in here to cry over the prayer for the new month.* Now the bosoms and the pearls didn't look as innocent. The dead foxes definitely had stories to tell. As for the men wrapped in their prayer shawls downstairs, who knew what they were hiding? I enjoyed measuring my height against my mother's shoulder, comparing the size of our hands. Years earlier, not much more than a toddler, I'd run to sit with my father and my brother in their special seats. When we stood in prayer, my dad draped us in his sweet-smelling prayer shawl, sneaked us candies from his pocket.

My mother watches us from her seat in the balcony. She plants a kiss on her hand, blows it down to us.

ORIT

I'm in my theater. It is an exquisite building with scalloped ceilings, ornate carvings peering at us, many cave-like spaces for props and costumes. I am in the costume shop. Embroidered brocades, gilded cords, silks and taffetas in all shades of pink, greens, and blues, whose colors shimmer and change as you touch them; velvets in the mustiest aquas and golds; tiaras, staffs, tangible manifestations of every sense or fantasy are here hanging on racks, draped over velvet sofas and antique tables, overflowing in baskets and cardboard boxes on the floor.

I am with my fellow workers, wading knee-deep in costumes. Someone is calling me. "Orit," the voice says, "others claim this space. The costumes and the props are no longer yours. You must give them away."

"No," I say depressed, and I wake, unable to face the day.

ELISHEVA

Hamzah and a Jewish patient named Arie have been recovering in my unit for a year. They limp around the patio, their hospital smocks inadequately tied behind them exposing everything they have. Hamzah is smoking. Arie is carrying coffee, more out of habit than need. I am conscious of them as I change the drip of my most recent patient because I hear their slippers slough across the concrete. Hamzah is on crutches. Arie's torso is in bandages. They're ogling Sarah, the student nurse, elbowing each other, boasting how manly they'll be when they get out of here. They lurch into the doorway, Arie's arm slung over Hamzah's shoulder.

"Hey, Elisheva," says Arie. "Guess what I just found out? *Hamzah* and *Arie* mean the same thing. We are both lions."

I wish I'd known Hamzah as his mother's cousin, not as his nurse. He's a gentle boy, looks much like my beloved Uncle Yehuda. We talked as his traction came down, as his bandages were removed. I asked him what he did in the army.

"My job," he told me, "was to go with my unit in the middle of the night to Arab houses to look for explosives and suicide bombers. We were acting on information the intelligence gave us. It was horrendous. We would wake them up. The women would scream hysterically. The children would cry and cling in terror to their mothers. In the short term, our job was essential because it never happened during the entire time of my service that we entered an Arab home and failed to find explosive belts ready to be used, and/or a suicide bomber hiding under the bed in which the children and the women slept. Not once. Each night that we burst into a Palestinian home, we prevented a bus or a restaurant from being blown up the following day.

"The tragedy is that in the long term, when the children wake in the middle of the night to see the 'evil' Israeli soldiers in uniform, in their home, their guns at the ready, they look into our eyes, and I know that at that very moment I have created a second generation of suicide bombers."

I stand in the corner as Hamzah talks. *How can that be?* I weep. *Little children seeing evil in Hamzah's eyes? In Uncle Yehuda's chocolate eyes? The fabric of our world is ripped beyond repair.*

BOOK SEVEN

ISRAELA

My children believe their actions will last forever, but I have seen. I know: history is their master. Two thousand years ago, Herod restored the ruins of Solomon's temple, rebuilt it, expanded it considerably for my people. He was one of my great megalomaniacs, a sentimental man who loved his family, who murdered his wife and his children out of fear and then cried over them, a broken man, a man serving two masters, wanting to please both the Romans and the Jews. Vanity.

It has not stopped. The killing. I was wrong. I am always wrong when I allow myself to forget. Elokim is not my lover. Not now. There have been many times like these, when He has abandoned my children. When He has abandoned me. When my children were left to fight alone. And yet I give birth to fruit and flowers. How can I still do that?

I appeal beneath the barrier of sound: my children have made mistakes. This, now, is my perspective: tell your sons and daughters that Egypt covers 1,009,441 square kilometers of land, that Syria has 185,180 sq.km, that Lebanon has an area of 10,400 sq. km, that Jordan has 96,188 sq. km. Iraq has 437,072 sq. km, and that Israel has 20,770 sq. km. Tell them my children cannot afford to give me away, but they'd share me with cousins who come in peace. Otherwise, tell them their children have been blessed since the days of Ishmael, that God has made them into many nations. They, the sons of Allah, have prosperous lands beyond my fragile borders.

ELISHEVA

I watch as victims of explosions lie in hospital wards alongside the perpetrators. Due to the severity of their injuries, they are not released from hospital care for a year or longer. For months, Palestinians and Israelis share the same bathrooms, the same bedside tables. After they've survived their initial trauma, recovered from the series of operations they've had to endure, they use me as an intermediary when they talk. At first, they're resentful, sullen, refusing to look each other in the eye. As they heal, I see them begin to compromise over TV programs, still wary, but offering each other the use of their toiletries, their tray of food. Next, they walk the hallways together, passing time. Later, they sit near the window, reading the paper, side by side. They show each other pictures of their children, their grandparents. Sometimes, I hear them argue, their voices low, guarded. Slowly, very slowly, they begin to exchange points of view. They play backgammon. They listen.

ORIT

I dream. I'm in a coffeehouse waiting for my sister. At the next table, with her back to me, is Shuli, my mother. I'm so excited to see her, I forget about Ruti.

"Ima," I call, and I lean to tap my mother on the shoulder, to embrace her. But before I've even touched her, the woman turns to face me: a toothless, fading smile, a waterstain on paper.

I'm obsessed by stories: Sammy was raised by Muslim parents in a Palestinian village on the other side of the Green Line. He objected to the hostilities of the Intifada.

"Keep your ideas to yourself," his father warned him, but within the confines of their home, Sammy persisted in his grumblings. His mother took Sammy into their back room, closed the windows and the doors.

"My name is not Saloma," she told him.

"What?" asked Sammy, wondering at the perspiration that was beading up on her forehead.

"I'm Shulamit," she said.

Dizziness washed over him.

"You and I both," said his mother, "we are Jewish."

The boy stared at his mother.

The next day, at dawn, Sammy and his mother crossed the Green Line into Israel where their names reverted to Shemuel and Shulamit. They have lived as Jews ever since. After the security checks, Shemuel joined the Israeli army, rose in the ranks until he was appointed major. So Sammy, from a hostile Palestinian village, became Shemuel, a "hot-shot" in the Israeli fighting forces.

During the worst period of the Intifada, Shemuel received a call from the security checkpoint.

"What's the problem?"

"Your father is here."

"Where?"

"Here at the checkpoint. Speak to him yourself."

"Son," begged his father, "since you left, my people have stopped trusting me. My life is in danger."

Shemuel made calls, assurances, conducted negotiations, pledged himself as a character witness for Khaled, his gray-haired father standing hatless in the middle of the road at the check point in the scorching wind that was blowing from the desert, a plastic bag dangling with his belongings from his hand. Asylum was granted. He was brought onto this side of the Green Line, since which time he has lived as a refugee with his Jewish family, in exile, in Israel.

I dream that I wake in the middle of the night to find the windows and doors of my home open. I'm naked, cold. I can't find the light switch. A wind is driving sand through the rooms, knocking my cups from the shelf, sweeping my papers from the table. Through the window, I see my sister in an open car. "Orit," she calls, as she blows away in the dark.

More newspaper articles: Dhaled was raised in a prominent Palestinian clan. He left his hometown, moved to Israel proper, and applied for Israeli citizenship. He couldn't have been considered a threat, because within the appropriate amount of time he became an Israeli citizen, married an Israeli woman, moved to live in a border settlement, became a respected member of society. Thirty years later, Dhaled disappeared, returned to live among his Palestinian friends in the place of his birth. Had Israel let him down? Had he grown to regard her as the worst mistake of his life? Did he miss his original people, traditions, way of life?

My nights are crowded with dreams. I'm standing in a field. Naked. A wall of thistles has grown around me. I can't see because a bandage is wrapped around my eyes, but whenever I turn, the thistles rip at my face, scratching my body and my limbs. I feel blood running down my face, into my open mouth so I can taste and smell it. I hear dogs growling in the distance. At the other end of the field, beyond the wall of thistles, I hear my sister's voice calling me. "Ruti," I answer. "Ratiba, I'm here."

Through my blindness, I can feel Ruti walk toward me, can smell her perfume, lavender, like our mother's. I feel Ruti's body heat when she stops near me, beyond the wall of thistles. But the voice that comes to me now is Shuli's.

"Come, babush, let Ima hold you. Come, dance with me."

I dance carefully because I'm frightened I'll touch the thistles. As I move, the thistles melt to the ground, my bandage floats away, white and graceful on the wind, and Ruti dances with me. I look at my sister: a mark, a knife blade, across her lip.

I read the news: Saloma was born to a Palestinian mother and a Jewish father. Her mother was murdered when she was born because she'd polluted the honor of her family by fraternizing with a Jew. Her father disappeared soon after that. She was left in a basket on the doorstep of a Christian orphanage. According to Arab law, a person is Muslim if his/her father is Muslim. Saloma's father was Jewish. A person is considered Jewish if she/he is born to a Jewish mother. Saloma was neither Arab nor Jew. One day, taking the bus to work, an eerie sensation took hold of her: she was being followed. The feeling stayed with her for days, stretched into a week and more, to the extent that she grew scared of walking alone. One afternoon, as she stepped out of the supermarket with a bag of provisions under her arm, a man addressed her by name, told her that he had information for her about her father's whereabouts, and coaxed her into a coffee shop to talk. He was a member of the *Shin Bet*.

"You are one of us," he said. "We need you." Saloma had never been needed before. "We need people who can give us information," he said. "You are the perfect candidate."

I dream: Jackals stalk around a circle of fire, their shoulders rounded forward, their noses sniffing the ground. Their haunches are folded beneath them like witches round a cauldron. As I look, I see that their eyes are clear, soft, human. They are the eyes of Elisheva, Ruti, and Naama.

"Listen to the mothers, Ority," they call to me.

Yes, I think. *That's it.* I look to the center of the circle of fire. A baby is lying there, swaddled in gauze. As I reach toward him over the flames, I break the circle of fire and wake up.

The situation is untenable. Palestinians are desperate for work, for independence, determined to make their voices heard, to fight until the country is theirs. Jewish settlers are intransigent, determined not to lose what they will never have again.

I'm scrambling up an embankment aiming for a fortress that runs across the horizon. That is where it will be. I reach the summit, hang myself over the wall like clothes draped to dry, and I look. Fields and hills stretch as far as the eye can see. No rocks or thistles, nothing parched by the sun. *Like Europe in picture books,* I think, *so lush, so blessed by rain.* My panorama is void of houses, of buildings or people. Not even an animal, a donkey, not even a bird. I don't hear any insects or see flying things. Nothing. Parallel rows of stones stretching as far as the eye can see, gleaming white in the sun, are all there is, stones, rows and rows of stones, standing, instead of people; white, immobile, gleaming on the grass in the sun. I look down and see my arm draping over the stones. I have lost my watch.

# ELISHEVA

Every day that ends without a suicide bombing is cause for thanks.

"Thank you, God, my God," I whisper into the evening air as I walk from the hospital to the bus.

It is 2007. The borders are closed. No one can get in or out of the Palestinian territories. Palestinians are unemployed and furious. After every suicide bomb that explodes in Israel, the Israeli forces zoom into the territories and demolish the home of the perpetrator. More. As a result of the Intifada and Israel's desperate need to prevent terrorism before it reaches its cities, Israeli forces strike the leaders of the Hamas from the air as they get out of their cars or as they sit in their homes sipping coffee. Often, bystanders, innocent people out to get their morning paper, their carton of milk, are killed along with the bad guys. This strategy, together with the wall we're building between the Palestinians and ourselves has reduced the amount of suicide bombers by 80 percent.

"Thank you for the peace we are experiencing at this moment. Thank you, God, my God," I say, when we wake in the morning to news about the birth of quadruplets or a tiger cub at the zoo seeking a foster home. Not wanting to tempt fate, I add, "Please, God, allow us to live in peace." Like one obsessed, I mumble, "Merciful God, thank you for not allowing an explosion this day." I follow that with, "God who breathes life into the dead," not even knowing what that means, "protect us from further violence." Conscious that I'm being a nag, I add, "I know. I know, God, you're wanted in Somalia. It's just that I need, we all need, to hold your hand."

ORIT

"Why are you closing us behind a wall?"

"Because we've had enough of your bombs, your killings."

"How can you determine where to build it? The fence is cutting into our land. You should have asked us."

"Yes? Whom should we have asked when we had no partner for peace? When you were sending suicide bombers against us?"

Ilan, the son of my very best friend, is demonstrating with the villagers of Bil'in, an Arab village near Ramallah. He called me a few days beforehand.

"Ority, come with me. See for yourself how things are over there."

So I'm here, with an open mind, I convince myself, on a shadeless lot at the entrance to the village. Against my better judgment, I've become embroiled in dialogue.

"We're human beings," the villagers tell me. "We want to live in peace, like everyone else. We have to defend our rights."

Every Friday, the Israeli military with their rubber bullets and their tear gas line up opposite Palestinian villagers. The villagers lock arms with their Israeli sympathizers, Ilan among them, to form a human chain, to force their way beneath the wire fencing. Together, they push the boulders from their border. Together, they defy the soldiers.

"Of course, they regard suicide bombers as holy martyrs," Ilan tells me, though I fail to see the "of course." To me, murder is murder. "The climate is changing," he tells me. "They know now that peaceful demonstrations have a better effect on our government, more influence over the outside world."

"But this demonstration is against us."

"Palestinians are tired of the violence," he insists, "tired of the poverty, of the lack of work."

I look into the faces of our soldiers. *Boys,* I think. *Little boys dressed up to fight.*

"Why do you bring tear gas and rubber bullets?" I ask the soldier nearest to me. "You can see this is a peaceful demonstration."

The boy dressed up as a soldier turns his body toward me, closing the Arabs out of earshot.

"Do you think we like doing this?" he says. "We hate it. Someone has to do it, so here we are."

The villagers are gathered in groups, chatting. *Like an outdoor market,* I think, *without the produce.* It's hot, though. No shade. I'm listening as Ilan talks with one of the villagers. But before I know it, a crowd has lined up opposite the soldiers, smelling of anger. A single voice, low, uncertain, calls out, "Take down the wall. Get out of our village." Someone else repeats it, louder, then another, and another. "Take down the wall!" they shout. "Get out of here!" "Take down the wall!" "This country, for Palestine!" Men, women, children, Israelis among them, Ilan and I among them—though my mouth is securely closed—calling out, "Take down the wall."

Before anyone realizes what's happening, a man's voice booms out, "Get out of here, you punks. You don't belong here!" A rock whizzes over our heads. One of the soldiers clasps his head. Blood everywhere. The soldier falls to the ground. Pandemonium. I can't see for the tear gas. I can hear, though. I can hear rubber bullets, the screams, the pounding of feet. I can hear orders being issued, voices dropping into silence. The stone-throwing demonstrator has been caught.

"His eye." Ilan's voice is tight. "It's his eye," he says. "The soldier has lost his eye."

My heart hurts. I limp away, rubbing at my own eyes. Stupidly, I tell a group of protesters, those who have not been rounded up, mainly women, that the soldiers are "doing their job."

A woman with a child in her arms thrusts her face into mine. "You think they're innocent?" she yells. "We have to walk through a fence guarded by Israeli soldiers to reach our own fields. You saw them shooting at us. They're out of control."

"Are you crazy?" I snap at her. "That soldier has lost his eye!"

"They shouldn't be here," says the woman next to her, her voice tense, breathing sour breath into my face. "If they would stay out of here, they wouldn't get hurt."

I lean into her, my vision still blurred by the tear gas. I snarl into the woman's face, aware that my breath is not one bit sweeter than hers, my temper snapped like an electric wire. "Maybe," I say. "Or maybe they're here because they've been hurt enough."

Ruti. It is Ruti, standing in her *hijab*, next to these women, the women in their *hijabs* and their robes, that's what they almost all wear nowadays. Ibrahim is standing by her, gaping at me.

Just like that, my anger vanishes. Ruti and I are opposite each other, Hamzah's wounds between us.

"For God's sake, Ruti," I say, holding my arms out to her. "Forgive me."

She draws herself from me. "My name is Ratiba."

"Ratiba, please."

Under her voice, "You stole my child," she says. "You put him in harm's way. You never even asked me."

"How could I have asked you?"

She turns to leave.

"Ruti, I'm your sister."

"My name is Ratiba. I don't know you."

I'm crying. I hate it when I cry. Lately, that's all I seem to do.

Ibrahim puts his hand on Ruti's back. "Talk to her," he says.

Again, she draws her body away from me, sucking air into her lungs. For a moment, I think she's actually going to spit. Instead, "Get away," she tells me. "Before I call the police."

Ilan rushes over from the other side of the lot. "What are you doing, Orit?" he whispers. "This is a peaceful rally." He pulls me away. *My life,* I tell myself, *it has lost its meaning.*

I almost go with him. I almost do. Then, *no,* I think. I yank my elbow from Ilan's grip, return to face my sister.

"You fell in love with Ibrahim while understanding differences, building a common language," I tell her. "That was noble. You were following our father's teachings. Then what did you do? You reduced your life to the level of your fears, emptying it of the good life."

She's not responding, I think, *but she's not moving away, either. Besides, I'm not finished.*

"It was against his better judgment that Ibrahim let you send me away," I tell her, guessing, aware that I'm taking a huge leap into what I don't know, "because he loved you. He hoped somehow things would work out. What has happened to his love? The love you lied to protect?"

And a new thought pops into my head.

"It wasn't me who stole Hamzah," I tell her. "Ruti, have you looked into his eyes? Into your son's chocolate eyes? Whom did we love, with eyes like those, if not our aba? Hamzah too dreams of a place where neighbors can understand each other. So, no doubt, do his sisters. They deserve it. See, Ruti, what we've done with our parents' dream? Our aba is weeping in his grave."

My strength has left me. I clutch Ilan's arm. "Now," I tell him, "let's go."

Last week, the Israeli Supreme Court determined that the fence around Bil'in is unconstitutional, that a section should be diverted because it's not essential for Israel's security, and it prevents Arabs from reaching their fields. This week, the villagers of Bil'in and all the surrounding villages are celebrating. Next week, Naama's children will demonstrate with their Palestinian cousins in the village of Al Walajeh.

ELISHEVA

A strange metamorphosis is occurring. The Yiddish lullaby that Shuli used to hum now runs on a regular basis through Orit's mind and body, and I watch as Orit steps into the shoes of her second spirit mother, the mother who raised her.

On the heels of success in hi-tech and fiber optics, engineering and scientific research, a privileged class emerges. On the heels of the Intifadas, with its loss of tourism and the withdrawal of foreign investors in Israeli industry, comes poverty. The middle is giving way. We have what we swore would never happen here, a society of "haves" and "have-nots," not on the scale of the countries of the West, but apparent just the same. Most years, Israel suffers from drought, but every four or five years the heavens open, and the rain pours down. The Ayalon River floods its banks down the center of the country; rush-hour traffic squeezes itself onto the peripheries of the freeway. Israelis smile at the skies and thank God for His blessings.

All that is, except the impoverished families who live in the lowlands of South Tel Aviv and Jaffo. Every deluge enters with a fury into the nooks and crannies of their homes, washing their beds, pots and pans, and whatever clothes they possess into the sewers.

I watch as Orit sets up a clinic in the south to teach the Bedouins how to eat a healthy diet. Once a week, she travels to the Bedouin community where they no longer live in black tents in the desert but in apartment buildings on the street near the shopping mall. Bedouin women no longer walk miles a day to their sheep shearing or to draw water from a well. Men sit on metal chairs in their stores or on the sidewalks, while the children slouch on their classroom benches, reveling in the junk food of city life. Yes, Orit teaches mothers in Beer Sheba the economic and health benefits of fruits and vegetables. She urges them to reflect on the lifestyle of their past and walk.

But for the period of the floods, Orit spends her days in Tel Aviv, battling with the authorities and banging on the desks of bureaucrats only to give up, roll up her sleeves, and help the poor salvage their possessions from the mud. She has developed an aptitude for social work. Wherever Shuli is, I know she is proud of her daughter.

Orit works with teenagers outside supermarkets, handing out lists to purchasers of the things most needed by the homeless. Together, they carry produce to the shelters. They tack collection boxes onto bus stops. Soup kitchens open around the country, catering to the indigent, to blue-collar workers and white-collar professionals who have lost their jobs.

It's Friday, my day off. Naama brought her grandson, Omer, to me because she was called back to the hospital while he was playing at her house. She said she'd only be a couple of hours and asked if I'd bring Omer back to her by noon. Omer is seven, has perfectly round eyes, eyes as black as beans, and a pointed chin. He manifests a peculiar interest in what happens to things at nighttime. "Why do your flowers close up when the sun goes down? Why do the moths fly around the light bulb? Does Dovy take his artificial leg off when he goes to bed?"

We're walking by the bus station on our way back to Naama's. Omer sees a homeless man dressed in rags with matted hair and a hand extended for coins. This is his first experience with the dark side of reality, and he bursts into tears. I drop a token coin into the man's palm and continue walking, clutching Omer firmly by the hand. But Omer is inconsolable. "Why is that man sitting on the sidewalk? Why is he so dirty? Why does he need money? Where's his family? Where does he live? Why doesn't his family come to get him? What do you mean he might not have a family?"

Naama has prepared pasta and ice cream, Omer's favorite lunch, but he refuses to eat. His lips are trembling. He wants to know how we can eat when the homeless man is homeless, hungry, sitting on the sidewalk, without a family.

Naama, Omer's Savta, suggests that we go back, find the man again, that this time we take enough money to help him. Omer likes that idea. He asks Asher to take him. Saba Asher and he walk down the side streets hand in hand. I'm walking with them, on my way home, feeling like Scrooge. They're discussing poverty, that there are people in the world who don't have blessed lives, that it is the duty of those who do to help those in need. The grandson challenges the grandfather; Asher answers as best he can until they find their friend. Omer hides his face as Asher introduces them both to the man on the sidewalk. I lag behind them. I watch them give their money to the man. I slink along home, offended.

Naama tells me that Omer isn't a demonstrative child yet, back home an hour or so later, he went into his grandparents' bedroom, threw his arms around the gnarled neck of his grandfather, murmured, "Thank you, Saba."

Naama tells me that she drew a blanket over her husband's knees, whispered to him that the song we all sung in the early days, has come back to mock us.

> Oh, oh! What sounds are those out there in the night?
>> Oh, the jackal is calling.
> Oh, oh! Why does the jackal call out there in the night?
>> Because he's hungry.
> Oh, oh! What sounds are those out there in the night?
>> Oh, a child is crying.
> Oh, oh! Why does the child cry out there in the night?
>> Because he's hungry.

ORIT

I was on stage, increasingly distracted from the role I was trying to play. The beams above the audience were dipping, forming a kind of ditch in the air. As I watched, a hawk flew in through an upper window, became trapped inside the overhead ditch. Immediately, a flock of smaller birds, also black, also birds of prey, swooped up and around the walls of the theater, round the wooden ditch, threatening, with their scratchy voices and open beaks, to peck the larger bird to death.

I couldn't tell whether the audience was ignoring the tragedy being enacted above or whether they didn't see it. I shouted for my fellow actors to stop their performance, for the spectators to look up, to save the large bird from disaster. No one heard me. The show continued. The manager called me from outside to tell him out of earshot what was happening.

I ran around the corridor. On my left was the playing area where the performance was continuing without me; on my right,

I passed prop rooms and rehearsal spaces, all empty. The director was ahead of me, out of sight. I ran round and around, away from the action on stage.

"Help!" I cried. I woke without having found him.

RATIBA

Finally, my Hamzah is discharged from the hospital. He doesn't see well, suffers from headaches. The doctor says he'll never be able to walk without crutches. Yet he's alive, thanks to God or to Allah. He's too big, he says, to move back in with us. He's learning Arab and Hebrew literature at the university, like I did. He visits us.

Kasim was in his workshop when it happened, smoothing a block of stone into a lintel. Luckily, at that moment, Ibrahim was standing outside the shop. Kasim groaned. Ibrahim heard a thump and a clanking sound as his father and the chair he was sitting on toppled over. He found him slumped on the ground, coffee spilt across the marble. Ibrahim screamed up to the house. "Ratiba! Latif! Samah!" his voice carrying across the courtyard like a gunshot. We brought the old man to Jerusalem, to the Hadassah hospital.

I've been respectful with Kasim, dutiful, but never comfortable. I'm frightened of the prayer shawl in his shed. The family has been hovering around him since his illness, but today, they are away, leaving me to sit by my father-in-law to keep an eye on the life-saving monitors. I watch him as he sleeps: a stern man. His face and hands lined by the sun and the winter winds, by the work with tools and stone that have become his life.

"You owe me, old man," I whisper, thinking of his secret.

"You're in charge now." His eyes are open, looking into mine. I don't respond. Then, "You must tell him, Ratiba."

"Tell who?"

Kasim stares at me.

"Tell what?"

"Tell your husband who you are and where you come from."

I turn to salt. I'm Lot's wife looking backward, running to save her life.

"You've not been fair to him," says the old man.

"How did you know?"

Kasim closes his eyes. He's having difficulty breathing. Again, he fixes his stare at me. "We make choices, all of us have to," he whispers. "But you've been standing at the crossroads for thirty years."

"When did you find out?" I whisper.

"Did you think I'd let my son marry without doing my job?"

"You've known all these years?"

"Yes."

"Why didn't you tell me?"

"It is your story. I was waiting for you." He's having difficulty speaking. Then, "You've done him a disservice."

"What about the prayer shawl?" A rush of defiance is making me bold. "Whose is it?"

"That was my story," he says. "You should have shared yours with your husband."

"I love him. I thought he wouldn't marry me, that you wouldn't allow him to marry me."

"You must tell him now. He will keep your secret."

Ibrahim is staring at me from the doorway. I rush past him into the bathroom, close the door behind me, lean against the tiles. Wheezing sounds, like the braying of our neighbor's donkey, are heaving from my chest. I'm unable to catch my breath. Cold. I'm fastidious about strange bathrooms and dirt, but now I slide down this germ-infested wall, curling into it as if to the embrace of a parent, until I'm crouched on the cement floor.

What the hell, I think, ignoring the pounding on my heart, and I lie with my face in a puddle.

Three weeks later, standing at the grave side, the call of the Muezzin whining round my ears, the winds whirling at our backs, I weep, more than I wept for my mother, more than for the father I adored, for the sister I'd banished from my life, for the people I loved in my younger days, whom I've incised from my heart. *Over thirty years,* I say to myself over and over. *Thirty years without my family,* thinking of the cursory note Kasim had left his sons, "There's a prayer shawl in the tool shed," it said. "Wrap me in it for my burial." That's all. Not another word. I could have told Ibrahim thirty years ago.

Ibrahim turned to ice when he read that final note. He wanted to throw the prayer shawl out. Wanted nothing at all to do with it.

"It was his final wish," I said.

"This is between you and my father," he told me then. "I wipe my hands of both of you." For the life of me, I can't work out why I intervened.

For three weeks, we've been busy with Kasim's illness, with his passing, so I've not said anything to Ibrahim about the conversation I had with his father. Not that he asks. He is more silent during these weeks than ever before, sharing nothing with me. I try to talk to him. Every morning, every evening, I beg him to share his feelings. He stares at me, wordless, a stranger.

After the funeral, when the neighbors are done with their con-
dolences, when Ibrahim is finished at the mosque, when he's at
some corner cafe talking with his men friends, when the girls are
off in their own world, I clear the clutter from the kitchen counter
and scrub every tile, tap, and corner of my house. The sigh of my
broom as I sweep reminds me of my mother, Shuli, of her death.
Then too I'd felt this compulsion to clean. *Order over chaos,* I think,
or is it the primal movement of rhythm, plain and simple? I cook Ibrahim his favorite meal of lamb and rice, meticulously cutting the
meat into cubes, chopping the mint leaves while gazing out the
window over the shady side of the hill. When I first met Ibrahim,
this hill was nothing but stubble for weeds to thrive on, for goats
to prod at with their old man beards. Now, it is covered in homes,
stone houses gathering like storm clouds around our own, stretching over the rocks till they fade into the horizon. As I watch, a
butterfly rises from the geranium pot flying off ghostlike into the
clouds. I set the table with a cloth and a candle as though I'm preparing for a celebration, but when Ibrahim comes home and we sit
down to eat, he refuses to talk.

A week goes by. Two. Two weeks of wordless routine. Nothing
will get Ibrahim to talk to me. Nighttime, his body lies like a fos-
silized tree, inert and foreign on the other side of our bed. Day-
time, I withdraw to the privacy of my closet to dress, as I would in
the presence of any man that is not my husband. The term *heavy
heart* keeps running through my head. "Heavy, heavy heart," I say,
over and over. My heart is so heavy; it has slipped, a shrouded
bundle, a stone in my lower gut that cannot be lifted.

A month. Two months. I unlock the storage shed to pull my
mother's suitcase, one last time, from its place among the baby
clothes, the obsolete garden tools, the cobwebs, and to lay a rose
over the wooden trunk for Fatima—the trunk with the wedding
dress that I should have worn, the one that held Kasim's prayer
shawl until his funeral, that still holds his secret.

"I tried," I tell Fatima. "I did. It's just too hard." I pull Fatima's dress from the trunk, rocking it in my arms. As I clutch it to me, a card flutters from the sleeve to the floor. On it, in childlike Hebrew, is written: "Itzhak, son of Sarah, daughter of Moshe Bilak." Beneath that, in smaller letters: "Hebron, 1929."

"Fatima," I say, gasping. "Thank you."

I pack the suitcase with my things. I leave a note on my table: "My darling Wadha. My most beloved Daifa, forgive me." Stepping from my washed front door, I pick my way down the path, down our Arab hill, between the thistles.

ORIT

"Yosef, I have a play coming up with a part for you."

"I'm sorry," answers Yosef. "I'm busy."

"Why? What are you working on?"

"Learning. To ease my mother's soul."

I feel my skin blush. Why don't we everyday people think like that?

Though it's over a year till Yosef and I see each other again, his gentleness is always in my thoughts. One afternoon in late spring, we arrange to meet for coffee near the cinema-tech overlooking the walls of the Old City. He's been eating too many cakes, his face pasty and unhappy. He has spent the year working gratis for his newspaper, waiting, like the gentleman he is, for their promises of payment to come through; battling with the authorities for legal ownership of the home in which he was raised; mourning the death of his mother.

"Are you writing?"

"No."

"No poetry?"

"Not really."

Our conversation revolves around the complexity of his identity.

"Are you Jew or Muslim?" I ask him.

"I live on the line dividing the two," he says, smiling. "I am nothing."

"You are both."

"How's that for a double whamo?"

I wonder about barriers and borders, about identities and divisions.

I look at his thinning hair, his honest eyes, at him, sitting in his favorite coffeeshop on the dividing line between the two sides of his city, smothering his ambivalence in cheesecake.

Why did you never marry? I wonder.

Suddenly, he says, "Come with me."

"Where to?"

"Never mind. Come. As an act of faith." He extends his hand to me.

"Now?"

"Of course, now. Come."

He takes me to the mountains over Jerusalem: the city behind us, the village in the valley beneath.

"Here," he says, chuckling a deep, brown chuckle, "let's dance."

"Here? Now?"

"Yes."

He has a yellow face. Dirty-blond hair laced with gray hangs across his eyes. *Some Cossack raped your ancestor,* I think, but I keep it to myself. His identity is over-taxed enough. He takes my scarf from around my neck, color of fire that I always wear, and starts to twirl, slowly, listening to some tune within himself, a tune I can't hear. Before long, he's standing on the tips of his toes, like a top, his arms spread out in his vintage "Peace Now" t-shirt like the leaf-bearing dove painted across his chest, dipping and swaying with a grace I've never seen, either in a man or a woman. He smiles, extends my scarf to me. I catch it, and we know we are enacting the dance of life over Jerusalem.

Without warning, I panic. I can't catch my breath. Waves, bucketfuls of air, surge from my stomach into my chest and shoulders, threatening to drown me, new waves crashing over me before the old ones have time to recede. Yosef reaches out to me.

"Let go," he murmurs. "Listen to the tune I'm humming and let go."

I fix my face on his as if my life depends on it. Slowly, I move through my whirl-tide, hearing only him, focusing only on his melody, until the waves wash out to the ocean that sent them.

New waves, different from the first, are flowing through me now, evaporating from my skin into the air, leaving me calm and light. Hatred, boys falling in fields, in the narrow alleyways of crumbling cities, patriarchs, mothers, politicians, all are phantoms now rising from the rocks, hanging like sleeping bats or molted feathers on the overhead branches till I feel as light as the scarf that wafts around me, coaxing me to fly. Yosef lets out a rolling laugh that curls around us with the breeze. Lights, like jewels, gleam in strings beneath us, 'round the mountain.

The only sounds are those our breath makes as we bend and straighten, or the crackle of the eucalyptus leaves as we crush them. We slow to a stop. Yosef leans into me. "We can't stop loving when our hearts are sore," he whispers. "Our hearts betray us when we stop loving."

The moon glows—predictably, a dirty-blond moon with the face of a middle-aged man.

"You were right," I say, leaning against a tree, looking down over the city. "It should be this simple." I'm silent then. For the first time in my life, I don't need to talk. I've said everything there is to say, and I've been heard.

"Just for today," I whisper into the darkness, "let it be good."

ELISHEVA

"Is this Elisheva?"

"Yes."

"My name is Varda."

"Yes?"

"I was Wadha. Ratiba's daughter."

"Of course, Wadha. My goodness. It is so nice to hear from you. How's your mother? Is everything okay?"

"Thank you."

"My goodness," I say again, stupidly. "How are you? How's your sister?"

"Daifa? She's fine. She's married now, with two children of her own."

"Wonderful. Congratulations. She is something, your ommy, why didn't she tell me? Whom did Daifa marry?"

"She married a man called Isma'il, a Palestinian. They've built a house in our village."

"Oh."

"My ommy wanted me to contact you. Well, actually, to come and see you."

"Of course. How is she? I haven't heard from her in the longest time.

"I don't know."

"I beg your pardon?"

"I don't know how she is. She left us six months ago."

"What?"

"Look, it's uncomfortable talking to you over the phone. Can I come and see you?"

"Of course. Come right now. I'm free, totally free for the rest of the day."

"Thank you. Yes. May I bring my boyfriend?"

"Well, of course. What a question … Is he also Palestinian?

"He's American."

This conversation is way too complicated, I think. *I've never even met Wadha.*

"Before she left, my Ommy wanted me to tell you," Wadha is saying, "his name is Isaac; the son of Zalman, your friend."

RATIBA

I take two buses. One from my village to Jerusalem, one from Jerusalem to Hebron, my fingers in my pocket all the way, clutching to what I now think of as "Fatima's note" with the strange Hebrew names.

I've never been to Hebron. The bus deposits me in front of a traffic circle near the outdoor market. A few Jews. Mainly Arabs. Dour-looking men and women going about their business. I walk past the vegetable stalls. Soldiers everywhere, the atmosphere palpably tense. I ask one of the soldiers where the Jewish area is.

"What business do you have there?" he wants to know.

"I am looking for someone."

"Who?"

"I'm looking for the house of prayer."

I have to show him my ID, have to show him the inside of my purse, let him scan me with his radar wand. Our country, on permanent alert.

"I have a message for Itzhak the son of Sarah, from his relatives."

He's not convinced.

"Come with me," he says.

It's not clear to me whether I am being escorted or whether I am under arrest, but he walks me through the marketplace until we reach the synagogue. The soldier follows me inside. Waits for me to conduct my business. Annoying.

A middle-aged rabbi is reading behind a table. "Can I help you?" he asks.

I show him my paper.

"This Yitzhak was here in 1929," says the rabbi.

"Yes."

"There were Arab riots at that time."

"Yes," I say. "I know."

"Who are you to this person?"

"I don't know yet. This is why I am here."

I ask him if he has records. He goes into the back room, my soldier still sitting in his corner behind me. The rabbi returns with a roster. In it are recorded the names of those who perished in the '29 riots. Without a word, the rabbi runs through the list, pointing at every name tenderly with his forefinger. "Yes. He's here. Yitzhak son of Sarah, daughter of Moshe Bilak, may his memory be for a blessing."

"Oh." I slump into the chair behind me, next to my soldier-watchman. "He was among the murdered." A sickness is seeping through me. I decide not to tell this rabbi about my dead father-in-law, about his secret.

"Not necessarily," the rabbi is saying. "D'you see this asterisk?"

"Yes."

"That means he wasn't found. Probably, he was killed, but he could have run away. How old was he?"

"I don't know."

"You don't know much about this person. Who is he to you? Who gave you that note?"

"Itzhak's mother was my aunt," I lie.

The rabbi looks at me in silence, the soldier's disbelief searing a hole through the back of my blouse.

"What about Sarah, his mother?" I ask. "Is she on your record?"

"This is a boys' seminary. Only boys and old men."

"What did you say her name was?"

I look up. The rabbi's wife is sweeping energy through the room.

"Sarah, the daughter of Moshe Bilak," I tell her.

Resting one hand on the rabbi's back, she takes a key from the desk drawer, shuffles into the adjoining room, beckons me to follow her, opens a cabinet drawer stuffed to overflowing with books, produces a file.

"There was a house here at that time," she tells me, "two streets over, the Street of the Generations. A woman was murdered there, in the 'twenty-nine massacre. She had a son who was never found." The rabbi's wife waves her arm at the soldier. "You can go, Haim," she says. "She's harmless."

"I'm staying," the soldier responds.

"See here," the rabbi's wife shows me. "Sarah, the daughter of Moshe Bilak, widow, immigrant from Lithuania, murdered in her home, Friday, August twenty-third, 1929."

"But what happened to Yitzhak, her son?"

"I don't know who you are, sweetness, or what relationship you have with this family," she says, "but it was a long time ago. There is no record of him. Maybe he escaped. Who knows? Maybe, with God's help, he is still alive somewhere in this wonderful country of ours, living the good life."

She doesn't sound convinced.

The soldier accompanies me past eighteen Street of the Generations to my bus. In place of a house, there is a low structure, a nursery school with children playing in the courtyard. On the gatepost, immediately beneath "Assistant Wanted," is a plaque: "Dedicated to the Children of Hebron, In blessed Memory of

Sarah, daughter of Moshe Bilak, and of her son, Yitzhak, who disappeared on Friday, August 23, 1929, the day of his bar mitzvah."

The air has collapsed in uneven lines in front of my eyes, like TV static with a malfunctioning cable. What were the names of this mother and son doing in my father-in-law's shed? Why the bloodstained prayer shawl? I can barely walk. My soldier-guide props me by the elbow, helps me, as though I were an invalid, onto the bus.

What am I doing? I ask myself, as I sink into my seat. *What has happened to our country?* The radio is on. Yehuda Poliker's song is playing. "Good evening, despair," he sings. "Good night, hope."

The bus is full. I peer through the windows, through my tears, as we bump our way back to Jerusalem, bulletproof panels clamped like claws to the windows, protecting us from guns, from rocks. Who was Itzhak Bilak? What happened to him? Whose prayer shawl was that, that Kasim took with him to his grave?

ELISHEVA

An elderly Arab is sitting in the waiting room when I get to the hospital.

"Remember me?" he asks. "I'm Wahid. I was your patient in Jerusalem when Avrohm was recording his life story on your machine."

"Wahid, of course I remember you. How are you?"

It took a while for Wahid to hear about Avrohm's passing. When he did, he went looking for me at my previous place of work. He told the staff there that he had urgent business to share with me. They wouldn't give him my whereabouts. It has taken until now for him to find me.

"I want to share the second half of Mohammed's note with you," he tells me.

"I thought you didn't have it."

"I didn't want to share it with you while Avrohm was alive."

"Why not?"

"I'd promised not to let Avrohm know about Mohammed's family."

"Can I hear it now?" I take Wahid into the nurse's room, hand him my recorder.

"I will start from the point at which Mohammed has just seen the woman, dead on the floor," he says, clearing his throat. He clicks the button.

"It was then," says Mohammed, "that I saw the child, because there, next to the woman, lying on a filthy, blood-soaked prayer-shawl, was a boy, his body twisted in a grotesque coil, bleeding, an open wound down the left side of his chest.

"I heaved the boy into my arms, the foul prayer shawl cling-ing to my grasp. With the call to prayer rising from the nearby mosque, I lurched from that place. 'Come,' I told the boy. 'I will name you Kasim.'"

The recorder clicks off.

That is the story. For the sake of that paragraph, Wahid has searched for me, has taken the bus from Jerusalem, to Haifa.

"Why are you giving me this?" I ask.

"You are a gatherer of stories, Elisheva. You will know what to do with it."

I throw my arms round Wahid. *This man,* I think. *This bearer of good tidings, he is my healer.*

The drawing Ratiba left on my dresser, I tell myself. *I have to find Ratiba.*

ELISHEVA

Who would have known she could be so secretive? First she hid Hamzah from us; then she hid Yosef, whom she's been dating for a year.

The day Yosef proposed, Orit left, traveling north to the synagogue hidden among the thistles. For days, she sat outside the deserted building with its "House of Prayer Available Needs Tending" sign on its door. Finally, she entered, wiped the chairs and the table as instructed by the sign, stayed to pray. For days, she prayed and sang, munched on pita bread and olives she'd brought in a linen pouch, slept in a sleeping bag outside, beneath the stars, waiting for her beautiful rabbi to appear, knowing, against all odds, that he would. He did. On the seventh day, just as the sun was setting, the beautiful rabbi walked into view from the rear of the building. On his head: the purple skullcap that was once his father's.

"Yes," he said, as he swung into earshot, a smile, she told me later, radiating from his face, "I will be happy to perform your wedding."

We can't find Ratiba. Ibrahim has placed advertisements in both the Israeli and the Arab newspapers. She hasn't responded.

Orit and Yosef are being ridiculous about their wedding.

"Elisheva," says Yosef, "all we want is to be married. We don't care about the arrangements. We want our close friends and Orit's rabbi; that's all," to which Orit adds, "We don't want any fuss, and we don't want a crowd."

"Elisheva and I want to arrange your wedding," Naama tells them.

They say, "Fine, do anything you like. We don't care."

"What kind of flowers do you want?"

"We need flowers?" When we insist that they do, Orit says, "Wildflowers. Bougainvillea from the side of the road."

Naama and I fantasize about a canopy covered in white roses or orchids or tulips or hydrangeas or…

Orit brings us a cloth, faintly yellowed with age, embroidered delicately in yellowing white thread. "It was my mother, Shuli's," she says. "I'd like it for my huppah." Yosef brings poles to hold up the canopy. He has made them himself, he says. Naama rushes into her "creative" mode.

"We'll wind climbing roses around the poles," she says.

"No," says Orit. "We want the poles to hold up my mother's canopy, unadorned."

No word from Ratiba.

The *huppah* is set on the cliff above the sea near Orit's house. It looks like some magnificent bird, an anomalous stalk or majestic pelican about to lift into the air. Nothing can be more beautiful than this stark white cloth, for in the outdoors it has absorbed the color of the clouds, its edges flapping joyously in the wind over four spindly legs.

Chairs are set up on the dunes. The water laps beneath us, extending as far as the horizon. Yosef walks down the aisle first so he'll be prepared when Orit arrives to welcome her into their *huppah* home. He is flanked on either side by his best men, Isaac and Isma'il, both of whom are dressed, I can't help thinking, like undertakers or waiters in suits and ties. Naama's daughter sits on the sand to the side of the *huppah*, playing her harp as Orit follows her groom. Naama and I accompany her, clutching protectively to her arms. I can feel Orit restrain the tears over the absence of her sister. Despite the ads Dovy and I placed in the newspapers, despite even an announcement over the radio begging her to come home, there has been no trace of Ratiba. We are berating ourselves for having let her slip so easily from our lives.

Migrating birds fly overhead as Orit's beautiful rabbi ushers our friends into marriage—Orit, elegant in her chiffon dress, her silver, newly cropped hair; sweet-faced Yosef inclining his head in the direction of his soul mate.

"Yours have not been easy journeys," says the rabbi. "It has taken you many lifetimes to find each other. Today, your guiding spirits can rest in peace."

A sudden gust of wind whirls around the bridal canopy, transforming its fabric into birds. Palm trees wave in giddy celebration; the tide runs along the beach in lapping tongues washing the feet of the guests, just as Abraham/Ibrahim washed the feet of his angels so they blessed him with children and children's children at the beginning of this, our story.

Ibrahim is here. He was reluctant to come, but Hamzah insisted that, as his parents are not legally divorced, Ibrahim is still Orit's brother-in-law, the closest to Orit of all of us, and Ibrahim can't say no to Hamzah. Hamzah has sent messages to Ratiba too, over the radio, begging her to come home for Orit's big day. "For Orit," the messages said, "the aunt who took me in, who loved me almost as much as you." But the very moment of the wedding has arrived, and there's been no answer. Ibrahim's brother and sister-in-law,

Latif and Samah, are here too, together with their own recently married children. They carry rose petals for the bride. Ibrahim and Ratiba's daughter Daifa is here with her children sitting in the second row next to her father. She's married to Isma'il, one of the two best men. Wadha says that Isma'il wants to turn Israel into a Palestinian state. We are nervous about what he might do. Or say. Samah, able as always to see through the diaphanous skin, through the skin and the clothes of a pregnant woman, extends her hand to Daifa's stomach, caresses its circumference and asks, "Three months, right?" Of course, she's right.

Daifa's sister, Wadha, now Varda, is here with her exposed bosom and her Jewish fiancé, Isaac. Isaac has brought his father, Zalman. Zalman stays with his friend Srulick when he is in Israel. It is many years since Srulick married Tanya, but Zalman flew in from America when they did because Srulick had saved Tanya from a closet when she was a little girl in the '67 war, and Zalman thought their love so romantic, he had to witness their union. So Srulick and Tanya are also at Orit's wedding. Our friend Avi is here, who never leaves his house now other than to go to the children's home where he works. The granddaughter in his arms is named Nurit, in memory of his murdered wife.

The groom has invited his friends from East Jerusalem, so Saloma and Fatima are here, Fatima standing, quiet and contained, next to her husband; Saloma, her limbs melting as ever beneath her voluminous robe, her face beaming happiness. Shoshana and Oshri, Yosef's friends from his student days at the Hebrew University, are here; Yosef stays at their home during the holidays. Orit's Ethiopian friend, Moshe, came with Ruhama, the doctor who volunteers in the Ethiopian community. Ruhama has brought her assistant, Lilith, who would be an attractive woman were it not for the scar that runs down the left side of her face. Itzik, Orit's roofer, who experienced such a drastic transformation in jail, is here with his wife and daughter, standing next to them, flirting with Lilith; Lilith, not wanting to hurt his feelings, trying to move away.

At least thirty people from the Ethiopian community are here, dressed in tunics with scarves wound colorfully around their heads, many of them with babies in their arms. Everyone is singing our latest national hymn as we wait for the bride and groom, when the couple is standing under the canopy, and later when we turn in an instant, staring behind us as a single, many-headed reveler caught in the flash of a camera, incredulous, thanking God for the greatness of His gift. "Shalom, salaam, peace," we sing, "will yet come upon us. Salaam," we pray. "Shalom, salaam—over us and over all the world."

Most present are the spirits that dance between the guests in specks of light, diamonds sparkling on previously drab grains of sand, piercing, in patches of color, any element they touch. They are windows into the world from which our parents watch us, alighting for the briefest moment on the wedding canopy, on a strand of hair that was dull, but that is now gleaming, that will fade again, instantly, when the spirit dances on. It is Uncle Yehuda and Aunt Shuli, and it is Ella—all of them laughing in their sparkle, celebrating their daughter's marriage. It is my parents, Dovy's parents, Naama's and Zalman's parents. Ibrahim's dead father, Kasim, and his dead mother, whose name, I think, was Fatima, are here, and so are Yosef, the groom's, parents; not in body, of course, but in their dreams. It is the dreams of our parents that wink at us from the water.

Naama is sitting in the front row with her grandchildren throwing candies at the bride and groom. I'm on the other side of the aisle with Dovy and my own large brood, a veritable tribe. I'd better not get into that, though; tribes are what got us onto the wrong path in the first place.

I am sitting next to my brother, Noam, the one person that has been here for me my entire lifetime. I thank God we still have each other. We are also throwing candies. So it is not such a small wedding after all, and it is wonderful. Naama and I are the matronly matrons of honor, but though we walk Orit down the aisle, the rabbi does not want us cluttering up the *huppah.*

We miss Ratiba.

All eyes are on Orit as she walks around her beloved, binding her life to him the way a Jew in prayer binds himself to God, the way God created the world in increments of seven.

"I will betroth you … forever with righteousness, justice, kindness, and mercy." The rabbi blesses their union. Yosef crushes the wedding glass. A snap, a rustle behind us, and we turn. It is Ratiba, plodding down the aisle of sand, her stiletto heels sinking with every step beneath the surface. In her fist, she's clutching a vintage suitcase, the kind everyone's grandparents carried when they ran away from places, the kind that tell stories in attics or museums around the world, the corners banging against her legs. It was her mother Shuli's suitcase, from Europe. It is the suitcase she used on her failed visit to me, small, shabby, sad. A giant bouquet of bougainvillea trembles over her heart until a second branch snaps off, and she's here.

Such is the power of family.

The wedding feast is set on rugs that Naama and I have dragged from our houses and spread, Bedouin style, over the dunes. The guests close in around Ratiba and Orit. Ratiba, it transpires, is living in Hebron now, working at a nursery school for orphans. She and Ibrahim assess each other from opposite sides of the circle. They remind me of a poster my daughter has on her bedroom wall of two stags confronting each other on a hilltop, wary, eyeballs still as glass. But there is no confrontation here, just time frozen in air. The afternoon melts into the pink of the evening. We relax, blend into the pensive mood of this wedding day. The sky turns purple, then darkest blue, streaked with the red of the setting sun. We sit cross-legged, chatting, or we lie with our heads in the laps of our loved ones, eyes closed, sipping wine, only half conscious of thunder, of lightning, of waves crashing beneath us, of sea water creeping, in black fingers, ever closer up the beach.